Books by James Aldridge

Novels

Signed with Their Honour
The Sea Eagle
Of Many Men
The Diplomat
The Hunter
Heroes of the Empty View
I Wish He Would Not Die
The Last Exile
A Captive in the Land
The Statesman's Game
My Brother Tom
A Sporting Proposition
The Marvelous Mongolian
Mockery in Arms

Short Stories

Gold and Sand

Nonfiction

Living Egypt (with Paul Strand)
Undersea Hunting for Inexperienced Englishmen
Cairo

MOCKERY IN ARMS

MOCKERY IN ARMS

a novel by

James Aldridge

Little, Brown and Company

Boston — Toronto

First American Edition

T 01/75

LIBRARY OF CONGRESS CATALOGING IN PUBLICATION DATA

Aldridge, James.
    Mockery in arms.

        I. Title.
PZ3.A3655Mo3   [PR9619.3.A5]   823   74-19387
ISBN 0-316-03121-6

Published simultaneously in Canada
by Little, Brown and Company (Canada) Limited
Printed in the United States of America

To Harry Sions, who made it all worthwhile

Though a large part of this novel takes place in Paris, the real story involves a Kurdish revolt.

Few people in the west know anything about the Kurds —a unique and divided people who live in Iran, Iraq, Turkey, Syria and the Lebanon. There are also a few in Soviet Armenia. There are about four million Kurds, and though they are a very old ethnic and cultural group they have never been able to achieve any kind of national cohesion or independence. Only recently have they been given a real degree of autonomy in Iraq, and achieved mere tolerance in Iran. In Turkey they are not allowed to call themselves Kurds.

I apologise to all Kurds for adulterating Kurdish names and places, but perhaps they will understand my necessary reason for doing so. I also hope they will forgive my liberties with their language and customs, and look kindly on my use of the Qazi Mohamed as a real character, though in different circumstances and with a different story altogether.

J.A.

PART I

Chapter One

Kathy sat in the old Westland helicopter watching Mac-Gregor struggling with the greasy, padded flying suit. He had made preparations to get into the suit methodically enough, but organised scientist though he was, there was something too ideological in him for any method to work perfectly for his elbows and knees. They would not fit, and never had fitted where they were supposed to. As the shivering metal hole of the helicopter vibrated noisily and tilted in take-off, Kathy slid across the aluminium floor and pushed an elbow and pulled a sleeve and got her husband into the suit.

'I can manage that,' he said when she tried to zip him up.

'Then don't get your shirt caught in it.'

He nodded impatiently and struggled alone with the zip.

'It's going to be sickening, I know it,' Kathy groaned as the plane swung to and fro.

It was a pale and yellow dawn, and she waited for the metallic air to freeze as the cranky old machine rocked them violently upwards along the deep ravines of the barren valley. She had been lifted into these Kurdish mountains before—a million acres of treeless highlands and sleeping alpine flowers and knuckled, endless, upright peaks.

'Do the Kurds still shoot down these helicopters?' she shouted above the rattle of the flying wings.

9

'Not this close to Rezaiya,' MacGregor said.

Ten months ago another helicopter of the National Iranian Oil Company had been hit with an 80-mm rocket fired by a Kurdish boy sitting alone on one of these empty peaks. The lucky shot had knocked the bottom clean out of the helicopter, and ten thousand pounds' worth of seismic prospecting equipment plus the Persian mechanic sitting on it had simply dropped out into the void. The pilot had been angry enough and skilled enough to get the machine back to Rezaiya, take another helicopter and a platoon of Iranian soldiers, and fly back and ferret out the marksman. They had shot the only Kurd they could find on the mountainside, a sixteen-year-old Begzadi shepherd. They had also slaughtered his flock with machine-gun fire, but they had failed to find his rocket launcher.

'He's going up the wrong side of the Chalchor,' MacGregor shouted, and climbed up the little aluminium ladder and put his head into the flight deck and began a noisy argument above the motors. Kathy heard the pilot say that they had seen Kurds on the hillsides, and they didn't want to get a rocket up their tail.

'Oh blast...' she said. She was tired and she was fighting off airsickness which had suddenly begun to affect her in her middle age.

But it was all over in forty minutes and they came down in a high treeless basin. The moment they landed, the mechanics opened the door as if they were under fire, helped them hurriedly off with their flying suits, shouted anxiously to hurry, helped them out, slammed the door shut, and then waved as the helicopter flapped off like a frightened pelican. They watched it slide over the peaks and disappear. Then they were alone in this cold blue heaven of silence.

'If Zadko is not waiting for us near that old Nestorian shrine,' MacGregor said, pointing to a ridge on the other side, 'we'll have to walk two days to Zinjan.'

'I'm not complaining, sweetheart,' Kathy said. 'I'm just happy to have my feet on something solid again.'

'That's not the point,' he said, as she helped him on with the rucksack. 'There are always Kurds somewhere up here, or even gendarmes, who may prefer that we don't get to Zinjan. You should have waited in Rezaiya.'

'Well I didn't. So make the most of it.'

He did not argue. He set a silent pace for them to go down the rocky valley and up the other side, and, apart from an occasional direction, they did not talk until they had reached their objective, a little rock pillar with a faded green altar carved into it. But there was no one waiting there for them.

'I'll make the coffee,' he said, taking a small primus stove out of the rucksack, 'and if Zadko isn't here in half an hour, we'll move on.'

Five months away from him, taking their children to European universities, and Kathy could look at MacGregor with fresh curiosity. Twenty-three years of marriage had still not dimmed her curiosity about him. But she watched his silent preoccupation as he prepared the coffee, and she decided that he was probably in more danger from himself now than he was from the Kurds.

'When did all this Kurdish trouble begin again?' she asked him.

'It never really stopped.'

'I know that,' she said. 'But there hasn't been open hostility and shooting between Iran and the Kurds for years. What made it suddenly flare up again?'

MacGregor shrugged. 'Hard to say. I think the Kurds are trying to set up an independent republic again.'

'In Iran?'

'I don't know yet.' He threw coffee grains into the water which was boiling in the aluminium pot, and then whisked it off the flame.

'I can see the prospects,' she said. 'Tribal Kurds and city

Kurds and political Kurds all cutting each other's throats for Kurdish liberation, while the Iranians slaughter them.'

'Don't be too hard on them. They did very well in 1946.'

'And look what happened,' she said. 'The Iranians hanged the Qazi Mohamed and his entire cabinet in the old Qara circle, and their great Barzani soldier had to run like a rabbit into Soviet Azerbaijan with his pitiful little army. Why on earth should they try to do it all over again? And with your help, if I know Zadko.'

MacGregor did not seem to hear her. He was standing up, absorbed in a bird which was wheeling in a tight aerial circle over a frozen patch of ground about half a mile away.

She watched him silently until his preoccupation irritated her. 'You're becoming a problem,' she told him. 'You don't even listen any more.'

'I'm sorry,' he said quickly. 'I was watching that Buteo hawk looking for a snow mouse.'

She kept her eyes on him, as if forbidding him to look away again. 'You're even taking on the coloration of the place,' she said. 'Your hair and your silly blue eyes and your boots and your clothes, and even that stubborn privacy you live behind these days. You just fold up into all this, don't you?' she said and waved a hand angrily at the mountains.

'Never mind,' he said gently. 'I missed you, and I'm really glad you came.'

He didn't want her to watch him too closely, so he took out a map and put on a pair of steel-rimmed spectacles and peered at the map and then at the mountains. But his china-skinned auburned face and thin, bony nose and hard pale forehead became preoccupied again.

'Oh for heaven's sake,' she groaned. 'Don't *do* that.'

'Do what?'

'Don't put those spectacles on and peer like that. Stay with me for a while.'

He put away his spectacles and folded the map. She knew that he was still, physically, a very shy man, and that he had never learned how to put up any kind of barrier against the embarrassment which she could easily use against him. But what better way to shake him?

'Anyway,' she said, 'Zadko obviously isn't coming, so we ought to get away from here before I become even more bloody-minded.'

'Give him another few minutes.'

'Didn't he at least tell you what he wanted?'

MacGregor shook his head. 'I kept getting dozens of urgent messages telling me to be in Zijnan before the 15th of the month if I were his friend and had the interest of all Kurds at heart, etcetera.'

'That's the typical Kurdish way of persuading you to do something for them.'

'It looks like it.'

'Haven't you any idea what they want?'

'No. But it's obviously something they consider desperate.'

'But you didn't just get up and leave Teheran because the Kurds asked you to come and see them?'

'No. I had to come up here for the NIOC anyway.' The NIOC was the National Iranian Oil Company, and MacGregor was the chief scientist for its Department of Exploration & Reserves.

Kathy zipped up her jacket and followed him down the slope again. 'The Iranians will throw you out for good if you start taking sides with the Kurds now.'

He raised his hands, but did not agree or disagree.

'And as you know,' she went on, 'I wouldn't be sorry if that happened. Not the least bit.'

'Now Kathy ... don't be like that.'

'You know what I mean.'

'I know you want me to pack up and go,' he said. 'But Europe can wait a little longer,' he said over his shoulder.

13

'No it can't.' She took a deep breath to catch her breath. 'You're fifty and so am I,' she said. 'And what used to be a youthful passion in this country has sunk out of sight in an oriental mess. It's all gone, Ivre,' she said as she saw his back stiffen. 'After twenty-three years of frustration, of being robbed of every possible use for your talents, of political confinement and house arrests, and God knows what— and of giving everything and getting back nothing, it's time to leave.'

'You're just back from six months in Europe,' he said lightly.

Kathy had originally gone to Europe to see their son Andrew into Balliol, and their daughter Cecie to the Beaux Arts in Paris, but she had stayed on for another five months because, after twenty-three years in Iran fighting one lost cause after another, the experience seemed finally to have exhausted her.

'I am *not* going to let you just fade into the landscape and disappear,' she told him. 'There's a perfectly valid world thriving outside all this.'

'Of course.'

'So there's no point in you getting involved with the Kurds.'

He didn't say anything. Then he noticed for the first time that she had cut and coiffured her hair. She had left Iran wearing it long.

'Why did you do that?' he said, amazed.

'Do what?'

'Cut your hair?'

'Because I was fed up with it the way it was. Anyway, you didn't even notice it yesterday when I arrived.'

He blushed angrily and turned around and continued their march route across the pale sloping rocks, treacherous because there was a thin skin of black ice on them. 'Careful how you put your feet,' he said to her when they reached a bad patch. Otherwise they went on in silence. He did not hurry, but he knew that she was steadily tiring in this high, thin air. They stopped for a long silent lunch, and in the early afternoon, still silent and preoccupied, he found the easiest paths over the interwoven slopes. But he seemed to forget sometimes that she was still behind him.

In the evening he lit a fire in a deserted Iranian police post which the Kurds had partly destroyed in the two open battles they had fought for their 1946 republic. They tried to keep warm while they ate a dinner of native bread and over-cooked rancid chicken which he had bought in the market at Rezaiya.

'It's awful stuff,' she said. 'I've finally lost whatever taste I had for bazaar food.'

'Nonetheless you need it,' he said. 'So don't try to taste it, just eat it.'

Kathy shivered and crouched over the miserable broken stove until MacGregor unfolded the two nylon sleeping bags, which he zipped together into a double one for warmth. He told her to get into it now before she lost all her body warmth.

She nodded silently with clenched teeth and went outside and stood in the darkness for a moment on the old roadway, feeling the clear, black, mountain sky biting at her bare ankles and bare hands and bare nostrils and lungs. And because the view, even in the starlight, was so still, vast, high, inverted, and clean, she thought it brutal to use any of it as a lavatory.

'I'm getting old,' she groaned miserably.

When she went back inside the dark police post she was still cold, and she asked MacGregor if she really had to undress.

'You'll freeze in the bag if you don't, and so will I.'

She crawled into the double sleeping bag and undressed and lay naked in the cold nylon envelope until MacGregor himself leapt in and she clung to him.

'I'll never get warm,' she complained.

'In a little while.'

Cocoon-like, they waited in the bag for warmth, and MacGregor asked her in the tangle of her arms and his elbows if their daughter Cecie had also cut her hair.

'No,' Kathy said. 'She's still yours. She won't cut it until you tell her to. Then she'll probably shave it off completely.'

'Is the Beaux Arts really what she expected?'

'When she got used to it.'

'But will she stick it out?'

'If she doesn't run off and marry some long-elbowed French boy.'

'Not another!'

'Don't worry,' Kathy said, untangling one of her arms. 'She's quite safe. She's much better off in Paris with Aunt Joss than going through all that mess with Taha and his Kurdish fancies in Teheran. I told her she must go over to London or Oxford every month to see Andrew, and I made him swear that no matter what happened he would not ignore her in that large brotherly way of his.'

'Don't worry. He'll do it.'

'He'll do it all right. But he's so sure of himself that he even bothers me. He wanders in and out of all the family living-rooms as if they were friendly railway stations, and he picks up all sorts of people and simply moves along like that in the usual flood of good friends and brothers.'

'He's a well-organised boy,' MacGregor said defensively.

Kathy was rubbing her naked hand up and down the ridge of his warm spine. Wrapped close to him, she was warm now and beginning to relax. 'What do Kurds call that?' she said to him softly, as if someone were listening.

'Call what?'

'Listen.'

They could hear a faint rustling on the flat dirt roof as a light mountain wind rattled the dry grasses and dead leaves on it.

'*Hus-a-hus,*' he said.

'Then what's the word for bubbling?'

'*Bilq-a-bilq.*'

'Whispering?'

'*Kus-a-kus.*'

'Snoring?'

'*Ker-a-ker.*'

She laughed. 'I remember that,' she said. She was finally relaxing into him, and she said: 'Those echoic things are all I ever liked in Kurdish; and those wonderful transliterations like a fiancé being a hand-holder. They say a spendthrift is hand-opened, and a stepfather a barren father. What's the word for handsome?'

'Sweet blood.'

'I always remember that day in the orchard near Lake Urmia. What did that Kurdish woman say to her husband when he shouted angrily at her?'

MacGregor had folded his wife's hair like some gentle, springy grass, and he told her in their naked warmth that the Kurdish husband had asked his wife furiously if she were devil or djinn, and she had replied: 'I am neither. I am a weeping woman...'

He felt Kathy's warm, inexplicable tears splashing his ear, and he cursed the circumstances and closed his eyes and tried, in married passion, to eliminate so many insoluble realities from their bodies and their minds, and when he had finished and she used her dry thumb to get rid of her tears, she said calmly, 'I came back determined not to quarrel with you. But how can we ever avoid it when we disagree so much on essentials these days?'

He heard a mountain dog bark very far away, the first sign of life that had touched them in twelve mountainous hours.

'Waiting for a moment when married people don't quarrel,' he said teasingly in Persian, 'is like a Shiah waiting for his never-coming Messiah.'

'Oh, those damned Persian sayings,' she said sleepily.

17

'You know, the nice thing about a hysterectomy,' she went on, 'is that, apart from all this stupid lack of energy, I don't have to worry or get up or think or even care a damn.' But before she went to sleep she said, 'Somehow, I'm going to find a way of getting you out of all this.'

Chapter Two

In the morning, they followed the dirt road along the mountainside, accompanied by the first noisy rifle shots. Sometimes a bullet splashed on the ridges above them, and when they reached a frozen mountain pond they saw a Kurdish horseman far off, moving up towards them from one of the deep valleys.

'The Begzadis still use horses,' he said, 'or it might be a mule.'

'Oh no,' she said. 'Not up here.'

'Anyway, it's not Taha. Taha wouldn't be seen dead riding anything less than a jeep.'

'Shouldn't we keep out of sight?' she said, disliking the rifle shots.

'You can't hide from a Kurd in his own hills,' he said. 'Better to be on the move and keep him in view.'

They watched him unsling his Lee Enfield rifle and carry it upright on his saddle. Kathy knew how menacing this was, and she was afraid now for MacGregor. Kurds were no more murderous than anybody else, but too many old scores were settled in these remote highlands to make the place safe for anyone who had his local enemies in Iran. And MacGregor in twenty-three years had supported too many complicated causes not to have enemies here.

The Kurd dug his heels into his bony and muddy Turkoman horse and galloped the last fifty flat metres. He stopped recklessly on top of them.

'Well, by God.' He was laughing like a child. 'You're

the ones all right.' He pointed his rifle at Kathy like a toy and asked: 'Do you speak Kurmanji, my lady?'

'No, she doesn't,' MacGregor said sharply.

'Then put her up behind me,' the Kurd said cheekily.

'You can carry my rucksack, and we'll walk behind you,' MacGregor told him.

The Kurd dug his heels into his little horse and scooped up the rucksack from the ground with his rifle, almost falling off because it was so heavy. 'By God,' he shouted. 'There must be gold in it.' And all the way down the valley he kept laughing and shouting at the top of his voice: 'There's gold in it.'

They followed him for an hour, until they could see a little stream ahead, where the road turned sharply out of sight. There the Kurd raised a whoop, dug his heels into his horse, and galloped down the road clinging to the rucksack. He disappeared round the bend, shouting and laughing. 'Goodbye to that,' Kathy said. 'He's gone off with everything.'

MacGregor did not stop but kept her walking along the road. 'It's just the local sense of humour,' he told her.

Before they had reached the corner an old jeep painted midnight blue swung recklessly around the bend and skidded twenty yards to a stop. 'It's all right. It's Zadko,' MacGregor said as Kathy gripped his arm.

The Kurd in the passenger seat leapt out of the jeep on very light dancing feet and embraced MacGregor with a wet enthusiastic kiss on both cheeks. 'Thank God,' he said like an actor, 'that you got my message.'

MacGregor laughed. 'The electric man,' he said affectionately to Zadko.

Zadko said 'Ahhh' impressively. Zadko was called 'dandy' and 'fine champion' by the mountain Kurds, who considered him their best soldier. He was dressed in a tribal coxa jacket with embroidered edges, blouse, striped cummerbund and wide Kurdish trousers. He was perfectly Kurdish, except for the Marks and Spencer carpet slippers which he wore on his tiny, swollen feet.

'Where's Taha?' Kathy asked him in Persian. 'Did you find him?'

Taha was Zadko's twenty-one-year-old son, who for five years had lived with them in Teheran while he attended first school and then University. They had both become attached to Taha, but at sixteen their daughter Cecie had fallen in love with him, and though they had kept the affair in check by vigilance and interference, they were glad when Cecie was safely in Europe and Taha had gone back to his father. But Taha had not gone back. Taha was a revolutionary, and he had taken half a dozen other Kurdish students with him and disappeared into the mountains above Rezaiya because he wanted revolution now, rather than the kind of hopes his father had for national liberation first.

'I found him all right,' Zadko said, walking up and down, cracking his knuckles. 'At the moment he's gone to the Begzada village to kidnap the Iranian Colonel Razmara on the 5th of the month.'

'What's he want to kidnap Razmara for?' MacGregor said incredulously. They knew Razmara and considered him a friend.

'Those boys want a hostage for the Kurdish students arrested by the Iranians in Tabriz last month. Imagine the stupidity of it,' Zadko groaned.

'God protect us all,' Kathy said sarcastically in Kurdish.

'Tomorrow,' Zadko said, 'when I've finished with this business up here, I'll go and get him out of the way before the Persian gendarmes trap him and murder him.'

Zadko sighed like an actor again and produced a packet of American cigarettes which he offered them. They refused, and they waited while he took out a diminutive pipe, plugged the cigarette upright in the bowl, lit it with a Persian match and puffed in and out with a far-away look in his eye. MacGregor knew Zadko had something to tell them, but first he was going to make them feel how important it was. They waited until he turned his little pipe sideways, blew out the remnant of the cigarette, and sighed dramatically again.

'What's it all about, Zadko?' MacGregor asked.

'Our *Komali-i-zhian*—our Committee of Life—wants you to do something for us,' Zadko said. 'That's why I sent for you.'

'I could guess that,' MacGregor said drily. 'But what is it they want me to do?'

'Something that might be difficult and risky for you,' Zadko said. 'But important to us.'

MacGregor waited.

'I can't tell you what it is,' Zadko went on. 'I'm sworn to secrecy. The Qazi has been waiting for you, but there are others...'

'You mean some of them are going to threaten him?' Kathy said.

'I'm saying that in the village there are Kurdish feodals and politicians and democratic party-ites and tobacco commissioners and soldiers and Kurdish tribal sheikhs and half-Arabs,' Zadko said. 'And even a Kurdish albino with funny fingers. All Kurds, but not all your friends. You understand?'

'Don't worry,' MacGregor said.

'*You* may not worry,' Kathy said to her husband. 'But I do.'

'You must listen to nobody but the Qazi,' Zadko said. 'Don't be put off by bad manners and by a Kurdish back-stabber who hates you. That's all.'

'You mean the Ilkhani? Is he here?' MacGregor said, surprised.

'Exactly.'

'What's he doing with the Committee?' MacGregor asked.

'The Qazi insists that Kurds must stop fighting Kurds.

Isn't that what you've always insisted on yourself? Unity...'

'Yes, but not with the one man above all who betrayed the 1946 republic.'

'He couldn't help that,' Zadko said, but it was a reluctant defence. 'The Ilkhani's a feodal. He just thinks he's lord of all Kurdish creation. That's all it is. I'd kill him myself, gladly, but maybe the Qazi's right. He's a Kurd at heart somewhere.'

'He's a rich and murderous old villain,' MacGregor insisted.

'Of course he is,' Zadko said vehemently. They got to the jeep and Zadko shouted at his unseen outpost: 'Don't keep shooting at those village dogs in the graveyard. It's bad luck, I tell you.'

They heard laughter from the mountains, and they drove into the dirt-piled, meandering cluster of Zinjan village where the stone shanties were roofed with earth and scattered like lumps of dirty grey sugar into a few narrow alleyways along a river bank. The jeep stopped dead on all four wheels before a stone hut with a threadbare curtain for a door, and Zadko leapt out of the jeep and pulled the curtain aside for them.

'Dusha!' he shouted.

An old Kurdish woman dressed in a threadbare bundle came from another door carrying a chipped enamel pitcher of water. She welcomed them in mumbled unintelligible phrases.

'Where's the soap?' Zadko demanded.

She put her hand reluctantly into the pocket of her coarse Kurdish dress and unfolded her fingers like a child to produce an old and near-dead piece of green soap.

'Where's the khanoum's sack?' Zadko demanded again. He used the Persian word *hoorjin*, which meant carpet-bag.

The old woman pointed to their rucksack in the corner.

'Who was the madman who ran off with it?' Kathy asked Zadko.

23

Zadko laughed the way he loved to laugh. 'That was Ahmed the carefree,' he said.

'Ahmed has a childish sense of humour,' Kathy said.

'He can't help it,' Zadko explained. 'He's a *Div* [devil] among us. Imagine that. But he's a brave boy who knows the mountains better than any true believer,' Zadko laughed. 'Welcome then,' he said formally.

'What do we do now?' MacGregor asked him.

'When you've washed and rested we'll come and call on you officially, and then we'll all eat, and then the Qazi will tell you what we want you to do, which of course you can refuse if you like.'

'After which, someone will cut his throat,' Kathy said drily.

Zadko laughed. It was a good joke coming from a friend and sister like Kathy.

Chapter Three

Zadko walked impetuously up and down a line of five men seated at a table in a dark, greasy, sheepskin storehouse with a low roof, addressing them the way he must have seen lawyers persuading juries in American films he had been to in Tabriz, or in the nomad cinemas on trucks that sometimes ventured into these hills, and whose screens were sometimes shot up by excited horsemen. The five men were seated under a white petrol lamp behind a long deal table covered with a faded, plastic cloth. An illegal Kurdish flag was stuck into a poplar branch in the middle of the table.

'This man,' Zadko was saying about MacGregor, 'is already known to all of you. We all know that Kurds don't like foreigners. And who can blame us? But this one is as good as any Kurd, because you will remember how, after 1946, he took in the sons of Abol Qazim and made sure that those Kurdish bastards and traitors, the khans of Zalako, didn't murder them. And my own son Taha lived with him like a son for a long time. So when I knock at this man's door in Teheran and he says *"Who?"* I always reply to him: "It is your brother out here." And when he says *"Who?"* again, I say back: "It is someone who respects you, whom you can trust, who would give his life for you if necessary..."'

MacGregor listened half-heartedly as Zadko went on with his character reference, which was the normal way a Kurd arranged for an outsider to be accepted into tribal confidence. MacGregor was more interested in the jury. He knew all of them. The Qazi, as its president, sat in the middle wearing a religious turban, and on one side of him was a tall old man wearing riding breeches. He had a stern, large, almost pugilistic and self-assertive face, with enormous ears that were pointed on top and bottom. He was a hetman, a Lord, the Ilkhan of the Megrik tribes. Next to him, like a dried stick, was a thin, sick, political Kurd who wore a crushed European suit. He was called 'the Iraqi' by all Kurds because he was a Democratic Party organiser for the Kurds of Iraq. He was an urban Kurd who had been born in the city streets of Mosul, and who hated the mountains and mountain lords like the Ilkhani. He had spent his short, sick life organising Kurdish oil workers. The Iranians and the Turks considered him an outlaw, condemned to be shot on sight. On the other side of the Iraqi was a fat plum-faced, iron-grey man in a well-cut double-breasted suit, a businessman who said nothing. Unlike the others this one was cleanshaven, and he looked a little startled. He was a rich Lebanese Kurd from Beirut, one of the Abbekr family.

'And now,' Zadko said to MacGregor as he finished his declaration and sat down, 'watch closely and fight back.'

There was a pause for spitting and coughing. Then:

'Mister . . .' the Ilkhan said rudely to MacGregor, and went on in Persian, 'You know me, don't you?'

'Yes I know you, Ilkhani,' MacGregor said grimly. 'Everybody knows you.'

'Why do you speak to me rudely?'

'There's no rudeness on my part,' MacGregor answered.

'What is between us?'

'Nothing.'

'Mister!' the Ilkhani began again contemptuously, but the others told him to speak in Kurdish, which he did reluctantly to this foreigner. 'You are very good friends of some Kurds here, aren't you?'

'Of course.'

'You would help your friends against me. That's how you feel about me, isn't it?'

'Certainly.'

'Why?'

'Because you've always caused trouble, Ilkhani. If it hadn't been for Zadko you would have taken over dozens of villages and half the wheat and tobacco fields of the Milani as well. Why should I agree with that, particularly after what you did in 1946...'

'That's got nothing to do with you,' the old man shouted angrily. 'You are a foreigner and I won't stand for that.'

MacGregor ignored the outburst. 'I also remember thirty years ago,' he went on, 'when you kidnapped me and my father and told my father, with a rifle in his mouth, to find oil in the Halali areas. You would have beaten both of us to death if the army hadn't interfered.'

'You are a foreigner and a spy,' the Ilkhan said again. 'What right have you to be here at all? Tell me that.'

'No right at all,' MacGregor said. 'If my friends want me to go,' (he stood up) 'I'll do so.'

The other Kurds told MacGregor to sit down, not to be offended, to be patient, it was the Kurdish way. But then Zadko leapt to his feet and said angrily: 'Qazi. It's time you interfered.'

The word Qazi in Kurdish meant judge, in particular a judge of religious jurisprudence which was still the fundamental law for all Kurdish disputes. In the white petrol lamp the Qazi from Saqqiz looked pale and grey because he was unshaven. He was dressed in a grey religious *djupa* which buttoned up to the neck, and he sat very still, like a man used to listening and then giving an absolute judgement.

'There's nothing to say,' he told Zadko.

'But...'

'It's only a rude quarrel. The Ilkhani is wrong. You

should not provoke,' he said to the Ilkhan, speaking in short sharp pronouncements. 'Are you upset?' he asked MacGregor.

'No. As far as the Ilkhan is concerned I can look after myself.'

'He's a foreigner,' the Ilkhani shouted at MacGregor.

'Be quiet, Amr,' the Qazi said gently to the old man. 'We need a foreigner in this, and one who is a good friend.' Then he turned to MacGregor and said, 'Let me explain our new policy to you, then if you agree with it and decide to help us, and if you're willing to swear yourself to the secrecy of it, I'll tell you what we want you to do. Does that sound reasonable to you?'

'Of course.'

'First let me explain the difference between the Kurdish decisions we've made up here, and those at Saj Bulaq in 1942 which ended in the fiasco of 1946. In 1946 we tried to set up a local republic in Iran. But this time we have decided to organise a national and political and military council which will prepare to establish a single Kurdish republic embracing all Kurds in all three countries, Iran, Iraq and Turkey.'

MacGregor took a deep surprised breath. 'It's a famous old idea, Qazi, but how will you go about it?'

'I'm telling you, Qazi,' the old Ilkhan groaned. 'Say no more to him.'

The Qazi simply shook his long, pointed, religious sleeves. 'This time,' he went on, 'we'll train and prepare an army which will not be simply a tribal force, or a local one in Iran or Iraq or Turkey, but will include all Kurds. And in particular our city and oilfield Kurds. We will train them up here in our mountains.'

MacGregor was aware that the room was filling up behind him, and Zadko whispered to him, 'In comes everybody. Tribal lords and Tabriz garage-owners and feodals and Saqqiz bazaar merchants and God knows who else. All

Kurds. But remember—they're not all friends.'

MacGregor nodded but did not turn around to look. 'Are you planning an uprising in all three countries at the same time?' he asked the Qazi.

There was a chorus of shouts behind MacGregor, telling the Qazi to say nothing more to MacGregor.

But the Qazi raised his voice. 'I really can't tell you more until you swear to the same conditions as the rest of us.'

'I understand,' MacGregor said. 'But before I go that far, can I ask you if the Kurds have decided yet who their main enemy really is?'

The sad Iraqi Kurd, the urban organiser, smiled as if sickness had always been part of his face. 'I remember all your arguments in Mahabad last year, sidi,' he said to MacGregor, sucking in his breath.

'Whom do you fight, Ali? That's always been the Kurdish problem and still is,' MacGregor said.

The Iraqi shrugged. 'The Kurds in Iraq have fought Iraqi governments, the Kurds in Persia have fought the Persians, the Kurds in Turkey have fought the Turkish governments. And behind all these governments in the past fifty years were the British and the Europeans, and now the Americans.'

'That's not my point, Ali,' MacGregor interrupted.

'I know what your point is,' the Iraqi said. 'You want to know whether we intend to fight your friends the Persians, since they themselves are trying to get rid of foreign domination and feudal rulers.'

'Isn't that still the problem?'

The Qazi interrupted them. 'I know it's a policy that you don't like,' he said to MacGregor, 'because you think like a Persian, and you want us to stay inside the Persian nation ...'

'Who is he to like or dislike it?' the Ilkhani shouted. 'He's a Baku spy.'

This time MacGregor heard the audience behind him

laughing at the old man. But some of them also shouted insults at MacGregor, and he turned around quickly to look at the rest of the assembly behind him. He could see only a mixture of Kurdish faces, tribal costumes, threadbare European clothes, army blouses, half-and-half mixtures, and one man holding a silent little transistor radio in his hand.

'I've told you all I can,' the Qazi said abruptly. 'But unless you accept the idea of a new republic, and all that it implies, I can't proceed.'

MacGregor said it was not that easy. 'It implies a great deal,' he said, 'so give me a little time to think about it.'

'We can wait three hours,' the Qazi told him, closing his briefcase. 'Is that enough?'

'I just need a little time to think about it,' MacGregor said.

He was about to leave, but the Iraqi stopped him and said in his faint, filtered voice: 'If you're thinking of the Persians...'

'Yes?'

'...remember that we have always had to fight the Persians and the Arabs and the Turks and the British, even to keep our own customs and to live in our own mountains and work in our towns.'

'I know all that, Ali.'

'How many Kurds in your lifetime have been hung or shot or beaten to death or murdered or bombed in their own cities and villages, and even in their own countryside. Just for being Kurds. Are you going to forget, sidi, that two million Kurds in Turkey are still denied their own culture, and are even forbidden to use the name Kurd? You know very well that our true national existence has been stolen from us. We have no doctors up here, no universities, no hospitals, no social cultivations, no theatres, no schools. Nothing of our own...'

'I know all that,' MacGregor said.

'I'm only telling you, habibi, that it can't go on. We have to revolt, even against our fellow victims, because very soon all Kurdistan will be choked to death. The world is closing in on us.'

The Kurds had been listening in silence, and though they had heard this précis of their predicament a thousand times before, and had thought of it themselves a hundred times a day, when the Iraqi had finished they began to grind their teeth and slap their hands on their knees and chant a famous Kurdish song about the Kurdish rivers that carried away the oppressed spirit, and the mountains which grew like stone flowers in the soil of murdered Kurdish martyrs.

MacGregor did not like it. He did not like being pricked by the thorns he had worn himself for many years, and as he left them biting the tips of their turban scarves and shouting heroic denunciations of their foreign oppressors, the Qazi caught up with him and took his arm gently. 'Don't let our emotion influence you,' he said. 'Think calmly about your feelings. Then, if you agree with us, we'll tell you what we want you to do.'

Chapter Four

When he left the sheep shed he was surprised to find that it was still daylight outside, and he found Kathy surrounded by mountain children in front of a village tea shop—a shanty with a broken deal table and seats. Kathy was turning the handle of an ancient Singer sewing machine, while a Kurdish girl of fourteen, with plaited hair parted in the middle and a white crumpled shawl over her shoulders, fed a length of polka-dotted cloth into its rattling little jaws.

'Who do you think this is?' Kathy asked him.

The girl looked up. MacGregor saw darting and cheeky Kurdish eyes, and the soft but wilful mouth of the marriageable Kurdish girl.

'Someone's red rosebud,' he said teasingly in Kurdish.

'It's Saqi's daughter—Kula.'

The girl stretched her shoulders back provocatively to prove she was now a young woman. MacGregor had to look amazed, and he was amazed. Saqi, her father, had been shot dead by a British agent in 1958 outside the door of the Ministry of Justice in Mahabad, where he had been charged with organising a local labour revolt among the oil company's ditch-diggers. Her mother had died two months later, and Kula had been brought to them in winter in Teheran, five years old, wrapped in a sheepskin blanket. She had a liver complaint, and Kathy had put her into the Russian hospital and had seen to it that she was treated and returned to her uncles among the Rawuz tribes. She was Zadko's niece.

'Have you forgotten your English?' MacGregor said.

The girl giggled, and then threw back her head and laughed like a bold-faced Kurdish woman; and she said in Kurdish to MacGregor, 'I said "Good morning" to Aunt in English. And what do you think she said to me? She said in Kurdish, "I don't understand your Kurdish any more."'

Two Kurdish children clinging with grubby hands to Kathy's skirts also laughed, and MacGregor watched his wife admiringly and wondered for a moment why all children and youths were instantly willing to clutch her skirts. Kathy never shrank from contact, was never frightened by physical appearance, and he supposed they knew it and felt safe with her.

'Don't ask the khanoum for sweets,' he told a six-year-old boy who had been holding out his hand.

'She's got her pockets full of them,' the boy said indignantly.

'You shouldn't ask for them,' MacGregor said. He asked Kathy if she had given the children sweets.

'Of course. They never see any sugar in these mountain villages.'

'This little devil is asking for more, and he'll get into trouble if any adult hears him asking.'

'Oh, nonsense,' Kathy said. 'He's not begging.'

'He's a Kurd,' MacGregor said.

'Your morals are always unnatural,' she said and put her hand into her jacket pocket and gave the boy a sweet.

MacGregor tried to ignore the children, and while Kathy went on turning the handle he told her in English that the Kurds had finally decided to organise a republic of all Kurds, and that they were preparing some kind of simultaneous uprising in Turkey, Iran and possibly Iraq.

'When?' she asked, unbelieving.

'They wouldn't tell me that.'

'How could they? They don't know themselves. Millenniums!' she said and repeated it with every turn of the Singer machine handle.

'Obviously it's a long way off,' he agreed. 'But they've decided to prepare for it now, and this time they might succeed.'

'What did they ask you to do for them?'

'They haven't told me yet.'

'I can guess why,' Kathy mocked. 'They want you to swear on your mother's grave that you are with them.'

'That's true.'

'You haven't, have you?'

'No.'

'Then don't,' she said. She stopped the handle when Kula said 'Stoppp' in English, and then started it again when Kula said *'skit-skit'*.

MacGregor could not compete with the sewing machine, and he took Kathy by the arm, telling Kula that her aunt had to leave for a moment. He walked Kathy along the river bank, and when the children refused to let her go he called to one of the women washing and beating clothes in the trickle of the water, and the children ran away. He kept a firm grip on Kathy's arm and took her up through the village. The village still had too many political and tribal Kurds in it who sat in the mountain sun nursing rifles or squatting over the fragments of dismantled trucks and engines. They were surrounded by skinny, dung-matted salukis, and they were drinking tea and laughing. On the flat dirt roof of a sheep pen a dozen Kurds were sitting around an 80-mm mortar whose open snout gaped upwards at nothing.

As they walked beyond the village MacGregor said, 'There's another factor in all this that's going to change the situation for them.'

'There's always another factor,' she said, 'particularly with you. You invent them.'

'Not this one.'

34

'You'll have to convince me.'

'Every big oil-consuming country is about to become very interested in these Kurdish mountains.'

'Why?'

'The NIOC has been drilling up here for months and we've made two very important discoveries. One is an extraordinary layer of oil that probably extends for about forty miles under these Kurdish hills, literally right along the Kurdish borders with Turkey, Iraq and Iran.'

'But you always knew about that.'

'I only guessed it. Now we've confirmed it by drilling.'

'So?'

'The other is even more important. It's a huge deposit of natural gas, a series of extended pockets that flow into each other at about 1,500 metres, which means that it will be fairly easy to exploit.'

'Who's going to bother with natural gas up here?' she asked him.

'In ten years there's going to be a world shortage of all hydrocarbons, so there's going to be a scramble for this find just as there is everywhere else these days when new deposits are discovered.'

'Do the Kurds know about it?'

'I think they do. At any rate they know I'm the person responsible for Iranian research into reserves up here, and they know I've been coming here almost every month for the NIOC. They've watched our drilling.'

'But aren't these mountains part of Iran's own concession area? So why should foreigners get involved?'

'Unfortunately,' MacGregor said, slowing down to make his point, 'it's part of the Iranian concession which overlaps everybody else's. So when the Iranian interest begins, all the outsiders will jump in. There'll be a big mess then between Kurds, Turks, Iranians, Arabs, Americans, British, and God knows who else. You can guess what's going to happen to the Kurds if they're not organised and ready for it.'

Kathy kicked a white pebble with a sudden stab. She stared distastefully at the bare mountains. 'All the more reason why you shouldn't get involved,' she told him. 'You can't stop it.'

'I'm not involved yet,' he told her.

'But you will be,' she said accusingly. 'And you'll be wasting years of your life again. After doing the same thing for the Azerbaijanians it was house arrest. This time the Iranians will be a lot harder on you if they catch you interfering.'

'Azerbaijan was different,' he said. 'And anyway, you were as deep in that as I was.'

'We were young then,' she said. 'Now you're too old to risk the same hopeless experience with the Kurds.'

'Maybe,' he said unhappily. 'Maybe ...'

They were half-way up the rocky slope above the village and he said after a while: 'It's difficult to just stand aside if you know what's going to happen. The worst always happens when foreigners become involved. And they will be involved. They'll find a way of dividing and emasculating the Kurds. It always happens that way.'

Kathy stopped walking up the slope and leaned forward. 'These bloody mountains,' she said vehemently. 'This whole stupid mountain idiocy.'

He waited for her to recover her breath. 'You used to like all this country even more than I do,' he reminded her gently.

'Now I hate it. Moreover, you get so ridiculously Rob-Royish up here.'

In 1952 MacGregor had been almost blinded by an explosion in the old Anglo-Iranian laboratory, and Kathy had read aloud to him Scott's preface to *Rob Roy*, in which he describes how the highland MacGregors, in particular Rob Roy, had been robbed of liberty, lands and birthright, and even forbidden by an act of parliament to use the name MacGregor.

'I'm not being Rob-Royish,' he told her, never taking her seriously when she said that, and also disliking it. 'I simply think it's going to be a hopeless situation for the Kurds if they don't do something.'

'Oh, I know. I *know*!' she said impatiently.

MacGregor took that quickly as enough consent to go ahead. It was reluctant, but it would do and they began to walk down to the slaty hillside in silence, arm in arm, when they heard two shots. Then someone shouted: '*Kuzan, Kuzan*' (Killer, Killer).

Almost at the same time they saw, as if it had just puffed out of the sky, a grey and khaki jet, unmarked, which poured itself over the low mountainside ahead of its noise, then levelled out and dropped three black canisters one after the other. As the canisters turned and twisted in the air MacGregor realised what they were. He gripped Kathy around the neck and pulled her to the ground and flattened himself beside her. A wall of hot air and black jellied smoke scorched their backs and pressed them into the ground and ripped Kathy's shoes off. It sucked all the cold air out of their lungs, and then poured back a blast of fire to replace it.

It was over in a few seconds, and when they lifted their heads, a hot sticky cloud of burning smoke had already floated up like a solid black balloon, and they could see an acre of fire eating up one end of the village.

'What was that?' Kathy said incredulously. 'What happened?'

'Napalm,' MacGregor said.

He pulled her to her feet and shouted. 'We're too exposed here.' He pointed to a trap of boulders above them and they ran towards them, Kathy holding her shoes in her hand. They flattened out between the boulders and waited for the plane to come back. But when it didn't appear again MacGregor stood up: 'It's no use cowering up here,' he said. 'We'd better get down to the village.'

They ran down the dirt road and along the river bank, and the black blanket of napalm which smelled of vaseline was burning the road and the fields and the end of the village. Even parts of the pale little river were on fire. They splashed through the unflaming stretches of the river to get away from the worst of it, and they reached the end of the village which was burning. It was already too hot to approach.

'Whose plane was it? Who would do such a thing?'

'Anybody. Everybody,' MacGregor said bitterly. 'They must've known the Committee was meeting here.'

The villagers and the rest of the political Kurds who had fled from the village were now running back, shouting and crying. Suddenly there seemed to be a hundred noisy men and women and children running about in the smoky panic in front of them. MacGregor and Kathy got near enough to the fire to see half a dozen bodies that were charred into smoking black lumps of burned meat, still burning with the intensity and stickiness of the jellied flame. They could hear screaming and moaning from some of the stone houses. Burned sheep, looking like charred old logs, were still smouldering.

'Look at that!' Kathy cried.

Two women whose flesh was still on fire were running in confusion, their legs and arms burned black. A woman ran from the river and ran into the hot fire and picked up a burned child and ran back towards the river with it, and as MacGregor went to help the men drag the others away, he shouted to Kathy, who had also run for the child: 'Don't let her put the child in the water. She'll kill it.'

Kathy chased the woman who had now caught the jellied fire from the child. She was shouting and beating at the unquenchable jelly on her clothes, and just before she reached the river Kathy pulled the child out of her arms.

But the flaming woman herself plunged in.

Kathy stood paralysed with the child on fire in her arms. Then she pulled off her sheepskin coat and wrapped the child in it to blanket the flame. But the coat itself caught fire and she took it off again and watched more fat running down the child's body from the melting flesh, where the jelly burned on, embedded deep. Kathy tried to pull the flames off the child with her fingers, but the unquenchable jelly stuck to her fingers and she had to rub the flame off her hand in the dirt. She found a stone and began to rub the burning jelly off the charred part of the child's arm, tearing the black and watering flesh to the bone until she had finally freed it from flame.

The child had been silent and conscious and in shock, but the moment Kathy had cleaned the flame, the girl slid into unconsciousness.

For an hour then, they were themselves involved in the same clutching mess. Panic and nausea followed and when Kathy eventually found Kula and the sewing machine, the girl's hair had been burned off, and her shawl was melted into her charred body. Kathy's unfrightened eyes closed, and in the waves of anger, not knowing for a moment what to do, she wanted to become part of the angry wailing confusion. But she fought it off. She had tried to make an intelligent effort to treat some of the damaged women, but she knew it was hopeless. Instead, she helped the other women who were rescuing bedding and kitchenware and clothes, and piling them together with the burned and the wounded and the dead.

She had lost sight of MacGregor, and it was almost midnight when she finally went through the village looking for him. She could no longer stand the smell and the taste of the scorched air.

'Ivre...' she called out several times.

He did not answer. Then, in the headlight of a jeep, she saw a mongrel saluki which had a hole burned into one side of its stomach. It stood perfectly still, looking around silently with pained eyes, afraid to move because if it did it knew all its intestines would fall out. Kathy squatted in front of the dog for a moment and stroked its ravaged, filthy head.

'Poor old boy,' she said. 'Poor old boy...'

When it nuzzled her slightly, as if it were puzzled about itself, she got up and went to one of the jeeps and took out one of the rifles which Kurds keep between the seats. And, hoping that it was true that they always kept a cartridge in the breech, she put the barrel against the neck of the saluki, who half turned around to look at her, and pulled the trigger. The shot carried the dog ten yards out of the beam of light she was standing in.

Chapter Five

MacGregor was no longer in the village. He was squatting on the floor of an old excise house on the main road, four kilometres down the mountainside. The Iraqi had already gone; so had the Ilkhani. But the Qazi and four blackened men were sitting under a petrol lamp, forcing themselves to finish their Committee business and get out before the Persian army came up the hillsides, or another unmarked plane came back at dawn. The Qazi had ordered the village evacuated. The wounded were being loaded in trucks and jeeps and taken down the mountain roads to Sewaz villages, where there was a Persian doctor.

'Zadko tells me that someone fired at you last night and said it was you who betrayed us,' the Qazi said to MacGregor.

MacGregor had been digging out a woman with Zadko's help when a shot had clipped the dust at his elbow, and the Kurd who had fired it in the darkness had shouted out 'Foreigner! Betrayer!' and had gone on firing until Zadko had fired his pistol at the roof where the shots were coming from.

'Who would believe such a thing, Qazi?' MacGregor asked now.

'Only a fool, and I apologise for him,' the Qazi said. 'Please don't worry about it.'

'I'm not worried about it,' MacGregor said. 'But I am worried about my wife.'

'Where is she?'

'Still in the village. Zadko left her asleep and exhausted in Dusa's house.' Zadko had found Kathy, and had insisted that she rest in the old house, and he had set his man Badr to guard the door.

'Nobody will harm her,' the Qazi said.

'Nonetheless, I'd like to get back as soon as possible.'

'All we need to know,' the Qazi said briskly, 'is your decision.'

MacGregor was about to reply when the Qazi interrupted. 'Don't allow what we have just suffered to influence you,' he said. 'Anger will not count in this.'

'How can I help it?'

'Nonetheless, it's not the best influence for what we want you to do.'

'I had made up my mind anyway,' MacGregor said. 'I'll do what you want done, Qazi, providing of course that I *can* do it.'

'All right,' the Qazi said, and he went on in a business-like way: 'I don't want to ask you to swear an oath of allegiance like the rest of us, but we'll take your word if you accept the six principles of 1946. Do you remember them?'

'Not exactly,' MacGregor told him.

'They're very simple. You must not betray the Kurdish nation, you will work for self-government for Kurdistan, you will not disclose any secrets, you will remain committed for life under these terms, you will consider all Kurds as brothers and sisters, and lastly you will not join another party or group against us. Can you accept all that?'

'Yes,' MacGregor said, but he knew that he was agreeing to something today that he might have been much more cautious about yesterday.

The Qazi looked at the other men in the room for a moment to be sure that they had not fallen asleep with exhaustion. 'In that case,' he said, 'I'll tell you what we want done, and though it may sound simple and unimportant, it is absolutely vital to us.' The Qazi hesitated. Then he added, 'It may also be unpleasant and dangerous for you.'

'I understand all that,' MacGregor said, impatient now with the repeated warning.

'We need help from a European, whom we can trust absolutely. In this case a Kurd would be too conspicuous.'

They heard a truck outside, and they waited for it to pass. Its straining, noisy engine seemed to press urgency on them.

'Last summer in Europe,' the Qazi went on hurriedly, 'almost three hundred thousand English pounds were stolen from us. Or we think it was stolen. All we really know is that it has disappeared, and with it the Kurd we sent to Europe to deal with it. Did you ever hear about it?'

'Never. I didn't know you had that much money.'

'I'll explain that later.'

'You mean it was money belonging to the Committee?' MacGregor asked.

'Of course.'

'What on earth were you doing with that amount of money in Europe, Qazi?'

'We were trying to buy arms with it,' the Qazi said. 'We've got to have modern arms if we are going to train and discipline a serious Kurdish army.'

'But you surely didn't expect the Europeans to sell you arms?'

'Yes we did. We wanted some small anti-aircraft and anti-tank weapons, a certain amount of ammunition, automatic rifles, machine-guns and some radio equipment.'

'But why Europe, Qazi? I can't imagine anyone in Europe selling you stuff like that.'

'Obviously you are not well informed,' the Qazi said calmly. 'There is a vast private arms business in Europe dealing with African and other countries. In fact the arms we wanted were originally bought by a European organisation for Biafra.'

43

'And you bought them openly?'

'No. We were doing it through agents. The arms were to go first to the Lebanon, and then they would be shipped secretly to us.'

MacGregor was beginning to recover from his disbelief. 'All right,' he said. 'What exactly do you want me to do?'

'We want you to find that money.'

MacGregor was not sure what that simple Kurdish statement meant. 'You mean you want me to find the money and then buy the arms with it?' he said.

'No. We don't want you to concern yourself with the arms. We won't press that on you. Just find the money and we'll do the rest.'

The Qazi explained that the Committee had sent the money to Europe with a young Kurd named Manaf Izzat, in the form of a negotiable letter of credit from a Lebanese bank on a Swiss bank in Zurich. 'Manaf was supposed to pay for the arms and arrange their shipment,' the Qazi said. 'But in fact he disappeared, and the money with him. We sent other Kurds, businessmen, to Europe to find out what had happened. But they were met with hostility from everyone, particularly the banks and the officials in Switzerland, France and Britain. Our men could find out nothing.'

'I can understand that,' MacGregor said.

'They were too obviously Kurds,' the Qazi said. 'So everything was hidden from them. That's why we would like you to do it, since you are a European and you will know better how to go about it.'

'I doubt that,' MacGregor said, and then he asked who else knew about the money.

The Qazi opened up his hands in a religious gesture. 'Obviously the banks knew about it, also political agents, governments, police. Too many people know about it.'

'You say Manaf Izzat disappeared,' MacGregor said. 'How do you know he didn't steal the money?'

'That's quite impossible,' the Qazi said, and the other

Kurds also protested sleepily, although Abbekr, the Lebanese, remained impassive. 'Manaf was an incorruptible and dedicated young man.'

'Then what do you think happened to him?'

'Most likely he has been assassinated,' the Qazi said.

'For the money?'

The Qazi hesitated. 'For the money and for the politics. As you know, Agha, everything to do with Kurdish politics becomes violent. Outsiders have always committed violence against us, and encouraged us to violence.'

'Then what's the point of pursuing it, since whoever assassinated him obviously got the letter of credit and the money?'

'But it wasn't quite negotiable,' the Qazi said.

'Why not? You said ...'

'It needed one other signature besides Manaf's.'

'Whose?'

'Mine,' the Qazi said. 'We had arranged for many safeguards and alternatives, because everything to do with that money had to be done cautiously.'

'They can forge anything these days,' MacGregor pointed out.

'I don't think it was done that way,' the Qazi insisted.

Again there was a moment's stillness, and MacGregor could clearly hear every man around him breathing. He knew that they were waiting for him to say that he would leave instantly for Europe, find the money and return it safe and sound. But he felt his original caution returning.

'Where did the money come from in the first place?' he asked.

The Qazi allowed himself a dry joke. 'Do you think we stole it, my friend?'

'Revolutions have been financed that way before.'

'Would it shock you in this case?'

MacGregor shrugged. 'No. But I'd like to know before I get involved in asking questions about it.'

45

'Qazi!' someone shouted through the door. 'You'll have to hurry. We can hear a mortar firing on the other side of the plateau.'

The Qazi simply opened his briefcase again and took out a document covered in cracked seals which were laced together by a green ribbon. 'This is the agreement signed between the Kurdish Committee and the Leoco Oil and Mineral Company of Beirut,' he said.

'Agreement for what?'

'It's an agreement to give the Leoco company a three-per-cent share in all the natural resources in Kurdish areas for ten years after they become available to us.'

'But you're not even a state yet, Qazi. You have absolutely no control over your resources. How could you make an agreement like that?'

'We have found friends who are willing to invest in our future.'

MacGregor glanced at the document in his hand which was written in the bird's-nest language of legal Lebanese French.

'Who controls the Lebanese company?' he asked. 'I've never heard of it.'

'There are a Lebanese Kurd, an Armenian living in France, a Syrian and a Swiss. Our Lebanese Kurd is here —Abbekr.'

Abbekr, the plump expressionless businessman, simply blinked his red-rimmed eyes. He was still cleanshaven and he was the only man who was not stained or dishevelled. He bowed a little to MacGregor.

'Forgive me saying so, Qazi,' MacGregor said caustically, 'but haven't you involved a foreign oil company in your plans for independence?'

'Do you object to that?'

'I know from experience in Iran and everywhere else that it's a very dangerous thing to do.'

'It may be dangerous,' the Qazi told him, 'but our prob-

46

lem is to buy arms. For that we need money. And if foreign businessmen are willing to gamble on our ultimate victory, then we ought to risk it ourselves.'

'Qazi! You must hurry...' the voice shouted again through the door.

Then Zadko came in nervously and said: 'Something on tracks is coming up the black road.'

The Qazi looked at MacGregor and waited.

MacGregor hesitated, but he knew that there was nothing to hesitate about. 'All right, Qazi. I'll do it. But I'll need a little time, and a lot more information.'

The Qazi thanked him simply in French, thus avoiding the flowery necessities of Kurdish or Persian. 'You will have to go to Europe on some other excuse,' he pointed out. 'Is that possible?'

'I am due for six months' leave from the NIOC,' MacGregor said. 'And my children are in Europe. Also, Kathy wants me to go anyway.'

They heard another truck passing outside, and Zadko was outside shouting at someone to turn his lights off. The Qazi got up and came around and stood with his thin hand gripping MacGregor's elbow.

'It's something I would not normally ask you to do, but it's really the Kurdish future that's involved, not just the money.'

'I understand...'

'And please don't underestimate the risks involved. One man has probably been killed already.'

'I'll need to know a little more,' MacGregor said again.

'Don't worry. Abbekr will give you more information. But when you are in Europe you will have to use your own judgement. You will have to act quite alone, without any help from us, since communication will probably be impossible.'

'I understand.'

'But as far as we are concerned you are acting for us, and

we will accept your judgement in whatever has to be done.'

'I'm not an expert in such things,' MacGregor began. 'And I can only use the methods I use in my own work, which is a cautious step by step approach. I'm not a diplomat, Qazi, I'm a scientist. So you're probably putting your case in poor hands.'

'You'll know what to do,' the Qazi assured him, and he added quietly, 'You must trust the Lebanese, Abbekr. The details are all in his hands, and he'll tell you where to begin and how to make contact with us. He's a good man. Never mind his thick business face. He's a Kurd. He will wait for you now in Mahabad. You know Hamid in Mahabad?'

MacGregor nodded and they shook hands as Zadko called him out to the jeep, and told him they'd better go up to the village to find the khanoum and then get out. But when MacGregor got in the front seat he was so exhausted that he fell asleep before the jeep had reached the village. He was awakened by Zadko leaping out in his carpet slippers and shouting 'Badr, Badr.'

There was no reply in the empty, smouldering, village street.

'Where the devil have they gone?' Zadko said, and he shouted angrily again, 'Badr.'

MacGregor went into the stone hut, expecting to find Kathy asleep. But when he lit the lamp he saw that the bed was empty and the sleeping bag lay untidily on the floor near the rucksack.

'Where are they?' MacGregor said anxiously as Zadko came in.

'I don't know,' Zadko replied, and they went outside and shouted in the dark empty village which still stank of burned-up habitation: 'Badr, where the devil are you?'

A dog sniffed hopefully at Zadko's feet. He kicked it out of the way and it ran off into the dark alleyways.

'Well, what's happened?' MacGregor demanded. 'Obviously something's gone wrong.'

'Badr must have gone off with the jeep that has the mortars. But I don't know what the khanoum did.'

'Then we'd better search the village,' MacGregor said, and unhooked the petrol lamp and surreptitiously and fearfully looked for bloodstains on the bed or on the floor.

'Don't think that, for God's sake,' Zadko said.

'You may remember that someone took a shot at me in the night,' MacGregor said.

'I know, but ...'

'And,' MacGregor went on grimly, 'Kurds are well-known kidnappers and murderers.'

'Don't imagine such things,' Zadko said. 'It's not possible. Why, I'd personally kill anyone that did such a thing.'

But MacGregor detected the same sort of panic in Zadko, and as they began to search the village in the darkness, shouting for Kathy and hearing their voices echo off the pale moonlit mountains, MacGregor knew that she was gone.

Chapter Six

They put the rucksack into the jeep and drove down the mountain to the Qazi, who said it must be a mistake of some sort. 'No Kurd would harm her. Please don't worry.'

'Unfortunately I haven't your confidence in Kurdish restraint,' MacGregor said. 'So I have to worry. I shouldn't have left her.'

He knew it was insulting for a Kurd to hear that from a foreigner, but he knew that the Qazi would forgive him, as Zadko did. The Qazi spoke to some of the Kurds sitting in a truck and sent for others whom he then took aside and questioned. Then he called to MacGregor.

'Mohamed says she went off with the young Dubas khan.'

'Who's he?'

'The Ilkhan's youngest son.'

'Do you know him, Zadko?' MacGregor said, getting into the jeep.

'Of course. Dubas the doll. As treacherous as the old man.'

'I mean, can you find him? Where would he be?'

'Qazi?' Zadko asked.

'Mohamed says that they have probably taken her to Kasta village, which is in their tribal area, and is a sort of spring outpost for them.'

'But what for?'

'I don't know,' the Qazi admitted unhappily. 'Kurds sometimes do stupid things. Unpredictable stupidities. I think Dubas is obedient to his father, but you should hurry and find her.'

MacGregor told the Qazi that he would catch up with the Lebanese Kurd in Mahabad, and as they went back up the mountainside to find the road to the village MacGregor shouted questions at Zadko: How far? How long?

'Kasta village is eight hours away. They've probably got about two hours' start, maybe more. But we can take a short cut on the Turkish side. We'll catch them before they reach their own territory.'

Zadko put a drum of petrol into the back of the jeep and they set off. The route they followed was a punishing, muddy, mountain track that ran along the mountain borders of Turkey and Iran, and by dawn they were travelling slowly in a white, wet, depressing mountain mist that drifted theatrically across the empty hills.

'Now that it's light,' Zadko shouted, 'I'll go down the mountainside.'

He swung the jeep off the potholed track and drove it straight down the side of a steep foggy slope in order to cut off a kilometre of winding road. But when they were half-way up the other side of the valley, climbing now, two explosions above them tore up lumps of rock and sludge. Muddy earth rained down on them from the mountainside.

'By God, that's a mortar from the river bed,' Zadko shouted, and stopped.

'Which side of the border are we on?' MacGregor asked.

'We're in Turkey,' Zadko said. 'But it'll save hours this way.'

'Then go on.'

'We can't. We'll have to get by those Turks, sitting down there on the river bank waiting for us.'

'Then go back. Only don't let's wait here.'

'Listen. It's just as dangerous going back. They could

catch us either way. And anyway, if we go back now we've lost too much time, maybe six hours.'

'All right. But what are you going to do with that?' MacGregor said.

Zadko had taken a Kalashnikov automatic rifle out of a sheepskin jacket in the back of the jeep, and he fumbled in the box that lay between them on the floor of the jeep and pulled out a clip of ammunition for it.

'There aren't more than ten or twelve men down there,' he said. 'All soldiers hate these mountains. So if I make a noise and frighten half of them, the rest will get out of the way.' He wiped the gun grease off his hands by running them along the engine cover of the jeep. 'Well?' he demanded.

'It's Turkey,' MacGregor protested.

'It's Kurdistan,' Zadko said.

'Can we do it some other way?'

'Listen, habibi. I don't want to worry you, but that young bastard Dubas can't be trusted, and we can't lose time with him. They can trail Kathy for weeks over the mountains, which will keep you here, chasing on behind. The old man hates you, and doesn't want you to go to Europe for the Committee. He's probably behind the murder of Manaf Izzat who was sent with the money. So we'd better get to him before he even knows we're there.'

'All right. Let's go.'

Zadko got back into the jeep. 'Give me a push,' he said, 'and then jump in. We'll creep up on them a bit.'

MacGregor pushed the jeep and leapt in as Zadko let it free-wheel silently and recklessly down the dirt road again. As they tumbled down in silence, MacGregor realised that Zadko had already seen everything tactically. But he was surprised when Zadko restarted the motor.

'They'll hear you,' he shouted.

'They won't have time now to know where it's coming from in the mountains,' Zadko said, and he drove the jeep at full speed into the shallow river and along the river bed until he had reached a bend. Then he pulled the jeep out of the water and stopped the engine. He leapt out in his wet slippers and squeezed between three large boulders. MacGregor followed, and he saw that they were directly behind the Turkish mortar crew of five or six men, barely a hundred metres away. They were clustered around their weapon on the open sand, looking up at the mountain, obviously trying to guess where the jeep was.

'It won't be difficult,' Zadko whispered.

He took his time. He walked back to the jeep and gave MacGregor an old Lee Enfield British service rifle and said, 'When I drive the jeep at them I'll stop when I'm almost on them. Then we can both fire and make plenty of noise. If you fire at the ground it makes no noise. If you fire at the rocks, the ricochets and the echoes make a lot of noise. Soldiers don't like ricochets. They don't understand them. They'll be surprised, and we will just frighten them a little and then drive on past them in the panic.'

Zadko put the Kalashnikov on his lap and drove out of the river, and as they came around the bend in full view of the Turkish soldiers the Turks were all facing the wrong way. Zadko drove on until he was almost over them. The soldiers turned around and Zadko stopped the jeep and began to fire, splintering the rocks above them. The explosions rocked the valley, and MacGregor fired the Lee Enfield clumsily at the rocks and the river, and he watched the mortar crew running for cover.

'Soldiers!' Zadko roared contemptuously. 'Soldiers!'

He drove the jeep carefully and deliberately through the camp, scattering petrol cans and equipment, and by the time he had reached the road and was speeding up the slope, the confusion behind them was more or less as Zadko had anticipated.

But what he had not anticipated was another jeep with four Turks in it coming down the mountain road which they were now going up. The two jeeps almost collided head on as they met on a shallow curve. MacGregor saw surprised Turkish faces flash by, and he also saw a machine-pistol in a soldier's lap.

'Take the automatic,' Zadko bellowed, 'and shoot at them when you can. If they catch us now they'll cut us down without asking any questions.'

Zadko pushed the Kalashnikov off his lap into Mac-Gregor's and as they groaned up a steep, rutted stretch, MacGregor looked back and saw the Turkish jeep, which was obviously in better condition than their own. It was already coming up the slope around the bends behind them.

'Look out,' MacGregor shouted involuntarily as the Turkish soldier in the front seat began firing at them with his machine pistol.

'Shoot them,' Zadko roared.

MacGregor watched, fascinated, at the next bend when he could see the Turk firing at them again.

'Will you *do* it,' Zadko roared again. 'I don't want a soldier's bullet up my arse and I don't want to be hanged by a Turk.'

MacGregor lifted the Kalashnikov and, forgetting that all automatics had to be fired low, he pointed it where he wanted to hit the jeep—at the front tyres. He pulled the trigger. The rapid flow of fire and the recoil, and the surprise of it, kept his finger firmly down. But the barrel lifted, and bullets smashed into the windscreen instead of the tyres. MacGregor saw the driver and the soldier next to him collapse backwards as if someone had slapped them hard. Then the jeep crashed into the rocky edge of the road and went over the side.

'Did you stop them?' Zadko had been repeating, trying to look around.

'I shot the driver,' MacGregor replied.

'Sweetheart!' Zadko laughed, and he went on calling

MacGregor sweetheart at the top of his voice until they were over the ridge and well on their way into the vast sheltering valley below.

Zadko simply kept going then until they were safely back in Iran, and by noon, when they had reached Kasta village, he swore they were in time. They parked across the highland dirt road, blocking it where it wound up a narrow defile, and they waited there for cars to appear on the road below them.

'Don't worry,' Zadko said. 'She'll be all right.'

MacGregor would say nothing, and Zadko guessed what the matter was.

'It was just bad luck,' he said. 'It was a mistake, habibi. Not your fault. .'

'It was stupid,' MacGregor said.

'You were a soldier,' Zadko said consolingly. 'You've won English medals, military crosses. Why be so upset about a few Turks?'

'Because I'm not a soldier any more,' MacGregor said angrily. 'It shouldn't have happened.'

'It was my fault,' Zadko told him. 'But now we'd better worry about the Ilkhan and his son. Do you know why we call Dubas a doll? Because he has no conscience and no fear, like an Englishman.'

Zadko stood up. A Volkswagen mini-bus was visible below, and Zadko started the jeep and kept it running. 'Let them get out first,' he said. 'Don't get down from the jeep, no matter what happens.'

He was nursing the Kalashnikov on his knees as the muddy Volkswagen roared up the hill. The driver was blowing his horn angrily. Zadko's jeep was astride the road, and Zadko was sitting in it shouting insults. The little bus stopped a foot from the jeep and four Kurds in embroidered jackets and wide Kurdish trousers and carrying rifles leapt out.

They looked. Then they laughed. 'It's Zadko,' they said. 'By God it's him.'

'Where is the khanoum?' Zadko demanded.

'Where do you think she is?' they said. 'Up our arse-hole?'

MacGregor had stepped down from the jeep, and he looked in the Volkswagen. She was not there. But an American car, covered in mud, had also stopped fifty yards away, and they saw someone get out of the front seat and walk up the road towards them, avoiding the puddles. He was a young, handsome Kurd and he wore the rich, pictorial European clothes which wealthy and sophisticated Kurds liked. He had very fine riding boots, a hussar jacket lined with sheepskin, an open-necked Byronic white shirt, a willow switch, and a nerveless body.

'That's Dubas,' Zadko said.

He did not hide his surprise to find Zadko sitting in a jeep waiting outside the borders of his own tribal area. 'You peacock, Zadko. You bastard,' he said calmly. 'What are you doing here?'

'Where is the khanoum, Dubas?' Zadko asked him.

'The khanoum is quite safe,' Dubas said, glancing at MacGregor but ignoring him at the same time.

'Where is she?' MacGregor said.

'Are you the husband?' Dubas said to MacGregor in perfect French.

'Where is she?' MacGregor said again.

'Don't be in a panic,' Dubas said. 'Come to my car. I have some cognac. You look quite sick.'

MacGregor knew he was filthy and unshaven and burned and grease-smeared and weary. And sick. 'It would be better if you'd tell me where my wife is,' he said, getting ready now for some kind of violence without knowing yet what it would be.

'Of course. But I hope you haven't been listening to everything Zadko says about me and my family,' Dubas

56

said good-naturedly. 'Zadko exaggerates. Zadko has a Kurdish tongue. He spoils everything.'

MacGregor knew that once upon a time a younger Zadko would have shot Dubas dead for a remark like that, but Zadko in carpet slippers simply called him *forfar the barmeesh*, which was sufficiently belittling and insulting in Kurdish.

Dubas laughed with his dark, attentive, unfrightened eyes that never left MacGregor's face. 'Do you really think I have kidnapped Madame?' he said, playing at the incredulous.

'Whatever you have done with Madame,' MacGregor replied, 'is stupid and dangerous.'

'But I rescued your wife from the awful business of Persian occupation. Their soldiers were only a few miles away from Zinjan village...'

'Where is she?' Zadko said again.

'She is safe with my father.'

'Where is your father?'

'Ah ... you're afraid of me,' the Kurd said happily.

MacGregor took the rifle from the jeep and said to Zadko that he was going down to the other car. 'If she's there I'll bring her back. If she isn't, we'll take this boy with us,' he said.

'I shall accompany you,' Dubas said.

'No,' Zadko told him. 'You stand quite still.'

MacGregor walked alone down the dirt road to the American car which was so splashed with mud that the windows were obscured. Only a small patch of the windscreen was clear. He heard Zadko and Dubas arguing behind him, and when he was a few yards from the car he called out: 'Kathy, are you there?'

He heard a commotion inside the car and then the back door opened and a Kurd got out. Then Kathy, who was surprised to see him.

'What for God's sake are you doing here?' she said. 'And

what are you doing with that?' She pointed to the rifle.

'Are you all right?' he said.

'Of course. Why?'

She had cleaned herself up and she was wearing a Zouave jacket similar to the one Dubas wore, and her hair was brushed.

'Why didn't you show yourself before?' he said.

'I didn't know it was you up there. I couldn't see through the car window.'

He was inexplicably angry with Kathy now for being here.

'Dubas, that boy, said it would be dangerous to show myself. What's happened?'

'You'd better come up to the jeep quickly,' he told her.

'Why?'

'Never mind now. Come on.'

'Wait a minute till I get my gloves.'

'Leave them,' he said and took her arm as the old Ilkhan got out of the front seat. MacGregor could hear him snarling, the way most Kurds did when they were threatening violence. He followed them up the road to the jeep.

'You look awful,' Kathy said to MacGregor.

'I feel awful,' he told her sharply, 'so don't quarrel with me until we're out of this.'

'Are you all right?'

'Quite all right,' he said.

But she knew that something had just damaged him and that there was something else in this odd drama she did not understand.

'Be careful,' she said gently to him, seeing the signs of rare temper, watching the rifle, and seeing Zadko with an automatic held in the pit of Dubas's stomach.

'Just don't say anything at all,' MacGregor told her. 'Nothing!'

The old Ilkhan, coming up the road behind them, roared in agony when he saw the gun in his son's stomach.

'What's this? By God! What's this?'

'This is your son, old man,' Zadko said.

'Shut up, Zadko,' Dubas said sharply. 'We don't want this to degenerate into a typical, bloody, Kurdish mess. Don't provoke him now.'

'But my God! My God!' The Ilkan turned around and shouted 'Hassan!' Two more men got out of the American car, also carrying rifles, and walked up towards them. There were now six of the Ilkhan's men around them, all armed.

'Let us pass, Ilkhani,' MacGregor said when Kathy was in the jeep.

'Who's stopping you?' the Ilkhan taunted. 'What are you afraid of? Are you afraid of Kurds?' That was a battle cry. 'Pass. Drive on if you are so brave. My God...'

The impasse now was one of pride and face. Neither side would risk moving now. But then Dubas said calmly to MacGregor in French: 'Get in the jeep and go.'

The old man was now ordering his Kurds to stand off at a distance, which would give them an advantage. But his son said at last: 'Be quiet, father. This incident is over. We can't get anything more out of it now.'

'What did you hope to get out of it in the first place?' MacGregor asked as he climbed in the back of the jeep. 'Money?'

That was an insult, but Dubas ignored it. 'We took pity on your wife,' he said contemptuously.

'You trick a woman...'

'Don't say such things,' Dubas said coldly. 'I assure you that your wife was always safe. He turned to Kathy. 'I hope you will tell him, Madame Kathy, that we behaved only with honour and courtesy.'

'Yes, that's true.'

'Our mountains,' Dubas went on in French, with a cold young smile and an affectionate gesture at the bare hills, 'may encourage us to behave differently from you, so I apologise for them,' he said with a mocking little bow. 'But I'll be in Europe soon myself, and perhaps then I will explain it to you, and we can redress the insults.'

And as Zadko started the jeep they heard Dubas laugh and say, 'May God go with you.'

Zadko did not waste any time, but put the jeep into its usual plunging dive. MacGregor hung on painfully in the back, holding the rifle in one hand and gripping anything else he could with the other. But he was longing now for this incident to be over, and for this journey out of these mountains to come to an end.

Chapter Seven

Zadko did not take them straight to Mahabad. He took them to the mountain portion of the black (asphalt) road fifty kilometres from Mahabad, where his son, Taha, planned to kidnap the Iranian officer Colonel Razmara, who inspected the road every month on the same day at the same time. Zadko left them in a little mountain karchani, a local tea house, where Colonel Razmara always ate his lunch. Zadko himself had gone to the village above the road to find his son before the boy came down on the tea house with his half dozen urban revolutionaries, none of whom was more than twenty-one years of age.

'If Razmara comes in first,' Zadko told them, 'for God's sake keep him here till I come back.'

'What happens if you don't find Taha?' MacGregor wanted to know. 'We can't just stay here, Zadko.'

'Don't worry. I know where he is,' Zadko said. 'Only don't let Razmara get in his car or go on his way until I let you know that I've put my thumbs on Taha.'

When Zadko had gone MacGregor sat at the old deal table watching his wife who was struggling to overcome the stale boiled atmosphere of the karchani. It had been raining, and every man who crowded into its mud walls sat at a table and steamed the air with the smell of trucks, horses, dogs, sheep, grease, tobacco, stewed meat and the gutted mixture of food and damp bread and kerosene.

Kathy had not yet tried to find out what had happened to MacGregor, and he was obviously not going to tell her unless she insisted. But now she was tired of his silence, and she asked him why he and Zadko had been in such a panic.

'Dubas told me he would take me to Mahabad, where you would be waiting,' she said. 'So what were you so worked up about?'

MacGregor watched the door, waiting for Razmara to come in.

'They were not taking you to Mahabad,' he told her. 'They were going to keep you moving around the mountains for weeks while I went looking for you.'

'But why?'

'Because the Ilkhani wants to keep me out of Kurdish affairs. Because he doesn't want me to do what the Qazi asked me to do.'

'What does the Qazi want? What are you being so secretive about?'

He told her then what the Qazi had asked him to do, and while he told her she watched him carefully but incredulously. 'I knew it,' she said. 'I knew they would suck you in.'

'They haven't sucked me into anything,' he said.

'Then why didn't you refuse?'

He would not argue with her, and she knew by looking at him that something else had affected him deeply. 'What happened before you got to me?' she asked him.

'I shot two Turkish soldiers,' he told her.

'*You* shot them?'

'Yes.'

'That's awful. How did you get involved with Turks?'

'We were on the Turkish side. They fired on us and I had no choice.'

'But that's awful, Ivre,' she said again.

'Of course it's awful,' he said angrily. 'We were taking a short cut because we were worried about you.'

'But I was perfectly safe.'

62

'You were not perfectly safe.'

Before Kathy could continue it an old woman who had been standing near them at the greasy window with a chador held up to her chin pushed a grubby piece of paper in front of MacGregor and began to mumble: 'Your Excellency. Your Excellency.'

'What is it?' MacGregor said.

'I can't read,' the woman said. 'Can you tell me what this says. It's a letter from my youngest son.'

MacGregor looked at the barely legible, illiterate Persian script and said: 'It's only a few words, mother. Your son says' (he peered closely at it, afraid to put on his spectacles) 'that you must wait here with two hens. Is it hens?'

'Yes. I have them.' She pointed to a cloth bundle on the muddy floor, and MacGregor could hear cawing in it.

'That's all it says,' MacGregor told her.

'But where is he?' she said, pointing to the paper.

'He doesn't say.'

'I've been expecting him here two days and two nights. He hasn't come.' She couldn't weep for him any more, she said, because all his life she had wept for him. Her eyes, she said, were quinces.

'Leave the two hens with me,' MacGregor said to her, 'and I'll see that your son gets them. You go on home, mother.'

'Give her some money,' Kathy said in English.

'What's your son's name?' MacGregor asked.

'Hassan, of the tobacco village Karseem.'

'Go on home, mother. It's stopped raining.'

'Excellency...'

'Give her some money,' Kathy insisted again.

MacGregor shook his head. He had never been able to give money to a victim. Kathy tucked a 100-Rial note into her dress and the old woman began to weep. Kathy took her to the door and sent her on her way.

'I can't even bear the sight of Persian misery any more,' Kathy said vehemently.

'You'll be all right when you get Europe out of your eyes,' he told her sourly.

'Europe's got nothing to do with it.'

'Nonetheless...'

'All right. Then I *have* Europe in my eyes, and the difference is real. So you can't blame me for feeling wretched when I see dirt and poverty again.'

'If you have to live with it,' he told her, 'thinking about Europe won't help.'

'How do you know it won't? That's a help you won't even try.'

He pushed away the rest of the cold grey mutton and looked at his beautiful and intelligent English wife and wondered again what had happened to them. When she had gone away to Europe he had wondered for the first time in his life if Kathy was still entirely his. Their long, tight marriage had survived their complicated loyalties to difficult causes in Iran, his house arrest (twice), and his in-and-out relationship with the old Anglo-Iranian company and with the NIOC. These difficulties had never divided them. Before her trip to Europe with the children they had never been apart, except for the four months he had spent at Cambridge eighteen years ago, finishing his second Doctorate of Science. But he knew that Kathy was finally tiring of it.

'All right,' he said to her now, as if he had just made up his mind. 'If you can ever convince me that we would be satisfied with Europe, then I'll stay there for good when I've finished this Kurdish business.'

She looked surprised and suspicious. 'What makes you suddenly say a thing like that?' she said.

'Just let me do what the Kurds want me to do,' he said, 'and then I'll leave here for good.'

'I can't believe it.' But when he flushed angrily she said,

64

'All right, all right,' as if his decision would fly away if she didn't accept it without question. 'If that's the only way to get you out of here, then all right.'

He still eyed the door, he still held the trussed hens which, head down, were cawing and struggling to be untrussed. The crowd in the sweat-filled inn was thinning. The sun came out and the shattered old German trucks, loaded like barges, were starting up, and the mud on the floor of the coming-and-going was already drying in clumps. The proprietor ran out shouting that someone owed him money, and MacGregor still held the birds, still watched the door.

'There's Razmara,' he said.

Colonel Razmara did not say anything to them. He bowed to them and then sat down at a table that had been kept for him. He ordered his lunch, and MacGregor was suddenly aware of four young men dressed like ragged truck drivers sitting at a table surrounded by bundles. He knew they were not truck drivers, and he decided that if Razmara had any sense he would also know they weren't truck drivers.

'What are we supposed to do now?' Kathy said.

'Just wait.'

Razmara was a long-faced man with no facial expression, no visible response, no embarrassments, no surprises; always a little disgusted. 'Well,' he said in English to them when he joined them. 'What are you two doing here?'

MacGregor shook Razmara's limp, disinterested hand and said he had just come from the Zinjan plateau where he had been looking at some of the gas drilling sites.

Razmara smiled sceptically. 'Did you know that one of those villages up there was bombed?' he said.

'We were there when it happened,' MacGregor told him, and he asked Razmara whose unmarked plane had done it: the Iranians, the Turks, the Americans or one of the half dozen foreign intelligence agencies that operated up there without any kind of control?

'I don't know yet. But I saw some of the wounded going down to the hospital in trucks. That's all I know about it.'

'It was brutal and disgusting,' Kathy said.

'In the present situation,' Razmara pointed out, beckoning to the proprietor to bring his food over to their table, 'the Kurds expect that sort of punishment when they plot rebellion. May I join you?'

'Of course.'

As he sat down, a plump *dehdar* (a local district governor), who had arrived with him and then disappeared, returned buttoning up his trousers. He was horrified when he saw Kathy, so that his little black moustache seemed to stand on end. The Colonel said a few sharp words to him, but the proprietor absorbed the embarrassment by spreading a damp once-white tablecloth and laying more knives and aluminium forks and bringing more tea and fly-ridden sweetmeats.

'Madame,' the dehdar said to Kathy. 'Aren't you wearing a Megrik jacket?'

'Yes.'

'It must belong to Dubas. That's what he wears. Where is he?'

'On his estates, I suppose,' Kathy said.

'Some day,' Razmara said as he dipped a piece of flat bread into the sweet hot tea, 'Zadko will kill that rich boy, and that'll be a good solution to it.'

'To what?'

The Colonel pointed out of the window at the mountains. 'It might absorb some of that insane violence up there.'

Razmara had ordered a bowl of pistachios to be brought and when it was on the table he pushed it towards Kathy and said: 'Do you agree with me, Madame Kathy?'

'With everything you say,' she said.

66

Razmara almost smiled. 'You don't agree?' he said to MacGregor.

'Kurds don't always fight among themselves, Razmara.'

'Maybe not. But they're far too violent to justify your affection for them.'

MacGregor felt Kathy's finger on his arm. Zadko and Taha had walked in, but MacGregor saw at a glance that they were unarmed, which put the danger upon them rather than Razmara. Zadko had a price on his head and was always fair game for army, police or anyone else, although there were times when everybody ignored it.

'I hoped I would find you here,' Zadko said familiarly to Razmara.

Razmara held up his hand in mock protest and defence.

'Don't worry,' Zadko said. 'It's perfectly peaceful.'

Razmara was looking keenly at Taha, who was not wearing Kurdish costume but was dressed in green fatigues, the uniform of the world's town and country jungle fighters.

'Has he joined the South Americans?' Razmara commented in Kurdish.

Zadko laughed and kissed Kathy's hand, but though Taha greeted his 'aunt' warmly he did not touch her. In Teheran Taha had been a clever, reckless boy with bright, hard eyes, and an almost gentle but cold-blooded concern for others. It was a natural, mountain courtesy, and Cecie, their daughter, had been an easy adolescent victim to its attractions. But now Taha was older and colder, and he was not going to be cracked by anything or by anybody.

'Much against my better judgement,' Taha was saying to Razmara, 'I give you this.' He gave Razmara a sheet of folded yellow paper.

'What is it?'

'A piece of dirty paper,' Taha said, 'full of protests against your imprisonment of Kurdish students. It demands their release. It objects, it denounces, it insists, etcetera, etcetera.'

'Who is it for?' Razmara asked.

'The Pad-i-Shah himself.'

'I'll deliver it in person,' Razmara said, and put it in his tunic pocket.

'I know exactly where you will deliver it,' Taha said.

'Good. Anything else?'

'No. That thing is my father's idea. Personally I was going to take you up in our mountains for a while and keep you there until our students were released from prison. And if they weren't released, we would have cut your head off.'

'That would have been stupid,' Razmara told him.

'We may do it next month,' Taha told him. 'Or in six months. You'll never know when it might happen.'

'By all means,' Razmara said. He turned to Zadko who had listened to the conversation with acute Kurdish pleasure. 'Why did you shoot those two Turkish soldiers, Zadko? What was the point? Or did he do it?' Razmara pointed contemptuously to Taha who was now sitting with the four 'truck drivers' near the door.

'What are you talking about?' Zadko protested.

'I heard it on the radio in my car half an hour ago. What made you do something so stupid? You knew there would be reprisals.'

'What reprisals?' MacGregor asked.

'This morning the Turks hanged four Kurds in the nearest village. One was a turbaned schoolmaster, and another was the father of eight children. I don't know what the others were.'

MacGregor barely heard Zadko shouting angrily, 'But my God ... isn't there any justice left on earth?' He was grinding his teeth in the Kurdish protest. 'But I know and swear that our Kurds died like heroes. I know that much,' he cried, and there were tears in Zadko's eyes.

'No doubt they did,' Razmara said drily. 'But you're not going to do that sort of thing up here. We won't tolerate it on either side of the borders.'

'Tolerate what?' Zadko said. 'Two million Kurds live like dogs in Turkey. Every year they shoot or hang God know how many. . . .'

'Don't kill Turkish soldiers on their own border,' Razmara insisted. 'It's not practical.'

He pushed away his unfinished meal and got up.

'Where are you going?' Zadko asked him.

Taha and Razmara had been eyeing each other across the room with obvious understanding and hostility. 'I'm getting out of this place,' Razmara said. 'And I suggest you do the same. It's becoming dangerous.'

'But I haven't eaten yet,' Zadko said.

Razmara put the remainder of the pistachios in his pocket. 'Get out of this place, Zadko,' he said. 'And your South American son also. I don't want you getting into trouble in my area.'

'There's not going to be any trouble,' Zadko said. 'Please sit down.'

'The dehdar has gone to tell my driver to radio the gendarmerie in the old frontier house above the cemetery that you are here.'

'No he hasn't,' Zadko said. 'The dehdar is sitting outside on a bench between two of my look-outs. So please sit down.'

Razmara hesitated, recovered himself, and then smiled an unfrightened sort of smile. 'In that case,' he said, 'I suggest you let him go. Then he and I will continue our usual inspection and ignore all this.'

'All right,' Zadko said obligingly, and Razmara bowed to Kathy and MacGregor as he went out, eating the pistachio nuts.

Zadko held MacGregor back when he was about to follow. 'Those murdered Kurds are our tragedy, not yours,' he whispered. 'It was my fault.'

'I don't care whose fault it was,' MacGregor said. 'It was done.'

69

'Please let us get out of here,' Kathy said to MacGregor. 'I can't take any more of this.'

'All right. Nothing's stopping us,' MacGregor said.

But Katherine pointed to the hens, still tied by the feet. 'What are you going to do with them?' she asked.

He looked at these wretched prisoners of starvation. 'I might as well turn them loose,' he said.

'Don't be crazy,' she told him. 'Someone will catch them.'

'I can't help that,' he said. 'We'll let them go.'

He took a knife from his pocket and cut the strings that tied the legs. He carried them outside and threw them into the air. They landed roughly and began to stagger around as if stuck to the mud. Then a naked-looking dog saw them and barked and gave chase, and the tough little birds ran down the hill croaking and cawing.

Zadko and Razmara were standing at the door, ringed by a dozen other Kurds and Persians, laughing at the spectacle; and MacGregor felt that his skin was shrinking, and his heart contracting for the sort of pain that only he seemed to remember any more.

Chapter Eight

Zadko went back into his thousand hills, leaving them with Taha and an old Peugeot that would take them straight to Mahabad, where Abbekr the Lebanese was waiting for MacGregor. But when his father had gone, Taha said he would now take them to a poor mountain village thirty kilometres away.

'What for?'

'It won't do you any harm, Uncle,' Taha said.

'I haven't time.'

'It won't take long,' Taha insisted calmly, and told them that they could meet some of his fellow revolutionaries who did not believe in united fronts with feodals like the Ilkhan, or businessmen like the Lebanese, or honest priests like the Qazi.

'Or your father?' MacGregor said.

'My father?' Taha said. 'He's got his own Kurdish ideas. What I really came down here with him for was to see you.'

'Oh...'

'It's that money, Uncle,' Taha said in English.

'What money?'

'Now that's childish,' Taha said as he led the way up the hill to the Peugeot. 'Everybody in these mountains knows all about that Kurdish money in Europe, and the arms. Everybody already knows you're going there to get it.'

'That's none of your business,' MacGregor told him. 'So don't even ask me about it.'

They were standing by the Peugeot waiting for Kathy

71

who had been using the mountains the way she hated to use them. She came back into their family argument and said that this was hardly the place for them to take up their old political quarrels.

'Nonetheless, Aunt,' Taha insisted, 'that money ought to go to the revolution, not to the Ilkhani.'

'It's not going to the Ilkhani,' MacGregor said indignantly.

'That's where it will end up,' Taha insisted. 'Somehow the old man will eventually get the money or the arms, and the Qazi can't stop it; nor can my father.'

They began to argue about it again, quarrelling about which should come first, Kurdish liberation or Kurdish revolution, until Kathy interrupted them impatiently.

'Well, you can't settle it here,' she said. 'And anyway,' she told MacGregor, 'Taha is right. You may or may not find that money in Europe. But it won't really help.'

'How do you know it won't?'

'Because it's the same old story. If the Kurds are ever going to succeed at anything, it won't be because of any help from you—a foreigner. And it won't be because of those cunning old men up there plotting among themselves. If anybody ever succeeds it'll probably be Taha—and without your help.'

'Taha wants a revolution even before they've got a nation,' MacGregor pointed out. 'What's the use of that?'

'It's irrelevant,' Kathy said as they got into the Peugeot.

They drove into the mountains for over an hour along a difficult muddy path until they came to herds of black goats that were usually the first sign of a poor mountain village. They stopped in the village, which was lived-in but empty now, and Taha's revolutionaries appeared from the wet rocks and stone huts like men who had been waiting there for some time.

'Why were you so long?' they asked him. 'What happened?'

There were six of them, and each wore the same kind of dirty green jungle uniform that Taha wore, and had shoes. Taha introduced his well-known uncle and aunt, and began to tell them that he had presented their paper petition to Razmara. 'With papa Zadko's help,' one of the boys said cynically.

'Never mind all that stuff about Razmara,' a boy wearing a worn pair of knitted gloves interrupted. 'What's the traffic like on the black road now?'

'Full of Persian army trucks,' Taha reported.

'Then we ought to move on.'

'Don't be in such a hurry.'

'Listen, Taha. The weather's too wet for us to go up any higher now.'

'We can wait here a little longer,' Taha told him.

'No, we can't,' the boy said. 'The army will be up in this village like locusts any day now. They always come through here after Razmara's monthly inspection.'

'What do you say, doctor?' one of them said to Mac-Gregor. 'Do you think we ought to get out?'

'I don't even know what you're talking about,' Mac-Gregor told him.

This embarrassed the youth, and MacGregor inspected them as they stood awkwardly in the village mud. One was bearded, another one was plump and hot and good-natured, one was a studious boy with a row of ball points in his shirt pocket and a pocket book in his belt, one looked too miserable to be dependable, one inspected Kathy with sensuous young Kurdish eyes, and the last of them carried a Russian automatic rifle as if it were a suitcase which he refused to part company with. The oldest was obviously Taha, who looked like a confident old man among them.

MacGregor asked him what, for God's sake, they were doing up here, armed to the teeth.

'This is a herders' village,' Taha said. 'The whole place, and everybody in it, is in fief to a feodal Kurdish landlord,

73

who is Kassim of the Beni Jaf. His agent lives in the next village and he takes every sheep and goat and skin and pluck of wool that comes off these hills. Five years ago the Beni Jaf landlord murdered three village elders up on the summer pastures because they asked for more grain and food and money. Two years before that two young women from this village disappeared, kidnapped by the same Beni Jaf feodals. They were never heard of again. Four shepherds were murdered last year for keeping back clips of wool. In bad years the children starve to death here, or rather they die of sickness caused by malnutrition, cold, and disease. This village rarely sees a lump of sugar or a sack of rice, it never sees a book or a doctor or a school or any of the Kurdish councillors the Government appoints. So they listen to us, Uncle,' Taha said, 'and when the time comes they'll know who to be in revolution against.'

'Using what?' MacGregor said. 'You're armed, but they're not.'

The boys laughed, and Taha said: 'All right. You'd better come and take a look.'

He led them to a small stone hut in a miserable clump of empty shacks. He undid an oiled padlock and opened the door and pulled down a board that blocked a small window. Inside, against the wall, there were four rifles, two sub-machine-guns, boxes of ammunition, mortar bombs, a pile of bayonets and six twenty-gallon drums of petrol.

'Where did you get it from?' MacGregor asked.

'In the last six weeks,' Taha said, 'we have made ten night raids on Persian army posts.'

'Who has?'

'We have,' Taha said.

'And what are they supposed to do with this stuff, Taha? Kill the khans?'

Taha ignored the sarcasm. 'If all these poor villages had arms, the Iranian Army would never come into these hills at all,' he said, 'and the Kurdish landlords would die of

74

fright. That's why we need that stuff you're getting from Europe, Uncle.'

'If the Persians ever find any of this equipment here, they'll hang every man in the village. You're playing games with helpless people, Taha.'

Taha kept his temper and said that no Kurd was helpless, and that the Kurdish revolution had to begin somewhere.

'Not this way,' MacGregor argued. 'You boys can disappear into those mountains. But these people would have to stay here and take the punishment.'

'I know all that,' Taha said. 'But the villagers must become involved.'

'Not this way,' MacGregor said. 'Not in isolated village revolutions.'

Taha had closed and locked the armoury door, and MacGregor looked down the row of mountain shanties and asked him where everybody had gone. Why was the village so empty?

'They're down at the river plateau,' one of the boys said, 'celebrating a sister-and-brother wedding.'

A sister-and-brother wedding among Kurds was the cheapest form of marriage common in all the poor mountain villages. A brother and sister of one family married a sister and brother of another family, which saved the bride price on both sides, and they could hear the ceremonial chanting as they went steadily down to the plateau. They could also hear a flooded little river rushing over stones and through tiny ravines—the sort of river that all Kurdish poets sang about as the true artery of Kurdish life. But before they got there they were met by the village dogs— not the usual dirty salukis, but huge headed, snarling mongrels.

'I hate these village curs,' MacGregor said to Kathy.

'Don't stop,' Kathy told him. 'They always know if you're nervous, and that makes them worse.'

She pushed her arm into his and walked him boldly towards them. The dogs went on snarling but allowed them to pass, and MacGregor noted that not only himself but two of the revolutionaries also got by under Kathy's protection.

'Oh no!' Kathy groaned when they came to the plateau. 'It's that lunatic Kurdish shuffle-dancing and they'll expect us to join it.'

The music was a sentimental wail, and the circle of men and women, shoulders locked, shuffled a few feet one way then the other, waving their bodies like wheat in the wind. They were all poorly dressed—part Kurdish, part European, but mostly with the discards of British, American, Iranian and Iraqi army uniforms. The women dancing looked sheepish, and the men looked conventionally lovesick.

'They're still mooney,' Taha said.

The *khatkhoda*, the village headman, who was sitting among the ragged children huddled in a greasy British army greatcoat, stood up and clapped his hands, and the dancing stopped. The dancers turned off their sheepish lovesick looks and began to laugh.

'Guests,' Taha told them. 'Friends.'

'Welcome,' the villagers said.

They began to slap the revolutionaries affectionately on their shoulders and backs, and then held their hands and wagged their heads. 'Welcome,' they said again as if they had not seen the boys only half an hour before. MacGregor and Kathy were held by the village girls who felt their clothes and pinched their wrists in affection.

'Taha's obviously made an impression here,' Kathy pointed out quietly, pursuing their argument.

'They're all nice boys,' MacGregor argued stubbornly. 'It doesn't mean much.'

'Nonetheless, the Chinese must have begun like this,' Kathy said.

76

'China is thick with people. Kurdish mountain villages are vulnerable little islands of poverty lost in the mountains. There's no comparison.'

The dancers were trying to reform again, and the girls had taken Kathy's hand to pull her into the circle. She was spared by a Kurdish boy who came running up the hill, along the bank of the river, hopping from stone to stone in his bare feet and shouting that two foreigners were on the path below, on their way up to the village.

Chapter Nine

MacGregor followed Taha, who immediately ran up a flight of crude steps cut into a high ledge over the river; from the top of it they could see two men following the river bed along a rough and difficult path. MacGregor looked long and carefully at them through Taha's field glasses, and Taha waited patiently because he knew that MacGregor could recognise many of the foreigners who came into these mountains.

'I think I know them,' he told Taha.

'Who are they?'

'It's an Englishman named Flanders,' MacGregor said, 'and his Persian serf.' He meant valet, but there was no Kurdish word for valet.

'What would he be doing up here?'

'I don't know. But he works for one of those international organisations that save starving children. *Children Unlimited,* I think it's called. Your father knows him. So does your Aunt Katherine.'

'He obviously knows his way up here.'

'He's been in and out of these mountains for years,' MacGregor said.

'Is he a British agent?'

'Probably.'

'Shoot him,' one of the revolutionaries said.

'Don't be foolish,' MacGregor said quickly, aware that any one of these boys would be perfectly capable of doing it.

They heard the old khatkhoda shouting from the river

below that he also knew the *Englisi*. The *Englisi* had been here several times before, and had sent them rice and dried beans and clothes.

'In that case we'll disappear for a while into one of the herders' shelters in the mountains,' Taha said.

Kathy had climbed the ledge, and when she heard that it was Flanders she said she didn't like it at all: 'Be careful with him,' she told MacGregor. 'He was on the plane with me coming from London. Or rather, he got on at Geneva. He and that Persian gladiator. He's bound to be looking for something.'

'Then you'd better delay them for a while,' Taha said as he went down the steps, 'so that we can get everybody out of the way.'

The dancers and the revolutionaries and the dogs were already hurrying back to the village, and MacGregor told one of the older village boys to run to the Peugeot and bring his rucksack down quickly.

'What for?' Kathy said.

'If Flanders is looking for something,' MacGregor said, 'He'll want to know what I'm doing up here myself.'

'He probably knows already.'

'It's more likely that he's heard about Taha and his village revolution,' MacGregor argued, and he stood up and watched the two men's agile rock-hopping. When the boy returned with his rucksack MacGregor took out maps and notebooks and instruments, and Kathy watched him as if she hated his organised stubbornness. He peered over a photometric graph and stretched his eyes at the horizon of empty hills, and at the bare and unpleasant little valleys, and he ignored her.

When Flanders came up the steps of the landing he showed no surprise at seeing them. 'What luck,' he said. 'I knew I'd run into you up here sooner or later.'

Their greetings were casual, and Kathy asked him what he was doing here himself.

'I'm counting sheep,' he said.

'Sheep?'

Flanders laughed. 'I thought that'd shake you.'

Flanders's lively blue eyes had already taken in Mac-Gregor's maps and notes and field glasses and instruments, and the long view over the ridges. 'You remember that very bad winter up here in 1963 which killed off millions of sheep and goats, and a lot of children died?'

'Of course.'

'I've just come from Geneva where my committee has agreed to buy ten thousand sheep and five thousand goats from Turkey to distribute in these remote villages.'

'That'll be useful,' Kathy said, 'particularly for the landlords.'

'The landlords won't get any of it,' Flanders protested. 'I'll be here myself to see that they don't. Anyway, if that's the system, that's the system.'

Flanders's professional eyes were everywhere, and Mac-Gregor felt his napalm-scorched boots being noted, and the grease marks on his jacket, left there by Zadko's automatic.

'You look a bit bashed about,' he said to MacGregor.

'Mountain work can be dirty sometimes,' MacGregor told him.

'I see your old man is still digging for the stuff, Kathy. I didn't think there was oil up here.'

'Not oil,' MacGregor said quickly. 'Natural gas.'

'Now that's interesting. How do you go about it?' Flanders gestured at the maps with a suède boot, and Mac-Gregor wondered how he had managed to keep himself so neat and tidy. Flanders was over sixty, but he was a vigorous, straight-backed, fresh-faced man. He was so clean-shaven that it looked as if he had never had to shave at all. The Persian with him was a neat copy of his master, though a little younger. He was known to be not only Flanders's valet but his masseur as well. In fact, Flanders always looked as if he had been freshly massaged around the neck and shoulders. Both were dressed in English tweeds, and MacGregor knew these two excessively fit old men still did judo together. Flanders was the nephew of Lord Oxted, and a friend of Kathy's family.

'How do you actually find the gas?' Flanders was asking him.

MacGregor could hear the village dogs barking and a car engine going away. But he delayed Flanders a little longer. 'Mostly it's a matter of hydraulics,' he said.

'You mean water?'

MacGregor nodded and pointed to the long line of high-escarpcd hills. 'There's a lot of water flowing underneath all these hills,' he said. 'And up here the underground water is usually mixed with oil and gas. If the flow of the mixture is blocked by a fault or fold at depth, which you can usually detect by the surface faults, the oil and gas and water build up in a sort of high-pressure underground reservoir. That's what we look for.'

'And then what?'

'What do you mean?'

'What do you do with it?'

'Drill it. Pipe it out.'

'But where to?' Flanders waved his hand at the barren mountains.

'To wherever it can be treated.'

'In Iran? Is that the scheme?'

'Of course.'

'What will your Kurdish friends think of that?' Flanders asked him. 'I hear they've actually formed a company, and want it all for themselves.'

MacGregor felt himself blushing, and Kathy had to save him.

'That sounds like one of those Teheran bar room stories you all love to invent about the Kurds,' she said to Flanders.

81

'But I know it to be a fact, Kathy,' Flanders said. 'The Kurds have actually sold a lot of fake oil and mineral rights up here for a fortune.'

'Who told you that?' MacGregor asked him.

Flanders laughed. 'You don't think a scheme like that can be hidden for long do you? Half a dozen people in Geneva told me about it.'

'Geneva?'

MacGregor decided to say no more, but Kathy asked Flanders exactly what they had told him in Geneva.

'The Kurds have banked a large sum of money in Europe from some crooked deal they've made. They've been trying to buy arms with it, and there's even a murderous quarrel going on among the Kurds about whose money it is, and who will get the guns. One Kurd has already been killed in Paris. Isn't that true, MacGregor?'

MacGregor would not reply, which made Kathy angry again. 'We'd better go on up to the village, Arthur,' she said to Flanders. 'It looks as if it's going to rain again.'

MacGregor gladly began to pack up his maps, while Flanders motioned to his Persian serf to precede them down the steps of the ledge.

'One of the most appealing things about this part of the world,' Flanders said as he followed the Persian, 'is the way sworn enemies on both sides just walk through all this hostility. Arabs and Crusaders used to do it. They'd be eating together one minute and cutting each other's heads off the next.'

He leapt athletically down every step, and when they reached the bottom he helped Kathy, who began to make a point of her own.

'I often wonder,' she said to Flanders, 'why you spend so much time up here yourself—coming and going through all the hostility?'

'Starving children,' he said.

'I thought you said dead sheep.'

'Same thing,' Flanders said.

'Very convenient,' she said drily.

'Kurdish children drink goats' milk and they eat cheese made of sheep's milk. That's the only reason I'm here, so stop being so bloody suspicious,' Flanders said good-naturedly.

'I'm only reminding you that Kurds are a murderous and revengeful lot, and you'll get a bullet in your back if you do anything here they don't like.'

'Such as?'

'I don't know ... betray a friend, or spy on them. Or something like that.'

Flanders laughed. 'I swear, Kathy, it's all above board.'

They were walking up the steep path to the village, and MacGregor was listening to their sportive bickering. Kathy went on warning Flanders to mind his own business. But while Flanders was getting a warm welcome from the villagers, Kathy said angrily to MacGregor: 'You see. Everybody knows about that money already.'

'That's why the Qazi wanted someone like me to go and find out what happened to it.'

'They'll find out about you too.'

'I suppose they will,' he said. 'But by that time I hope to know where it is and get it back for them.'

They said no more about it, and they watched Flanders at work among the villagers, speaking broken but adequate Kurdish, even making jokes to the women. He said he was up here to count sheep, goats and children.

He inspected .very part of the village and made notes and asked questions while MacGregor kept his eye on the armoury. When Flanders caught sight of the well-oiled padlock he suddenly threw back his head and laughed as if he had guessed its secret.

'All right,' he called over to MacGregor and Kathy. 'I've finished here. If you want a lift to Mahabad, there's my Landrover.'

His Landrover had come to the village by the same mountain track that Taha had used, and MacGregor followed Kathy up the path to the car, avoiding the dogs but lagging behind a little because he was beginning to feel the effects of no sleep and too much tension.

'Do hurry,' Kathy said irritably to him. 'It's starting to rain, and I hate getting wet up here. It's impossible to dry out.'

He caught up with them and pushed a hand through her arm, ostensibly to help her, because she was beginning to be short of breath again. She let his hand drop and finally took her arm away.

She went on laughing and joking with Flanders in the front seat of the Landrover, which Flanders drove. The serf was put in the back seat with MacGregor, who listened to Kathy's and Flanders's cynical teasing of each other until he couldn't keep awake any longer. He went to sleep as they rolled comfortably down the mountains to Lake Rezaiya, and he woke up when they had arrived at the old police station in Mahabad, which was where MacGregor had asked Flanders to deliver them.

'So long, you two,' Flanders said gaily as they got out. 'I'll drop in and see you in Teheran. Lots of questions I want to ask you,' he said to MacGregor. And as the Landrover drove off he shouted: 'About oil...'

MacGregor watched the car until it had completely disappeared. Then he picked up his rucksack and pointed down the dusty road ahead. The house he was looking for was almost on the outskirts of the town, on the banks of the Suaj Bulaq river. It belonged to a Kurd named Hamid the Stitcher; a rich, invisible, city Kurd who had made a fortune after the war from four big stitching machines he had bought from U.S. army surplus, and which sewed up anything from motor tyres and parachutes to silk stockings and tents. It was a new house, an ugly cement villa, but it had become a collecting place for Kurdish nationals, Kurdish moneyed businessmen, and friends like MacGregor.

But there was no Hamid. A servant opened the door and they were shown into a stitched Persian living-room with coloured glass ornaments and carpets on the walls, one of them a gaudy souvenir of Mecca. They waited for ten minutes, and Abbekr the Lebanese came in looking as if he had just been awakened from a deep sleep.

'I apologise,' he said in a delicate businessman's sort of courtesy, 'for the lack of welcome ...'

They went through the usual Persian protestations, then they took coffee, and finally Abbekr told MacGregor what he knew about the money, where it had been deposited, and the steps they had taken to find it. Then he put in front of MacGregor, on the little inlaid table, the bank letters MacGregor needed, with credentials for himself, and a yellow envelope stuffed with a thousand English pounds for his expenses.

'I don't want the money,' MacGregor told Abbekr and pushed it back across the table so that it just touched Abbekr's neat, round stomach.

'You'll need that much and probably more,' Abbekr said, pushing the money back again.

'I don't want it, Abbekr, so don't insist,' MacGregor said.

Kathy prodded MacGregor from the stitched couch. 'Take it,' she said. 'Europe is much more expensive these days than you think.'

He did not know whether Kathy was being cynical or serious. He didn't want to know, because he would refuse to take the money in any case.

'Are you afraid that someone will accuse you of being a paid agent of the Kurds?' Abbekr asked him gently.

'Perhaps.'

'In that case I shan't press you. But will you at least promise that you'll go to Monsieur Ajoukir at the Bank Ismaili in Paris if you need money?'

'If it's necessary,' MacGregor agreed, and got up.

But as Abbekr went ahead to get them Hamid's car, Kathy told him he was mad to spend his own carefully stored savings on this Kurdish fantasy. 'If they've got all that money, then for God's sake let them at least bear the expense of finding it,' she said.

'I'll manage without it,' he told her.

Abbekr told them the car was ready and they followed him out of the house. It was dark and still and cold outside; the sky looked like a purple pincushion and the large walled garden was full of muddy shadows and a soft provincial silence. Long before they had reached the high wooden gate they heard shouting from the top of one of the walls. MacGregor heard someone say in Kurdish: 'Don't let them out yet, Rashid.'

'We'd better wait a minute,' MacGregor said to Kathy.

'What's the matter now?'

'I don't know yet. Just wait.'

There was a sound of scuffling, and they heard someone running along the street outside. Then a car started and roared away.

'Rashid,' Abbekr shouted from behind them. 'Where are you?'

'What's happening?' MacGregor demanded.

A Kurd in tribal costume and armed with a machine-pistol came into the light of the gateway, breathless from running. Then he laughed when he saw them. 'Don't be scared, doctor,' he said. 'It's all right now.'

Abbekr told them to wait a moment and he went out cautiously through the high gate.

'I hope you're enjoying all this,' Kathy said to Mac-Gregor. 'Because I'm not.'

'Oh, it's just Kurdish exaggeration,' he told her.

'No it isn't. They're a murderous lot when they do this sort of thing.'

'Kathy!'

'I mean it.'

Abbekr had returned and he said it was quite all right. 'All that money, you see,' he said apologetically.

'It's not the money,' Kathy said angrily. 'It's him,' she said and pointed at her husband.

'No, no,' Abbekr said, and he helped them into the clattering diesel Mercedes and told Kathy that though Kurds were too provocative and too noisy and too medieval, they were not murderous. And as they drove off, Abbekr waved the tips of his plump fingers at them, delicately, as if to prove how gentle Kurds could be.

Chapter Ten

In Teheran, in their living-room under its low ceiling, and surrounded by their old, creaking house and its dirt garden full of dry leaves, dry cyclamens, dusty bougainvilias, roses, eucalyptus, little dirt canals and a high mud wall, they tried to come to some sort of emotional working agreement which would get them through this.

'How will you tell Jamal Janab that you're abandoning them, and throwing in your lot with the Kurds?' she demanded.

Jamal was the director of *Resources and Reserves*, Mac-Gregor's department of the National Iranian Oil Company.

'I don't know what I'll tell him,' MacGregor admitted.

MacGregor sat in the elbow of a thousand Persian identities, in the house where he had been born and brought up, and he wished that one of their children were here, not only because he missed them but because Kathy would be easier on him if the children were around.

'You'll obviously have to lie to Jamal,' she went on relentlessly.

'If I did he'd only see through me,' he said.

'Then what are you going to say, since you're sworn to Kurdish secrecy?'

He got up and stood by her as if to calm her. 'Don't get angry, Kat,' he told her gently. 'I'm not going to deceive an old friend like Jamal.'

'He's protected you for years.'

'I know,' he said, and though he sifted the cut ends of her hair through his fingers, he was absorbed in some far-away point she couldn't see. 'I'm still sorry you cut your hair,' he said. 'It makes you look like your brother.'

He was surprised when he saw her eyes fill with tears. She pulled away and said: 'Don't start being gentle with me. You're only trying to avoid trouble.'

'That's true,' he said and left her alone.

In the afternoon he tried not to lie to Jamal Janab. The Persian was a plump, jowelled, startled man who knew with the sensitive flesh of a nervous man that MacGregor had something important to say to him, something, in fact, he could not say. They left the Survey room where MacGregor had been showing Jamal the graphs of four of the proposed drilling sites in the Kurdish areas, and they went up to Jamal's glass office in the glass shoe-box building of the NIOC. They sat down at the end of the long conference table where they had held their weekly planning discussions for the last five years, and MacGregor took off his glasses and said as simply as he could: 'I want to go to Europe for a while, Jamal.'

Jamal dropped his thick chin down into his neck in surprise. 'My dear chap,' he said. 'You mean now?'

'It's short notice, I know,' MacGregor went on, 'but I only made up my mind about it after Kathy came back.'

'Ah ... the children,' Jamal said hopefully. 'They need you.'

Jamal was a sentimental family man himself. He had two fat little sons and a plump little daughter with blue rings on her fingers against the evil eye, ringlets, and plump little legs. Jamal liked to find the same soft centre of family sentiment in all his friends. Wasn't that what friendship was for?

'No, it's not that,' MacGregor said. 'I simply want to go away for a while.'

'How long?'

'Six months. Maybe longer.'

'You don't say!'

Jamal got up and walked behind MacGregor and looked nervously out of the window through the plastic lathes of the sun-blind. Then he stared at his daughter's drawings of veiled women which were paper-clipped to the leaves of a giant rubber plant.

'Six months,' he repeated. 'It must be something serious.'

MacGregor did not turn around to follow Jamal's movements. 'In fact, it might even be better if I resign,' he said.

'Why?' Up went his hands. 'Why, in God's name, would you want to resign? What's the matter?' Jamal said in Persian.

MacGregor hesitated. 'Difficult loyalties, I suppose.'

'You mean politics?' Jamal said wretchedly. 'Oh no!'

When MacGregor had been under house arrest the second time, Jamal had been imprisoned for a year. That was when the Iranian oil fields had been denationalised and returned to the foreigners who had made sure that any passionate advocates of nationalisation like Jamal and MacGregor had been locked up. Now Jamal wore his old enthusiasm and his genuine courage disguised under layers of contempt for politics, and MacGregor knew it, and didn't try to break into Jamal's protective surface. But he knew he had to explain himself to Jamal.

'What did we really want when we were young, Jamal?' he said.

'Don't remind me,' Jamal said, cracking his plump fingers in a Moslem ablution. 'Revolutions, liberations, socialism, our national right. Why do you ask?'

'Because it seems to me that we lost our nerve too soon.'

'Now how can you say that?' Jamal demanded. 'After all—we rescued something. We rescued this...' They had rescued the portion of Iran they were sitting in. The NIOC was the only fragment left in Persian hands—less than a third of the national oil resources.

'But look at us.' This time MacGregor raised his arms at the glass walls that surrounded them. 'This isn't really what we had hoped for, is it?'

'But we haven't given in yet,' Jamal insisted.

'Haven't we?'

Jamal understood. 'In that case I don't want to know why you're going to Europe. Don't even tell me.'

'I'm sorry, Jamal.'

Jamal pulled out the drawer of his teak desk and took out a sheet of paper with typed Persian script on it.

'You'd better listen to this,' he said, and read in Persian: 'Inform us if it is possible that one of your senior officers, Dr MacGregor, was with the Sherki Kurd Zadko Jelal Zahib when he murdered two Turkish soldiers near the Sindoi border post. Ascertain if you can Dr MacGregor's exact movements on the 14th and 15th of the month, and do so without revealing the purpose of this enquiry.'

MacGregor felt the hot wind of pursuit, but he knew he could not be distant with Jamal about it. 'Must you answer it?' he asked Jamal.

'I'll tell them anything you say,' Jamal replied. 'But why did you get involved? Why the Kurds, habibi? Why?'

'What's the difference who it is?' MacGregor said to him. 'In the last ten years we've all been waiting for some mysterious event to come along and change everything by a sort of timely miracle. Nothing's come along. Nothing has happened.'

'But what *can* happen?' Jamal said with a large shrug.

'I don't know, but it has to begin again somewhere.'

'All right, all right. But I'm a Persian, and to me every Kurd, no matter where he is, has always been a curse and a nuisance. Let them have anything. Everything they want. But don't, for God's sake, involve yourself with them.'

'Don't worry,' MacGregor said. 'I'll be careful.'

'You say things like that,' Jamal said in exasperation, 'and you look so English. But you frighten me with your primitive determination.'

MacGregor laughed. 'That's why you should let me resign, Jamal.'

'I won't let you resign,' Jamal said. 'You have six months'

leave, which we owe you. What you do in that time is your own affair, not mine.'

'That's not a wise way of looking at it,' MacGregor warned him. 'You ought to fire me. I've tried to give you good reasons for doing so.'

'No. No. I refuse, absolutely. Anyway, what does Kathy say to all this?'

'She doesn't like it.'

'She's quite right. Thank God for that. She's suffering too, like me. I know it. She'll never agree. But I'm not going to let you resign. You belong here with me. There's going to be a big conference on reserves this year, and I think, finally, you and I will be given our proper place, after all these years of being tricked and deceived and ignored and punished.'

'Kathy wants me to leave Iran for good,' he told Jamal.

'Ahhh . . . Kathy! She just says that. I'll talk to her. You can't leave us now. We have just begun to be justified and recognised. You will get something important now. I'm sure of it. Anyway, what would you do somewhere else?'

MacGregor shook his head. 'I don't know. In fact I don't even know what will happen once I get to Europe.'

'Then I don't want to hear anything more about it. You go. Take your leave and let happen whatever happens. Then you can come back. Only you'd better look after yourself, because I know what Kurds will do.'

MacGregor began to say something, but gave up.

'No. No,' Jamal said. 'Please don't try to tell me anything. Don't precipitate anything, I beg you.' He was turning the ruby ring he wore on his little finger around and around. 'Just let us leave it as it is.' And he used both his hands to cut the air.

'All right,' MacGregor said and got up to go.

Jamal escorted him to the door so that there would be nothing more said, nothing more decided. 'When will you be going?' Jamal asked.

'Immediately.'

Jamal waved his plump fingers and dropped his eyelids over his black eyes and said, 'All right, all right. I'll arrange everything,' and he closed the door after him.

When he walked down the corridor MacGregor found Kathy waiting for him in his office. He locked up the new German document safe and pushed his rolled maps into their long, black, plastic pigeon holes and then put out the lights, locked the door, and followed her along the corridors out to the parking bay.

Kathy drove them silently home through the rush-hour traffic of early Teheran eventide. He watched a dry drift of pulverised horse manure swirling along the road before them. The Peugeot taxis, which Persians called time-suckers, swerved in and out of the traffic jams.

'I hate those stupid Peugeot drivers when they do that,' she said vehemently. 'What did you tell Jamal?'

'I told him that I was leaving, and we had a discussion about politics. But I didn't lie,' he added hurriedly.

'But what *did* you tell him?' Katherine persisted.

'Not much. He guessed the rest.'

Another taxi swerved in front of Kathy and she said irritably: 'Did he also guess that you had killed those two Turks?' But before he could reply she let out her breath and said: 'Oh blast. I didn't mean to say that.'

MacGregor kept quiet.

She blew the horn. 'Don't become silent and tight-jawed,' she said to him, 'just because I've said something stupid. Tell me what he said.'

'Nothing much. But he knew about the Turks. He had a message from army or political Intelligence about it. I even offered to resign, but he refused to listen.'

'That's a big help.'

Kathy drove well. She concentrated on what she was doing. But at the next traffic lights she hit the steering wheel impatiently with her hands and said: 'All right. I suppose

I'll have to accept it.' Then she raised her hands to the heavens. 'But my God—Kurds in Europe.'

'It's not the Kurds who are in Europe,' he pointed out as lightly as he could. 'It's their money.'

'And the violence will follow,' she said grimly. 'Anyway, how do you think you're going to find that money?'

'I don't know.'

'Do you want me to do it for you?'

'No, I don't.'

She moved the car six feet. 'You'll do it all wrong,' she told him. 'You'll go into it naked and innocent and pure, like a lamb to the slaughter. If you have any sense you'll let me use everything there is at our disposal—my family...'

'No,' he said.

'... my friends,' she went on, 'and whatever influence they've got. You're not going to get far with your kind of effacement.'

'Just let me do it my own way,' he said.

'All right,' she said. 'All right. Anything to get you out of here.'

He didn't say anything more because he was determined that Kathy's unconscious English contempt would not upset him. He wanted the old shattered streets of the city to get the better of him just once more. This was, in fact, the best part of the day to him. Every time he made this journey home with Kathy, the bare mountains of the Elburz seemed to slide down in their soft evening dust and close off the end of the day for him, wrapping him up in the dim streets of the half-lit city. He had, at times, a recurring, morbid thought that he would probably die in those purple hills. But he didn't really believe it.

When a big Mercedes followed the example of the taxis and swerved in front of Kathy, she groaned. 'Everybody's doing it,' she said. 'I'll be so glad to see the last of this anarchic, stupid, oriental mess.'

94

PART II

Chapter Eleven

In her five months' absence in Europe with the children, Kathy had not taken over one of her family's houses in Chelsea or Belgravia or Holland Park, where the family trust had some of its properties. She had bought instead a sooty, three-storied house in Battersea. She had cleaned it up and put in proper plumbing and central heating and furniture, and then left it like a broody hen to await their arrival. He knew that was Kathy's method to get him over his distaste for her wealth and keep her family out of the way.

'But I'm not going to let you go crawling down the political back alleys where people wait for you with a knife—particularly Kurds,' she told him. 'We'll do it by the front door or not at all. So just relax into it, sweetheart,' she begged him. 'And please don't let's quarrel.'

'I'm quite relaxed,' he said unconvincingly. He was sitting in the study she had furnished for him in the Battersea house, trying to pretend that he felt at ease and at home and not boxed in by black streets and dull skies.

'Just let things happen by themselves for a while,' she went on appealingly. 'Don't rush into this yet.'

'But I can't leave it too long,' he said. 'What's the point in waiting, Kathy? Where is it getting me...?'

'You can't just walk around asking people where the money is,' she insisted. 'That's not the way to do it. Let me establish some sort of believable presence here, and in Paris. Otherwise you'll only be at a disadvantage from the outset and nobody will tell you anything or take any notice of you.'

'I don't want you to get involved in any of it,' he told her.

'But all I want to do is get you through it as quickly as possible,' she said. 'That's my only interest in it.'

'All right,' he said. 'Do what you like.'

But he knew he was already at a disadvantage. He had to fit into her English life. There were no bare mountains, no skin-and-bone poverty, no mud-walled cities to reassure him.

One of Kathy's government cousins in a striped shirt said to her: 'I don't like being judged by all that silence. What's he up to? What's on his mind? He looks dangerous.'

'Oh, he's always like that,' Kathy said, choosing the ridiculous rather than nothing. 'You just don't understand him.'

'How can you understand a man who comes from Tibet?'

It was true. Kathy knew MacGregor was out of place. She had expected it. Nonetheless, she took him at weekends to white houses in Hampshire and to stone houses in Gloucestershire, and to the rivers and hills and farmlands enclosed by deeds and heritage and habit. Finally they went to see Kathy's mother who lived like a stone in three cluttered rooms of their corner house in Belgrave Square. On charity days she was wheeled out on the S.W.1 pavement in a stainless steel invalid chair by a butler and an Australian nurse, and left there for half an hour, speechless, to sell a charitable marigold or poppy or paper lifeboat with pins she could not lift, or handle, or jab into coat lapels. She was deaf and almost blind, and though she hardly recognised Kathy, and did not really know who MacGregor was any more, Kathy said that it was not the failure of her eyes and ears so much as the old skin of her privileges and her insensibility which were outlasting her intelligence and her faculties.

'That's the strength you so despise,' she said to MacGregor, who denied any kind of judgement like that.

In fact, standing before her in the vast faded rooms of the rich old house, and dressed on a cold spring day in a new double-breasted overcoat and new, fine shoes and a blue shirt, MacGregor had penetrated her emptiness for a remarkable moment.

She smiled at him and said, 'Has Katherine put her hat on yet?'

He didn't know what that meant. Kathy was permanently hatless. She obviously meant some schoolgirl Kathy. He did not know what to shout in her ear in reply, so he took the amazingly living hand from the chair in the oriental way and held it awhile until Kathy came in, looked startled at the scene, and shouted in her mother's rag-like ear: 'We're going now. Don't forget to brush the dog.'

Kathy picked up a Scotty as worn and as dead as its mistress and so mangy that only Kathy's unfrightened flesh could have handled it calmly. She put the incontinent wreck in her mother's lap, a mutual therapy, and then said to MacGregor: 'Come on, before that wretched dog messes all over her.'

MacGregor hurried out behind her, leaving the paralysed pair waiting for something to dissolve them into the stuffed old treasure-house of things which would be sold up the moment they were both dead.

It depressed him more than it should have, and the next day, as if to get rid of the kind of influence it was going to have on his life, he took the train to Oxford to see his son Andrew.

Even as a child Andrew had been his easiest companion: a logical boy without any kind of temper, and so sure of himself that he never needed to be upset by anything. Kathy thought him too sure, too calm, too much in control. But now, at nineteen, he was so naturally gifted that he didn't have to worry about a doubtful future, or a failed opportunity. He knew he was able to do anything he wanted, and he had accepted his talents modestly, and without thinking too much about them. The day after his own arrival in England, MacGregor had been walking along the cluttered side of Battersea Bridge Road with Andrew, and they had seen a thin, small, man dressed neatly but poorly in black, walking alone on the edge of the roadway with his clenched fist held up in a sort of relaxed salute.

'There's Arno the anarchist,' Andrew said to his father.

'What's he doing?'

'Arno's on a victory parade,' he said.

Arno's eyes were smiling happily and his face was preoccupied with a sort of modest pride and shy embarrassment. His face told all. He was not only marching in a huge victory parade, but around him in the ranks were his comrades, and on the pavements were happy cheering people who had just been liberated. He raised his clenched fist in a shy salute, acknowledging the applause and the cheers.

'Arno,' Andrew shouted to him.

Arno hesitated only a moment. Then he broke mental ranks and cut across the road through the marchers and shook hands happily and modestly with his friend on the pavement. This great day...

'Is it better, Arno?' Andrew asked him as if Arno was recovering from some wound.

'Okay,' Arno answered, holding his side. But he was obviously anxious to get back to the march. He shook hands warmly in a congratulatory way with MacGregor, and then put his arm affectionately round Andrew while they all walked across the road, dodging through blocks of marchers. Arno fell back into the ranks, joining his revolutionaries tramping through the dead papers and blown bus tickets and chocolate wrappers that were strewn along the route, and they marched with him for a little while along the roadway until Andrew decided they could tactfully break ranks. He simply waved a hand to Arno as they stepped up on the pavement, and they watched him until he had turned the next corner.

'I took him home to lunch last Christmas,' Andrew said, 'and afterwards we marched all over Clapham up to our calves in snow. But no matter what you do you can't penetrate the illusion. He never makes a false move and never really says anything that isn't normal and sane. If it's a dream, then old Arno certainly lives thoroughly and happily in it.'

Andrew's affections were casual but extensive, and at Oxford MacGregor didn't find him in his rooms, but in the Blackfriars Priory, packing plastic bags of fresh warm blood which was being collected for the NLF in Vietnam. The bags were being handed to him by a large young friar in white linen robes and monkish sandals.

'This is Father Joseph. My father,' Andrew said, and MacGregor noticed that the friar looked at him with a curious smile, as if the father was worth knowing because of the son.

'We're in a bit of a mess,' the friar said.

The seminary was filled with doctors and nurses, and students giving blood. They were lying on camp beds and on tables, with arms dripping drop by drop into the little plastic bags hung on the blankets under them.

'I hope blood doesn't upset you,' Father Joseph said.

'Not in bags,' MacGregor said.

MacGregor helped them stack the filled bags of blood into the refrigerator in the large kitchen, where other friars were cooking large pots of vegetable soup and stewed apples.

'My God, you're stewing apples again, Father,' Andrew said.

'Apples every Sunday,' Father Joseph said.

The sweet and pleasant smell of the apples mixed with blood, plastic and soup was too much, and MacGregor was glad when Andrew was allowed a break and they walked across St Giles into the arms of Balliol. MacGregor asked him how he had mixed himself up with the priests.

'I admire them,' Andrew said. 'Oxford isn't a good place for morality, but at least these Dominican priests practise a little of what they preach.'

'Collecting blood for Vietnam?'

'Why not? Who else in this city would lend their seminary to blood collectors for the NLF in Vietnam? Half an hour in that priory and you can forget that this whole town is only an academy for rigid convention.'

'Oh? What particular rigid convention are you talking about?'

'Any one you like—political, moral or religious. They're all the same. There aren't any heresies here.'

'I thought you came to Balliol because it was heretical.'

Andrew laughed. 'So I did. But what a joke. They only teach you the heresies at Balliol in order to help you with the orthodox. It's an education in how to make it work better.'

They had passed into St John's, and MacGregor looked at the stained stone cloisters and the chapel, and he remembered why he had felt imprisoned at Cambridge: too much brick and mortar, pointed arch, mullioned window, bell and eventide. 'Can't you get out of it what you need and discard the rest?' he asked.

'I don't think so,' Andrew said. 'In fact, I don't think politics should be taught like religion or medicine. That's what they do here, so they turn out the curers and the magicians.'

'Don't be too hasty,' MacGregor warned him, knowing it was superfluous advice because his son was too much in the grip of his own intelligence to be hasty about anything.

They stood for a moment in St John's, and in Laud's quadrangle, and MacGregor felt the Gothic arches closing over his head again like a sotted stone blanket.

'You have to have faith in this place to get the best out of it,' Andrew said, as they went back. 'And that's what I'm finding difficult. Maybe impossible.'

'You'll grope your way through it,' his father said, but without much conviction.

At Blackfriars, Father Joseph was now lying on one of the couches, his joyful young stomach pushed upwards, his religious arm bleeding into a plastic bag with a map of Australia on it. The Holy Father's blood would end up in some burned-out child, or in some lacerated woman lying in the mud of a Vietnamese village where gunships and green men and marines made Christian insertions into other religions.

Chapter Twelve

MacGregor and Kathy left England the next day, a warm April day, and crossed the Channel to stay in Paris with Kathy's maternal Aunt Joss, with whom Kathy had installed Cecie six months before. When they were in the taxi on their way across Paris from the Gare du Nord Kathy warned him again how *not* to behave in Paris. 'Don't try to go cap in hand through the political back doors. Let me use the people I know—the ones I've known most of my life.'

'It's taking too long, Kathy,' he told her. 'I can't put off doing something much longer.'

The taxi was breathless, and Kathy clung to his arm. 'I'm in more of a hurry to finish this than you are,' she said. 'But you won't get anywhere if you start hurrying it now. Be patient a little longer.'

Aunt Joss's house was in a silent little side street called Barbet de Jouy in the 7th arrondissement: *un hotel particulier* that was high-walled, high-gated and enclosed like a seminary. This was 'the Paris House', where Aunt Joss had lived for forty years, even through the occupation— another house among the family houses in town, in the country, in Italy, in Switzerland, Bermuda, Peru, Venezuela. They were kindred to each other like the family itself, and this one was first cousin to the London house in Belgrave Square.

Inside the high walls, Aunt Joss's house was a small and beautiful survivor of pre-Haussmann Paris, one of three

Parisian villas left in the wasteland of ministries, offices and glass banks in this part of the 7th. The gatekeeper and doorkeeper, Monsieur Marin, sat all day in a filthy broken chair in front of an old puffing Mirus, in what had once been a coach-house. The courtyard was pebbled and permanently damp, and there was an outside stone staircase that curved romantically up to the front door. It was Madame Marin who opened the door, a thick-legged, ageing Breton peasant dressed in black.

'Aunt Joss?' Kathy called when they were standing in the hall.

'Is that you, Cecie darling?'

'No. It's me—Kathy.'

Aunt Joss was a voice that came from somewhere else, from behind walls or doors or through curtains. She lived in one little room behind the stairs, and it was her invisible presence that tied the house together with disembodied questions. 'Are you there?' 'Is that you?' 'Are you going out?' 'Is it raining?' The palazzo-and-walnut hall was the communications centre of the house, and when, an hour later, their daughter Cecie arrived, slamming the front door behind her, she shouted in the hall to no one in particular as she kissed her father: 'I've just bought an old Citroën for my birthday, and I'll keep it in the coach-house.'

And Aunt Joss's voice: 'All right, Cecie darling.'

Voices to Cecie darling...

'How do you manage this?' MacGregor whispered to Cecie, wondering how he was going to manage it himself.

Cecie was intent on taking him out into the old courtyard to see her old black *traction*, and when she was outside she said: 'I love it here. I love Aunt Joss. She doesn't question me about anything I do, just as long as I announce it at the top of my voice in the hallway.'

That was not the reply MacGregor wanted. Whenever he saw Cecie after being away from her, even for a few days, he was momentarily frightened for her. She had a long bony frame with fragile legs and elbows, and fingertips that seemed to do all the work for her, they were so insistent. Sometimes she would grip her thin thumbs angrily inside the rest of her fingers. And someday, something would snap Cecie in half across the middle. Her soft blue eyes and skinny limbs and long flowing hair predicted it. But when she shouted for Marin to open the gates, Marin ran to do as he was told, and when she drove the old *traction* out of the gates (using knees and elbows like gears) the car did as it was told. They leapt into the traffic of the Boulevard des Invalides as Cecie put the Citroën into the speed and anarchy and violence of Paris exactly the way she wanted it. That was when MacGregor forgot all about the breakable limbs and the doe-like eyes and the probing fingertips. Cecie, he knew, was tougher than any of them, and there was nothing, really, but her wilfulness and adolescent passion to worry about. And as he sat back and watched Paris undoing itself around them, he felt safer and more at home here than he had felt in London.

But he already knew, in the grip of this impatient city, that he was going to make one quick attempt, on his own, to find that money.

Chapter Thirteen

Kathy said, 'All right,' with a little shrug of irritation and resignation, and let him go.

MacGregor felt like a child who was being allowed to burn his fingers in order to be taught a lesson, and it was not the most encouraging feeling to have when he arrived in the bank-filled streets of Zurich, which was where the money had last been heard of. He went to a hotel in the old part of the city, and then walked across the Limmat and simply walked into the Bank Mercantile with his papers in his pocket. He asked at a small glass counter to see Herr Goetz, the name Abbekr had given him.

'What's it about?' the girl at the desk asked him.

'A letter of credit,' MacGregor said. 'A large sum is involved.'

Only when he was facing Herr Goetz across a metal and glass desk with drawers that fitted like a watch-case did he present his Kurdish credentials. Herr Goetz read the spidery Lebanese French, and then put the letter on his desk and placed his open hand nervously over it as if to hold it down in a high wind.

'But you're not a Kurd, Mr MacGregor,' Goetz said.

'My authority is from the Kurdish Committee who negotiated the original credit with you,' MacGregor said.

'I can see that. But what is it you want of us?' He tapped the letter. 'This doesn't say.'

'I simply want to know where the money is, Herr Goetz.'

Goetz read the credentials again, obviously giving himself time to think before he said anything.

'I can't possibly tell you anything about it,' he said finally.

'Why not?'

'Because I don't really know who you are, despite this letter.'

MacGregor took out his passport, but Goetz held up a protesting hand and said: 'I don't mean that. I mean, I don't know who you really speak for.'

'Surely that's clear.' MacGregor pointed to his credential.

'That's only a letter,' Goetz told him and pushed a button on a grey console and said in German that someone called Hoechst should be sent in.

Two men came into the sound-dead room and sat down near the door, and MacGregor felt that he had just been locked in. Herr Goetz got up, excused himself, and taking MacGregor's letter he went out like a man on the way to consult someone in a hurry. The two men at MacGregor's back said nothing, and MacGregor waited. It was hot, so he took off his top coat, and he felt two hands holding the collar as he pulled it off.

'Thank you.'

There was no reply, and while MacGregor waited he inspected the perfection of this Zurich banking office. Every time he came to Europe from Persia he was enthralled with the perfection and precision of line and fit and colour and kerbstone and paint. All Europe was built on a hard, straight line, whereas Persian streets and houses and interiors still seemed to have in them a memory of mud compounds, even in the perfectly-built banks and villas, and rich indulgent houses.

'Mr MacGregor . . .'

Goetz had returned with another fine-suited German-Swiss banker, and MacGregor was glad that Kathy had made him go to a good tailor in London and get a well-cut suit, because he knew that any respect he got here was for his English sleeve rather than his Kurdish credentials.

'This is Herr Muehler,' Goetz was saying. 'He will explain the situation.'

'Unfortunately,' Muehler said quickly in perfect English, 'there's nothing to explain. We can't really help you, Mr MacGregor.'

'But surely you must know where the money is.'

'There's nothing I can say,' Muehler said firmly, as if that was all he intended saying. 'We have no authority to give you any information.'

'Then who has the authority?' MacGregor asked.

'That's hard to say,' Goetz told him. 'In any case we are no longer responsible.'

'Then who is responsible, Herr Goetz?'

They were now standing together in the centre of the room, on the perfectly fitted carpet. They were making sure that MacGregor had nothing to sit down on, and with MacGregor's letter still in his hand Herr Muehler balanced on his heels as if he were anxious to leave. For a moment MacGregor had forgotten which was Muehler and which was Goetz.

'There's nothing we can discuss and nothing we can do, Mr MacGregor,' Muehler said again. 'I'm very sorry, but that's all I can say.'

MacGregor hesitated. 'All right,' he said. And as he pulled on his coat he held out his hand for his letter. Herr Muehler shook his head.

'I think we must keep this,' he said.

'You can't do that,' MacGregor said sharply.

'I'm afraid we must...'

'It's a personal credential,' MacGregor said. 'So let me have it, please.'

'I feel this letter would be better left with us, Mr MacGregor...'

MacGregor pulled the letter out of Muehler's hands.

'You're mistaken, Herr Muehler,' he said, and he knew he was red-faced.

There was a moment now when MacGregor, wanting to leave, was aware that all four men in the room were hostile. But he walked determinedly to the door and was surprised to find that it was not locked. He went out through the glass corridors, out into Bahnhofstrasse and then down to the Limmat where he stopped to recover his nerve. It was not the incident that had undone him, as much as the realisation that he should never have walked into that bank at all.

The real extent of his mistake became clear when, two hours later, in his hotel along the quay under the chiming clock that sounded like a peal of alpine cow bells, two men in business suits showing police cards with large red crosses embossed over them asked him if he wouldn't mind coming with them to an office just along the quay.

'I do mind,' MacGregor said, still tense and angry. 'I'm not going anywhere with you.'

'I see. Do you speak French or German, Mr MacGregor?' one of them asked.

'No,' MacGregor lied, knowing the advantage of sticking to his own language.

'In that case, will you come downstairs to the manager's office?'

'No, Monsieur. I will not go anywhere with you,' he said.

The policeman hesitated. 'Then we'll have to talk here.'

'By all means.'

'Please sit down.'

'You can sit down if you like,' MacGregor told them. 'I prefer to stand.'

'As you wish.'

They looked like Americans, but they spoke like Swiss; and while one of them did the talking, the other looked young, serious, sullen and observant. The one who spoke had red hair and he behaved as if he knew the real purpose behind MacGregor's search for the money.

'Do you have some sort of identification?' he asked Mac-Gregor.

MacGregor gave them his passport, which the spokesman glanced at briefly and then held casually in his hand as if he would keep it.

'Is that all you have?'

'Yes.'

'I understand you have a certain letter, Mr MacGregor.'

MacGregor said nothing.

'Could we see it please?'

'The letter you're talking about has nothing to do with the Swiss police,' MacGregor said. 'It's a private matter.'

'Could you tell us who signed it then, and where it was written?'

'I'm not going to answer questions like that, so please don't ask me,' MacGregor told him.

'I must tell you, Mr MacGregor,' the policeman said, 'we know there are Kurdish terror organisations in Europe, and here in Switzerland.'

'I know nothing at all about terror organisations. That's nothing to do with me.'

'We understand that your letter is an authorisation from a Kurdish organisation.'

'My letter is simply a private introduction about a letter of credit. That's all it is.'

'From whom?'

'I don't think I have to tell you that either,' MacGregor said. He had been perfectly still in a way that orientals simply stand still to outwait an opponent. He did it unthinkingly because he had done it from childhood unthinkingly. But he was suddenly aware of it, because these two policemen were obviously irritated by its hint of implacability.

'I have to tell you that we don't like foreign organisations operating in Switzerland and using Swiss facilities,' the redhead said.

'I suppose not.'

'That's all we are asking you to discuss with us, Mr MacGregor. So why don't you come with us?'

MacGregor shook his head. 'You'll have to arrest me if you want me to go anywhere with you,' he said.

Nobody moved for a moment.

'We don't want to do a thing like that,' the policeman said. He was putting MacGregor's passport ostentatiously into his pocket.

'My passport, please,' MacGregor said, holding out his hand.

'You can have it back later. We want to check a few things.'

'No. Please give it to me now. Or give me a receipt for it.'

They gave him back his passport, and MacGregor was grateful for all occasions when he had been questioned by Persian police.

'All right, Mr MacGregor,' the redhead said. 'We don't want to force anything on you. We know you are here on behalf of an illegal Kurdish organisation in Switzerland, and though you are free to come and go, there's a limit to our toleration in a situation like this. What happens in Turkey is not our affair. But what happens here is.'

MacGregor felt the inescapable grey shadows of two dead Turks following him into the streets of Europe. His anger had gone. His fear of being trapped and confused had returned, and he depended on his silence now to protect him. He simply stood still: deliberately, implacably still.

'We suggest that you leave Switzerland as soon as you can arrange it,' the redhead said, and that was the end of it and they left.

MacGregor let out his breath, and he was thankful that Kathy had not seen any of it. He was not surprised when, at the Zurich airport, his passport was handed over again to the redhead and his sullen young companion, waiting for him at the barrier. After a delay of half an hour the passport was returned and nothing said, and he was allowed to go. But he knew that he was now in that grey, plastic-covered book that Swiss passport officers referred to when known criminals, prostitutes and revolutionaries arrived at their red and white borders and asked to be let in.

Chapter Fourteen

Kathy guessed what had happened when he gave her a safe outline of it. He left out the details, but she told him, as he expected her to tell him, that he had exposed himself stupidly and for nothing.

'I said again and again that was *not* the way to do it,' she reminded him. 'That way you'll only make a victim of yourself and have every policeman in Europe after you.'

He knew she was right, and what worried him now was not so much his mistake, but the fact that the frontiers as well as the front doors of Europe would be closed to him if he behaved as clumsily as that again. So he said: 'I know. I know. You were right, and I was wrong.' And once more he let Kathy organise it her way, agreeing to wait until she had planned for Aunt Joss's household to admit the influence of the city.

In fact the old house had originally been fitted for rich and serious Edwardian entertainment, but Aunt Joss had simply closed it all up. She had locked away its treasures and had lived happily under the stairs, attended by Marin the slippered gatekeeper and Madame Marin, who cooked and washed and shuffled breakfasts and lunches and afternoon teas into Aunt Joss's secret corridors and then disappeared like Aunt Joss into her own room behind the kitchen. But when Kathy pulled out the beautiful, knobbly old crockery and the weighty silver and linen from the cupboards, she had to employ a girl named Sylvaine from one of the employment agencies to help, because Madame Marin in the kitchen was a good Breton cook but refused to serve anyone except Aunt Joss, and anyway her liver was bad. So it was Sylvaine from Provence who crossed the frontiers between kitchen and dining-room, which was heavy with curled walnut, dim rich tapestries, and vast dusty chandeliers which Kathy ordered taken down and washed free of fly dirt in methylated spirits.

Kathy set about it knowing unthinkingly who should come, and to whom they should go. And though MacGregor knew that the French bourgeoisie rarely opened their living-rooms to strangers, even in Teheran, he discovered that the upper classes of Paris were lavish with their salons. Most of Kathy's friends were the same sort of friends she had in England: house-owning land-owning families, bankers, courtier families turned diplomats or high officials, colonisers, Cognac gentry, and unclassifiable men, none of whom cared what republic it was, fifth, sixth or seventh, or what the bourgeoisie did in their little corridors of power as long as they kept out of the way and did what was expected of them. And MacGregor fitted as badly into this network as he had into the country houses of England.

Yet he attracted them. His role was inexplicable to them when they tried to understand his mysteries. They knew what he had done. But why did he keep himself so still? Why was he so blue-eyed and silent? What was he hiding in his intense detachment from them, and in that preoccupied and uncompromising face? He behaved, Kathy said, the way the French thought all Englishmen should behave, though they rarely did.

'What other way am I supposed to behave?' he said self-consciously.

'I'm not complaining,' she said, and MacGregor lost track of what glass dining-tables he had eaten at, whose salon he had leaned against with a glass of something in his hand, what meticulous French coffee he had been drinking on high, tiled balconies overlooking the Quai d'Orléans or the

Cours Albert or the Parc du Champ de Mars. But he knew
that in this milieu it was only a matter of time before Kathy
decided who was the man they needed, although he suspected that Kathy had known who it would be.

The man they wanted was a merchant banker named
Guy Moselle.

MacGregor had already had Moselle explained to him,
and strictly speaking, he was more than a banker. In the
1880s the Moselles had deserted their old aristocratic and
feudal positions as court officers and braided diplomats, and
they had established throughout the Empire a vast monetary
and political Intelligence service for French banks which
had become as indispensable to France's international
monetary policies as the Deuxième Bureau was to France's
national security. As if to fit its present role, Guy Moselle
had an anglicised surface rather than a French one. The
barons, counts, marquises and chevaliers had gone. The
old French face had gone. Only the lean, rich authority
remained, and in Moselle's leanness and authority was another France. Moselle still kept family estates in Normandy,
but he did not consider them worth bothering about because
the French peasant tenure system made profitable capitalist
farming too difficult. Kathy said he only bothered with his
farms for their feudal contact with the land. He ran them
ruthlessly and well, because that was the only way he knew
how to run them.

'He's a sort of Tommy Barban,' she warned MacGregor.
'So be careful with him.'

'A what?'

'You remember the Frenchman in Fitzgerald's book?'
she said. 'The one who fought wars, any wars, because that
was all he was good for. Guy's only good for his established position in the French order of things, and he's
almost untouchable and knows it.'

MacGregor remembered Barban, and Barban's charming
loyalty to his simple ideas and to his complex training. But

Moselle was a leaner and more talented man. He ran every morning in his jogging suit around the bridle paths of the Bois, sometimes followed by his eighteen-year-old daughter on a retired Garde Républicaine mount that looked far too big for her. In summer he went north or east or west when everyone else went south; and in spring and autumn he flew himself down to Cannes in an American Beechcraft for long weekends on the top of the unfashionable but private pine hills above Mandelieu in a house that preserved a little of the long-lost Riviera twilight.

'It's a house for misfits,' he said to MacGregor with dangerous, twinkling eyes when he invited them to go down there with him for a late spring weekend. 'Like you and me,' he said to MacGregor. 'We should get on very well.'

MacGregor liked Moselle: it was impossible not to like him. But if there was a brotherhood of misfits MacGregor doubted if he and Moselle would be in it together. Nonetheless, Kathy insisted that Moselle was their man.

'If he decides to help you,' she said, as she lay in the old bathtub at Aunt Joss's preparing for their weekend, 'he'll do it without blabbing it all over the place. And he won't betray you to anyone, no matter what's involved. That's part of his ridiculous code....'

'His code is obviously something you admire,' he said, looking at his wife's abdomen rising just above the white crest of the soapy water and provoking his own jealousies.

'Why not?' she said. 'I've always liked honest men, and that includes you. I told you. I've known Guy all my life, even before I knew you.'

He wanted to ask her what Moselle's superior price might be for his help. Something considerable, no doubt. But he didn't ask her because he did not want to hear her answer. She had made it clear that they would definitely fly down to Cannes in Moselle's Beechcraft for the weekend, regardless. And because MacGregor was silently hostile to it she pressed it a little harder on him. 'He already knows you want something of him, so at least give him a chance to find out what it is.'

'What about Cecie?'

They were worried about leaving Cecie. She had told them that morning over breakfast cornflakes that she was going to a big student demonstration that day in the courtyard of the Sorbonne.

'There's bound to be a *bagarre*,' Cecie had told them. 'Cohn Bendit and all those Trotskyists of the faculty of letters at Nanterre are coming down to organise it, and the right-wing "occident" crowd have sworn that they'll break it up with their usual tactics.'

'What tactics?' MacGregor had asked her.

'Oh, they'll beat up a couple of students. Or they'll set fire to something, or provoke a fight.' Cecie's thin white fingers had run themselves like an ivory comb through her long fine hair.

Kathy got out of the bath now and said to MacGregor: 'Don't worry about Cecie. She's got a dozen protectors by now, and there's nothing you or I can do about it. She's been to other demonstrations.'

'Nonetheless...'

He could not forget what happened to rebellious students in Teheran, and if there was any worldwide logic to police-student relationships, the French police would be sent to the Sorbonne to beat up the demonstrators and break up the revolt with baton charges and tear gas.

Cecie had ridiculed his fears. 'Don't be silly. This isn't Teheran. It's different here.'

'How different?'

She had laughed.

Now, at Orly, strapping himself into the little grey box of Moselle's Beechcraft, he watched Moselle's capable brown hands and perfectly-cuffed wrists manipulating throttle and control column and tiny earphones and switches, and talking the air traffic jargon of pilots. And he wondered again how different any of this problem was from his Persian problem, or how different were the characters of the men involved in it, including Moselle himself. The Frenchman had seated Kathy beside him. He was explaining what he was doing, and MacGregor was tucked away safely behind and out of the way.

For three dense hours MacGregor sat silent in the back worrying about Cecie until the plane landed on the little Cannes airport in a funnel of spring mimosa. Moselle's modest Simca was waiting, and it took them across the autoroute and up through the pebbly hills of Mandelieu to the top of the blue pine crest, where the Moselle house in Mandelieu sat upright and protected. It was a clever house, close enough to the sea to keep Cannes and Cap d'Antibes in view, but high enough to keep clear of the hot tourist mess which had spoiled the Côte. In daylight it seemed almost outside the Midi, but at night it became an outpost overlooking the pearly, seafront cities, whose diamond lights twinkled wickedly on the horizons of autoroutes and Esterels.

'I'd forgotten such places existed,' Kathy said to Mac-Gregor, when, after dinner, they sat in the darkness of the round balcony, enclosed in glass, staring at the Mediter-ranean with the stars lapping at the window panes.

Moselle ignored the view and went on offhandedly ex-plaining France to them. There was obviously going to be trouble, and because France was a private matter to Moselle, some sort of personal explanation from him was necessary.

'What we used to do in France as a right,' he was saying without resentment or regret, 'we can only do now as a privilege, which is inefficient but inevitable.' Moselle's ath-letic lithesomeness and perfect face and perfect shirt and perfect French manners made sense, whereas France's failure to behave did not.

MacGregor listened tunelessly, and he looked at the

stars and listened to the Provençal dogs barking in the little valley below, which cut off the distant traffic of the autoroute. From a distance he heard Moselle asking him what he had been doing in Switzerland, and why had he been looking for information at the Bank Mercantile.

'Why didn't you come straight to me?' he said.

MacGregor abandoned the dogs and said that he had not realised at the time that Moselle could help him. In fact they had not even met at the time.

'Kathy should have told you,' Moselle said.

'I didn't want to walk in on you,' Kathy said, 'and say *"Hello Guy. Here's my husband. Help him."* That would have been rather crude.'

'You could have done it,' Moselle insisted, and he managed to flatter Kathy rather than reprimand her. 'Anyway, what's it all about?'

MacGregor told him about the disappearance of the Kurdish money, and the peculiar silence and hostility which the Kurds had met when they tried to trace it. 'They thought someone like me, with a European name and face, might be able to find out what had happened.'

'Fascinating!' Moselle said. 'But is that all?'

MacGregor hesitated. 'That's all,' he said. 'I've simply been asked to trace the money.'

Moselle was smiling his distant, friendly smile at MacGregor. 'I wonder if you have any idea what sort of reputation has preceded you,' he said to MacGregor.

'Reputation?' MacGregor said nervously. 'Why? Is it important?'

'Apart from the mystery of your involvement with the Kurds, and the silent way you seem to fit into it, you're supposed to have come down out of those mountains with a bigger purpose than money.'

'I'm here to trace the money. That's all.'

Moselle laughed. 'Not romantic enough,' he said.

'Oh, for heaven's sake,' Kathy said.

'You don't understand,' Moselle told her. 'The best way to handle something like this is to create mystery, not deny it.'

'No, Guy,' Kathy said firmly. 'No romantic nonsense.'

'But the romantic nonsense is already there, Kathy, so I suggest that you take advantage of it.'

'What romantic nonsense are you talking about?' MacGregor asked.

'The tantalising curiosity about you. There are wonderful rumours that you have killed Turks, that you have been fighting in the mountains as a Kurdish guerilla, that you are, in fact, a dedicated, committed soldier in the Kurdish cause; etcetera, etcetera.'

'Oh, that's absolute nonsense,' Kathy said.

'Is it?'

'Of course it is.'

'Then don't underestimate the attractive possibilities of it,' Moselle told her. He pointed to MacGregor, who was frowning and keeping quiet. 'MacGregor has a remarkable air of renunciation,' Moselle said, 'and since renunciation is the real strength of all ethical systems, it's what people are beginning to admire again these days. Don't you think?' he said to MacGregor.

'What am I supposed to have renounced?' MacGregor asked.

'Who knows?' Moselle said with an amused but friendly smile. 'Look at these women.' He tapped two bronze Germaine Richier women behind him on the balcony. 'They're powerful in themselves because they're a sort of renunciation of themselves.'

Kathy laughed. 'I've never heard such nonsense in all my life.'

'I'm serious,' Moselle said, still smiling. 'You don't understand the French, Kathy.'

But Kathy dismissed it. 'You're just being clever,' she said.

'I've read MacGregor's dossier,' Moselle pointed out.

Moselle had pushed a button. A servant came in to take away their glasses, and as they watched the equatorial moon raise one huge eye above the green bay of La Napoule, the servant said: 'The ORTF, Monsieur,' and went inside to switch on the late night TV news.

They sat in Moselle's English study near the fire which, in this Midi spring, was the sort of anachronism that worked. But then they saw masked medieval CRS charging like halberdiers down the badly-lit Parisian boulevards into a student peasantry waiting behind primitive barricades near the Place Edmond Rostand, where they had gathered (the reporter said) after they had been expelled from the courtyard of the Sorbonne.

'It's going to be a massacre,' Kathy said, sitting up.

They were both tense, looking for Cecie in the flying hair and in the knocked-out figures who were dragged off senseless and bloody into the *paniers à salade*. There was no broken Cecie visible in that mess.

'We'd better telephone Aunt Joss to see if she's all right,' Kathy said.

'She'll be all right,' MacGregor told her, suddenly regaining, as he always did, his confidence in elbows and knees that did what they were told.

When they explained it to Moselle he said: 'Of course.'

He dialled Paris and then he got Aunt Joss. 'Hello, Aunt Joss,' he said. 'It's Guy Moselle. I hope I didn't wake you up so late, but Kathy wants to ask you about Cecie.'

Kathy took the phone and MacGregor picked up the *écouteur* and heard Aunt Joss report that someone had telephoned to say that Cecie had been arrested at eight o'clock, inside the Sorbonne.

'Did they tell you where they've taken her?' Kathy asked.

'I didn't ask, Kathy darling. They're sure to let her go when they find out who she is.'

Kathy groaned at Aunt Joss's contact with a lost world,

and she asked Aunt Joss who it was that telephoned her. But Aunt Joss hadn't bothered to find out.

'Telephone me here,' Kathy told her and gave her the number, 'if you hear anything from anybody. And please question them next time, Aunt Joss.'

'All right, Kathy darling.'

MacGregor hung up the *écouteur* and told Moselle that he would like to return to Paris tonight, if possible. If they could find out when the next plane left Nice, perhaps Moselle could get him to Nice airport, where the normal traffic to Paris left from.

'It may not be necessary,' Moselle told him. 'They've probably taken her to the commissariat at Saint Sulpice. If you wait a moment I'll find out.'

'All right,' MacGregor said. 'But I'd better go back anyway.'

'Wait,' Kathy told him. 'Guy can probably do it the simple way.'

The simple way was from top to bottom, and MacGregor listened while Moselle found the number of the Saint Sulpice commissariat, then heard him talk to one person and another until he reached the man he expected to speak to. Did they have *une anglaise*, Cecilia MacGregor, among the students arrested? After some delay Moselle said sharply to the policeman at the other end to look at the lists, and after a moment's wait he nodded. He put his hand over the mouthpiece.

'She's at Saint Sulpice,' he said. 'But they're going to move them over to Notre Dame des Champs....'

'Is she all right? Was she hurt?'

After another sharp conversation Moselle reported that she was all right. 'Do you want me to try to arrange for her release?' he asked MacGregor, who was glad he was asked even though it was Kathy who said: 'Of course!'

Moselle asked the policeman if he would release the girl on his word now. Or would he telephone the Minister to

123

arrange it? Moselle listened to the reply, and again he blanketed the mouthpiece and said to them:

'They say that they've been told to get an expulsion order for any foreigner like Cecie caught demonstrating. They've agreed to let her out of prison now, tonight, but they say that if there's a *procès* there'll be a record, and then she'll be in danger of expulsion from France.'

'Can you stop a *procès*?' Kathy asked him.

'Yes. But I don't want to do it on the phone.'

Kathy and MacGregor exchanged a glance. 'I ought to go back anyway,' MacGregor insisted.

'I'm sorry, Guy,' Kathy said.

'It's all right. We'll leave first thing in the morning, and I'll see that there's no *procès* and no record. Please don't worry.'

'Are you sure that's all right?' Moselle asked MacGregor.

'We can go right away if you like. But I won't be able to do anything till morning anyway.'

'No. That's fine,' he said. 'It's very kind of you.'

'Cecie's a bit of a handful at times,' Moselle said, and MacGregor felt that Cecie had now been removed from his protection, and put under Moselle's.

When he went downstairs with Kathy to go to bed, they deliberately said nothing to each other about Cecie. Why quarrel now? In the early morning, crystal and pure at 13,000 feet, they sailed up the blue shaft of the Rhone, and it was nine o'clock when Moselle finally dropped them off at Aunt Joss's. He said he would go and settle the business of Cecie immediately, although it might take a little time, since it was Saturday.

'Come to lunch Monday at Pillet-Will,' he told Mac-Gregor, 'and I'll let you know what I've found out about your Kurdish money.'

'Where is Pillet-Will?' MacGregor asked. 'What is it?'

Moselle laughed. 'It's a little street between Rue La Fayette and Rue Laffitte, just behind the Boulevard Haussmann. Just ring the bell at number 5A. You'll have to wait for someone to come down, so don't worry if it takes a few minutes. It's my personal entrance.'

MacGregor thanked him, and thanked him for the abortive weekend, and Kathy was kissed. When Moselle had gone they banged on the wooden gate to wake up Marin. It took him some minutes to get his trousers on and they waited in silence because they still had nothing to say to each other.

Cecie was not only at home, but up and eating breakfast with Aunt Joss when Kathy announced their arrival in the hall, and she came out dabbing a napkin at a slightly swollen lip.

'What happened?' Kathy said, holding Cecie's face.

'Oh, someone pushed his elbow into my mouth,' Cecie said offhandedly.

'You mean the police?'

'I don't know. You couldn't tell in that mess.'

'You were told to keep out of it.'

'I did keep out of it,' Cecie protested. 'I was standing with a big crowd in the Sorbonne on the steps under Victor Hugo when they just swept me up with everybody else. They were after one of the boys, and they collected me as well. That's all.'

They had remained in the hall, and Kathy said she was lucky they hadn't beaten her up properly and locked her away for a month.

'Oh heavens, Mama,' Cecie said. 'They didn't even ask me any questions.'

'Because Guy Moselle got you out.'

Cecie looked surprised, and then indignant. 'Is that what happened? I thought it was because I was the only girl in the group.'

'Guy has gone this morning to stop the *procès*; because if there is a *procès* you'll be expelled from France.'

Cecie hesitated a moment. 'Oh, blast Guy Moselle,' she

said angrily. 'I didn't realise he was getting me out.' She turned to her father then and told him that Zadko's son, Taha, had turned up last night.

'Where? Here?'

'Yes. He's upstairs asleep,' Cecie said.

'How did he find you?' Kathy asked.

'Oh, I'd written to him from here a couple of times. But he expected to find you,' she said to her father.

'Now it's perfect,' Kathy said to MacGregor. 'Quite perfect! But he's not going to stay here, Cecie, so don't ask him to.'

'He doesn't want to stay here. He's got to find one of the Iraqi Kurds who's in the faculty of medicine, but all that trouble yesterday made it impossible.'

'Then you'd better go and wake him up,' Kathy said.

'Someone else has been asking for you this morning,' Cecie told her mother. 'It's that rich Megrik, the Ilkhani's son.'

'Dubas?'

'Yes. I thought I'd wait till you came back before I told him where you were. In any case he and Taha ought to be kept apart.'

'I hope you're listening,' Kathy said to MacGregor.

MacGregor was listening.

'They've not only followed you here,' she said, 'they're bringing their stupid Kurdish rivalries with them.'

'They can't do much in Paris,' MacGregor argued.

'How do you know they can't? They want that money. And being Kurds they'll do anything to get it.'

She went into the kitchen to tell Madame Marin to cook them breakfast. 'What's she so upset about?' Cecie asked her father.

'You ...' MacGregor said.

'But why is she being so hard on Taha before she's even seen him?'

'She's not being hard on him. She doesn't want trouble.'

He knew in fact, that Kathy would be glad to see Taha.

Taha would always be the closest attachment they both had after their own children, even though she had taken a great deal of trouble to remove Cecie from his influence. But there was obviously a lot more than that to worry about now.

Chapter Fifteen

When Taha came down he looked as if he had just walked in from some poor mountain village. He wore a thin sports jacket which showed his wrists, and cheap grey trousers which had been creased like a paper bag. But those hard young eyes revealed nothing and admitted nothing, and they watched everything.

'You can't walk around Paris in those clothes,' Kathy told him.

'I don't want to pay sixty francs for a pair of French trousers,' Taha replied.

'I'll give you the money,' Kathy told him.

'Thank you, Aunt,' Taha said with a little bow which rejected her offer, so that Kathy said irritably: 'Oh, then please yourself.'

'How is your father?' MacGregor asked him quickly. 'Did he give you any message?'

'He just said to tell you that he doesn't approve of me being here,' Taha said. 'But since you knew that already it's hardly a message.'

'How did you manage to get a passport?'

Taha leaned forward and said in an undertone: 'Lebanese.'

'Where did you get the French money from?'

'I haven't got much.'

'Yes, but how did you manage to get it?'

'Do you think we stole it, Uncle?'

'Did you?'

'What does it matter?' Taha said with a little laugh.

Kathy interrupted them. 'Before I go and have my bath,' she said to Taha, 'would you like to tell me exactly what you hope to do in Paris?'

Taha looked from MacGregor to Kathy. 'I thought Uncle ought to have some help. But I don't want to talk about it here.'

'Why not?' Kathy asked.

'Cecie says your house is bugged. So please don't ask me serious questions, Aunt,' Taha said.

'In that case you and MacGregor had better talk out on the street,' Kathy told him, 'where your secrets will be safe.'

'Naturally.'

Kathy left them, and MacGregor knew she was going upstairs to question Cecie who was washing her hair. Kathy would want to be sure that Taha had not, in one night, recaptured a passion which had put Cecie in such jeopardy a year ago but was over now.

Taha had also watched her go, but he refused to say anything until they were outside the wooden gate and walking up Boulevard Saint Germain.

'You didn't know, did you, that Zadko was shot in the chest two weeks ago when he was driving through Helali village,' he said.

MacGregor stopped dead the way Persians stop in their tracks when they are told of accidents or illness or death. 'No. I didn't hear. Is he all right?'

'It was a small carbine, so the bullet took a little piece of his rib clean out through his back. But he's all right.'

'But who did it?'

'It was that crippled religious idiot named Kahmi Belud. He tried to get away in Zadko's jeep, but my cousins shot him dead, which was a stupid thing to do.'

As they joined the Simcas and Citroëns and Peugeots surging like salmon upstream to some secret breeding ground, Taha said it would have been better to have kept the ass-eyed cripple alive. 'We could have squashed him until he talked. The only point in killing a murderer like that is to shut him up.'

Taha himself would have kept his head, but his unrevolutionary cousins were, he said, wild and medieval men who wasted their tempers on silly revenges.

'Obviously someone else must have been behind it,' MacGregor said. 'That maniac would never have thought it up by himself.'

'We'll never know if it was the Americans, the British, the Iranians or the Turks,' Taha said. 'But whoever was behind it, the Ilkhani was the one who actually organised it. The old bastard has sent his son to Paris, and they'll be watching everything you do now.'

'Let them.'

'Be careful, Uncle, even though you're in Paris,' Taha said offhandedly.

'Careful of what? What can they do?'

'Every Kurd in this city must know by now that you're looking for that money. And they also know that the money will be used to buy arms with.'

'That was inevitable from the outset,' MacGregor said.

'And it's also inevitable that the money and the arms are going to end up with the Ilkhani if you're not careful.'

'Now don't start that, Taha. The Committee will be responsible...'

'The Ilkhani is going to get control of the Committee.'

'How?'

'By isolating the Qazi and my father from it. By forcing them deeper into the mountains. Why do you think that religious maniac took a shot at Zadko? The Ilkhani is trying to frighten them.'

They had turned off at the Odéon and were coming into the Latin Quarter from the Rue Racine. There was a small demonstration at one end of the Boulevard Saint Michel and there was something nervous about the people on all the Left Bank streets. Every side street they passed was stacked like a chess board with mobile guards and CRS and gendarmes. A woman standing in the doorway of her boulangerie with a cat clasped in her arms pointed to the police and said bitterly to MacGregor: 'They've surrounded the whole quartier. They've *bouclayed* us in with all those filthy students. Now they'll start breaking my windows.'

'I think we'd be wise to get out of this,' MacGregor told Taha. 'You won't want the police looking too closely at your papers.'

'Put me on the Métro to...' he pulled a piece of paper out of his jacket pocket and said: 'Vaugirard.'

'What do you want to do there?'

'That's where Hakim, the medical student, has his room —near the ateliers of Vaugirard,' he read.

They stopped at the next Métro entrance and looked at the large map on the staircase. When they had navigated a route to the Vaugirard ateliers, MacGregor went down to the train with him, and while they waited for it he asked Taha if he needed money.

'No. Nothing, Uncle.'

'How long do you intend to stay?'

'It depends on you,' Taha said, 'and on whether you get that money.'

MacGregor sighed and put him on the Métro to Montparnasse. For a moment Taha was locked in the little glass cage of Paris, and MacGregor watched the boy take his seat on the *banquette* of the Métro among the clerks and typists and salesmen in their European city. Taha seemed to see nothing of it, as if there was nothing in this city he need be bothered about.

Chapter Sixteen

Pillet-Will was a little dog-leg of a street. At one end the Rothschilds had just built themselves a stone and glass box for their merchant banking business. At the other end were the solid battlements of the National Assurance Company built fifty years before. Between them were two Parisian houses. One of them MacGregor identified from a worn brass sign which said 'L. F. & Cie'—Lazard Brothers —the other great merchant banking house of Paris. And on the other house, which was opposite, a plate the size of a visiting card said: 'Moselle'. It was a tall red house with too many tiny windows.

MacGregor rang and waited, and an old man in a leather apron opened the door. Without saying anything he showed MacGregor into a perfectly preserved Louis Napoleon salon smelling of furniture polish. The old man disappeared for a moment and when he came back he pointed to a double-doored lift, and they went up to the top floor of the house which became a different place. The corridors had grey painted walls, thick carpets, painted doors, and all the aseptic surface that Moselle lived with. Mac-Gregor heard typewriters, but they were almost a domestic sound, and Moselle was waiting for him in a dining-room that looked like a beautiful Dutch kitchen. It was softly white, with a black and white tiled floor and an attractive Dutch fireplace.

'I don't usually have an apéritif before lunch,' Moselle said, 'but if you want one...'

MacGregor shook his head.

'Then we can eat at once, and then you can come along with me to the Seigneurie where I've arranged for you to meet someone who may help you. I'm assuming, of course, that all you want me to do is put you on your way.'

'That's right.'

They sat down at the table with a chequered cloth and stiff white napkins, and a woman in a white coat brought them a white leek soup. 'We have a fixed menu here,' Moselle said, 'but if you don't like anything you don't have to take it. Just leave it and we'll find something else.'

MacGregor said he wasn't fussy.

'Before we discuss anything,' Moselle went on as he tasted his soup before actually eating it, 'there is one thing I would like to know, in strict confidence.' He smiled disarmingly at MacGregor. 'It's something that keeps cropping up in your affairs.'

'Please.'

'Personally I don't care one way or the other, and it won't change anything as far as I'm concerned, but I like to know how to deal with a situation.'

'I understand,' MacGregor said, knowing what was coming.

'Did you shoot those Turks? I mean you personally?'

'Yes, I shot them,' MacGregor said.

Moselle looked at him with a curious little smile, as if expecting more of an explanation. But when MacGregor didn't offer one he said: 'Amazing. You continue to surprise me.'

'What's that got to do with the Kurdish money?' MacGregor asked.

'The man I'm taking you to meet after lunch is a Turk named Colonel Seroglu.'

'That sounds Greek.'

'No. He's very much a Turk,' Moselle said. 'He's a sort of Turkish counter-something-or-other in Europe, and he works with a surprisingly large budget. Some of it probably comes from the Americans, although he obviously hates them. The point is, he's the man who may ask you the same question.'

'But why a Turk? What's he got to do with the Kurdish money?'

'Seroglu's got all the original documents and letters of credit which your Kurdish friend had—the boy who disappeared.'

MacGregor had been erecting silent barriers against any more involvement with Turks, but he knew it was useless. He asked Moselle how the Turks, of all people, had got hold of the documents.

'Search me,' Moselle said with a shrug. 'He's got the documents but he hasn't got the money.'

'Do you happen to know where the money is now?' he asked Moselle.

'It's in a Paris bank. Or rather in the Paris branch of the Persian Banque de Fars.'

'I've never heard of it.'

'It's a private bank, set up in Paris about twenty years ago.'

'No Kurd would deposit that money in a Persian bank,' MacGregor pointed out. 'It's too risky.'

'I hadn't thought of that,' Moselle said.

MacGregor's half-eaten soup had been taken away with Moselle's empty plate, and he stared at the naked body of his suffocated trout.

'Tell me one more thing,' Moselle said, pouring MacGregor a glass of Swiss grape juice. 'If you do manage to get hold of that money, what the devil are you going to do with it?'

'Give it back to the Kurds,' MacGregor replied.

'Yes, but what do they want that money for? To pay for the arms they bought?'

'That's not my problem.'

Moselle shrugged. 'It may very well become your problem,' he said ruefully. 'There are two arms dealers also looking for the documents of that young Kurd. One of them is a Dutchman named Seelig, and the other, his partner, is an Englishman named Strong or something like that. Forte, I think. Have you ever heard of them?'

'Never.'

'They've heard of you,' Moselle told him. 'They're what we call offshore set-up men. Does that mean anything to you?'

'No.'

'They go around the defence establishments of Europe and the arms manufacturers setting up deals for offshore trading for anything they can get their hands on—discarded jets, used tanks, mortars, ammunition, rifles, automatics: anything. They know everything that happens in the surplus arms business. Most of it goes to Africa and the Middle East, but some of it goes to people like your Kurdish friends.'

'Are they anything to do with Seroglu?' MacGregor asked.

'No. Except that Seroglu's got the documents they want.' Moselle pushed a bell for the domestique. 'You'll probably be wondering before you've finished with all this why everybody worries about legal documents, and the legal appearance of everything.' He waited for the serveuse to come and go. 'But the legal façade is what they all operate with in these affairs, even governments. The more doubtful the affair, the more legal they all want to appear. So you won't get far unless you're willing to join in their bitter legal contests.'

'I think I know the method,' MacGregor said.

'Good. See what you can do first of all with Colonel Seroglu. But for God's sake be careful. He's a very single-minded Turk.'

They finished the meal in red grape juice, a thick small steak and a spoonful each of green beans. Then, telling

MacGregor that on their menu coffee was never served after lunch, he sent MacGregor into a pretty but antiseptic waiting-room with washroom attached, and then disappeared. When he came back he was dressed in riding habit—jodhpurs, a polo-neck sweater and an old hacking jacket which was badly torn on the sleeves and the pockets.

'Let's go,' he said, and this time they went down a bronzed metal lift to an underground garage to Moselle's Rover. He drove them out along Rue La Fayette and beyond the Gare de l'Est across the old boucherie canals where the new and useless slaughterhouses of Paris had been built. They went up Avenue Jean Jaurès to Pantin where the old suburban church looked like a genuine landmark in what, out here, was an ugly city. MacGregor had expected the Seigneurie to be a bank or some sort of public building. It was an athletics' stadium in the working class district of Pantin.

Moselle drove in through the main gates, and up into the little dirt park to the second of two arenas, which was covered with black cinders. A groom in an English cap was already waiting with a shaggy and nervous pony, whose tail had been braided into a thick black loaf.

'Undo that tail,' Moselle told the groom sharply.

'But he shits all over it,' the groom said.

'Then don't let him. Whack his rump every time he forgets to lift his tail up.'

While the groom undid the plaiting, Moselle took off his hacking jacket and suddenly, without any kind of warning, he threw it over the pony's head. The pony tossed it off angrily, and Moselle whacked it across the top of the ears with his riding crop. Then, with the help of the groom, he got the coat across the eyes and fixed it in place with a rubber luggage holder tied around the jaw.

'The point of this operation,' he said to MacGregor, 'is to break him of his habit of skidding wide when he turns. A very unpleasant and useless habit in a polo pony. He gets my smell from that coat, so he knows it's me. But he can't see what he's doing. So every time he refuses to obey without question, I hit him over the ears.'

MacGregor was interested, but for the moment he was more interested in the well-kept but empty old stadium. Was this the place where the Turkish Colonel was going to see him?

'Seroglu'll be here in a little while,' Moselle assured him. Then he mounted the pony and looked quizzically at MacGregor. 'It's none of my business,' he went on as he struggled with the beast. 'But it's never wise to be silent with a woman, no matter how long you've been together. Do you mind me telling you?'

'Not at all,' MacGregor said stiffly.

Moselle dug his heels into the pony's quivering flanks and the four shaggy legs left the ground together. Moselle pulled hard on the right rein and the blinded, angry pony did a sort of gallop sideways. Moselle hit him over the ears, and went on hitting him, until he turned properly. Then he went on implementing his policy around the black arena while MacGregor watched, fascinated. Rider and beast went on lashing at each other across the stadium until Moselle finally drove the pony along a wooden fence so that every time the pony turned wide, he hit the fence hard.

'It's a form of religious instruction,' Moselle said breathlessly when he came near. 'Faith! Otherwise harsh chastisement.'

'Mr MacGregor.'

MacGregor had not noticed the arrival of a small alert man barely five foot three or four inches high, who looked neat and delicate and troubled but determined to overcome any weaknesses of that sort. He wore a double-breasted camel-hair coat and stood very upright, the way small men stand upright.

'Seroglu—MacGregor,' Moselle said hastily and took the pony off again.

Seroglu shook hands formally. 'You don't look like a military man,' he said to MacGregor. 'And that's what I was afraid you'd be.'

'Aren't *you* a military man?' MacGregor asked him.

'Yes, but I hate dealing with soldiers. I prefer intellectual men.' He was watching Moselle's violent performance. 'Moselle on that horse!' he said. 'What's he doing to it?'

'He's trying to break it of some sort of swerving habit,' MacGregor said.

'He loves meddling with nature.' Seroglu's little body stood firmly and aggressively in defence of nature. 'Did you know that my son is at the Beaux Arts with your daughter?'

'No I didn't.'

'Does your daughter come home with nihilistic ideas? Smash everything?'

'No,' MacGregor said. 'Nothing as bad as that.'

'My other son is a schoolboy at the École Alsacienne. They want to occupy the school. By next week, he says, every faculty in France will be occupied by students, his school as well. I don't quite know what to do, and I wanted to ask you how you protect your daughter.'

'I haven't had to face that yet,' MacGregor said evasively.

'I'm terrified the police will beat them up in a demonstration. They're both small, like me.'

Seroglu's little Turkish body quivered with anticipation and distaste. He stood away from the fence as Moselle returned on the pony which was lathered in sweat and cinders, and was blasting hot, wet air through its nostrils. It tried to toss the jacket off its head again, and Moselle whacked it lightly across the neck. Then he leapt off and undid the rubber bands and pulled off the jacket and stroked the pony's head affectionately, talking English, not French, into its twitching and resentful ears.

'You've met,' Moselle said, taking a towel from the groom and wiping his perspiring face. 'Did you ask him, MacGregor, how he got those Kurdish papers?'

138

'Not yet.'

'Well, how did you get them, Kemal?' Moselle said to Seroglu, wiping the legs of the pony with the towel.

'Perfectly legally,' the Turk said. 'Manaf Izzat, the young Kurd who had them, was a Turkish citizen. So his papers were handed to us by the Sûreté.'

'How did the Sûreté get them?' MacGregor asked.

'The boy died of typhoid in a hospital in Lyons, and the police found his documents and informed us. There's no mystery about it.'

Moselle laughed. 'Never any mystery, Kemal. Everything legal. Everything open at both ends for all to see.

'Of course.'

'Then I ought to point out,' MacGregor interrupted, 'that the documents did not belong to Manaf personally, nor did the money covered by the letters of credit.'

'How do you know?' Seroglu asked.

'Because the documents and the money belong to the Kurdish Committee of Life.'

'I know all about that Committee,' Seroglu said. 'But what have you got to do with it?'

'I've been authorised to act for them,' MacGregor said. 'So I'd like to have those documents back.'

'Do you know where the money is?' Seroglu asked him.

'Of course we know,' Moselle put in. 'And though you've got the original documents, Kemal, you can't get the money out of the Banque de Fars without establishing your right to it under French law.'

'On the other hand,' Seroglu argued, 'nobody can get at the money without the documents we have. I've got that in writing from the Banque de Fars.'

'The documents belong to the Kurdish Committee,' MacGregor put in. 'And as far as I can see you have no right to hold them.'

They had walked to Moselle's car, and Moselle leaned on

the Rover as if he were impatient to go, or as if he wanted Seroglu to come to the point.

'We can only release those documents, Mr MacGregor, on two conditions,' Seroglu told him.

'Then let's have them,' Moselle said.

'You can have the documents,' Seroglu said, 'providing the Turkish Government agrees to whatever use the money is put to.'

'That's not possible,' MacGregor said. 'It's out of the question.'

Seroglu ignored the rejection. 'We also insist that the assassins who shot our two Turkish soldiers on the frontier near Sindoi must be handed over to the Turkish authorities at Saray, where they will have to face a *procès*.'

Moselle laughed and MacGregor blushed.

'No Kurd will ever agree to those conditions,' MacGregor said to Seroglu. 'And you must know it.'

Moselle opened the door of the Rover. 'Is that your last word on it, Kemal?'

Seroglu was unhappy. 'What else can I say?'

'Nothing, I suppose.'

Seroglu put out his tiny, delicate hand to MacGregor and smiled. 'Let's not quarrel over someone else's money. I'd like my son to make friends with your daughter, and I'd like our families to meet to discuss the best way to protect our children. I admire English methods...'

'Of course,' MacGregor said politely.

'May I ring your wife?' Seroglu said.

But Moselle had cut him short by starting the Rover and immediately driving through the gate, waving a casual goodbye and leaving the little Colonel alone in the empty hole of the old stadium.

'I'm sorry to cut that short,' Moselle said when they were out on Avenue Jean Jaurès, 'but it's the best way of dealing with Seroglu. He's such a dedicated Turk that everything else is a disguise.'

'Why was he trying to be so friendly? Do you think he hopes to get some sort of information out of me?'

Moselle shook his head. 'Seroglu wants to be liked and respected in Paris. And you need never worry about those dead Turks as far as he's concerned. I mean morally. Seroglu himself has killed quite a few of his own countrymen in his time.

'Your real problem,' Moselle went on when MacGregor had remained silent, 'is to get around those documents.'

MacGregor knew that Moselle wanted him to ask for his help, but at the moment he was incapable of asking Moselle for anything.

'You might get some help from that offshore Dutchman and his English partner,' Moselle went on. 'In fact I'm pretty sure you'll find them sitting at home in your living-room.'

'Unlikely, with Aunt Joss,' MacGregor said.

Moselle laughed. 'Don't be too sure. Aunt Joss is a very keen ghost. But they said they were going to call on you, and if I were you I'd listen to them. They probably know much more than Seroglu does.'

They passed the Châtelet, and a group of students marching along the edge of the *trottoir* hit the roof of the Rover with their open hands and shouted: *'La Presse complice. Figaro fasciste.'*

Moselle put his head out of the window and asked the students what they were doing over here.

'The flics blocked off the Boul' Mich and the bridges,' they said. 'So we came over here to bark like dogs.'

Moselle immediately turned down the next side street. 'I'll let you off at the Pont Neuf,' he said. 'I don't want to get tangled up in any mess on the Left Bank. Can you find your way home from there?'

'Of course.'

'I'll tell Kathy I put you on the way.'

'Are you seeing Kathy now?' MacGregor asked him.

'Didn't she tell you?' Moselle said as he stopped. 'She's coming over to meet my daughter at four o'clock. I want them to know each other. She's probably there now.'

There had been other times when he had returned home to find Kathy out, but never before had it felt so ominous. The emptiness of the old house was a message. Walnut and granite and marble were denunciations. Why had she gone to Moselle, and why hadn't she mentioned it? He left the house again, and as he opened the gate to the street he was met by two men who called him by name and introduced themselves: Seelig the Dutchman and Strong (not Forte) the Englishman—the offshore set-up men whom Moselle had told him to expect on his doorstep.

'We didn't want to meet you with Moselle,' the Dutchman said, 'because his sponsorship is expensive and quite unnecessary.'

'What do you want?'

They were standing near the gate. Strong suggested that they go back inside.

'That's impossible. Just tell me what you want.'

'I'm not going to tell you anything out here, old boy,' Strong said. 'There's a café around the corner. Let's go there.'

MacGregor walked between them to an unpainted little café which had a small billiard table in the back, with three cats and a panting pekinese sitting on it.

'*Tiens...*' the Dutchman said and went straight to the dog. He ignored its growls and snaps, and patted its head and pulled its fur. MacGregor heard the Englishman mutter under his breath: 'Oh, Christ, Seeley, the dog hates you, so leave it alone.'

MacGregor wondered which of these two men was the

important one. The Dutchman was an abnormally bleached man—bleached skin, bleached hair and eyebrows, white fingernails and white eyelashes, almost an albino but not quite. The Englishman was playing a bluff, healthy and fleshy role he had obviously invented for himself. MacGregor kept his coat on and ordered a coffee when they asked him what he would have.

'Thank God,' Strong said, 'that you're English. Your Kurdish friends have a horrible habit of always cheating and lying to us, because they claim that all Europeans cheat and lie with them.'

'What kind of Kurds have you been dealing with?' MacGregor asked him.

'All kinds,' Strong said in his loud English voice. 'They're all the bloody same, though.'

MacGregor asked them again what they wanted, and the Englishman said that they understood from various sources that he had an authorisation from the Kurds to find the money they had banked in Europe to buy arms with.

'Is that right?' he said.

'Partly.'

'We know it's right,' the Dutchman interrupted. 'We have here...' he unzipped a black folder and opened it carefully on the café table. 'We have here the protocol of an agreement we signed with the Kurdish agent, Manaf Izzat, before he died in Lyons. We have here the manifests of what he had agreed to buy, and what we had agreed to deliver.'

'You mean arms?'

'What else?'

'I don't know anything about that side of it,' MacGregor said. 'I have no authority to talk about arms.'

'Well, you'd better give yourself the authority,' the Dutchman said, 'because we have over two hundred thousand pounds' worth of equipment which your Kurdish Committee ordered from us, but which they haven't paid for.'

The Dutchman put his finger on the documents. 'We expect you to pay for the equipment, and to arrange for its delivery.'

MacGregor glanced at the blurred, flimsy carbon copy: lists of arms which he did not even want to look at, because he did not want to know what they were.

'Why do you call this an agreement?' he said. 'I don't see any signatures on it.'

The Dutchman found another document in his brief-case. 'This is the original letter of intent, signed by the Kurd, Manaf Izzat.'

He gave MacGregor another flimsy typewritten sheet in French. Scrawled across the bottom of it were a series of signatures including one in Persian script—Manaf Izzat. The latter said that the parties involved had agreed to come to terms on a list of equipment which had been prepared as a separate document.

'It only says that you agree to come to terms,' MacGregor pointed out. 'Where is the contract itself?'

'That is the contract,' Strong said, and tapped the letter. 'In French law it is considered binding.'

'You'll have to prove it,' MacGregor said, finishing his coffee. 'In any case,' he said, 'I can't help you with any of this because it's none of my business.'

The Englishman put up his hand to stop the Dutchman's outburst. 'Wait a minute, old boy,' he said to MacGregor. 'We understand your situation.' It was one Englishman to another now. 'In fact you haven't got the money, have you? So you can't promise to pay, can you?'

'Perhaps...'

'We know you haven't got the money,' Seelig insisted. 'But if you'll agree to honour this contract, we'll help you get that money out of the Banque de Fars.'

'How?'

'Take our word for it,' the Englishman said. 'We can do it. No problem.'

The pekinese barked and Seelig went over to it.

The Dutchman shouted across to MacGregor, 'Did you actually know that the money was in the Banque de Fars, MacGregor?'

'Certainly.'

'That means you've already talked to Colonel Scroglu,' the Englishman said. 'But I'll bet our offer is a better one than his.'

MacGregor got up. 'The trouble is you've got your offer back to front,' he said.

'Oh?'

'If you help me get the money,' MacGregor said, 'then I'll try to find out if the Kurds will honour your contract. Not the other way around.'

He was leaving before they could make further propositions. But the Dutchman stopped him, and the three of them stood together near the door. 'You don't really know who put the Kurds' money in that Persian bank, do you?' he said.

'No.'

'Moselle didn't tell you that, did he?'

MacGregor shook his head.

'Then I'll tell you. First of all, it was never put in the Banque de Fars at all. It was originally transferred by Manaf from the Swiss bank in Zurich to the Bank of Famagusta, which is Cypriot. Did you know about that?'

'No.'

'We had agreed, with Manaf, to make the Bank of Famagusta the stakeholder, pending settlement of final details of this contract. You didn't know that either?'

'No.'

'But in December, before the signature of the Qazi could be put to our agreement, the Bank of Famagusta was bought up by a consortium of three other banks—Persian, Greek and French. And the Persian bank in that consortium was the Banque de Fars. So it was a simple matter for them to get the Kurdish deposit into their account and block it. A very neat trick, don't you think?'

'Very. But who organised it in the first place?' Mac-Gregor asked.

'Ask your friend Moselle,' the Dutchman said.

The Englishman put a friendly hand on MacGregor's sleeve and said: 'Never mind all that. What's done is done.' But then he gripped MacGregor's arm firmly. 'Listen, Mac-Gregor,' he said. 'You're obviously a bit over your head in this kind of dirty business, so let me give you a word of bloody good advice.'

'I'm simply trying to get that money,' MacGregor pointed out. 'That's all I'm interested in.'

'The money you're looking for is already tied up in an arms deal,' Strong pointed out. 'In fact, you can't disentangle the guns from the money any more, and you'd be a fool if you tried to.'

'Maybe . . .'

'Do you know what you'll have to do to get that money?' Strong insisted.

MacGregor was buttoning his coat. 'I can guess,' he said.

'Guess away,' Strong said. 'But you'll have to get involved with us. Do you see my point?'

'More or less.'

'In that case you ought to realise that we're offering you the best and cleanest way out.' Strong still kept Mac-Gregor's arm in a tight grip and spoke now in a low, persuasive voice. 'The manifests are perfectly legal,' he said, 'and the only question left open is their delivery to a Lebanese port. So you'd be saving time if you let us act for you. It's logical, for Christ's sake.'

'I'll have to think about it,' MacGregor said, trying again to leave.

The Dutchman laughed rudely. 'You'll have to think quick, MacGregor, because other people are also interested.'

'Shut up, Seeley,' the Englishman said.

146

'Where can I get in touch with you?' MacGregor asked Strong.

'Here,' the Englishman said. 'Just walk in and tell Louise.' He nodded towards the woman who had served them, and then MacGregor realised that the café had been kept empty. The café door had been bolted, and Louise was opening it for them. She was respectful and pleasant, and she smelled faintly of artichokes and vinegar. MacGregor guessed it was all of one piece.

'Do you own this café?' he asked the Englishman.

'The building...'

'Is your office upstairs?'

'My office, like Abraham Lincoln's, is in my hat,' Strong said, and MacGregor realised that the only time he had felt anything strange in all this was when they unbolted the door to let him out.

Chapter Seventeen

In the early morning, when he was still in bed, he heard someone going up the stairs to the top of the house, and then he heard Andrew and Cecie laughing.

'Did I hear right?' Kathy said, sitting up.

'He must have come over on the night ferry,' MacGregor told her sleepily.

Kathy got out of bed and went upstairs. MacGregor lay relaxed for a rare moment, feeling all his family around him. Then he heard Kathy's angry voice arguing with Andrew, and he pushed his head into the pillow. When she came back she said in her driest, flattest, English voice: 'With his first year exams a month off, he says he's come over to Paris to see what's happening.'

MacGregor lay still. 'Don't worry,' he told her. 'He's never failed an exam in his life. There's no question of it now.'

Kathy stood at the door of the bathroom, looking accusingly at him. 'He doesn't intend to take his exams,' she said. 'He doesn't even want to go back to Balliol next year. So you'd better get up and face that one.'

MacGregor sat up. 'Is he serious?'

She disappeared into the bathroom. 'Who knows?' she said. 'Who knows what idiocy that wonderful mind is preparing for us now.' But then MacGregor heard her cynicism crack and she was muttering passionately to herself: 'My God, how I hate self-willed people.'

MacGregor knew it was really meant for him. He shaved silently, and Kathy bathed silently. But there was now a

quarrel between them—the one they had avoided yesterday
when she had come home after supper from Moselle's and
he had asked her nothing, and she had told him nothing.

'Did he tell you when you went up to Oxford that he'd
had enough of Balliol?' she asked him when she was dressing.

'Not exactly.'

'He says he did. Why didn't you tell me?'

'I honestly didn't think it was that serious.'

Kathy stood facing him across the bed. 'He says he explained it to you. Explained what?'

'He made some sour comments about Balliol,' MacGregor
said. 'That's all I remember.'

'Then you'd better talk him out of it,' she ordered, and
they went down to breakfast.

Andrew was already reading the morning papers to Cecie,
and nothing was said between father and son until Cecie
had gone in to see Aunt Joss and Kathy had gone to get
ready for some appointment with a couturier or coiffeur
in the Faubourg Saint Honoré or the Avenue Montaigne.

'Paris is going to have some sort of huge upheaval,'
Andrew said. 'And I want to see it. That's all.'

'What about your first year exams? You're out if you fail
them.'

'I don't intend to take them,' Andrew said.

'Why not?'

'I told you. Balliol's a political seminary and I don't
want that.'

MacGregor kept his temper. 'The first year at any university always seems pointless. At Cambridge, in my first year,
I already knew more than they could teach me. It took me
another year to realise how little I really knew.'

'You were studying a natural science, and that's different.'

'The result is exactly the same,' MacGregor told him.

'All right,' Andrew said. 'But the truth is I actually don't
want to *know* what they teach me,' he said. 'I've seen it,

and I don't want it. I'll only stay on if I can switch to one of the natural sciences like you, or even to maths. No humanities, no ethics, no politics, no moral philosophy...'

'You think you can just switch over to science like that?'

'If I have to.'

'Which one?'

'It's irrelevant,' Andrew said calmly, knowing, as his father knew, that he would succeed at any one of them if he wanted to.

'That's a pointless way of choosing an education.'

'I know,' the boy said. 'That's why I'd like to just walk out on everything.'

'You're not going to walk out on anything,' MacGregor told his son. 'So don't expect me to be reasonable about it.'

'Don't worry. I'm not going to do anything stupid. I simply want to change direction before it's too late. So let me see what's happening here for a while, and then I'll make up my mind what to do.'

MacGregor hesitated. 'All right,' he said. 'You can stay for a while. But only so that I can talk you out of it.'

Andrew laughed and said he was going straight to the Sorbonne where the students, Cecie had told him, were going to decide how they were going to extend the student strike to all the academies of France.

A moment later, when Andrew had gone on his way, MacGregor heard him talking loudly to Marin in the courtyard. He went out to see what was wrong and found the old man shouting at someone outside the gate. Marin was saying that he would call the police if whoever-it-was didn't go away. The stranger outside asked in French for Monsieur MacGregor, and MacGregor told Marin to wait. He called out through the gate that he was MacGregor.

'What do you want? Who are you?'

'It's impossible to talk through this wooden wall, Mac-Gregor,' the man said indignantly in French. 'I can't shout my business in the street.'

MacGregor unlatched the big gate and was about to open it when the man began to push hard on it to force it open wider. MacGregor and Andrew instinctively resisted and pushed it back as Marin said angrily: 'That's what I mean. He's trying to break in.'

'You silly bastards,' the stranger shouted. 'Let me in.'

As all three of them pushed the gate closed, Andrew asked his father what it was all about.

'I haven't the faintest idea,' MacGregor said.

'But he knows your name,' Andrew said.

The voice over the gate was still shouting in French. 'You can't hide in that place forever, MacGregor. Come on out...'

'What does he mean?'

'I don't know,' MacGregor said, 'and I don't want to know.' He told Andrew to come back into the house, and as they reached the steps he spoke very forcefully to his son: 'Don't ever let anyone in that gate unless you know who it is,' he said. 'Particularly if they come asking for me. And don't talk to strangers outside it, or go off with them if you don't know them. Do you understand?'

'Yes. But why?'

'It ought to be obvious to you.'

'You mean even here in Paris...?'

'Just don't do it.'

'All right, but it's not like you to get in such a panic.'

'I'm not in a panic,' MacGregor said angrily, but he realised that he was. 'And don't be so sweet and reasonable, because it's very irritating.'

'Don't worry,' the boy said.

Kathy was standing at the top of the steps with Cecie. They were asking what was wrong.

'Nothing,' MacGregor said. 'Some crank, that's all.'

But Kathy had heard it. 'Guy warned me that this sort of thing would begin to happen.'

'Nothing's happened,' he said sharply. 'It was nothing.'
'All right, all right,' she said soothingly. 'Don't get upset.'

He knew he must keep his temper, otherwise he would say the wrong thing to Kathy and she would make a fool of him. He went into the old study and, forcing himself to stay there, he read the morning papers until he heard Andrew and Cecie test the gate. Finding there was nobody outside, they drove off together to the Sorbonne.

He forced himself to wait again until he heard Kathy go out. Then he knew he must make some gesture in the direction of the Banque de Fars, if only to find the last known place where the money had actually existed.

He found the bank's address in the Bottin and took a Métro to Château d'Eau in the 10th arrondissement, which was the leather-and-hide district of Paris. He found the street and the house number of the bank, but not the bank itself. 'Hilal & Fils' was written on the windows of the peeling old hide-and-skin warehouse where the bank should have been. A plaque on the side of the door said: '*Société Anonyme de Meshed.*' But all the paintless doors were closed and locked with padlocks. He asked a woman who was sweeping the doorway of the next building—which looked like an iron interior from Captain Nemo's Nautilus —but she said there was no bank here.

'Try the Crédit Lyonnais on the corner,' she told him.

It seemed pointless, but he asked at the Crédit Lyonnais, and the serious clerk, whose plump little fingers were already stained with the morning's money, said: 'No Banque de Fars in this quarter.'

'It could be a private bank for the leather importers,' MacGregor suggested.

'Not here. You've made a mistake, Monsieur. I would know.'

He thanked the man and walked back through the narrow streets of hides, leather, and buzzing little sewing machines worked by pale girls and women, surrounded on

152

the floors by scraps of leather, cloth, hides and the smell of stain and dye that seemed ready to explode in their faces.

He was glad to get out of it because he knew he had been to the back door again, and this time it seemed not only hopeless, but depressing and ridiculous as well.

But he did not know how he was going to get back to the front door of Europe without Kathy's help or Moselle's. And he didn't know how to ask her, because at the moment they were neutralising each other. They were avoiding the bad subjects: Moselle, Andrew and the Kurds, and the result was a lack of communication. But Kathy solved it for him by asking him, with accusing suspicion, if it was true that he had gone to see the Dutchman and the Englishman who sold arms.

'Yes, I did,' MacGregor admitted.

'Guy told me you'd seen them,' she said, 'but I didn't really believe it. What are you dealing with people like that for?'

He told her that Manaf the Kurd had done business with them.

She stretched her lips in revulsion. 'You keep away from arms-dealers,' she told him. 'If you're looking for the money —all right. But if you're going to get involved with people like that I'm going to stop helping you.'

'If that money is already committed to people like that,' he pointed out, 'I haven't much choice, have I?'

It was mid-morning and he began opening the large stack of brown envelopes of survey material for the conference on reserves sent by Jamal Janab from Teheran. He guessed that Kathy had gone to telephone Moselle, because in half an hour Moselle himself telephoned and said that he had changed his mind about the Dutchman and the Englishman.

'They're really a waste of time,' Moselle said.

'Why?' MacGregor said. 'They've promised to honour their contract with Manaf Izzat, and that's something.'

He heard Moselle's dry little laugh. 'They can only honour what French law allows them to honour,' he told MacGregor. 'The real decision is out of their hands, so you might as well talk with the people who will really decide it.'

'Who, for instance?'

'There's one man you'll have to meet eventually,' Moselle said. 'And only yesterday he asked me to arrange a meeting with you.'

'Who is he?'

'An American named Caspian,' Moselle said.

'I know Caspian,' MacGregor said.

'Do you know him well?'

'No. But I've known of him in Iran for years.'

'Then you probably know that he's responsible for a lot of American thinking on the Kurdish problem. He'll give you some idea of what you're really up against. It may even persuade you to think again about going on with it.'

'That sounds like Kathy,' MacGregor said drily.

'Of course it's Kathy. But I wonder myself how much farther you can go,' Moselle told him.

The air was dead between them for a moment.

Moselle said: 'Are you there?'

'Yes.'

'Well?'

'I'll go as far as I can,' MacGregor said. 'Then I'll stop.'

'Fair enough,' Moselle told him and said that Caspian, the American, would be lunching at the old Ambassador Hotel just near Pillet-Will at one o'clock. If MacGregor would give his name there he would be expected. 'I'll try to get along, but Kathy and I are going riding at one, as you probably know.'

He didn't know, and he looked critically and accusingly at Kathy when she appeared half an hour later in jodhpurs and elastic-sided ankle boots.

'What did you do about Andrew?' she asked him, sensing his anger with her.

'I argued with him,' he told her. 'He says he might switch to a natural science.'

'Well?' she demanded.

'Let him stay in Paris for a while,' he said. 'There's no point forcing him to go back now. He'd deliberately fail his exams anyway.'

'And what's the future in that?'

'I'll try to talk him out of it,' he said.

He was looking closely at his wife. It was obviously a coiffeur she had been to yesterday. A French mind was at work on Kathy, because her beautifully-cut hair was closely fixed around her attractive English face. And though she had always been beautiful, with nothing ill-fitting about her, she had obviously become an exciting discovery for someone who was adding French perfection to the original English outlines. Kathy was looking at herself in the mirror with a slight frown, as if she didn't quite approve of the result. She tried to disorder her hair a little and she wiped off some of the faint eye shadow. Then, seeing his close interest, she shrugged.

'I'll have to get used to looking normal again.'

He nodded.

'You don't approve, do you?'

'You look very beautiful.'

'But you don't like it.'

'It's different,' he said, and went back to the documents he had stacked in orderly piles on the desk.

But she came around and sat near him on the desk and told him in the affectionate voice he had lived with for twenty-five years but hadn't heard much of lately: 'Don't let's quarrel about the children, whatever else happens.

And please don't let Andrew do anything stupid or over-confident.'

'All right,' he told her as if it were a formal agreement: they must not quarrel about the children whatever else happened.

He heard Moselle's Rover arrive in the courtyard. He watched her go, he heard her get into the car, the door slam, the gate open, the Rover drive off, and the gate close again. After that he went to work on photometric surveys until he heard Cecie tooting commandingly in the *traction* for the gate to open. He got up and went to the front door and watched old Marin rushing out in his slippers to open the gate.

Cecie had Taha with her, and when they came in the front door he could see that Cecie was bruised and her arms were grazed. Her dress was also spotted with some-one else's blood, and she told her father before he could say anything that the police had rushed them on the foot-path along the Boulevard Saint Michel, when they were watching the student demonstration against yesterday's police brutality.

'I was just watching it,' she told him.

MacGregor got angry for the second time. 'You're extra-ordinary,' he said. 'Can't you get into your head, Cecie, that if you're arrested again you're going to be expelled from France...'

'Oh, that's nonsense,' Cecie said.

'No it isn't. Anyway, I told you to keep away from demon-strations.'

'The whole Left Bank is now one permanent demonstra-tion,' she said, 'so how am I supposed to keep away?'

'Try.'

She went inside and they heard Aunt Joss call out: 'Is that you, Cecie darling?'

'Yes, it's me,' she said and went in to Aunt Joss, saying, 'Look what the flics did to me...'

156

Taha had been watching MacGregor with amused, impersonal eyes. 'It won't make any difference what you say to her,' he said. 'She won't listen.'

'Then why don't you speak to her?'

Taha laughed. 'I came here to talk to you.'

'If it's about the money,' MacGregor told him, 'don't bother.'

'The money doesn't matter any more,' Taha said. 'They've already got it. It's the politics of it you'll have to deal with now.'

'What politics? What are you talking about?'

Taha shrugged. 'Obviously they'll start approaching you now with their political offers.'

MacGregor was putting on his raincoat. He could no longer sit still in the old house, which everybody else seemed to have left to him, to hold up and breathe in while they were away.

'Why should anyone start approaching me with politics?' MacGregor said. 'The situation is no different now than it was before.'

'Why did Aunt Kathy lunch yesterday with Dubas—the Ilkhani's son?' Taha asked him.

'Did she?'

'What did they talk about, Uncle?' Taha persisted.

'How do I know? Ask her yourself, Taha.'

He was on his way to the Ambassador Hotel to hear what the American, Caspian, had to say, and Taha walked across the courtyard with him, saying again as they parted company at the half-opened gate: 'The whole thing is going to get very dirty, so you ought to be careful.'

'I'll be careful,' MacGregor said. 'There's nothing else I can be.'

Chapter Eighteen

He was ten minutes early at the Ambassador Hotel and he crossed Haussmann and watched French workmen, *en bleu de travail,* unloading rolls of newsprint from Berliet trucks into the high black windows of *Le Monde.* There was something in the tackle, the trucks and the method of using wedges and levers that was so French that MacGregor wondered whether national character wasn't, after all, a technological thing.

He went into the old hotel and felt as if he were walking into the condition that Aunt Joss lived in. The Ambassador had been built to fill solid, stable space, but it was now an amber-coloured ocean with fading tapestried walls and neat little gatherings of Empire gilded chairs and tables waiting for guests. He asked at the desk—an island in the middle of this old sea—for Mr Caspian, and a bellboy showed him into a restaurant that was like any other restaurant in any of Paris's four-star hotels. Caspian was seated at a corner table, and he looked as if he was in his permanent place. He was reading from a pile of letters and papers that were scattered along the *banquette,* and on the table.

MacGregor was surprised by Caspian, and he felt how much Americans had changed in his lifetime. The American missionaries and doctors and geologists and archaeologists and diplomats his father had known in Iran had all been older, country-looking men: Presbyterians and Quakers. The Americans he knew now in the NIOC or in the consortium looked more youthful and codified, as if they were far more successful at copying each other.

But Caspian was different.

'You're just the same,' Caspian said, glancing quickly at MacGregor but then looking restlessly everywhere else as if nothing was worth looking at for long.

'How are you?'

MacGregor remembered Caspian before the war as a tall, thin, disbelieving young man with a sharp nose and a cynical, edgy, aggressive manner. He had come to Iran as a poorly-paid American teacher, which seemed ludicrous, because he was a brilliant linguist, speaking and writing Persian, Arabic and Turkish, as well as most of the European languages. After the war MacGregor had seen him once or twice teaching at the University in Teheran, and he seemed then to be living on some inborn insult, as if he had a great deal more intelligence than the world wanted of him. His fellow professors and teachers had treated him as cynically as he treated them, and MacGregor had always felt sorry for him, although he would have hated to have clashed with him.

Now he was a rotund man in a loose, light-coloured American suit, with plump cheeks, relaxed lips, and a sort of snarling but good-natured disbelief in everything around him. His restless eyes seemed to be disposing of everything as they wandered carelessly around, unseeing, untasting. He moved uncomfortably in his seat when MacGregor answered his questions about Kathy. Answers were not the main part of Caspian's interest.

'Sit down,' he said, and told the waiter to take the papers and letters away. 'I let him do that,' Caspian said to Mac-Gregor, as the waiter gathered the papers, 'just to show the natives that we've nothing to hide.'

'You haven't changed,' MacGregor told him. 'Except your shape.'

'I took to drink,' Caspian said.

But he looked quickly at MacGregor as if he had guessed all the trials, troubles, difficulties, stupidities and other wasteful problems in MacGregor's life.

'You're about fifty now, aren't you?' Caspian said.

'Fifty-two.'

'There ought to be a law that at fifty a man owes nothing to anybody. Then off he goes.'

'That's all right if you haven't got children,' MacGregor said.

'I escaped that frightening hazard,' Caspian said gloomily. Then he took a deep breath as if to cheer himself up. 'Let's get the food, then we can solve all the outstanding problems of Kurdistan. Do you want steak?'

'All right.'

'Okay, Michel,' Caspian told the waiter, as if MacGregor's confirmation was all a good waiter needed. He leaned forward, and without looking at MacGregor for more than a second at a time asked him why he had got himself mixed up with Kurds. 'You know what reckless nuts they are. All they can do is cut each other up like a pack of dogs.'

'Why did you get mixed up with them yourself?' Mac-Gregor asked.

'I'm not mixed up with them,' Caspian said. 'I've got no interest in them.'

'I thought you were the American expert on the Kurds. That's what I heard.'

'I'm the U.S. expert on everybody—Persians, Turks, Arabs, Azerbaijanians, Russians, Armenians, Kurds, Nestorians, Lebanese, etcetera, etcetera.'

'Does that mean you work for the CIA?'

Caspian was shaken out of his restless indifference. 'Now why would you say a thing like that to me?' he said as if he was genuinely upset.

'I was told...'

'Then you were told wrong. So don't, for Christ's sake, connect me with those boy-scout butchers. Please!'

'Sorry...' MacGregor said.

'Anyway, what were you doing yourself, shooting up the Turkish Army?' Caspian said appreciatively. 'My God, I'd love to have seen that.'

'There was nothing to see,' MacGregor told him. 'So let's leave that out of it.'

'Why?' Caspian said. 'Let the Turks get a little blood on their noses for a change,' he snarled. And, speaking perfect Suleiman Kurmanji, he quoted a Kurdish proverb which said that if you cut a tree in half you can build a house. But if you cut a man in half all you can do is bury the bastard. 'So why worry?'

'Quite right,' MacGregor said, aware that Caspian was looking for a short cut through his thin skin in order to get at his sensibilities.

'Your mother was Persian, wasn't she?' Caspian said.

'No. She was English.'

Caspian didn't hear. 'I can't remember her.'

'She died when I was fourteen.'

'I remember your father. You're the same sort of blue-eyed nut.'

The steaks came, and Caspian ate and drank whisky at the same time and seemed to forget MacGregor. 'What does the Qazi really think his chances are?' Caspian said to MacGregor when his plate had been cleaned of beans, meat, and potatoes.

'He's an optimist,' MacGregor said.

'What about you? Are you doing all this for the Persians?'

'The Persians?'

'You're a Persian at heart, MacGregor,' Caspian told him, looking quickly for denials or embarrassment. 'You're not much of a Kurd.'

'Same place, same problem,' MacGregor pointed out.

'Do you want some pie?' Caspian asked him.

'All right.'

'Michel...'

The 'pie' came, and Caspian attacked it like a man who had waited for nothing else. But he took only a mouthful and left the rest. 'Why can't you persuade the Qazi to accept our help and leave it at that?' he said.

'What sort of help? You mean American military help?'

'Don't get nervous. Eat your pie,' Caspian said, and called for another whisky. 'We'll be quite happy to see the Kurds organise their liberation, but we think they ought to do it in sensible stages.'

MacGregor laughed. 'That's too old a story, Caspian. It wouldn't convince anyone, and I'm surprised you talk that way.'

'I know. I know. But take Iraq. Obviously the Kurdish problem is forever there. So if the Kurds want to get involved in Iraq, we'll be glad to give them a hand. It's as crude as that.'

'Why Iraq? Why should they start there?'

'Now don't let's you and I start spelling out this stuff. You know very well why I'm saying Iraq.'

'Why not Turkey?' MacGregor said.

'Because we can't do anything against our Turkish allies, and you know it,' Caspian said. 'Tell the Qazi he can slaughter the Turks later on. In the meantime, why don't you tell him that we'll accept his special notion of the Kurdish national question if he'll accept a little bit of guidance on how to go about it.'

'Now that *is* crude,' MacGregor said. 'You know they won't listen to anything like that.'

Caspian shrugged. 'You know what we want, so why should I try to wrap it up for you. Why don't you talk to them a bit?'

'What about?'

'Jesus, I don't know. Talk about anything. Just give them a chance to understand our interest. Even our self-interest. Isn't that possible?'

'I doubt it. They'd never trust you.'

Caspian had now arrived at his cigar. 'I know! I know! We've been stupid. We've always supported the worst elements. And what a lot of shit we've shovelled on ourselves. But this time I'm trying to do it different.' He raised his eyes to heaven. 'I swear it....'

MacGregor was beginning to understand that there was a serious method in Caspian's lurching disparagements. Everything was stupid. Therefore everything for everybody was a matter of self-interest.

'Anyway why do you want me to talk to the Qazi?' he said to Caspian. 'You've got your own agents up there.'

Caspian laughed and his eyes wandered around the room again. 'Do you think you can get that money without our help?'

'Probably not, since you're the people who stole it.'

'Please...'

'Who really owns the Banque de Fars now?' MacGregor asked him.

'You must be kidding,' Caspian said.

'It's no joke to us,' MacGregor said.

Caspian shook his head. 'I'm sorry, MacGregor. That bank business was not my doing. But the point remains. Do you want the money?'

'Of course.'

'Then we can easily get it for you.'

'How?'

'For Christ's sake, does it matter? We can have the money transferred to you personally. It's not a major financial operation. Buying a postage stamp. We'd put it entirely into your hands.'

'That's nice. But in exchange for what?'

'Just tell the Qazi that we support the revolution.'

MacGregor watched the half-eaten apple 'pie', now soaked in cigar smoke, being eaten with relish. 'A lot of other people also support the Kurdish revolution,' MacGregor pointed out. 'The thing is—what are you supporting it for?'

'Anything you like. So we can get the gas, the oil, the politics, the place. Take your pick. Maybe we want to use the Kurds to outflank the Arabs, or the Russians.'

'In that case, it's not my business.'

'Even if you get that money?'

MacGregor blushed. 'I'm not supposed to get it on terms like that, and you know it.'

Caspian's response was excellent. 'I guess I deserved that,' he said, and put four teaspoons of sugar into his coffee. 'You're a deceptive man,' he said. 'I think I begin to believe some of those stories about you.'

MacGregor was not going to be tempted to ask him *what stories*; and when Caspian let his eyes wander like tangled searchlights around the room again, he said to MacGregor, 'Okay. Let's leave it there for the time being.'

'By all means.'

'It's not a bad start,' Caspian went on.

'Not bad,' MacGregor said.

'We can meet again when you've had time to worry about it, what do you think?'

'Why not?'

Caspian inspected him frankly for ten seconds. 'The trouble is I'm so used to dealing with petty little Machiavellis that I've forgotten how to talk to a man with a cause in his mouth.'

MacGregor had watched a thousand shapes forming in Caspian's complicated plump face, and he realised that Caspian had not thickened with drink or food, but with pleasure. After a bad start in life, Caspian had obviously found the one thing that satisfied his intelligence and his abilities. He was perfectly happy now in his profession, and MacGregor felt glad for Caspian's sake. He was obviously good at his job, and was likeably if cynically honest about it. But MacGregor wondered if Caspian's honest propositions were any safer than the other kind which came wrapped in the hundred skins of hypocrisy.

164

'Anything more to say?' Caspian asked.

'No. Nothing.'

The rest was silence until MacGregor saw, across the restaurant, Flanders of Children Unlimited whom he had last seen in the Kurdish highlands with his Persian masseur. Flanders caught his eye and waved casually and went on talking to a woman, who also looked up as if she had been told about MacGregor and wanted to see him.

'Do you know that bastard Flanders?' Caspian asked him.

'We meet from time to time.'

'Talk about the CIA,' Caspian snarled as if everything to do with any Intelligence agencies was the red rag to his bull. He waved at Flanders. Or rather he raised a flat hand and let it flop down worthlessly again.

MacGregor waited politely for Caspian to finish his coffee, then he would go. But Caspian kept him a little longer. He called for more coffee and told MacGregor about his American father's attempts, from Turkey, where Caspian had lived as a boy, to prevent the 1925 Kurdish revolt, led by the Dervish Sekhs. It had ended predictably with the execution of Sekh Said and forty-six other Kurdish leaders, and the slaughter of hundreds of Kurds by the Turkish army.

'Hundreds,' Caspian said as MacGregor finally got up to leave. 'The usual bloody end to all Kurdish revolts,' Caspian said without standing up himself. 'And that's what I don't want to happen again. Honestly...'

'I believe you,' MacGregor said and he shook Caspian's offered hand which was limp with non-communication.

Chapter Nineteen

Taha brought with him next day, 8th May, a delegation of four Kurds to warn MacGregor about the risky manoeuvres that were going on. They waited outside the gate until MacGregor went down to let them in. Two other men who were not with them (Belgians, they said) tried to speak hurriedly to MacGregor in French, one of them saying that they had tried to telephone him.

'We have seven light Swiss aircraft, less than a year old, which would be ideal for mountain use. We can adapt them to carry rockets, and we can even provide pilots...'

MacGregor ignored them, and let the young Kurds in. Then they all sat down in the stony dining-room around the walnut table, looking and behaving uncomfortably as if this old imperialist room was another oppressive country and another oppressive culture. MacGregor had easily recognised the Kurd in every face. Marin the gatekeeper had mistaken them for Algerians, *bicots*, and had refused to let them in. Algerians in this city were pigeons in the street.

'Do you have anything to tell us?' Taha began, speaking Kurdish.

'Nothing,' MacGregor said. 'You don't expect me to explain myself, do you, Taha?'

'But you went to see an American yesterday. What did he want?'

'That's not your business,' MacGregor said, 'so don't ask me.'

One of the four Kurds was a medical student whose name,

Zayid Jahiz, was Dervish. 'We simply want to explain what is happening here among the Kurds in Paris,' he said, 'because you probably don't know how serious it is.'

'In that case you're obviously going to repeat Taha's ideas about revolution first, and unity afterwards.'

'It isn't that,' the boy said, and though he had a soft and gentle face and a fine skin, he had the classic, glittering, Kurdish-Dervish eye. 'The Americans have been busy among us lately. So have the French and the English, the Turks, and the Iranians. They've all suddenly begun to be interested in the Kurds in Paris. What for? They're all beginning to promise us something, anything, if only we will be friendly to them or influence Kurdish affairs the way they want them to be.'

'Who listens to them?' MacGregor asked. 'Why are you so afraid?'

'Listen, Uncle,' Taha said. 'There's a secret faction among the Kurds here who are working with the Americans. That's why we want to know what the Americans offered you.'

MacGregor heard footsteps coming down the polished marble steps and he knew that someone in the family would put their head through the door at any moment to see what was going on.

'All I agreed to do in the first place was to recover the money,' he told them. 'And that's all you need to know, and all you need worry about.'

'We already know how the Americans got hold of the money,' Taha said. 'So why are you talking to them?'

'There are ways of getting it back,' MacGregor said. 'And I've got to do it in my own way.'

'Whether you get it back or not we can't let you hand over these arms to the Committee. That's really what we came to tell you.'

'How do you propose to stop me?' MacGregor asked.

They did not reply.

'Are you thinking of murdering me, Taha?'

'Please don't joke, Uncle.'

'Then don't talk nonsense,' MacGregor told him, like an angry father to a demanding son. 'I can only do what I have to do, Taha. There's no use trying to frighten me out of it.'

Taha was calm with his cold eye. 'Who's trying to frighten you?'

'You are—in typical Kurdish fashion.'

It was Cecie who put her head through the door, and she held up a student poster printed on thin cheap paper with letters cut from a stencil which read: *'Enragez-vous.'*

'Well?' she demanded.

She knew them all, and MacGregor watched the Kurds become sheepish.

'Go away for five minutes, Cecie,' MacGregor said to her briefly. 'Until we've finished.'

Cecie looked surprised and hurt. She left them, and in a few moments they heard the engine of her Citroën in the courtyard and MacGregor knew it was a mistaken way to do it. They were all vulnerable, Cecie in particular; even these boys with mountain faces.

'Let me make clear,' he said, 'that I also have to think about the Kurdish choice, and about what it is. I can't ignore it.'

They got up from the table and Taha said in a purely informative way. 'You're too practical to be a Kurd, and too single-minded to be a good revolutionary, Uncle.'

'I'm not supposed to be a Kurd or a revolutionary,' MacGregor said. 'I'm supposed to get that money. Or what the money has already bought.'

It was the Dervish who gave him a final gentle warning. 'Please don't give anything to the Committee, Agha. We beg you. The Committee isn't safe any more.'

'You want me to break my word to the Qazi?'

They said nothing to that, and MacGregor saw them out through the gate, Taha making his farewell with a mocking little bow.

When he came back, Andrew was waiting for him with a visiting card in his hand. 'While you were in there with Taha, we had a visitor. He's in the study.'

'Who is he?'

'A French security man.'

'How do you know he's a security man?'

'Will you bet?'

'I'll just wash my hands from the gate,' MacGregor said. 'Marin's been oiling the latch.'

'Take your time,' Andrew told him. 'Mama's in there softening him up a bit.'

MacGregor needed the time to shift his nerves from Taha to a French policeman, but he was also worried about Andrew, who was taking it for granted that he should know everything that was going on.

'What you ought to do,' Andrew was saying as MacGregor dipped his hands in the little washbasin behind the stairs, 'is use their secret rivalries against them.'

'What rivalries?'

'The French hate the Americans....'

'What's that got to do with it?'

'Just keep it in mind.'

Andrew would have followed his father into the study, but MacGregor said 'No' and closed the door behind him.

'Monsieur...' the Frenchman said, and offered a light hand.

Kathy's eyes warned MacGregor to be careful. 'This is Monsieur Guérin,' she said.

Guérin did not waste time. 'I was telling Madame that we want you to come down with me and explain a few things,' he said. 'We're not far from here.'

'Explain what?' MacGregor asked. 'And to whom?'

'To us,' Guérin said, and tightened himself a little with a French smile. He produced a white card in a plastic folder with a red and blue stripe across one corner. It said that he was from one of the political sections of one of the bureaux of the Department of Security and National Procuration.

'Procuration?' MacGregor said. 'What's that?'

'You know, of course, our responsibilities?'

'No, I don't.'

Guérin twitched a little, as if ignorance like that was hopeless.

'Do you want me to come now?' MacGregor asked him.

'Naturally.'

MacGregor did not ask any questions. 'Then let's go,' he said.

'I'll get your Burberry,' Kathy said, and as she did so she said in Persian to MacGregor: 'I'll call Guy...'

'No,' he said.

'Don't be silly,' she said.

'Leave him out of it,' MacGregor insisted.

But she told him in French, for the benefit of Guérin, that he must be back by six o'clock because they were going to a cocktail at Jizzy Margaux's, Guy Moselle's sister, reminding him also that a Minister whom she named would be there expecting to see him. 'Don't be late,' she said. 'And the Americans also expect you at six.'

Margaux, Moselles, Ministers and Americans: they were Kathy's family hints and family warnings for Monsieur Guérin. MacGregor followed Guérin out to the gate where Marin, already primed by Guérin's air of police authority, was waiting to swing open the portal like an old soldier who knew whom he served.

Chapter Twenty

Political Intelligence men were not a new experience for MacGregor but he knew he was dealing here with a different type: a European, not the pale sick men who seemed to operate their sickness for the benefit of the prisons of Teheran. These were respectable men, ministry men, like the India Office men or Foreign Office men he remembered in his youth. The French treated most foreigners as if they were ridiculous, hostile, or simply not there. Six Frenchmen at their desks ignored him when he sat down in a room which was en route to something else. Then three more ministry men in the next room ignored him with Quai d'Orsay manners. That was a little better. They were young men of family working in their white nylon shirts, and one of them smiled at him. Then he was conducted by a man who looked like a retired *Garde Républicaine* into what was an eighteenth-century French drawing-room with a fine carpet and beautifully decorated walls. Two men were sitting slightly sideways on the edge of a gilded couch, and MacGregor recognised one of them.

'We met last week at the Belgians',' the Frenchman said in English. 'Guy Moselle introduced us. Do you remember? I'm Antoine Cumont.'

'Yes, I remember,' MacGregor said.

At the Belgians', Moselle had made a point of taking MacGregor to meet Cumont; and later Moselle had said that Cumont could be trusted with anything that was a bit off-beat. He belonged to the one faction in the Quai d'Orsay that wanted to deal openly with liberation movements. 'He's the sort of man you've got plenty of in England, but we haven't in France,' Moselle had said. Kathy had also told him that Cumont came from one of the six monarchist families of France. So here was Monsieur Cumont, sitting on a Louis XIV gilded couch in the Département de Procuration, with black silk socks stretched tight across his dainty ankles. He was a waxen old man, and he had an old man's passive authority.

'This is my colleague, Major Schramm,' Cumont said.

Schramm was the contradiction. He was a tough little peasant-like gabardine soldier. Where were the tall lean St Cyriens of Cumont's own class in their sky-blue képis? Not here. Schramm watched; and he watched with an aggressive smile on his hard young face as if he was about to be amused, but most likely never would be. He leaned forward with his little smile and plucked a fragment of Paris dust from MacGregor's blue jacket.

'Guérin,' Major Schramm called.

The *agent* who had brought MacGregor came in immediately with a silver tray of drinks and glasses, which he put on a little table with minutiae, and then went out again.

'How is Madame MacGregor?' Cumont said in slow but good English. 'And your children? Are you enjoying your stay in Paris?'

While he gave Cumont his polite answers, Schramm was pouring him a vermouth and adding a little Campari and no ice.

'All right?' he said to MacGregor.

'Perfect.' How did Schramm know what he liked?

'I hope you'll forgive me,' Cumont went on, 'if I tell you that we know what you are doing here in France, and that we can't really approve of it. But I suppose you guessed that.'

'Did you bring me here to tell me that, Monsieur?' Mac-Gregor asked.

'Not really. In fact, we appreciate your interest in the Kurdish problem, because we have our own interest in it as well. We'd just like to know a little more about it, and why you are involved in it.'

MacGregor looked from one Frenchman to the other. 'I'm an old friend of the Kurds,' he said, 'so they asked me to help them.'

'Of course,' Cumont said, 'that's really why we want to talk to you.'

MacGregor knew why Cumont was in this, but he wondered why the little French soldier was here. He had a feeling that whenever he stopped looking at Schramm, Schramm watched him even closer.

'Will you answer one thing for me about the Kurds?' Cumont was saying.

'If it isn't political,' MacGregor said.

'Oh?'

'I can't talk about internal Kurdish politics,' MacGregor told them.

'It's really an historical question,' Cumont said. 'I'd simply like to know the reason why all Kurdish uprisings in the past have ended in division and failure. Are they always naturally at loggerheads with each other? Or are they just unlucky, and do the wrong thing at the wrong time?'

MacGregor told Cumont that it was difficult to answer. 'It puzzles the Kurds themselves,' he said. 'All Kurds want the same thing. But they've never been able to find a way of deciding how to do it.'

'And now?'

MacGregor rubbed his knees. 'It will be different,' he told Cumont. 'In the long run, anyway.'

'But what exactly are they trying to do?' Cumont asked. 'We have so many conflicting reports.'

MacGregor hesitated. Cumont's questions were simple and direct, and he wanted to answer them without appearing evasive. 'They want to establish an independent republic,' he said.

'You mean by force?'

'By any means they can.'

'Where?'

MacGregor shrugged. 'Anywhere they can,' he said. It was only half an answer, but it was all he was going to give.

'I see....' Cumont ignored a door which had been opened a crack and hurriedly shut again. 'You say that you can't speak politically for the Kurds,' he went on, 'but can you at least tell me what sort of international allies the Qazi and his Committee are looking for?'

'You mean, what is their attitude to France?'

'Yes.'

'I've never even heard France mentioned,' MacGregor said.

'What do they really feel about the Russians?' Schramm asked.

'The same as they feel about everybody else,' MacGregor said. 'Friendly if the other side's friendly, hostile if they're hostile. There's nothing secret about it,' he said irritably to Schramm.

Cumont had a violet-coloured file tied with faded pink tape on the couch beside him, which MacGregor had not noticed before. Cumont put on a pair of large gold French spectacles, untied the file with china-doll fingers, and glanced at it with his careful old eyes. 'We have our own sources of information,' he said, 'so please don't think I'm asking you to give away secrets of the National Iranian Oil Company where you work.'

MacGregor waited.

'Is there really such a large deposit of exploitable gas and oil in the Kurdish highlands?' Cumont asked. 'Have you actually plotted it?'

174

'What does your independent source tell you?'

'That there are probably huge reserves there. Is that so?'

'We can't hide the fact,' MacGregor said. 'So I'm not telling you anything you don't know.'

'But obviously you know more about it than anyone else,' Cumont suggested persuasively. 'Considering your experience there, how exploitable do you think the deposits are—in the short term?'

'All the deep layers of natural gas are rather sulphur-saturated, but modern processes can cope with that. The oil ...' He shrugged. 'It's very deep but it's just a matter of investment.'

'And pipelines?'

'What pipelines?'

'Would they be safe?'

'From whom? Going where?'

'Going anywhere. Would they be safe from the Kurds themselves?' Schramm asked on his keen, French edge.

Again MacGregor felt irritated by Schramm. 'They would be safe if the Kurds got some benefit from them,' he said. 'Otherwise the Kurds would obviously blow them up as often as they can. Anyway, what pipelines are you thinking of? There aren't any at the moment, nor are any planned as far as I know.'

'It was just a general question.' Cumont closed the file and turned to Schramm. 'Do you have any questions before we get to the real point of this?'

MacGregor felt himself on the other side of some line from Schramm. 'We know all about Kurdish guerilla methods,' he was saying to MacGregor in military French.

'Do you?'

'We know enough,' Schramm said confidently. 'But we don't know what they plan to do. Strategically, I mean. Do they aim to create a large mobile force in the military sense? Or do they plan to use small units, and the usual methods of hit and run?'

'If I knew the answers to those questions I wouldn't tell you. But in fact I don't know.'

Schramm bent his head a little in a sort of pugilistic acknowledgement. 'I can understand that,' he said. 'But what I'm really trying to find out is their military capability. What is it?'

'I can't really say,' MacGregor replied. 'But it's a lot better than most people think it is.'

'Where will they begin, for instance?'

MacGregor didn't answer.

Schramm smiled. 'In Iran, Iraq, Turkey?' he said.

'I couldn't tell you that either. You're asking impossible questions, Major Schramm.'

Schramm's professionalism was better than his hard young face, because he laughed. 'Perhaps there's one thing you can answer, Monsieur MacGregor. I notice in the list of arms the Kurds have bought that there are a number of British .303 service rifles. What's the point of that?'

For a moment MacGregor wondered if he should go on pretending ignorance, or simply refuse to answer. But there was something in this relationship of Cumont to Schramm, and in Cumont's birdlike attention, with a cigarette burning in his delicate fingers, that made MacGregor feel the nearer honesty he was with these men, the safer he would be.

'Range and accuracy and durability are what the Kurds want in a rifle,' he said. 'That's all I know about it.'

'But surely they could do the same thing with an American M.6. And you can get plenty of M.6's from the offshore dealers....'

'Have you ever seen the Kurdish mountains, Major Schramm?'

'No. But I hope to pay them a visit really soon. I even know a little Kurdish.'

Cumont stopped it by holding out his hand for Mac-

Gregor's glass, and MacGregor knew that they didn't believe in his military ignorance.

'No more, thank you,' he said, handing Cumont the empty glass.

Cumont listened for a moment to a chanting noise outside the window. Then he said to MacGregor: 'Do you know what happened to all that military equipment the Kurds bought?'

MacGregor said he didn't know.

'It's stored in Swiss railway trucks in the SNCF yards at Lyons,' Cumont told him. 'It's costing the Englishman and the Dutchman about ten thousand francs a week for use of trucks and siding. So you can see why they are anxious for you to take delivery of it.'

'They're anxious to be paid,' MacGregor pointed out.

'That's true,' Cumont said. 'But that side of it is a very delicate situation.'

'You mean with the banks?' MacGregor said.

Cumont made a gesture of distaste. 'What those banks did to get that money is quite illegal in France,' he said. 'In fact we may be able to restore that money to your Kurdish Committee.'

Cumont got up then and walked to the window to see what the chanting was in the street below. He beckoned to MacGregor and Schramm to come to the window. About a hundred schoolboys in short raincoats and duffle coats, and carrying banners and placards, were marching in the street below. The banners said they came from the Lycées Buffon, Condorcet, Paul Valéry and Charlemagne, and they were shouting that they were on strike against the continued occupation of the Sorbonne by the police.

'Gide didn't inspire *that*!' Cumont said sourly as the boys of Lycée Condorcet disappeared down the Rue de Constantine. 'At this rate, we'll have a next generation of intellectual deformities.'

They went back to the gilded couch, and MacGregor

knew they had reached the real point of this meeting. 'Are you suggesting that you can restore that money to the Committee?' he asked Cumont.

'In certain circumstances,' Cumont said.

'What circumstances?'

'If we can decide who genuinely represents the Kurds in this.'

'I do,' MacGregor said firmly.

Cumont smiled at MacGregor's sudden rush of *folie*. 'I'm sure you do,' Cumont said. 'But we must be sure of the credentials.'

'I think my documents will satisfy you,' MacGregor said.

Cumont put the thumbs of his fine yellow hands together. 'Do you have them with you?' he asked.

'No.'

'Where are they?'

'At my home.'

Schramm and Cumont exchanged a glance. 'You should be careful with any sort of document you have from the Kurds,' Cumont told him. 'You know what happened to the Kurdish boy.'

'Not exactly,' MacGregor said.

'The boy had typhoid, but we couldn't discover how he got it.'

'I knew that he had died in Lyons, and that the French Sûreté handed his documents over to the Turks.'

'That's not true,' Cumont said with sudden anger. 'The Turk, Seroglu, insists that the Sûreté gave him the documents. But they were stolen. And unfortunately we have no way of forcing Colonel Seroglu to hand them over to us without an incident.'

'I see,' MacGregor said, but he knew it sounded more cynical than he meant it to be.

'In fact we don't really need Seroglu's documents, providing you have the proper credentials,' Cumont told him, and he stood up to bring it to an end.

'And if they do satisfy you?' MacGregor asked as they waited for a moment around the little drinks table.

'France has a strong Mediterranean policy, Monsieur. And it includes all the periphery interests in Iran and Iraq and Turkey and the Persian Gulf. And of course that would include the Kurdish areas.'

'You mean the oil....' MacGregor said as they walked to the door.

'We can discuss all that when we've seen what sort of credentials you have....'

They shook hands, and this time it was Schramm who led him through the antichambers and the clerks to the Citroën. They stood for a moment in the little courtyard while Schramm said to MacGregor in Kurdish: 'The world is a rose garden. You must always go through it with a friend.'

MacGregor had to laugh. 'Where did you learn that?' he said.

'From a Kurd....' Schramm's watchful eyes seemed to be looking for effect, because he went on to say in Kurdish what else he had learned:

'Goat-sucker, toadstool, dirty hem, pederast, womb, bladder, lover, cry-baby.' Schramm's hard eyes never left MacGregor's face. 'I suppose you know all that.'

'Yes. They're all Kurdish four-letter words.'

'Funny language,' Schramm said, as he closed the door of the Citroën and waved to MacGregor. The driver turned out of the gate as if he knew, for sure, that there was nothing in front, on the sides, or behind him.

Chapter Twenty-one

It was twelve o'clock when he got home: French lunchtime. Kathy was not at home, and Aunt Joss did not call
out. She knew who it was from the vibrations on stone and
wood, so he did not announce himself in the hall. Considering that they had last seen him taken off to some unknown
future by a French policeman he wondered why there was
no sign of anybody. There was only a note for him on the
dining-room table where his luncheon place was set.

'Cold lunch in the ice box. Open some wine.'

He ate his lunch, and then decided to walk across the
river to the Place de la Concorde, to the bank where he had
transferred what foreign currency he had. It was an American bank, and he always liked going into it because he liked
the American banking method. It seemed to believe in
itself and its money. Today he would sign one of their blue-
backed cheques for $500, and then store the francs he got
in his inside pocket to pay what he could of the household
expenses: some of the drinks or the food or the transporta-
tion or the extras they entertained with; Kathy would not
take anything more than that.

'Good afternoon, Mr MacGregor,' the clerk said. He was
a Greek-Lebanese-American who would exchange a few
words with MacGregor about Beirut and the latest news
from Iran—if there was any news. Or about the clerk's
interest in mountain-climbing.

Today he raised his first finger and rubbed his thick
black eyebrows as if making a secret sign to MacGregor.
'I thought you might come in today,' he said. 'I hoped
you would.'

'Why? Something wrong?'

The Greek did not lean forward or make anything look too unusual, but he said quietly to MacGregor: 'I'm not supposed to let you know this, but you're a friend. Somebody,' he said, 'is enquiring about your account with us, and there have been Telex messages coming and going to Teheran and Washington and London. I thought you'd like to know.'

MacGregor thanked him. 'I suppose it's the usual financial check on something I wanted to do,' he explained.

The Greek understood, and he nodded and slapped down a bundle of fifty-franc notes. He counted out the rest in smaller bills and change, saying loudly when he had finished: 'Goodbye, Mr MacGregor. Glad to have seen you again.'

MacGregor waved his fingers, and as he walked around the bloated traffic of the Concorde he wondered who was prying into his bank balance. He knew it was probably just another pressure on him, but it depressed him and he didn't want to go home with it. He went shop-gazing on the Right Bank, and sat in a café opposite the Louvre, calculating the volume of lead pollution in the Paris streets. At their present levels, the nitrous oxide from Arabia and Persia would eventually kill every living thing in Europe— men, women, children, trees and flowers. But he could shrug it off in his present mood. Poetic justice...

When he got home again Kathy was locked in the bathroom preparing for their dinner at Jizzy Margaux's. She shouted through the bathroom door that he ought to get ready.

'Had you forgotten?'

'No. No.' he lied

He waited until she had emerged like a plucked flower. She did not ask him what had happened or where he had been taken to.

'Where were you?' he asked her.

'I told you last night. I went riding with Guy in the famous hippodrome. It's the silliest place. All sorts of sawdust and bandy-legged French grooms wearing English caps, and stable dogs named Bob and Jock.'

When he had gone off with Guérin he had left her tense and worried. Where was the worry and concern now?

'Don't you want to know what happened?' he asked her.

'I know what happened,' she said. 'The moment you left I rang Guy. I had to. He told me it was all right, that a friend of his wanted to talk to you. It was Cumont, wasn't it?'

'Yes.'

'I told Guy it all looked so sinister that I was convinced you were not coming back. But he just laughed and said it was the idiot French way they did things. What did Cumont want? Did he ask you to help them with the Kurds?'

'Something like that.'

'Did you agree?'

'Not directly,' he said. 'It didn't really get that far.'

She was pulling on a rust-coloured dress which was new, holding it delicately over her head before letting it slide like liquid over her shoulders. He guessed that it had come from one of the haute couture houses in the 8th arrondissement, and he was perplexed as he had been all his married life by his wife's complexity. There was something savage in the way Kathy was returning to her old life, so that even the line of her body and neck and face seemed to be obliterating everything that he knew of her before.

'Zip me up,' she said to him.

Once it would have been an excuse for affection; she would have leaned happily if briefly against him. But Kathy was not going to lean against him now, and perhaps never would again.

'I think it's time we left Paris,' she said, but he couldn't tell how serious she was. She had said this before. She began to pull at her French coiffure with disrespectful English fingers. 'I know what Cumont's department does,' she said, 'and you're going to get thoroughly out of your depth.'

'Is that what Moselle's been telling you?'

She turned to look at him. 'I don't need Guy to tell me. He doesn't know you, but I do.'

'I don't see what you're so worried about,' he said.

'Now you're involved with political Intelligence departments. And you'll be demolished by experts.'

'Perhaps...' he said, but he knew she was right.

She put on her lipstick very carefully. 'Harold Essex is also here to see you. I saw him this morning.'

'Essex...'

'Essex,' she repeated tauntingly. 'The reluctant patron of our happy marriage. Do you realise it's twenty-three years since you first arrived in Moscow with him on that ridiculous mission.' She glanced at him through the gateway of the old mirror. 'Do you really think that you're any better equipped now than you were then to match your political wits with Essex's?'

'But he must be a very old man now.'

'Harold's never too old to be cunning,' she said. 'And he probably gets better at it as he gets older. He has to cover up more.'

'What does he want?' MacGregor asked, feeling already the embarrassment that Essex always made him suffer.

'He wants what they all want at the moment. You.'

MacGregor bent over his shoes and talked to the floor so that Kathy could not see his wretched face. 'Essex won't bother me,' he said.

'Put your jacket on,' she told him gently, 'and let's go.'

He did as he was told, and as they went downstairs Kathy pulled his shirt cuffs below his coat sleeves.

'Essex is either going to ask you for one of his clever

favours,' she said, 'or he's going to put Foreign Office pressure on you.'

'How?'

'Ahh...' she said cynically in the hall. 'They all have such high hopes for you, including Essex. Such bribes. Essex will know what to do, and it'll be fascinating to see how you cope with him after all this time.'

They stood in the hall for a moment and Kathy, perfect herself, put finishing touches to his collar, his hair and his tie.

'You see! Everything I told you would happen is now happening,' she said, her clear, cold English eyes never leaving his. 'Only it's going to be a lot worse than I thought.'

'Well I think it's just beginning to unravel itself,' he argued.

She held up her gloved hands to stop any more explanation. 'All right. All right,' she said. 'I'm not going to argue. Do it your way.' Then she called out: 'Aunt Joss. We're both going to Jizzy Margaux's for cocktails and dinner. We'll probably be home late.'

'All right, Kathy darling. But where are the children?'

'Reoccupying the Sorbonne, I think. I don't really know,' Kathy said.

'Must I worry about them?' Aunt Joss asked.

'No. I'll ring in an hour to see if they're safely back.'

'All right, Kathy darling. All's well...'

All's well.... That was new, and as they turned down Rue Barbet de Jouy looking for a taxi they could laugh a little more affectionately on each other's arms for a moment because they had suddenly infected each other with their fresh clothes, perfumes, haute couture, and their bright new shoes glittering on the pavement. A little glamour, after all, could overcome almost anything.

Chapter Twenty-two

But the dry mountains of his youth got the better of him again in the first ten minutes at Jizzy Margaux's. He was geographically misplaced among the generals, bankers, Ministers of the Republic, diplomats, women, brandy exporters, bankers, and the high civil servants of Europe who were putting their affairs in order over Jizzy Margaux's goblets and *amuse-gueules.*

The middle of the house was drilled clean through by a remarkable, gracious, circular staircase which simply cut a wide hole up through each of the five floors, so that the whole house seemed to be built around a whirlpool. They were on the top floor, where the walls were silk, painted with a Japanese garden. Above them, on the fanlight, painted exotic birds flew in and out of delicate bamboo leaves. He would decide, later on, that the beautiful Jizzy and her house were Japanese twins.

He kept out of the way and watched all the other women with Kathy in mind, trying to decide what they were here for, and what Kathy was here for. In two minutes he discovered that the women were also watching him, as if they knew something about him that he didn't know himself. French, Dutch, German, English, American, Spanish, Indian and South American women; and one Burmese girl who grew like an exquisite plant out of the green carpet. She was so still that the men and women talking to her obviously found it difficult not to stare at her. She even listened like a plant, apparently hearing nothing, registering nothing and saying nothing.

'Those Burmese women are really the end, don't you think, MacGregor?' someone said to him. 'I suppose it comes from all that exotic relaxation which the Brahmins force on their women. Isn't she a beauty?'

MacGregor knew it was Lord Essex without turning around, and he knew better than to treat it as anything but a casual reunion as of yesterday instead of their first meeting for twenty-two years.

'Who is she?' MacGregor managed to ask calmly.

'Some Burmese General's wife, a Kachin. I think her husband's name is U Tha, or something like that. He was once a big shot in U Nu's 'Clean Wing' party, but now he's one of the leading lights in the anti-communist coalition, and she's supposed to be rich with corruption. Definitely not your cup of tea, MacGregor.'

MacGregor felt an usurpation already taking place. The better man was establishing his position.

'I didn't think I'd find you mixing with this lot,' Essex went on. 'There are more reactionaries standing around on that flashy green carpet than I've seen in one place for years. What's Kathy up to, bringing you here?'

'Kathy knows the family.'

'I know very well who Kathy knows,' Essex said. 'But she's not playing this upper-crust game in Paris for nothing. What's she up to?'

'Heaven knows,' MacGregor said.

Essex chuckled. 'She seems to be enjoying it anyway. She's going about it as if it were something of her own.'

Kathy was sitting on a white couch with Guy Moselle on one side and an Italian on the other. Two American men in silk suits were seated dangerously on a low glass coffee table in front of her. Kathy's décor was excellent, and her poise was better than any other woman's in the room. 'She hasn't changed a bit,' Essex said, 'except that she has that colorado colouration that comes with all that dry mountain air. You both look like plumed eagles among this lot.'

By now MacGregor had been able to inspect the old man and he was amazed to find that Essex too had hardly changed in twenty-two years, except that his clothes had moved with the times. His gay shirt collar was large, so was his tie, and his hair was longer as if to prove that he still had it. He was sunburned, as if that too were important, and wrinkles, cracks and ridges were obliterated by the stain of the sun. It was only when MacGregor took a closer look that he saw that Essex's skin resembled a snake's. It was smooth, but it was about to crack. His neck was dry, his mouth was just beginning to get lost in his teeth or his jaw, and his eyes were slower to move. But five feet away, and again he seemed hardly changed. Essex had instinctively stepped away a little when he felt Mac-Gregor's sudden inspection.

'That's Moselle, I suppose,' Essex said, nodding towards the couch.

'Yes.'

'It's funny, but I never met him. Is he your current problem?'

MacGregor was caught unaware. He blushed and stumbled with his answer. 'What problem do you mean?'

'Yours. You can't tell me you haven't had problems with Kathy in twenty-two years of marriage.'

'Kathy's an old friend of his.'

'So you said before,' Essex said, still smiling. 'But cheer up. She must be aware that all the women in this little Japanese jungle are looking at you.'

There were three women twenty feet away, young women —two of them Parisiennes who were perfect to their perfect little heels. They were inspecting MacGregor and obviously talking about him. He wondered why, and he had to discipline himself not to inspect himself for a fault.

'You know what they're fascinated with, MacGregor?' Essex said.

'No. . . .'

'Your fighting reputation.'

'Then they must be mad,' MacGregor said.

But Essex was delighted. 'They're tingling all over with feminine fascination because they've heard that you've been killing Turks in those wild hills. They've heard that you dress like a Kurd and gallop all over the mountains like a Riff. And here you are, looking properly out of place. It's great.'

MacGregor knew he was being fooled, but he tried thereafter not to look at the long-necked women and the pretty women and the hard women, because he knew that they too had been fooled. He stared over their heads at the wall, and he knew that Essex was watching him and laughing at every thought that was in his head.

'I'll be seeing you Saturday,' Essex was saying. 'Kathy's invited me to lunch.'

They were swept apart then because another group standing nearby had waited to interrupt them. But just as the two young Parisiennes were about to talk to him, MacGregor felt his arm being taken by Jizzy Margaux herself.

'You don't remember who I am, do you?' she said to him. 'You've forgotten me in half an hour since we met at the door.'

No one who had ever seen Giselle Margaux would forget who she was. She had the most natural and startlingly beautiful face MacGregor had ever seen. She was not young —she was now in her early forties—but her soft French beauty suggested untouchability. It was too much. MacGregor remembered Moselle telling Kathy, in an unhappy way, that his sister had never had any real human contact with anybody at all, not even with her husband.

'It's that same gap you find between animal and man,'

Moselle had said. 'There may be affection, even love I suppose. But what is finally missing between a man and his dog? What is it that really divides us from them? In any case, Jizzy has never been able to break through it, and that's what she had to live behind, like my mother did. I think she's always looking secretly for someone to make her human.'

In fact the beautiful Jizzy had two faces. One was the maquillage of a Parisian craftsman which was a work of art in itself, and the other was the natural face that was buried underneath it: there somewhere, but only hinted at as an indestructible foundation.

'I am . . .' Jizzy began.

'Don't,' MacGregor said quickly in embarrassment.

But she seemed disappointed, as if she would have preferred him to have forgotten who she was.

'Kathy shouldn't have dragged you here,' she told him.

He didn't know what he was supposed to say. 'That's all right,' he said. 'I'll go over there in a minute.' He pointed unthinkingly to the window.

'Why don't you just go home? I won't mind.'

He wanted to get away from her. Her restless, life-seeking look was on him, and he was not sure that he could cope with it. Even her bright eyes had a peculiar animal film over them, as if she saw everything like a dog and without any lasting contact with it.

'I'll wait for Kathy,' he said. 'Then I'll go.'

'Go on down into my husband's library,' she said, and her French mouth got hopelessly tangled in the English words. 'I didn't know,' she said in French. 'Kathy should have told me.'

Told her what?

He glanced at Kathy. Until now Kathy had ignored him, but he realised that she was now watching him intently. She signalled him with her eyes. She looked at her watch. Then she got up, and he saw her excusing herself. He

189

knew she was going somewhere to ring Aunt Joss to find out about Cecie and Andrew.

'Would you excuse me for a moment,' he said to Jizzy Margaux. 'I must go and see what's been happening to my son and daughter.'

'Why? Where are they?'

'I'm not sure. Kathy's gone to telephone. They've been demonstrating at the Sorbonne.'

'Oh, that...' She kept a tight grip on his arm, and in some curious way he found himself relaxing, as if Jizzy was not going to let anyone get at him. She took him to a door that was not marked in the wall at all. Then he was inside a little round room with a cupola of glass in the ceiling. 'Kathy,' she said. 'Here he is.'

Jizzy's strange eyes were still waiting for his to take hold of hers. But MacGregor looked elsewhere, and he knew that when she went back to her salon and closed the door behind her she would become something else, and their messages would be different.

Kathy had already dialled the number, and while she was talking to Aunt Joss she pointed to the *écouteur* for him to listen in.

'Where are they?' Kathy was asking Aunt Joss.

'Cecie's car broke down near the Beaux Arts,' Aunt Joss said. 'She came back and got Marin to go and help her.'

'Is she all right?'

'Of course. She said to tell you that the *professeurs* are going to hold a big *manifestation*. Is that important? She said that someone called Taha or Jaha has gone to Lyons.'

'When?'

'How do I know, darling? She didn't say. Is it important? She'll ring me back, she said, in an hour if she doesn't come home.'

'Listen, Aunt Joss,' Kathy said. 'When you talk to her, tell her she's got to be home by midnight.'

'But Kathy darling, she says everything here begins at

midnight. And I think she's right. It's all very interesting for them. . . .'

'Midnight,' Kathy insisted.

'All right. All right.'

'Where's Andrew?'

'There's a note he left you. Just a minute.' Aunt Joss then read the note. Andrew had gone to Lyons with Taha and they were not to worry. 'That's all it says.'

Kathy looked at her husband. 'All right, Aunt Joss,' Kathy said, and told her goodbye and hung up.

For a moment they both kept perfectly still.

'Isn't Lyons where those arms trucks are?' she said to him.

MacGregor had not told her about the trucks being in Lyons, and he had only just discovered it from Cumont. 'How do you know where those arms trucks are?' he asked her.

'Oh, for heaven's sake,' she said.

'Is there anything Moselle doesn't tell you?' he said to her angrily.

'Never mind that.' Kathy's quiet, flat, efficient fury was worse than her temper, because it was part of an inborn ability to insult him with her family manner and contempt. 'Now that you've involved your own son in this,' she said, 'I suppose you'll finally recognise your stupidity.'

'I've been trying to keep all of you out of this,' he told her.

'Well, you haven't, have you?'

'Andrew won't get involved,' he insisted. 'Whatever he's gone down there for, he knows what he's doing. If he's gone with Taha there must be a good reason for it.'

'Like your good reasons.'

'Oh, he'll be all right Kathy,' he said. 'And I'll talk to him when he comes back.'

'Why don't you leave now, this minute, and go after them?' It was not a suggestion, it was an order.

'There's no need to panic like that,' he told her.

'I'm not panicking,' she said. 'I'm telling you what to do. So go.'

'No,' he said. 'They won't do anything stupid, neither of them. Taha won't risk anything silly with Andrew.'

'All right,' she said getting up. 'You seem to know. But I'm telling you now—when Andrew comes back I'm going to take both the children to London.'

'But nothing's happened,' he insisted. 'Look, Kathy. Just wait a little until you see him. If they've done something reckless, then all right, let's all go back. But don't keep saying we ought to leave. I can't leave. I simply can't. Not yet.'

She seemed to let everything ebb away from her, as if she had finally exhausted herself. 'All right,' she said with a shrug. 'Why should I go on bothering? By all means stay. Let us do everything you want. Personally I don't care any more. But if Andrew does get into trouble I'll never forgive you.'

'He won't get into trouble.'

They were now standing up to their ankles in this exotic little observatory, shouting at each other in whispers. A rich, fat ginger cat began to manoeuvre itself around their legs, and then the door opened and Colonel Seroglu the Turk was standing with them saying to MacGregor: 'Please introduce me to your wife, Mr MacGregor. We have only met on the phone. How do you do,' he said to Kathy, and Kathy had her hand kissed as Seroglu went on, 'Please let us make a firm appointment. It's such a shame that our children don't become friends. I'd like mine to go to England. Let us try next week....' He had taken out a very fine, thin, leather diary and he began to go through dates until Kathy interrupted him.

'I think we may be leaving Paris in a few days' time,' she said. 'Perhaps when we come back.'

'All right, all right,' Seroglu said, and closed his book.

'But in the meantime I must talk to you,' he said to Mac-Gregor. 'Important business,' he added.

'Yes. If you can ring me tomorrow...' MacGregor began.

And while he was talking to Seroglu, Kathy left him, to return to the white couch where Moselle would be waiting for her.

Chapter Twenty-three

They did not quarrel again when they returned at midnight because they could not. And, recognising his difficulties with Kathy, Jizzy Margaux had left him alone at dinner, although she obviously considered him worth a lot of trouble. Over the intimacy of the warm little dining-room they had all eaten like passengers in a railway compartment, but an hour after they left the dinner MacGregor remembered nothing that was said except a brief conversation he had had with an Italian diplomat who said that the English diagnostic method in medicine was the best in the world. The English, he said, considered you healthy until you proved yourself sick, whereas continental doctors diagnosed you as sick until you proved yourself healthy. The Code Napoléon of medicine.

Cecie came home at one a.m. but he did not call her in, although he was sitting in bed reading more of the material that Jamal Janab had sent him from Teheran. He slept badly, and when the phone rang at seven o'clock in the morning he leapt out of bed and Andrew told him that they were on the way back to Paris. Everything was all right. There was nothing to worry about.

'They're on their way home,' he told Kathy.

She groaned and turned over and went to sleep almost immediately as if that part of the day was finally over and done with.

She was still asleep when he went down to breakfast, and Cecie reported to him over cornflakes that the Paris students were going to go on demonstrating. 'Even the *gens du quartier* think it's degenerating to keep the police in the university.'

MacGregor had always enjoyed Cecie's outbursts because he did not have to quarrel with her, or protect himself. But then she said, 'What's going on between you and mother?' Cecie's face was bent over her plate, as if that gave them enough secrecy to discuss family affairs. Her long hair made a tent for her cornflakes. 'You were obviously arguing last night. I saw your light on.'

'We were not....'

'Then you'd been quarrelling at Jizzy Margaux's.'

'We have to quarrel sometimes,' he said. 'Anyway, it wasn't important.'

'It's been going on too long,' she told him.

'A few months in a lifetime isn't very long, Cecie. It'll pass.'

She dug determinedly at thick blobs of orange and green and yellow paint which had solidified on her sweater. 'Why is she suddenly taking up that sort of *bois* horse riding? With people like the Moselles. I hate Guy Moselle. I don't like any of them except Jizzy, and she ought to have been a nun.'

MacGregor knew he had to be very careful. 'When your mother married me she had to abandon almost everything she was brought up with. And now that she wants to relax a bit and enjoy some of it again, why not? She gave up a great deal, and we went through some very difficult times.'

'I know all that,' Cecie said. 'But this isn't like her.'

'Whether it is or not, it's not doing her any harm.'

'It's not doing her any good either.'

'It doesn't *have* to do her any good, so let's not talk about it.'

'But you hate it, don't you?' she said.

He did not reply. Cecie had passed so quickly from clinging childhood into long-limbed adolescence that he no longer remembered how it had happened, or when. He still saw her as an unblown rose.

'Don't worry,' he told her. 'It'll solve itself after a while.'

'But you're going back home to Teheran, aren't you, when you've finished getting that stuff for the Kurds,' she whispered in her anti-bugging voice.

He looked at the tapestried walls, at microphones he could not see, at tape machines he could not stop. The ragged mountains above Saqiz seemed a long way away now, and so did the peach and almond orchards of Mirabad and the open valleys in the stony rivers, and the broken-backed Turkoman horses with filthy, hairy legs huddling in the winter snow. Or the tea shops without communication wires or electronic devices in the ceiling. Was mountain poverty the only genuine, unobtrusive liberty left?

'Your mother wants us all to go back to London,' he told Cecie.

'That's stupid,' Cecie said calmly. 'Anyway, you'll have to go without me.'

She got up, leaving it happily with the sort of incompletion that children can live with.

'Where are you going with all that stuff?' he asked her, pointing to the rolled-up posters and tins of paste she was picking up off the floor.

'Denfert Rochereau.'

'Listen, sweetheart,' he said, following her out. 'Please ... *please* keep out of the way of the police. For my sake.'

'All right,' she said. 'But I have to do something for this demonstration, because most of the students locked up in the Santé are the ones who were taken when I was arrested, and I know what's happening to them there.'

MacGregor let go this small branch of his deeply-rooted tree and went back inside. He poured out a cup of coffee, put one spoon of brown sugar in it and carried it upstairs to Kathy who was lying awake as if she didn't want to get out of bed, or had been waiting for him to come up with his appeasements. He put the coffee on the bedside table, pushing away the books she had been reading, and sat on the bed near her.

'Aren't you well?' he asked.

'I'm all right,' she said. 'I'll just stay here a while.'

He did not press the point because he knew that when she was relaxed like this she wouldn't make an issue of anything which was better avoided for a little while longer.

'Do you want me to put Essex off?' he said.

'No,' she said, and he told her that he was going now to see Seroglu.

'That ridiculous man.'

'But he still has the documents.'

She stared into her coffee cup, but as he went out she said: 'What time is Andrew due back?'

'Some time early afternoon,' he said.

When he closed the bedroom door he stood still for a moment to allow his nerves to slide into their proper place. Then he went to see Seroglu.

Seroglu lived near the Observatoire where the plane trees of the Boulevard Saint Michel came to a dead end, and the gravel part of the footpath under the trees was stacked with parked cars. Seroglu's card said in French, *Push bell and mount to the first floor.* He pushed the bell. He heard a child running down a passage, and a small girl of ten opened the door. Behind her was Seroglu himself, looking urgent and occupied. He told his daughter that Madame Claire, below, would send up another complaint if she ran like that down the passage.

'Come in,' he said to MacGregor, and the daughter held his coat as they went into a room across the hall, which was domestic and comfortable, with a fireplace and a couch and French tiles over the fireplace right up to the ceiling.

'My wife is with my other daughter at Clichy,' he said.

MacGregor nodded. Seroglu told his daughter in English to go and get the coffee, and he turned to MacGregor and asked if he would prefer an apéritif, or maybe tea.

'No. No. Coffee's fine.'

Seroglu's passionate desire to bring the world close to his family had its attractions. MacGregor did not feel out of place in this oriental sort of domesticity, even though it was trying hard to be European.

They sat down in deep armchairs, Seroglu almost disappearing into his, and he began to tell MacGregor about the students who, last night, were parading outside and throwing plastic bags filled with water over the wall of the Catholic orphanage on the other side of the avenue. 'It was like a Marxist carnival,' he said. 'The noise! Where is all this anaesthetising of France going to get them?'

The daughter brought the coffee on a large tray, and MacGregor tried to take it from her, but her father said, 'The maid is sick, but she can manage. She's like an English girl.'

She managed very well, and when they were sipping coffee Seroglu began. 'It seems to me that you and I can talk about it sensibly,' he said, 'because you understand our problem. But these others...' Seroglu's bitterness was directed at everybody out of sight who failed to understand the Turkish difficulties.

'What is the problem?' MacGregor asked him.

'What it's always been. The weight of the Kurds is always around the Turkish neck. It's the curse on our future. Every Turk knows it, and every Kurd fails to understand it.'

'Why should they?' MacGregor said. 'You've always treated them badly, and, if I may say so, brutally.'

'Perhaps we have been single-minded,' Seroglu admitted. 'But have you ever been to the old Kurdish part of Turkey?'

'Not for some time.'

'Yet you...'

MacGregor knew what Seroglu was going to say, but the

Turk seemed to discipline himself with an effort.

'Our Kurds are changing their habits,' he said. 'The old tribal authority and the mad recklessness is disappearing. We are settling them down. We are finally giving them a sane and sedentary life. They are becoming Turks, which is what they should be. Why, all the dockers of Istanbul are Kurds.'

MacGregor was not going to argue the historical tidiness of the Turkish solution, so he waited for Seroglu to come to the point.

'The real enemy of the Kurds is not our republic,' Seroglu went on, 'but all the foreigners who want the oil and gas in the Kurdish highlands, part of which are in Turkey. That's the problem, and that's what you and I can do something about.'

'How?' MacGregor asked him.

'Mr MacGregor,' Seroglu went on, leaning forward awkwardly in his deep chair. 'Why don't you arrange some sort of a dialogue?'

'I don't follow you,' MacGregor said, and he heard the front door opening. The little girl ran along the hall again, and then another of Seroglu's gestures to the world came in wagging its tail and making a fuss of him: a bitch cocker spaniel who obviously adored the master. Seroglu embraced the dog and said: 'Ah, Bobbee. Go and say hello to *M'sieur l'Anglais.*'

The spaniel stuck to her master and fell at his feet, tongue hanging out, eyes faithfully on his brown shoes.

'What sort of a dialogue are you suggesting?' MacGregor asked him. 'Do you mean between Kurds and Turks?'

'Why not?' Seroglu said. 'Our department for these affairs might be willing to support some sort of Kurdish republic.'

MacGregor leaned forward. 'The Turkish authorities would actually talk about a Kurdish republic?' he said incredulously.

'I said they might. It's not easy to clarify our position.'

'I think you'd need to clarify it considerably,' MacGregor said. 'I can't quite believe it.'

'We might be willing to come to terms with some sort of Kurdish autonomy in Iraq and Iran, providing we could get some sort of assurance, a textual guarantee, that such a Kurdish republic would renounce all claims on Turkey.'

MacGregor laughed at the spaniel's soft brown eyes and remembered that spaniels were gun dogs and could carry a bird tenderly in their teeth and deposit it uncrushed and unbroken at the master's feet.

'No Kurd would ever agree to abandon one and a half million Kurds in Turkey,' he told Seroglu. 'You must know that.'

'But let us be practical,' Seroglu protested. 'I know that you want the documents I was given by the Sûreté when that Kurdish boy died in Lyons.'

'They belong to the Kurdish Committee,' MacGregor said.

'You can have them,' Seroglu told him. But after a moment's hesitation he said: 'You can have them if you will bring from the Qazi an incontrovertible guarantee that Kurdish aspirations end at the Turkish borders.'

'I could never get a guarantee like that,' MacGregor told him. 'And I wouldn't even ask for it.'

'Then what do you suggest?' Seroglu said indignantly. 'What is your solution?'

'I can't suggest anything,' MacGregor replied, 'except that you ought to hand over those documents.'

'But we can't allow the present situation to go on. I tell you the foreigners—the Americans, the French and the British—will make an awful mess up there.'

'There's an awful mess there now.'

'But it'll get worse, now that they're all so interested.'

'That's true,' MacGregor admitted.

'That's why you and I should work together,' Seroglu insisted. 'We could settle this problem once and for all.'

MacGregor tried one sortie of his own. 'If you hand over

the documents, Colonel,' he said, 'I'll persuade the Qazi to meet anybody you like so that they can talk about Turkish problems.'

'That's not what I meant.'

The little girl put her head in the door and asked them if they wanted more hot coffee. She spoke French the way French children speak French, with a sort of high, petulant lilt.

'Go away, *chérie*, for a little while,' Seroglu said.

'What did you mean, then?' MacGregor said when the girl had gone.

'We can't talk to the Qazi about Turkish problems. That's out of the question.'

'Then what is there to talk about?' MacGregor said.

'We can talk about the area as a whole.'

'And leave the Kurds out of it?'

'No. Just don't make an issue of them. And if you agree to that we'll help you with the documents. Everybody is watching you, Mr MacGregor. The Kurdish rivals are watching you. The foreigners are watching you. Everybody wants to know what you'll do, because you're the one who will decide a great deal.'

'That's only because everybody knows why I'm here,' MacGregor pointed out.

'Well...' Seroglu clasped his hands together like a priest. 'Sooner or later someone will want to kill you,' he said unhappily. 'And you should think of your family and your children.'

MacGregor got up. He did not want to know if Seroglu was being a family man again, or reminding him of his vulnerability. 'I'd become a nervous wreck if I started worrying about things like that,' he said lightly as he watched the little girl opening the front door for him.

'Please remember your children,' Seroglu said, his large eyes wide open in appeal.

'My children are in no danger,' MacGregor said. But he

added: 'No more than you are, Colonel Seroglu.' He hoped that it sounded ominous enough.

As he shook hands with the little Turk and met his troubled eyes, he couldn't quite believe that Seroglu was anything more than a family man with a family security in mind. But once outside, Seroglu became another voice talking to him of war and politics, and he knew that the Turk was as dangerous in his self-interest as the Kurds were in theirs.

Chapter Twenty-four

By now there had been so many warnings of provocation and danger, that when something finally happened Mac-Gregor did not really expect it.

Essex had arrived by taxi for lunch, and he had ordered the taxi to drive right into the courtyard.

'What an extraordinary sight to see outside any front gate in Paris,' he said to MacGregor.

MacGregor went out to see what it was, but there was nobody on the street. 'They must have gone,' Essex said. But about ten minutes later Marin puffed into the dining-room with a broken bottle in his hand and told them that there was fighting outside in the street in front of the gate. MacGregor told the others to wait, and he ran down to the gate and let himself out. Eight or nine dark-eyed badly dressed men were facing each other across opposite foot-paths and shouting at each other in Kurdish. The street itself was littered with broken glass.

'Go back inside,' someone shouted at MacGregor.

MacGregor recognised Jahiz, the gentle dervish boy who had come with Taha to see him.

'What's going on?' MacGregor demanded. 'What are you doing here, Jahiz?'

'We can manage this,' Jahiz told him. 'Please go back in, ya doctor.'

The other two Kurds with Jahiz had been part of the same delegation. But facing and opposing them were five unknown men with Kurdish faces, Kurdish eyes, Kurdish hair, Kurdish European clothes, except for one who wore a well-cut dacron suit.

'Tomorrow,' one of them shouted at MacGregor, 'we'll quarter you.' He drew his first finger from his forehead down to his groin and then back again, saying *phht, phht* with each gesture.

In the meantime Essex had appeared behind MacGregor. 'What on earth is it all about?' he said.

MacGregor ignored him. 'Who are they?' he asked Jahiz. 'These are the ones who tried to kill Taha yesterday.'

They began to shout at each other again—the usual insults about America, dogs, donkeys, Russians, cowards, honour. But when they heard the *pam-pom* of a police wagon they all began to run down the street. One stopped long enough to throw a last bottle over the wall and to shout at MacGregor: 'We can easily get over that wall.'

By the time a sergeant and an agent leapt out of the police van the last of the Kurds was out of sight, except for Jahiz who stood calmly talking to MacGregor.

MacGregor explained hurriedly to the Garde Mobile that there had been an argument between some students. Then Essex took over and said to the sergeant. 'I can vouch for this man.' He pointed to MacGregor.

The sergeant insulted them all, and when the blue van disappeared, Jahiz touched his heart in farewell and he too disappeared.

Essex thought it a huge joke. 'Now you've got Kurds throwing bottles at each other in the streets of Paris. Amazing...'

It put Essex in a good mood, and over lunch he reminisced on their days together in Moscow and Teheran. He asked Kathy if she ever wondered what would have happened to her if he had never brought MacGregor with him on that mission to Moscow.

'I'd be dead with boredom by now,' Kathy said.

'You mean you enjoy that amazing sport we just saw outside?'

'Why not?' Kathy said.

MacGregor waited for Kathy to divert or stop Essex's irritable teasing. But Kathy was enjoying it, and she went on giving and taking the details of her life with MacGregor as if it was all fair game. Eventually it was Essex who tired of it, and he told Kathy that the last time he had been in Aunt Joss's house her Uncle Pierre (Aunt Joss's husband) had been alive.

'He used to chew the ends of his cigarettes and leave the mess on the plates...'

'That's revolting,' Kathy said. 'I don't even want to hear about it.'

'And that *femme de ménage*, or whatever she is ...'

'You mean Madame Marin,' Kathy said firmly.

'It always amazes me,' Essex went on, 'how Paris is still full of old women like Madame Marin who still look as if they're waiting for the tumbrils to start rolling again.'

MacGregor could contribute nothing to this kind of family fascination, and he was glad when they heard the front door slam, and Andrew shouted in the hall for the waiting ghosts: 'I'm home.'

'Thank God for that,' Kathy said to MacGregor.

Andrew stood at the dining-room door, dishevelled and dirty from Lyons, but nonetheless tidy and organised. He said he would go and wash up and have some dessert with them, and when he came back Essex said he was a good mixture of both parents, but favoured Kathy a bit. When Andrew had washed and changed and joined them for dessert, Essex asked him how many languages he spoke.

'Three,' Andrew said, as if it were a matter of course, like all things.

'English, French and Persian, I suppose,' Essex said.

'Yes.'

'I hear you're very clever.'

Andrew looked at his mother as if asking her if she had been talking.

'I didn't say a word,' Kathy said.

'You could obviously do very well in the Foreign Service, Andrew,' Essex told him. 'Why don't you think about it?'

'No thank you,' Andrew said politely.

'Why not?' Essex persisted. 'I could fix it in a jiffy if you want me to.'

Kathy poured the coffee.

'MacGregor?' Essex appealed.

'He can do as he likes,' MacGregor said.

'No, he can't,' Kathy corrected sharply. 'He's not going into the Foreign Office, Harold, so don't try to steal the son because you lost the father.'

'But we never had his father,' Essex said. 'MacGregor was only a temporary war loan from paleontology.'

'Nonetheless...' Kathy said, and MacGregor was surprised that she was taking it so seriously. They both knew that Andrew would not think of going into the Foreign Service.

'You're certainly a tight little family, aren't you?' Essex commented, and he asked MacGregor what he was a student of now. And had he read Mauriac, Camus, Chesterton, Eliot, Koestler, Sartre, Deutscher, Thomas Mann...?'

'Of course he has,' Kathy said.

'I was only trying to find out what sort of a man your husband is now,' he said.

MacGregor kept quiet. He knew that Kathy was not only defending him but was also defending herself against Essex's teasing implication of a colossal failure in her life.

'Okay,' Essex said to MacGregor. 'As I remember it this house had a library. We've flexed our muscles long enough, so let's go in there for a private chat.'

'You'd do better in the breakfast room,' Kathy told him. 'It doesn't smell of musty curtains and dead leaves.'

The breakfast room was the only room in the house that MacGregor liked. It was good to eat in, good to talk in, good to drink tea in or read the papers in or listen to his children in. He was on home ground here, and he watched Essex adjust the wide lapels of his shirt collar with the middle finger of each hand. It was a high-collared, pinkish shirt.

'You and I have never wasted words, MacGregor,' Essex was saying. 'So let me ask you straight out if your Kurdish friends imagine that they can actually succeed with this new idea for their independence.'

'Why not? Sooner or later they'll get some sort of autonomy or independence. It's inevitable.'

Essex hugged his elbows—an old habit. 'Everything on earth happens sooner or later. But what about now? Can some sort of independent Kurdistan actually take shape?'

'Of course.'

'So you want to speed it up with guns and revolution?'

MacGregor reminded him that guns and revolution were nothing new in that part of the world.

'Of course,' Essex replied. 'But why are you, of all people, suddenly involved in Kurdistan and Kurdish affairs?' Essex sat back in the old wing chair and stretched his hands above his head.

'That doesn't need any explanation,' MacGregor said 'I've been involved in the same thing all my life. There's nothing new about it.'

'But it doesn't seem like you,' Essex persisted. 'That money for instance. How could you have got yourself mixed up in something as foul as that?'

'I'm waiting for you to tell me what you want,' Mac-Gregor said.

'All right...' Essex sighed and wriggled in his chair. 'Let me tell you what we are *not* interested in. We are not interested in plans to exploit Kurdish oil and natural gas, nor do we want the sort of political alignments the Americans are keen on.'

'No oil and no alignments,' MacGregor repeated.

'All we're after is an open door,' Essex said. 'It would help for instance, if you could explain to us what the Kurds are thinking.'

'With pleasure.'

But Essex went on quickly. 'What we want is a genuine contact with the Qazi which would be open at both ends. Obviously you're the best person to make it. That's all.'

'What do you want to contact the Qazi for?' he asked Essex. 'What do you want from him?'

'Nothing at all,' Essex insisted. 'We simply need a contact we can trust. And one they can also trust. That's you.'

MacGregor had taken a handful of salt from the old silver cruet that was permanently on the breakfast table. 'Are you offering the Kurds some sort of recognition?' he asked Essex.

'I'm offering them nothing at all. That's the sort of thing you eventually work up to in diplomacy not what you begin with. Have you forgotten?'

'You mean there's some eventual hope of recognition?'

'I'm not even promising that. How can I? But if your Qazi knows what diplomacy is, and I believe he does know, then he'll see that what we are proposing is a better prospect for him than any short-term commercial or political deals he could make with the French or the Americans. Do you agree?'

'Perhaps,' MacGregor said cautiously.

'Good. Then you ought to be able to come over to London and tell some of our experts exactly what you think. They're anxious to hear it.'

'I'm not going to do anything like that,' MacGregor told him.

'Why not?'

'If you want to suggest something quite specific to the Qazi,' he said, 'I'll tell him about it. But I'm not going to set myself up as a go-between for you.'

Essex got up and took an apple from the bowl of fruit

that Kathy kept opulently full on the sideboard. 'Isn't that a silly way of looking at it?' he said. But then he added: 'Wait. There is something specific you could mention to him.' Essex bit the apple noisily.

'What?'

'Money,' Essex said.

'What money?'

'£250,000. Isn't that the amount your Kurdish friends are trying to recover?'

'Something like that.'

'We can advance you that much tomorrow,' Essex said. 'You can tell your friend the Qazi that.'

'Advance it against what?'

'Nothing. It's up to you.'

'You mean you'll pay the Kurds that money if I become your agent?'

'Just a contact,' Essex corrected.

'What sort of a bribe is that?' MacGregor said calmly.

'It's not a bribe,' Essex said. 'It's blackmail. Think of the alternative for you.'

'A few more difficulties won't make much difference.'

'Don't be too sure about that. Nobody's taken your passport away, have they? Or frozen your bank account? Or thrown you out of France? That sort of thing. Everybody's got some sort of weapon they can use on you if they want to.'

'Use any weapon you like,' MacGregor said.

'Me? Why should I do anything so ridiculous? But I do know that your situation in Iran is already a difficult one. I'd hate to see you having more trouble there.'

'Put your apple core in there,' MacGregor said and pointed to a thick parchment waste-paper basket.

Essex disposed of the apple core and wiped his hands on his large red handkerchief. 'Anyway,' he said, 'I'll leave you with the thought. But if I were you I'd clear this up as quietly and as quickly as possible. And we would help you do that, if you'd be a little more reasonable about it.'

'Of course,' MacGregor said, and escorted the most reasonable man he knew to the hall where Essex called out, like a member of the family, 'Goodbye, everybody...'

'Goodbye...' Aunt Joss said from the bowels of the house.

When he went back in, MacGregor called Andrew down and asked him why he had gone to Lyons with Taha. What exactly had they done there?

'Mama's been at me already,' Andrew said. 'So don't you start getting upset as well.'

MacGregor looked enquiringly at Kathy who had followed her son into the room.

'He refuses to tell me anything,' she said.

Andrew raised his shoulders. 'Ask Taha,' he said. 'He'll tell you. He'll be here in a minute.'

'I want *you* to tell me,' MacGregor insisted.

'But it's not really my business.'

'Both you and your father,' Kathy said, 'have a marvellous way of narrowing yourselves down when you feel like it to what-is and what-is-not your business. If it wasn't your business why did you go with him?'

'Because Taha's not very safe in France. He looks like an Algerian—a *bicot*. So I thought I'd buy the tickets there-and-back and go with him.'

'To do what?' MacGregor demanded, knowing that he could persuade Andrew to answer, whereas Kathy would make an issue of it and the boy would calmly but vigorously resist her.

'He just wanted to look at those trucks. Or rather, we tried to find them but couldn't. Then Taha saw some of the Kurds studying at the University of Lyons. That's all.'

'You're not to do anything like that again,' MacGregor told him. 'And that's because of me, not because of you.'

'All right.'

'Is that all you're going to say to him?' Kathy put in. 'Why don't you tell him that he's not allowed to have anything more to do with the Kurds—any of them.'

'Let's not take it that far,' MacGregor argued. 'He knows what we expect of him. And you've got to understand,' he said to Andrew, 'that you're putting all of us in danger when you do things like that.'

'Who paid the fares and the hotel?' Kathy asked him.

'I did.'

'With whose money?'

'With my own grant money of course.'

The boy kissed his mother affectionately and went outside to let in Taha who still refused to talk in this bugged house, so they went outside to the courtyard and crunched around on the damp limestone pebbles.

'You're a fool,' MacGregor told him.

'But I had to see those trucks,' Taha said in Kurdish.

'Why?'

'Because I had to be sure they exist. In fact they've been shifted to Marseilles.'

'Are you quite sure?'

'Don't be so suspicious of me, Uncle,' Taha said. 'The trucks have gone to Marseilles.'

'Then someone else has probably got hold of them,' MacGregor said. 'But how?'

'The Americans. They've obviously paid the arms dealers for those trucks, and they've been handed over to Dubas and the Ilkhani.'

'You don't really know that . . .'

'But it's probable,' Taha said.

'I suppose it is.'

'Don't you see?' Taha had a grip on MacGregor's arm. 'That's why it's the trucks we have to worry about. Never mind the money now, Uncle.'

'I'm only interested in the money, Taha. And if you're

thinking of blowing up those trucks, you'd better think again,' MacGregor warned him. 'It would be suicidal to try anything like that in France.'

'Why?'

'The French will be expecting you.'

'Of course. But that doesn't make it impossible.'

'Even if you succeeded,' MacGregor argued, 'they'd catch you. And after that, you wouldn't see the light of day again.'

Taha laughed. 'You're such a single-minded man yourself, Uncle. Difficult to tear away from your purpose. Well, I've learned it from you.'

MacGregor knew better than to argue the philosophy of action now. 'Just one more thing,' he said.

'Yes?'

'Keep Andrew right out of it. And I mean it, Taha.'

'Andrew's got a mind of his own. In fact he surprises me sometimes.'

'He also surprises your Aunt Kathy. But I don't want him anywhere near any Kurdish plots.'

'That's not likely,' Taha said.

'Look, Taha,' MacGregor said. 'Why don't you wait a little. Let me find out first what is happening to those trucks. Then you can do what you like.'

Taha hesitated. 'All right,' he said. 'I'll wait a little. But I can't wait for ever, Uncle.'

'Just give me a little time.'

By next morning MacGregor knew what he had to do, and he was anxious to get out without any questions being asked. He left quietly after breakfast. He expected to be accosted at the gate by the usual Kurds and speculators who came every day now, but there was a gendarme posted outside. He saluted MacGregor as if he knew who he was, and MacGregor wondered if Aunt Joss had asked for him, or whether Kathy had asked Moselle to have him sent around to keep an eye on things.

MacGregor walked around to the café where the set-up

men ran their business, and Louise, the woman who ran the place, asked him which one he wanted: 'Mister Strong, *l'Anglais*? Or Monsieur Seelig, the Dutchman?'

'Either one,' MacGregor said.

He sat down at a shiny formica table and she brought him a glass of vermouth, which he sipped gladly until the Englishman arrived.

'I thought of you only the other day when I was flying over the Alps,' Strong said. 'Those mountains! Someone was telling me all about the Kurds; I never knew much about them before, and I don't know much about them now, but I'm beginning to understand your interest in them. It's funny how the English are the only people who can produce men like Lawrence or Gordon or Wingate, or odd-sods like you. Bloody odd, if I may say so.'

'Nothing like that applies,' MacGregor told him.

'Nonetheless...' Strong said suggestively, his eyes smiling like a schoolboy's at MacGregor who looked solidly at the vermouth before him. 'I was a gunner myself,' he added in confidence.

'I always thought you were in the RAF.'

'Oh that's just my breezy professional manner,' Strong said, and puffed out his cheeks and laughed. 'You have to acquire a pretty thick skin in this business.'

MacGregor wondered what sort of man was behind that pretty thick skin.

'I admire honest soldiers,' Strong went on. 'And personally I don't care how many Turks you butchered. I've got no time for Turks.'

'I'm not a butcherer of Turks and I am not a soldier,' MacGregor pointed out.

'Don't worry. It's the neutrals who are the real butchers in this business. Take the Swedes and the Danes. They're all bastards when they become mercenaries. The funny thing is, the English are probably the most corrupt of the whole bloody lot, I mean the money part of it. It's the Germans who are the most honest mercenaries in our business.'

MacGregor tried again. 'I'm not in your business,' he said. 'I'm dealing in something else.'

Strong laughed. 'I know. You're a man with a cause. And that's why you're having so much trouble.'

'That's got nothing to do with it,' MacGregor said. 'All I want to know is why you shifted the trucks to Marseilles.'

'How did you know about that?'

'Did someone else buy those arms from you?' he asked Strong.

The Englishman shrugged. 'Let's say we sent those trucks down to Marseilles because they were too hard to protect in Lyons. Marseilles is a proper port. It's got much better yarding facilities for security.'

Strong turned to two waitresses who had been talking and laughing, and he told them to go to the kitchen.

'Yes, but who paid you?' MacGregor persisted.

'How do I know?' Strong said.

'You must have some idea who is behind it?' MacGregor tried again.

'I've got dozens of ideas.'

'Are other Kurds involved?'

'Obviously,' Strong said.

'Where are the arms going to be shipped to?'

Strong laughed. 'Oh no,' he said. 'You can't press questions like that on me. All I can say is that they'll be shipped out of Marseilles on the last day of the month unless you can come up with something.'

MacGregor said: 'All right. Perhaps I can. Will you stick to your original agreement with the Committee if I get the full amount of money?'

'How would you get it?'

'Never mind how I get it. Will you give me until the end of the month?'

'You're asking a lot, aren't you?' Strong protested.

MacGregor shrugged impatiently.

'Well...' Strong made an elaborate show of making up his mind. He groaned and wriggled. 'Jesus Christ,' he said. 'I can't stand that other lot. They disgust me. But if I give you till the end of the month, you'd better do something yourself about those trucks.'

'What do you mean?'

'There are a couple of Kurdish maniacs who want to dispose of that stuff with a bomb. You know about them?'

'Yes.'

'Well, whoever they are, you'd better persuade them not to touch the stuff in the meantime.'

'I'll do my best. But they have different ideas about it, and they don't mind very much what they do.'

Strong sighed as they stood up and shook hands. 'You're the first man I've trusted in twenty years,' he said, and smiled with his breezy, RAF smile. 'But I'd lose my simple faith in man if you did the dirty on me.'

Chapter Twenty-five

'*Plus je fais l'amour, plus j'ai envie de faire la revolution,
Plus je fais la revolution, plus j'ai envie de faire
l'amour . . .*'

MacGregor was reading student slogans on the walls of
the Soeurs de Saint Vincent de Paul as he walked home
along the Rue Babylone where he had been buying the
morning papers. He had also read, as he walked, a five
line despatch in *Figaro* from Teheran which said that two
days ago, in a clash between Iranian frontier gendarmes and
Kurdish rebels, four Kurds were reported killed.

He had been out before anybody else in the house, but
when he got back Kathy was up and dressed, and instead
of asking him why he had been out so early, she told him
that she was going back to London. She was already packing
her suitcase.

'Guy will fly me there,' she said. 'I want to see the doctors
at St Thomas's. I don't trust these French doctors. It's all
chemistry to them. I'll go and see Dr Taplow and see what
he says.'

'Is it much worse?' he asked her.

'I don't know. Taplow told me I would still have some
bad moments, but he didn't say anything about feeling as if
I had a lorry rolling over my stomach muscles.'

'Are you sure it isn't tension?' he said tentatively.

'What tension?'

'There's a lot of it about.'

'There always is,' she replied. 'Anyway there's nothing

really wrong with me. I just want to go and make sure, that's all.'

'Then I'll pack and go with you.'

'No you don't. That would really make me tense. You want to stay here, so stay. I'll take Cecie. She's much better out of all this violence, and the Beaux Arts is more or less closed anyway. You can look after Andrew.'

He didn't argue. She had made up her mind.

At two o'clock Guy Moselle's Rover called for them, but Cecie had already refused to go. 'If you think there's nothing really wrong with you,' she said to her mother, 'it's pointless me leaving here now.' But Cecie said quietly to her father: 'She doesn't really want me to go with her. She wants to be on her own. Let her go. It'll do her good.'

When Kathy was seated in the Rover and firmly under Moselle's protection, he said to MacGregor, 'I have something to tell you. I'll be back at seven or eight. Come and have dinner with me at the old house at nine. Cecie knows where it is. You come too,' he told Cecie. 'Thérèse will want to see you.'

'I'm busy,' Cecie told him.

'Then just get your father there.'

When Moselle's fine brown hands had turned the car out of the drive MacGregor realised that he had said no more than a faint, pecking goodbye to Kathy, and it left him clinging a little longer to Cecie. He told her he would go with her to her atelier. 'Just to take a look.'

'Are you all right?' Cecie asked him.

'Yes. Why?'

'I don't know. But don't get upset about Mama,' she said. 'Women have to feel like that sometimes. They long to be alone.' Then she shouted, 'Aunt Joss!' Her eyes stared at some distant vanishing point.

'Yes, Cecie darling...'

'We're going to the atelier. If Andrew comes in, tell him to join us there.'

217

'All right, sweetheart...'

Long before they reached the atelier, which Cecie shared privately with five other students, they had to go around the road blocks and barricades which the students and the CRS were erecting against each other. The Sorbonne and the boulevards and the little *pavé* streets and alleyways around the university were piled high with rubbish, benches, *poubelles*, chairs, fruit boxes and the slices of iron lemons that usually lay under the trees. The paving blocks had been torn up, and the clean white sand that lay underneath the granite *pavé* was exposed like a baby's skin.

'You'd better watch out tonight,' he said to Cecie as he leaned out of the grimy window of the atelier and looked down on the battlefield. 'They're obviously preparing for another pitched battle, worse than the last one,' MacGregor said. 'They're crazy.'

'But the police are asking for it,' Cecie said. 'They ought to get right out of the whole quartier.'

In the grimy little atelier he watched Cecie marking out a piece of cardboard and cutting a stencil from it which read: '500,000 workers to the Latin Quarter.'

'Why should 500,000 workers come to the Latin Quarter?' he asked her. 'This isn't their affair.'

'But it should be.'

'It sounds a bit remote, doesn't it?' he said.

'It won't be for long,' she told him. 'Sooner or later everybody in France is going to get involved in this.'

He sat by the dirty window and watched her for a little while longer, still trying to overcome the misery of Kathy's abrupt departure. When he knew he was not going to get the better of it, he told Cecie he was going home. 'But don't be late this evening,' he said to her.

'I'll be home at eight-thirty to drive you to Moselle's house at nine,' she said, and as he walked down the old corridor to the stairs she followed him. 'I'm tempted to take you somewhere else.'

218

'Where?'

'Anywhere,' she shouted after him, 'except to Guy Moselle's.'

But at nine o'clock she delivered him obediently to Moselle's as she had promised.

Moselle's Paris house was a genuine old Parisian mansion. Some of the other houses between the Avenue Foch and the Avenue de la Grande Armée were more like large suburban villas than city mansions but Moselle's had been a genuine country home built in the early 1830s before the rebuilding of the avenues by Thiers and MacMahon. It was red-brick, almost English, surrounded by old brick walls, yew trees, and an English lawn which, in May, was still nailed down with daffodils, snowdrops, aconites and crocuses. Budding roses snaked up the tight old walls with scentless city petals. The Mandelieu house, the new house, the Geneva house, the Normandy house, the Villancourt house. This was the old house, the Paris house. . . .

The gates were electrically sealed and operated, and Cecie pushed the button and shouted into the little speaker that it was M'sieur MacGregor. The buzz and the click of the Parisian *entrée* followed, and Cecie said: 'Goodbye. Don't be late,' and got back into her Citroën and left him walking up the brightly-lit gravel path.

He heard dogs barking and a door banging and he could see a girl of Cecie's age, neatly dressed and rather petite, walking the way only a French girl can walk—a demure passion in every step.

'*Le mari de Madame Kathy,*' the girl said. Then she went on in English. 'Where's Cecie? Didn't she at least come in?'

MacGregor knew it was Moselle's daughter, Thérèse. 'Cecie couldn't wait,' MacGregor said. 'She was in a hurry.'

'Cecie's always in a hurry when she comes out here,' the girl said. 'She doesn't like my father.'

'I wouldn't say that,' MacGregor said.

'My father has been waiting for you,' Thérèse said. 'Never mind the dog.'

The dog, like the unhappy girl, seemed intent on getting the better of him. But in the house Moselle looked fresh and organised and friendly. He told MacGregor that Kathy was all right. A car had been waiting for them at the airport, and he had seen her safely home to the Belgrave Square house. MacGregor straightened his badly-knotted tie, sought for his handkerchief which was lost in his top pocket and unbuttoned his jacket.

Moselle laughed. 'You looked much better the way you were,' he said. 'In fact I'm always tempted to sneak a look to see if one of your shoelaces is undone.' He looked at MacGregor's shoes.

MacGregor kept quiet as Moselle took him through the silk-walled hall into a neat little study. He gave MacGregor an American Martini and said he had just been reading all the student magazines. They were on the table near his chair: *Zoom, Cinq Colonnes, Caméra iii*.

'What strikes me,' Moselle said, hardly pausing, 'is their lack of any educated logic. There is absolutely no sequence to anything they say. They don't argue. They simply present a piecemeal case without any method or proper shape to it at all.'

'These days they prefer declamation,' MacGregor suggested.

'Maybe,' Moselle said thoughtfully, as they sat down. 'But it surprises me, because Marx is such an excellent teacher of logic. And there's no sign of Marxian logic in any of this stuff, except the clichés and the revolutionary phrases,' he said. 'I should think that even your Kurdish friends have a better sense of political reasoning than this lot.'

Thérèse opened the door and said if they didn't come to dinner straight away they would miss the ten o'clock news on the ORTF.

'They're middle-class boys,' Moselle went on as he took MacGregor into the dining-room, 'crying hang-the-bourgeoisie.'

They sat in an oval dining-room at one end of a small oval table, softly lit, and they ate without eating, the way healthy, disciplined, rich men eat. This time they were served by a woman in a white cotton housecoat: a family meal; and Thérèse, sitting like Miss Muffet, was asked by her father what was the latest situation at her faculty of letters. Thérèse said that all the students were putting up posters for the general strike on Monday, which the students' union and the teachers' union and the CGT and the other trade unions were organising.

'About fifty militants of the March 22 movement came and occupied our faculty at Censier,' she said. 'And by the time I left there were almost five hundred there.'

'Well, Pompidou's just back from Iran,' Moselle told them, 'and he said privately that he was bowled over by what's been happening in Paris. He's going to announce the reopening of the Sorbonne on Monday.'

'Then he's stupid,' Thérèse said.

'Why?' MacGregor asked her.

'Will he call the police out of the Quartier Latin?' she asked her father.

'Unlikely,' he said.

'Then the leftists won't allow the Sorbonne to open and there'll be fighting all over the place,' she said.

MacGregor had been watching Thérèse and wondering why Cecie did not like her. 'Which side are you on, Thérèse?' MacGregor asked her.

She looked up at her father. 'Go ahead,' he said sharply. 'I'm not going to quarrel with you. Tell him what you think.'

'I'm a reactionary,' Thérèse said. 'I don't like the violence. I hate the communists, and all the anarchists and Trotskyists from Nanterre. You should see them when they get

221

together. They're like wild animals. And they don't really care about France or the faculties. And I'll tell you something else about them. They're all denouncing exams and the *examen de passage*. Nobody will be able to get his Bac this year or his degree, because they've sabotaged everything. But not before most of the militants had themselves passed their own *examens* or their Bac the year before. They're like this all day...' She flocked out her hair with quivering fingers.

'You shouldn't be frightened by appearances,' Moselle told her.

'Their appearance is exactly what they are,' Thérèse insisted. 'They don't care who or what gets hurt.'

'Shush ...' her father said gently.

On the way here, Cecie had told her father that Thérèse was convent-bred and convent-nerved, and that this house was a convent, her wealth was a convent, her father's authority was a convent.

Thérèse got up and said: '*Oui, papa,*' when he told her to go and get the coffee. And though it was obviously the true Catholic devotion of a good daughter, MacGregor could see that Moselle did not really like it or want it that way.

When supper was finished they sat in the library and Moselle asked him cautiously if he knew that his friend the Qazi had been shot and wounded.

MacGregor took a moment to recover. 'No, I didn't,' he said. 'I read in *Figaro* this morning that four Kurds had been killed. That's all.'

'I didn't see *Figaro,*' Moselle went on, 'but we had a Telex about it from Iran this morning. The message said that the Kurds were fighting among themselves, and that the Qazi had been forced to flee and is now in hiding. Does that sound likely?'

'It might be,' MacGregor said, 'but I doubt it.'

'Your friend Zadko is also in trouble. The report suggested that the whole Kurdish front is collapsing, if that's the way to put it.'

'That doesn't sound right,' MacGregor replied. 'There isn't any Kurdish front. In any case I doubt if it's as simple as that.'

Moselle gave him a cognac. 'Personally I don't know what it's all about. I don't understand it the way you do. In fact I am only repeating textually what was said.'

'Why did they report it to you?'

'Because of something else. They wanted to know, from Teheran, if you were still in Paris. And even more extraordinary—if you were, in fact, still alive. That's why I didn't say anything this morning in front of Kathy. I didn't want to scare her.'

MacGregor raised his hands, fingers open in stiff astonishment. 'Who would ask a weird thing like that?'

'Heaven knows. We don't usually specify clients on our Telex, not even by their code numbers.'

MacGregor rubbed his eyebrows and his ear with the tips of his fingers. 'Obviously someone expects me to be dead already,' he said, 'but it sounds too exaggerated—all of it.'

'Well ... there are obviously some pretty violent rivalries among the Kurds in Paris,' Moselle said, 'as you discovered for yourself a few days ago.'

'Did you ask for a gendarme to be put on our gate?' MacGregor said.

'No. It was Cumont. We're both very concerned about Kathy. All this violence is beginning to upset her. That's why I encouraged her to get away for a while.'

'Violence of this sort isn't exactly a new experience for either of us,' MacGregor said. 'So I wouldn't exaggerate its effect on her.'

'Nonetheless, I think it does upset her,' Moselle insisted. 'At this particular moment in her life physical violence suddenly becomes quite frightening.'

'Don't judge Kathy by your daughter,' MacGregor said caustically.

Moselle did not say anything for a moment, obviously surprised by MacGregor's harsh reply. But then he smiled. 'Thérèse is rather nervous,' he said. 'And I suppose it does influence me. She needs a mother to give her some sort of emotional help and independence, which she hasn't had since her own mother died three years ago.'

The phone rang as if it had been timed to ring, and Moselle picked it up and nodded before he had said a word. Then he said, 'Hello, Kathy.'

MacGregor listened and got up and looked at the spines of Moselle's books. Louis de Broglie's *La Mécanique Ondulatoire à la Théorie de Noyau*. Wasn't it de Broglie who had pushed wave mechanics into the study of nuclear forces? What was Moselle's interest in that...

'No, Kathy,' Moselle was saying. 'I didn't see Cecie. She wouldn't come in. Yes, he's still here.'

He gave MacGregor the phone and MacGregor felt Moselle's warmth all over it. He heard Kathy saying: 'Hello, hello,' as if they had been cut off.

'It's me,' MacGregor said, and he waited to hear her reply so that he could guess what part of herself she was exposing to him.

'Why didn't Cecie stay there with you?' she asked.

'She said she was busy.'

'Did you let her go to one of those demonstrations?'

'No. She went to the atelier.'

'Where's Andrew then?'

'I haven't the faintest idea. I think he's with her.'

Barriers had already built themselves up along five hundred miles of barbed telephone wire.

'Have you seen Dr Taplow yet?' he asked her.

'Not yet. Ten o'clock tomorrow.'

'Then ring the moment you've seen him.'

'But I don't expect him to say anything startling.'

'Nevertheless...'

'All right. All right...'

She hung up, and Moselle said. 'There's no need to worry about Kathy. I assure you she's perfectly all right.'

MacGregor ignored it, and after a decent delay he said it was time he went.

'I'll get the car,' Moselle offered.

'No. No. I'll walk a little,' MacGregor said, 'and then get a taxi.'

'You'd better be careful,' Moselle said.

'I'll be all right,' MacGregor said.

They shook hands at the gate, and as he walked out into the blue Paris vapour of midnight, MacGregor was aware of someone crossing the road in the speckled mess of mercury light and chestnut shadows. There was no doubt that the figure was coming towards him. MacGregor stopped and looked for an escape route. There were lines of parked cars along the streets, and fast traffic flying along the avenue. There was no one else in sight.

'It's me....'

It was Andrew, and MacGregor knew from the rivulet of sweat above his eyes how tense he had been. 'What, for God's sake, are you doing out here at midnight?'

'I thought I'd better come and get you,' Andrew said.

'What for?'

'You shouldn't be on your own.'

'Now don't start exaggerating,' MacGregor protested, but he knew how glad he was to see Andrew.

'You were obviously expecting something,' Andrew said. 'You looked as if you were about to take off.'

'Just nerves.'

As they walked down the steel-walled street Andrew told him that someone had flung a bottle of sulphuric acid at their wooden gate. 'I was in the courtyard talking to the old man, and we heard a Vespa. Then the bottle smashed to pieces on the gate.'

'Acid!' MacGregor said incredulously. 'How do you know?'

'You can't mistake the smell. We got the hose on to it fairly soon, but most of the paint will be off the gate by morning.'

'That doesn't sound like a Kurdish trick,' MacGregor said. 'Acid! I've never heard of them using acid.'

They walked out of the Avenue Foch. The top part of the Bois was black behind them, and Andrew said that when he and the old man were winding up the garden hose near the coach-house, the Vespa had come back. 'This time the bottle came over the wall and landed in the courtyard, a couple of metres from where we were standing.'

'My God...'

'Luckily it didn't burst. This one was filled with somebody's piss. It wasn't acid, anyway.'

'Where was that gendarme who'd been posted outside?'

'He turned up later. I asked him where he'd been, and he said that he had heard someone crying *au secours* around that little corner, and he had gone to investigate.'

'But acid ... That's a foul way to do it.'

When they had reached the Champs Elysées MacGregor said he needed to sit down for a while. They picked one of the late-night cafés near the BOAC office and sat in the electric light on the pavement under the awnings, drinking iced beer in glasses that wet their hands.

'You don't really fit in this city, do you?' Andrew said to his father.

'At the moment,' MacGregor said lightly, 'I feel as if I've lost contact with everything *but* this city.'

They watched dark and wingless chariots racing up the Champs Elysées, and when they had finished their beer they paid their bill and walked on under the shadowless trees.

'The trouble is,' MacGregor said unhappily, 'there's no time left now. Somebody is trying to assassinate the Qazi, so I've got to take a chance and do something pretty quick.'

'That doesn't sound like you,' Andrew told him.

'I know. But I realise now that you can't use careful scientific methods on a problem like this. There comes a moment when you have to plunge.'

'Be careful,' Andrew said.

'I've got to go to the French,' MacGregor said. 'There's no other way.'

'The French?'

'All the French want is commerce,' MacGregor explained, and he knew that he was talking this way to Andrew because he could no longer talk this way to Kathy. 'I can't trust any of the others. None of them...'

They walked straight on down the middle of the vast esplanade of the Invalides, and Andrew did not say anything to him for a long time. Then he said, 'Doesn't it sicken you the way the European mind still has the world by the throat? I'm beginning to hate it. In fact the longer I live in Europe the more non-European I feel.'

'Listen to me,' MacGregor told his son. 'Your mother wants you to think like a European, and she's right. Your future is here, not there. So don't start getting tangled up with oriental loyalties the way I've been all my life. Leave them alone.'

Andrew said nothing, and they walked home in silence as if there was something in this that they both wanted to avoid.

Chapter Twenty-six

Kathy phoned him from London at eight o'clock the next morning, Sunday, and she said she was going to St Thomas' Hospital with Dr Taplow for X-rays at eleven o'clock on Monday morning.

'I forgot to tell you yesterday,' she said, 'that the Ilkhan's son, Dubas, wanted to talk to you. He rang me up after I lunched with him and I told him you would contact him. He's staying with Flanders.'

'You mean Flanders of the Children Unlimited?'

'Who else?' She gave him Flanders's telephone number.

He asked her now why she had lunched with Dubas.

'Because I didn't want you to have one more personal enemy with a private grudge against you,' she said.

He knew she was trying to sound relaxed, but he didn't believe it. He had decided even before he said goodbye to her that he would join her in London when he had seen the French and talked to Cumont. There was no other way of dealing with this tension between them.

He ate a silent breakfast—Cecie and Andrew were still asleep—and he walked out to look at the acid stain on the big gates. The *agent* said it was the work of Maoists, anarchists, communists, who hated the big houses owned by the old families. MacGregor said, 'Do you think so?' to be polite and then went back inside. He would have to talk to Aunt Joss about it because he was now exposing her to risks that were serious. He stood in the hall and called out: 'Aunt Joss ...'

'Yes?' a voice came from the wall.

'I want to talk to you about last night,' he shouted at the ceiling.

'What about last night?'

'Someone threw a bottle of acid at the gates.'

'I'm quite aware of that. What do you want to say?'

'I think it would be safer for you if I left you and went somewhere else for a while.'

Aunt Joss was silent for a moment, and he wondered if that was her way of agreeing with him. But then her echoes came through the doors and walls and staircases. 'If you leave here now I'll never forgive you,' she said. 'You wait till Kathy comes back, then you can leave.'

He smiled at the ceiling and called out: 'All right, Aunt Joss.'

At ten o'clock he phoned Cumont, who did not answer. It was Sunday and nobody at the Department of Procuration knew anything. But MacGregor gave them his name, and in five minutes Cumont rang back and told MacGregor to come around to the old Hotel Voltaire on the Quai Voltaire.

'I expected you to call,' Cumont said. 'I suppose you've got something to tell me.'

'When can I see you?'

'Come immediately. I'll be waiting.'

MacGregor took the Qazi's letters of introduction from the jacket where he had hidden them and he walked through the late, dull Sunday streets of the 7th arrondissement to the 6th, avoiding the noisy quayside which had long ago been eaten up by traffic and cement.

He imagined the old hotel still using brass bedsteads, although its entrance hall was modern and expensive. Cumont was sitting by himself in a corner of the breakfast-room, sipping coffee from a bowl. Today he was a dry, thin country gentleman. He held a cigarette in the thin speckled fingers of his right hand, but so delicately that it seemed as if a tighter grip would snap his fingers in half.

'Can you imagine where our friend Schramm is?' Cumont asked casually as MacGregor sat down.

'No.'

'Kurdistan. But that's strictly between you and me. We sent him off three days ago.'

MacGregor was impressed. 'How did you get a French officer up there?' he asked Cumont.

'I'll explain that later,' Cumont said. A waiter brought coffee, sugar and spoons, and the white cloth was dusted with a napkin. Cumont waited until he had finished and then said he was sorry to hear that Madame MacGregor was ill and had gone back to London for treatment. Moselle had told him. Moselle had been very worried about her.

MacGregor let it pass.

'Have you been in touch with your Qazi?' Cumont asked.

'No. It hasn't been necessary.'

'You heard that he'd been shot?'

'Yes. But I don't think that changes the situation.'

Cumont looked puzzled. 'Then I think you'd better tell me what you wanted to see me about.'

'My letters and credentials, which you asked for,' Mac-Gregor said and put them, folded, on the table.

'Your credentials?'

'Yes. You said that if you could accept my credentials, you would be willing to come to terms about those trucks or the money.'

'Yes, of course.'

MacGregor knew then that something else had happened, and that Cumont was going to hold him off.

'I think I can persuade the Qazi and his Committee to agree to what you want,' he said to Cumont.

'I see, I see.'

'You said that under French law the banks who seized those Kurdish funds could be ordered to hand them over.

230

It was your own suggestion.'

'Yes, I did say that,' Cumont admitted. 'But since then we have had word direct from the Qazi. That's why I asked you if you had also heard from him.'

'You got word here, in Paris, from the Qazi? You mean through Schramm?'

'No. No. We have been speaking to a young Kurd from the Committee called Dubas.'

'Dubas...' MacGregor laughed as if Cumont had deliberately meant it as a joke. 'Dubas is not a member of the Committee,' he told Cumont. 'Did he claim that he was?'

'Not exactly,' Cumont said. 'But he has their letters and credentials. In fact his credentials specifically state that all other documents including yours are cancelled.'

MacGregor kept as calm as he could. 'The Qazi would not give Dubas any sort of credentials,' he said. 'And he would certainly not cancel mine in favour of Dubas. It's quite impossible.'

'Perhaps. But someone on that Committee gave him valid letters. I assure you they are authentic.'

'How do you know they are?'

Cumont hesitated before MacGregor's forthright questions. 'We have our own means of checking that. We don't need to doubt them.'

'Do you have your means of checking Dubas himself?' MacGregor said angrily.

Cumont put his freckled old hands on the table. 'Yes,' he said. 'We know very well that he is sponsored by the Englishman, Flanders. And Flanders, as you know, is an agent of the Anglo-American consortium.' MacGregor did not know it, he had only suspected it. But he found himself inspecting Cumont's clever old eyes.

'Do you know who finally paid the offshore men for those arms?' Cumont asked him.

'No.'

'This Englishman, Flanders,' Cumont said.

'Children Unlimited,' MacGregor said.

'Yes. So you can see that there is obviously a conflict of interest here,' Cumont went on. 'We don't know what faction among the Kurds has the authority now. We have heard that the Qazi is in hiding. This boy Dubas says the arms must go to his father, the Ilkhani. Obviously something is wrong. That's why we sent Schramm to the Kurdish areas. But until he gets back I can't really discuss anything with you.'

'You can't believe Dubas,' MacGregor insisted. 'He can't speak for anybody but his father.'

'We don't believe him,' Cumont said. 'But we don't disbelieve him either. We must wait to make sure.'

Cumont waited for a Berliet truck to pass along the Quai.

'Do you think that Schramm will manage to find the Qazi?' he said to MacGregor. 'Assuming of course that he gets into the Kurdish areas.'

'He might,' MacGregor said. 'But I doubt it.'

'Would you be willing to go there yourself and bring back some sort of clarification?' Cumont hesitated. 'Or rather, find Schramm and take him to the Qazi. Then we'll be able to decide this immediately.'

MacGregor said he was not sure that he understood. 'Is that the only way to do this?' he said.

'I can't see any other way,' Cumont told him. 'In the meantime I would see that those trucks do not leave France. If you do go...' He looked at MacGregor who made no sign, no acceptance. '... you'll have to be back here by 31 May, because after that it is out of my hands.'

'That wouldn't give me much time.'

'We can put you on an Air France jet for Teheran at five o'clock tomorrow morning, if you can manage it. There'll be a ticket for you at Orly, with Air France.'

'It's not easy for me to get away at the moment.'

'I understand,' Cumont said.

'I'll let you know...'

232

'You don't have to,' Cumont said. 'The ticket will be there if you want to use it.'

They were shaking hands and Cumont gave him back the Qazi's letters, unread. 'There's one thing I should mention,' he said. 'There are some young Kurds in Paris who want to blow up those trucks in Marseilles. I suppose you know about it.'

'I've heard about it.'

'If you know any of these young imbeciles, please warn them not to do it. We will not tolerate that sort of thing in France.'

At the door of the breakfast-room MacGregor asked him how he had managed to get Schramm into Persia and into the Kurdish areas.

'He's gone there as a correspondent for one of our pulpy journals,' Cumont said, smiling.

'And the Iranians let him in?'

'We had other influences—after the Prime Minister's visit.'

'You'd need them,' MacGregor said.

'Anyway, Schramm will be pleased to see you. He's fascinated with all that medieval *niaiserie*. He also admires you, so you should make an interesting pair in Kurdistan. But please be careful. Think of your lovely wife, and your young family.'

Chapter Twenty-seven

When he told Cecie he was thinking of returning to Iran for a week or two, she said, 'What about Mama?'

'She'll understand,' he said. 'There are good reasons.'

'Don't be too sure,' Cecie warned him. 'Women aren't like men when it comes to understanding good reasons.'

MacGregor knew that Cecie was right, and when Kathy telephoned at two o'clock and said that Dr Taplow couldn't find anything wrong with her except muscular fatigue, MacGregor said he was thankful for that. But he did not mention that he was thinking about going back to Iran. He had no real hope now of discussing it calmly with her, and he wasn't going to put it to her *fait accompli*.

'There's something you'll have to do,' Kathy told him on the phone. 'You'll have to go to the Opéra Comique tonight with Jizzy Margaux.'

'With who?'

'Guy's sister. Don't pretend you've forgotten her.'

'No. No. I remember her.'

'I had accepted her invitation days ago, and I forgot to cancel it. I just rang her now and she said it didn't matter. Her husband's away, and you could take her yourself.'

'Is it absolutely necessary?'

'Yes it is necessary. Why? Are you doing anything else?'

'No.'

'Then please do it,' she told him.

He did not want to quarrel with her about something so unimportant now, so he asked Kathy where he was supposed to meet Jizzy Margaux.

'Go to her house for a cocktail at six.'

She sounded relaxed. She was feeling better. But MacGregor knew there was now a disciplined silence between them. He went out and walked around the Sunday streets trying to decide what to do. But Paris on a Sunday could not help him, and when he went back to dress for Jizzy Margaux and the Opéra Comique he was still undecided.

He was almost ready when Andrew shouted up the stairs that the Megrik Kurd, Dubas, was here and wanted to see him. He put on his jacket and went downstairs.

'Dear friend,' Dubas said in perfect French, and with youthful sport in his Kurdish good manners. He was standing in the hall without his riding switch, looking like a young Frenchman who had just stepped out of his Jaguar. 'I have come to Paris.'

MacGregor led the way into the breakfast-room, and Dubas asked after Madame Kathy and made offerings of conciliation, while MacGregor waited for him to come to the point.

'You'd better look at these,' Dubas told him.

He showed MacGregor his letters from the Committee. MacGregor read the script very carefully and the six signatures under the seal of the Committee. But neither the Qazi nor the Iraqi had signed them.

'The Qazi was ill,' Dubas said. 'He was wounded. So he couldn't sign it. But I've been sent to relieve you of your unpleasant responsibility for that Kurdish money. This will explain.'

He gave MacGregor another letter which was written in red ink in the priestly and highly literate language of an Imam or scholar; it was addressed to the French Department for Iranian Affairs at the Quai d'Orsay and said that all previous credentials issued by the Kurdish Committee were cancelled.

MacGregor handed them all back. 'They don't mean anything to me,' he said.

'Not to you,' Dubas said. 'But they mean something to the French.'

'I'm not going to take any notice of these letters,' Mac-Gregor told Dubas. 'Nor will the French. Because without the Qazi's signature they are all worthless, and you know it.'

'The Qazi was ill, wounded . . .' Dubas said again.

'I know what happened to the Qazi. But if your father thinks he's going to get control of the Committee . . .'

'God forbid,' Dubas said.

'Your father will never get those arms, Dubas, because I'll do everything possible to see that he doesn't.'

'But why do you go on bothering with our dirty and barren Kurdish mountains when your family lives here in safety and comfort?' Dubas said. 'Why bother with us, my friend? I just don't understand you.'

MacGregor stood up abruptly and said there was no point in talking about it. He went out into the courtyard and opened the big gate and he stood there for a moment in the warm Parisian evening, a little wet with rain, looking at the two men who leaned against a crumpled American car at the end of the street.

'Your friends?' MacGregor asked Dubas who had followed him.

'My cousins from Geneva,' Dubas told him. 'The policeman wouldn't let them come any nearer. What are you afraid of, mon ami?'

MacGregor pointed to the blistered patch of paint on the door which looked like a large raw blemish on human skin. 'It was a repulsive thing to do,' he said.

He watched the young Kurd's face, but there was no sign of horror on it and no sign of innocence.

'City warfare,' the Kurd said contemptuously.

'Goodbye, Dubas,' MacGregor said.

Dubas smiled. 'To live in this rich and beautiful city...' he said as MacGregor closed the big gate on him. 'I'll be going over to London next week,' he said from the outside. 'May I call on Madame Kathy?'

'Please do,' MacGregor told him and waited until he heard the car start before opening the gate again.

Although MacGregor had not forgotten how beautiful Jizzy Margaux was, he had forgotten the rest. But now that he was alone with her he could look at the perfection of her extraordinary face and realise how right Guy Moselle was about her. Tigers, panthers, lions, leopards and perhaps even bears and gazelles could pace up and down in a cage and look out of it without ever seeing the human being staring at them from the other side. The untouchable Jizzy seemed to suffer the same disconnection. She looked out on the world as if she was pacing behind it, as if there was nothing at all in front of her.

She put two glasses of champagne on the marquette table of her salon. 'I don't like American cocktails,' she said. 'I don't understand how anybody can drink them. They remind me of thick meat and hot faces, and men with belts around fat stomachs.'

She handed him his glass and he thanked her.

She sat down. 'First of all,' she said, 'let me tell you that after you were here the other night I kept thinking about you. But then I decided I'd better stop, because I don't really understand you.'

MacGregor said that was a pity, and asked her about Caracas, where her husband was.

She dismissed it as a worthless city and said, 'What's wrong with Kathy? What's happening to you two? Everybody told me it was so perfect.'

MacGregor resigned himself to the sort of conversation it was going to be. 'Nothing's happening to us,' he said. 'Why do you ask?'

'Kathy is obviously fooling about with my brother Guy,'

Jizzy told him. 'So what do you think about it?'

'I don't think anything at all about it,' he said.

'Then you'd better,' she told him. 'Guy is not someone I would trust. Not that way.'

He touched the champagne with his tongue and looked away.

'You should be afraid of Guy,' she persisted.

'What good would that do?' he said.

'I don't know. But your marriage looks very successful, and Guy only wants something that succeeds. That's why he wants Kathy.'

MacGregor asked her then if it wasn't time they went to the opera.

'Oh, let the stupid opera go,' Jizzy said. 'I just want to talk. I've decided I can talk to you, because I know it won't go any further. Normally I never can tell anything to anybody. The only other person I can trust never to repeat anything I say is my daughter, but she's only ten years old and I can't say everything to her yet. Do you talk to your children?'

'Sometimes.' He couldn't help smiling at Jizzy.

'But you can't talk to Kathy any more,' she said. 'Is that what's wrong?'

He refused to talk about Kathy, and Jizzy put her long fingers up to her face as if she were about to pull something off it. 'Why don't you look at me?' she said. 'I mean at my face.'

He looked at her face cautiously.

'You don't like it, do you? Does it embarrass you?' she said.

'You speak French so quickly that I hardly understand you,' he told her, trying to avoid everything she was saying to him.

But that seemed to be the answer she wanted. 'I was going to ask you a lot of questions,' she said. 'But all that can wait now.'

238

She said she would be back in five minutes, and while he waited he decided he had better keep a tight grip on himself.

She came back dressed in raw natural silk. *'En avant...'* she said, and they left the little salon and plunged down the stairs through the core of the house. They stood in the street together for a moment, and she took his arm. They got a taxi, which was another enclosure, and MacGregor began to feel the real attractions of this Frenchwoman without being able to recognise exactly what they were.

The opera was *Werther*—Goethe's tragedy of a gothic German marriage. Jizzy sat in silence beside him, as if she was too emotionally engaged in this German romance of Albert and Charlotte and the irresponsible Werther to be of any use to him. *'Laissez couler mes larmes,'* Charlotte sang with French suffusion, and Jizzy said in a whisper to him, 'I hate it. It hurts me.' And MacGregor was surprised to see Jizzy snatching two lush tears off her eyelids before they could lap over and ruin her maquillage.

She said nothing on the way to her house, and MacGregor was beginning to be aware of the real puzzle in this woman, who seemed to be fighting against the very nature of her face. It was only when she was making coffee in the expensive glass kitchen that she decided to talk again.

'They always make *Werther* a tragedy, but that kind of bourgeois marriage was just stupid,' she said, as if she had to explain why she could weep over a German romance set to French music. 'And I'm sure Goethe meant to say so.'

'I always had the feeling when I read *Werther* that Goethe was attacking romantic love, not marriage,' he said.

'How can you say a thing like that?' she said. 'Germans have always been hopelessly sentimental about love, even Goethe.'

'Maybe. But on the whole Goethe liked a good marriage, without thinking much of love.'

They were sitting at an aseptic table, and he realised that

pristine cleanliness must have been part of the Moselle up-bringing. He watched her precision and order, doing kitchen work and servants' work in a Givenchy dress, grinding coffee beans, filling a glass *cafetière*, wiping it, putting it down, lighting the gas. She was so preoccupied with what she was doing that she seemed to have forgotten him.

'I don't know what Goethe thought about love,' she said to him. 'But I do know that it's marriage that's stupid. I was married at twenty for love. French love is made in the mouth. It's so disgusting. French men are very good with their mouths and their hands. But I hate it. Sometimes that sort of passion can become love—I mean quiet love without hands in it. Then it's all right and goes on forever. But if it just stays with its hands and its mouth, it just becomes quiet hate. That's what it did to me. All my *surface*...' She ran her hands down her body. 'Nobody knows, not even my husband, about me. I am normal. I have a good French *surface*. Not so?' She waited. She was demanding an answer.

'Of course,' he said.

'But when I tried to love him quietly, he killed me with his hands and his mouth. Let him do it to others, but not to me.'

She sat down opposite MacGregor and he realised that he no longer found it difficult to look at her or watch or listen. The beautiful Jizzy, who was so desirable, did not want to be desirable at all, and it relieved MacGregor of any bother about it. But what did she want?

'English marriages are supposed to be different,' she went on as she poured him coffee with neat, feminine care. 'That's why I don't understand about you and Kathy. Don't you have a devotional marriage? What do you say?' she demanded.

He laughed. 'Marriage is hard work in any language,' he said.

'Why do you say that? I think being in love with you

would be very simple and without all those other stupid tortures. That's what I would like. I would fall in love with you very slowly if you like. Very quietly. And nobody need ever know, not even Kathy.'

Jizzy was looking at him as if she were appealing desperately to his reason and to his own kind of untouchability. She was not suggesting something amoral or evil, or asking him to cheat. MacGregor wondered if this was what Guy Moselle meant when he said she was always trying to find some sort of lost connection with the human race.

'Does it embarrass you?' she said with concern.

He pointed to the coffee which was boiling.

'Be careful,' he told her. 'You're too near it.'

Jizzy had put her arm near the hot steam and she pulled it away. Then she came back and sat near him again, wiping her arm but never taking her eyes off him. 'You don't know what I mean when I talk about French men, do you?' she said.

He shook his head.

'You'll never understand what that did to me when I was young. I thought love like that must be normal, so it killed me. I thought I was dead,' she said again. 'But now I've been thinking about you. I've been looking at you very carefully, and I decided that if we ever did come together nothing like that would ever happen to me again,' she said. 'Don't you think you would feel the same?' she asked him.

'It's too late for anything like that, Jizzy,' he said with a faint smile, refusing to treat it seriously.

'You mean because of Kathy?'

'Certainly.'

Jizzy's perfect eyes glazed over. 'But she need never know. Why should she? I shan't hurt her. Nor will you. We shan't hurt anyone. I've been waiting so long, just to feel something again. I don't mean love,' she said, and shrugged. 'I just mean what is happening to me now. It's been coming for such a long time, and now I think it's finally here. Just a moment,' she said.

Jizzy got up and went to the shiny kitchen sink. She turned on the polished taps, bent her head over the sink, and washed her face with kitchen soap. MacGregor could see the skin of the maquillage pouring like brown sunlight into the stainless steel bowl. She took a towel from the side of the sink and came back to him drying and rubbing her face.

'I'll never wear that again,' she told him. 'Is it better?'

MacGregor was startled at the transformation of one beauty to another. Jizzy's clear, tawny face was lightly and attractively freckled, like tiny petals on other petals; and now the puzzled, innocent, preoccupied and mature woman was visible. If anything she was even more beautiful than she was before.

'But why on earth did you do that?' he asked her.

This time she laughed, but MacGregor knew how serious she was. 'I wanted to look like you.' She put her hands to her face and said between her teeth: 'I swear I'll never wear maquillage again as long as I live. Are you hungry?' she asked him.

'As a matter of fact I am,' he told her, and he knew that she was letting him off lightly in some way.

'Why didn't you take me to dinner? Did you forget?' she asked him. But she didn't let him answer. 'I didn't really want you to take me anywhere,' she said. 'I was determined to bring you here.'

She went to the giant refrigerator, a temple in this white, tiled palace. She took out roasted chicken and olives and put down some plates and napkins. Everything glittered and shone. Then she sat down and they both picked delicately over a chicken bone between sips of coffee. With her mouth half full two tears splashed like grapes on the shiny table top between them.

'Don't be embarrassed,' she said. 'It's just happening to

me like that. I understand all about you. You live...' She swept the tears off the table with her napkin. 'You actually live with some sort of true abnegation, don't you, and that's what I need. I think that's why I always admired de Vigny,' she said in French and then went on in French: 'My brother Guy thinks that you will bury yourself and die in those Kurdish mountains, like a poor priest doing his duty. I'd do that myself if I were a man. And I'd do it with you as a woman if you were at all interested.'

'What makes your brother think I'll die in the Kurdish mountains like a priest?' he asked her, confused by Jizzy but also aware that she was trying to help him.

She shrugged and licked her fingers. 'He says you're that kind of English—Englishman. He thinks that's what's wrong between you and Kathy. Is it true that she wants to come back here and live like this?' Jizzy gestured at their glittering surroundings.

MacGregor felt that he was hearing second-hand some of Kathy, pouring out her heart to Moselle. And Moselle casually passing it on to his sister. 'Yes. She wants to come back.'

'But what for?' Again Jizzy gestured incredulously at her rich house. 'My God,' she said, 'I'd give anything to finish with all this. I hate it.'

Jizzy then began to strip off her jewellery, pulling at her ears and her fingers as if in quick divestment there was some sort of liberation. She dropped her jewels on the plate with the chicken bones.

'Let me tell you now about Kathy,' she said.

'Maybe it's better that you don't,' he said.

'But you should know,' she insisted. 'Because even Kathy's suffering from the same sickness as everybody else. Everyone in France these days lives in some sort of personal or sexual trauma. A few clever words, phhttt, and Kathy'll be gone like everybody else. You agree?'

'Not at all,' he said.

'You'll never understand why she wants to come back to all this, will you?'

'But I do understand,' he said.

'Why, then?'

'Because she was too long away from it,' he said. 'It was never very easy or safe or pleasant for her in Iran. You see, Jizzy, almost nobody knows what Kathy's been through in the last twenty years. Nobody.'

Jizzy's perfect, animal eyes looked at him calmly. 'You don't understand women at all, do you,' she said.

'Maybe not.'

'Then you'd better watch out,' she said, 'because Guy understands women very well. He's French, and he'll know what to do with Kathy if you ever have to go away and leave her behind.'

The glass kitchen was quiet and hot.

'You're underestimating Kathy,' he said. 'She's not likely to collapse into his arms like a naïve young girl.'

'Don't be too sure,' he said. 'Oh my God, no ...'

He got up to go. She did not try to stop him, but she faced him sadly with her beautiful, stripped face and her freckled, petalled cheeks. He remembered a Persian play on words which said that if you lived a life of pride and wealth it was all so much life wasted, and if you didn't believe it then just read the Persian word for fortune backwards and it meant unattached and lost.

'Please stay,' she said to him. 'It won't hurt you to stay.'

'It's not quite so simple,' he said gently.

'Why isn't it?' she said. 'I don't mean love ... I mean that other marvellous thing. And if everything fails with you and Kathy. We wouldn't hurt her.'

'Nothing's going to fail,' he said. 'It's not like that.'

'But it might. You know it might.'

He undid his hand which she had casually tucked into her arm where the silk and the flesh and the perfume met. She replaced it with her own hand in his, and led him

244

slowly down the stairs through the crater to the bottom of the house.

'Do you know what Valéry said in *L'Abeille*?' she asked him when they reached the bottom.

'No.'

'He said that everybody in love needs torment, because a pain that is quickly over and done with is much better than a slow and sleeping anguish.'

'Is that meant for me or for you?' he said lightly to her.

'I think it's meant for me, but it might be meant for you too. In any case you and I are not like the others. We do not suffer from the sickness of Europe, do we?'

He left it all as a mystery, and he got himself out of the door with no more than Jizzy's untouchable lips gently against his. As he walked, and as the taxis grazed him on the crossroads where he didn't see them, he wondered if Kathy had known what would happen with Jizzy Margaux, and if she had deliberately arranged it that way.

He walked slowly to the all-night PTT office behind the Bourse where he could be sure of privacy among the clochards. He telephoned her at the Battersea house although it was now one o'clock in the morning, and when she answered he kept his nerves together and said: 'It's me. Don't worry. Everything's all right. I just wanted to tell you that I'm going back to Iran at five o'clock in the morning.'

There was a long silence. 'What for?' she said in a far-away voice. 'What happened?'

'Nothing's happened. It's just that I have to finish with this business, and this is the only way to do it.'

'What does that mean? How long will you be there?'

'About ten days, that's all.'

'And the children?'

'They're quite all right,' he told her. 'Don't worry. They can look after themselves.'

'How can you say that?' she said. 'The TV says that there's going to be a general strike in Paris tomorrow, and

245

that's something they ought to be kept out of, particularly Cecie.'

'I'll talk to her,' MacGregor said. 'She'll be all right. Andrew will watch out for her.'

'And who'll be watching him? I'll come back tomorrow.'

'No,' he said sharply. 'Just leave them. They have to be trusted by themselves sooner or later. They're all right, Kathy.'

'Oh, go ahead then,' she told him wearily. 'But you'd better prepare yourself to live with the consequences when you come back.'

'What consequences?'

'If you don't know there's no point in telling you.'

'Don't be like that.'

'Well I am like that,' she said.

'When I come back this time it'll probably be for good,' he told her.

He could hear her breathing, but she didn't comment. She asked him if he was going into the Kurdish areas.

'Of course. That's the point.'

'How do you know it isn't a trick?' she said.

'It might be,' he admitted. 'But it's unlikely.'

'Then for God's sake don't go,' she said. 'Do something sensible for once.'

'I have to go, Kathy,' he said. 'The whole thing is at stake now, and I honestly want to get it over and done with and then clear up whatever it is that's between us.'

'All right, go,' she said. 'By all means go. Go! But don't be sure of what you're coming back to. That's all.'

PART III

Chapter Twenty-eight

When MacGregor pushed open the gate of the old barracks at Maradesh he didn't expect to see Schramm squatting in the mud among the Kurdish mechanics and donkey drivers who were talking and laughing quietly around a dung fire.

'I suppose you've been looking for me all over the place,' Schramm said in his hard French.

'No,' MacGregor said. 'Someone like you can't travel far in these mountains without half the population knowing all about it.'

'I set out four days ago in a hired car from Rezaiya with this chap, Gala.' Schramm pointed to one of the Kurds at the fire. 'But he keeps taking money from me for petrol and food and bribes, and that's all. He seems to be intent on getting everything I've got. Even my clothes and my pocket knife. One of these Kurds speaks a few words of German. Otherwise I don't know what they're saying because my Kurdish is too primitive. Do they all speak different dialects?'

'Of course. But what brought you to this place?' MacGregor indicated the abandoned barracks.

'I don't even know where I am.'

'You're about ten miles inside Iraq,' MacGregor told him.

The Frenchman laughed and slapped his dusty paraboots. 'You don't say. Well, I didn't pass through any frontier posts, so you won't have to convince me who these mountains really belong to.'

MacGregor kept his eyes on the Kurds and wondered if any of them understood French. 'Nonetheless,' he said to Schramm, 'the Iraqi patrols will shoot you on sight if they catch you.'

'What about you?'

'I'm not a French soldier in civilian clothes and I don't carry a pistol in my hip pocket.'

'How did you know about that?'

'In two days, we not only found out where you've been and where you've been trying to go,' MacGregor said, 'but what you ate, how you dug a hole to relieve yourself in, how you shaved every early morning with a battery shaver and without water, and that you are obviously curious and dangerous with maps, note-books and a silver biro with a ring on the end of it. You're very conspicuous,' MacGregor told him, and walked over to where Gala the driver was lying down near the fire.

'I was looking for your friends of the Committee,' Schramm said as he followed. 'But I can't get anyone to tell me where they are, so I haven't been able to do anything yet.'

'Yes you have. You've been to see the Ilkhani,' MacGregor said. 'You were with his men two days ago when they were attacking some of the Qazi's men.'

'Is that what it was?' Schramm said with a shrug and his tough little smile. 'Anyway, I just ran into the old man, so to speak.'

'No you didn't. You were looking for him and you were taken to him.'

MacGregor told the Kurds around the fire who he was. He asked the driver why he had taken the Frenchman to see the Ilkhani. What sort of a Kurd was he?

'He paid me to do it,' Gala said with a shrug.

MacGregor remembered now who Gala was. Gala had fought with the Mullah Barzani against the Iranian army in 1946, but since then he had become a professional mountain smuggler and guide to other smugglers or intelligence agents or anybody who wanted something in the mountains. He had the reputation of paying off all the border guards in cigarettes and transistors and electric irons to look the other way, and sometimes he would betray a rival smuggler by sending anonymous messages to Iraqi or Iranian border guards. He used donkeys and was known as a donkey thief, but he never carried a rifle. MacGregor accused him now of stupidity and self-interest.

'Why did you bring him across the border?' MacGregor said to Gala. 'That was stupid and dangerous.'

'But he wants to see the Qazi,' Gala said, 'and the Qazi is somewhere near Amaradiya in Iraq. So I brought him here. He paid me....'

'Where's your car now?' MacGregor asked him.

'I loaned it to Murad, who is just back from a pilgrimage and is now a Hadj.'

'What a lie,' MacGregor said, and told Schramm he'd better pack up his bed roll and get ready to go.

'Where to?' Schramm asked.

'We'd better get out of here while it's still dark,' MacGregor told him, and he said, 'Come on, Gala' and led the way out of the old barracks gate and down the steep, rutted road to a battered old Mercedes.

'But *merde*, that's my hired car,' Schramm said. 'Where did you find it?'

'It brought me up here.'

'But how?'

'Never mind that now. Get in,' he said, and he got in the front seat himself and told Gala to go down the mountain road as far as the river, and then follow the black road up to the old Nestorian village where the caves were.

MacGregor went to sleep, waking and dozing until they drove through a hail of splashing mud and pebbles up a steep wet slope which was grey and slaty in the headlamps.

They stopped at the outskirts of a large village where two armed Kurds, obviously Zadko's men, told them to get out. One of them recognised MacGregor and asked him if they had any weapons in the car.

'Give me your pistol,' MacGregor said to Schramm. He handed it to the Kurd who tucked it in his belt as if it were now his. He told MacGregor that Schramm should stay where he was, and that MacGregor should come alone.

It was a short, dark, stumbling walk uphill to a mud-brick hovel, where there was another Kurd squatting sleepily outside. A lamp was lit and MacGregor walked into one room and then another, with ceilings a few inches over his head. In the third room he saw the Qazi lying on a wooden bunk which was covered with old mats. Over him was a grey army blanket, which the Qazi pulled around his shoulders as he sat up. He wore wartime RAF cotton socks, but no shoes.

'Welcome,' the Qazi said, taking MacGregor's hand. He apologised for his appearance and the place and the discomfort, and added: 'I heard that you were on the way.'

'I hoped you would,' MacGregor said. 'I tried to send messages ahead.'

The Qazi was thin, and his face was a pale, stony grey, the colour of the blanket around his shoulders. His throat was wrapped in a dirty bandage, and his beard had been shaved off and was growing again in a stubble. So was his hair, which had been clipped up to the crown, which was also wrapped in a bandage.

'Are you well?' he said tiredly to MacGregor.

'Yes,' MacGregor said. 'But you, Qazi. You don't look well.'

'I'm perfectly all right again now,' he said. 'It was difficult for a while.'

'I'm sorry to see you like this,' MacGregor told him.

'Oh, it doesn't matter now. We've been rather harassed.

The Ilkhani has been trying to kidnap me, chasing us from one place to another, sending up messages that he only wants to protect me.'

'My God ...'

'But of course he wants to use me like a cap in his hand, and he wants to prevent Zadko establishing himself in some place where he can operate safely. He's been giving Zadko a lot of trouble, hounding us from one place to another, using his motor cars to ambush us and trying to kill Zadko. I have had a very difficult job avoiding his provocations.'

'Avoiding his provocations?' MacGregor said. 'Is it worth it, Qazi?'

'Of course,' the Qazi said, holding his bandaged throat for a moment. 'We have to have a principle, and if unity is the principle we have to stick to it. So we must avoid fighting among ourselves, otherwise there's no Kurdish cause at all. I won't let even the Ilkhani change that.'

'But sooner or later he will kill you,' MacGregor argued.

'I don't think so. He simply wants to force me to agree to his methods and his policies and his ideas of the Kurdish nation. But I'll never do that. Some day he will have to accept our ideas, our genuine purpose, and I won't spoil that now by trying to confront him.'

The Qazi called in one of the guards.

'Take our friends up to the dry caves,' he told the guard, and he said to MacGregor that they would be comfortable up there, and that they should also meet privately and briefly in the morning before he saw the Frenchman.

'Where is Zadko?' MacGregor asked.

'He is on the roadway below Haldasht,' the Qazi said, and he told the other guard to go and find Zadko and bring him up to the village.

'And the Iraqi?' MacGregor said before going.

'He's here,' the Qazi said, 'but he's not very well.' The Qazi lay down again. 'We can discuss all this tomorrow.

253

You'll need a rest after your long journey all the way from Paris. I'm pleased to see you, my friend, and grateful too.'

In the early morning the Qazi wore a clean turban and a clean burnous. He was waiting for MacGregor in another cave, which had been swept out and furnished with an old deal table, cane chairs, and a large black radio set standing silent in a corner under a yellow hurricane lamp. MacGregor knew it was all fake, but he hoped it would impress the Frenchman, who might recall other oriental guerilla caves in other oriental liberations. The four guards in dirty Kurdish costume and wearing bandoliers were more convincing, although MacGregor could not avoid the feeling that there was something hollow even in the soldiers. Only the Iraqi and the Qazi gave it the lean and authentic look that was expected.

'Well then,' the Iraqi said to MacGregor. 'What happened in Paris? Is it complicated?'

'I'll explain what happened, and then you'll see what the problem is,' MacGregor said, and he told them step by step what he had done in Europe. The Iraqi and the Qazi sat tense and still at the dusty old table, listening without interrupting. But when he had finished the Qazi could not hide his confusion.

'It's a mess,' he said. 'So tell us what it means there, not here.'

'That's more difficult,' MacGregor said. 'Every government in the west is suddenly interested in the Kurdish future, and every one of them wants to meddle in it.'

'That's not new,' the Iraqi said, his sick face looking sour.

'No, but for the first time, Ali, they all accept the idea of Kurdish independence, even the idea of a national Kurdish existence. And that's quite new.'

'In that case,' the Qazi said, 'we have progressed. So what is the problem? Why don't they help us, or at least let us buy arms?'

MacGregor wished that he had better explanations than those which had seemed obvious in Europe but were difficult and remote up here. Two Kurdish women with a sick child had approached the Frenchman that morning, thinking he was a foreign doctor. (All foreigners ought to be doctors, they said.) Schramm was full of pity, but he had to tell them sadly that he was not a doctor, and that he couldn't help, so the women spat at him and called him a donkey's arse.

'The trouble is,' MacGregor said to the Qazi, leaning his elbows on the dusty table, 'that they'll only accept the idea of the Kurdish revolution if they can buy an interest in it.'

'With what?'

'With anything: money, arms, promises, politics, corruptions. Anything that will give them what they want. Only the French seem to want the oil and the gas for purely commercial reasons. That's why I thought the French would be more useful to us than the others.'

'Are the French honest?' the Qazi asked.

MacGregor laughed. 'How can you ask a question like that, Qazi?' he said sadly. 'The French are the weakest, that's all.'

'It's difficult to understand the European mind,' the Qazi said unhappily.

'Europe is changing very rapidly, Qazi,' MacGregor said to him. 'Once it would have been easy for them to control you with bombers and soldiers. But it's not so easy any more, and they're surrounded everywhere by their own upheavals.'

'And the arms?' the Iraqi said. 'Who's got them now?'

'Nobody yet.' MacGregor heard a jeep's engine behaving as if it were in distress. He knew it was Zadko arriving from somewhere, and in a moment the Kurd walked in, looking around the dust-laden cave to see what was going on.

'Are you well?' he said, embracing MacGregor. 'I know you saw Taha in Paris; I know that much.'

MacGregor excused himself to the Qazi and told Zadko about Taha. Zadko listened patiently (today he was being patient) and he only interrupted once when MacGregor mentioned Dubas. 'So it's true, by God. The Ilkhani's son is there too.'

MacGregor told them about Dubas and his fake documents.

'You see, Qazi!' Zadko said. 'Did you tell him that we're being hounded in our own mountains?'

'Yes, I told him. But there's no reason to exaggerate it. Let us talk to the Frenchman,' the Qazi said, and told one of the guards to go and get him.

'Just a moment,' MacGregor said to the guard. 'I'd better warn you before you see him, Qazi, that this Frenchman thinks like a soldier. Moreover, he's disappointed in what he's seen so far.'

'Then how should we treat him?' the Qazi asked.

'I think he'll listen to you,' MacGregor said to the Qazi. 'But let Zadko impress him with something as well.'

'What do you mean?' Zadko said indignantly. 'Why should we try to impress a Frenchman?'

The Qazi looked enquiringly at the silent and sick Iraqi.

'I don't like this Frenchman,' the Iraqi said.

'What do you say?' the Qazi said to MacGregor.

'That Frenchman is the reason I came all the way from Paris,' MacGregor said.

'Very well.' The Qazi touched his bandaged throat which was hidden by a thick woollen scarf. It was obviously painful for him to talk: 'We'll do our best,' he said.

Schramm had cleaned the mud and manure off his boots and though he did not actually salute, he stood erect and his eyes were watchful and cautious. MacGregor introduced him in French and told Schramm that he could speak French to the Qazi and the Iraqi.

256

'I have letters, Qazi,' Schramm said and gave the Qazi two letters which the Qazi read quickly and then put aside.

'Do you want me to explain our situation, Monsieur?' the Qazi said. 'Or do you want to ask me your questions?'

Schramm was brisk. 'All I want to know is how much authority you have, and what you plan to do next.'

The Qazi thought for a moment before he replied. 'The only way you can find out about our authority,' he said, 'is to ask any Kurd who it is he considers his true spokesmen to be.'

'I can't do that,' Schramm said, 'because I don't speak your language well enough.'

'Then you'll never know much about us, will you?' the Qazi said.

Schramm took it very well. 'Perhaps,' he said. 'But I'm really more interested in what you yourself plan to do now.'

The Qazi raised his relaxed hands. 'That's difficult to say,' he said. And as the Qazi and the Frenchman began to juggle questions and answers back and forth, Zadko pulled MacGregor's sleeve and asked him what was being said.

'The Frenchman is asking the Qazi who exactly the Kurds want to fight,' MacGregor told Zadko.

'What does he mean?'

'He's trying to find out if you're more interested in fighting the Ilkhani or the Iraqis or the Iranians or somebody else.'

'Ahh.'

'He wants to know if you have contact with the Russians,' MacGregor translated.

'Tell him we've got Russian guns.' When MacGregor ignored it, Zadko insisted. 'Go on. Tell him.'

'Why should I tell him a lie like that?'

Zadko pointed to the new Kalashnikov automatic rifle with a neat brown butt and webbed straps which the Kurd on guard was holding.

'Where did you get that?' MacGregor asked.

'We stole it from the Iraqis,' Zadko said.

'Who did?'

'I did,' Zadko said. 'And since the Frenchman's obviously recognised it, tell him what you like. Let him think there are thousands more,' Zadko said, and then whispered: 'Let's go outside for a moment. I have something important to tell you.'

MacGregor hesitated. But he knew that the Frenchman expected to be left alone with the Qazi, so he went outside into the sun with Zadko who told him that it was all very well for the Qazi to talk unity and to hide himself as a way of preventing the Ilkhani from shooting fellow Kurds.

'But what that old arse, the Ilkhani, did last week was to tell the Iranian gendarmes where we were. Then he killed one of my telescope men on look-out post.'

'The Qazi told me what happened,' MacGregor said.

'Yesterday I was on the Iranian side,' Zadko went on, 'and the Ilkhani was still hunting us up and down like dogs. The Iranian gendarmes are letting him do it.'

'But what's he doing it for? What suddenly pushed him so far?'

'Somebody outside is encouraging him,' Zadko said. 'He was in the village of Juria a week ago and he stood on the roof of a village house waving his big ears and a German pistol and shouting at the villagers that he would shoot my men whenever he saw them and he would shoot anyone who shielded us. He's going to kill me and the Qazi sooner or later, unless I kill him first.'

'What does the Qazi say to all this?'

'He says it's foreign provocation.'

'He's probably right,' MacGregor said as they sat on a loose stone wall overlooking the village. 'If you start fighting among yourselves now, only the foreigners will benefit.'

Zadko turned his back on the sun. 'Well. I don't know.'

he said. 'Sometimes Taha is right when he wants to kill all the feodals.'

'Taha is wrong,' MacGregor insisted.

Zadko pointed to the township of Arbebil which they could just see far below. 'That used to be a tribal town,' he said. 'In summer it used to be shut up, and everybody went down to Sulav to escape the dust and the heat. It's an old town. It has many old Kurdish buildings and two barracks in ruins, and walls two kilometres high. It has gates, the Mosul gates. It was a Kurdish tribal fortress. But now it is a mechanics' town, and it has asphalt roads and markets and tea-houses and a big mosque. You can see there how our Kurds are changing every day.'

'I know....'

'They are losing the mountains, habibi, and now they live like beggars on the roadways and in garages, and they buy and sell and work like dogs in oilwells and drive buses and trucks and paint their houses. How long will they live like that—in asphalt poverty?'

'I know all that,' MacGregor said again. 'But change like that is inevitable, Zadko, and it's got nothing to do with your problem at the moment.'

'Why, for God's sake, does it have to be inevitable?' Zadko said. 'Summers and winters don't matter any more. You see how we change? So who can show the Frenchman that, when even Kurds themselves don't always understand what is happening to them? Taha is right. We are becoming a city people, so we have to revolt like city people.'

'I understand all that....'

'But what other foreigner will ever understand it, or understand what we are all quarrelling about? How will a foreigner like that Frenchman ever know what we want, what we would like to see for our future? I said to Taha before he went away to Paris: *Nobody had ever broken the bond of Kurdish honour, so don't you do anything wrong.* But he said: *What a ridiculous thing to say. In fact I* only meant that we Kurds must have honour, or we have nothing. I meant that we must remain incorruptible men. I wanted him to remember that in Paris. But no Frenchman will ever understand that. How can he? Europeans don't understand honour.'

'That's true,' MacGregor said.

'I know the worst about these mountains.' Zadko gestured at the horizons around them. 'But we will lose everything if we don't defend our mountains and our cities against everybody. That's why I want to kill that gelded pack-horse the Ilkhani. He makes everything so hopeless.'

They had walked back to the cave mouth, and MacGregor stopped for a moment and leaned against the raw, warm rock, looking out over the hillsides which were covered now with fresh green gorse, alpine moss and heather. He could smell charcoal from the village below and he could hear the slap slap slap of women washing clothes in some muddy pool. The bold raucous laughter of the women told MacGregor all about their vulgar jokes and their open faces and their fierce equality with any man.

Zadko suddenly held MacGregor's arm and listened. There were four shots in quick succession.

'You see. That's what's been happening everywhere we go.'

'What is it?'

'It's Ahmed telling us that there is an Iraqi army unit coming up the asphalt road. They're probably coming from Ardebil.'

'I thought the Iraqis were leaving you alone?'

'They do and they don't,' Zadko said. 'Go and get the Qazi and the Frenchman,' he said. 'We'll have to do something.'

MacGregor went into the cave and called the Qazi, and when they got outside, Zadko told the driver of the hired car to take the Qazi and the Iraqi away from the village, up one of the tracks. Then he put the Frenchman in the back of his blue jeep, and with MacGregor in front nursing rifles he drove down through the village and told his look-out men to fire shots down the valleys to warn the others.

'What's he going to do?' Schramm shouted.

MacGregor did not risk an answer because Zadko had taken them off the road. He went over the steep broken edges and down and across a sliding slope like a downhill skier. Twice they nearly turned over.

'He'll kill us,' Schramm bellowed.

'Just hang on,' MacGregor shouted back. 'And keep quiet.'

When they had plunged downhill through chasms and around boulders Zadko stopped the jeep on a ledge and shouted a few words across a slope. Then he fired a signal shot to some unseen Kurds, and took the groaning jeep back up the perpendicular slope to where they could look down on the asphalt road and see four Iraqi trucks and an armoured car. Zadko fired another shot which echoed in the mountains.

'For Christ's sake explain it,' Schramm said to MacGregor.

MacGregor knew what would follow, and he simply pointed to two mortar shells, bursting on the roadway a few yards in front of the Iraqi armoured car.

Schramm laughed. 'Can you imagine the sort of communication system it would have taken us to organise mortar shots like that?' he said.

'Communication up here is just mutual understanding,' MacGregor said.

The Iraqi column had not taken cover. They could see an officer in the armoured car looking up at the hillsides through field-glasses. Zadko shouted at the top of his voice so that they heard the echo across the valley: 'Mahmoud...'

One more mortar burst followed, landing behind the column this time. They could hear the Iraqi soldiers shouting angrily and quarrelling. But nobody took cover. Then there was a burst of heavy machine-gun fire from the armoured car, not at the mortars but at Zadko who was standing up in full view of the armoured car.

'What's he exposing himself like that for?' Schramm shouted again as the heavy-calibre bullets crumpled rock and dirt around them.

'For God's sake wait,' MacGregor said impatiently. 'It'll explain itself in a minute.'

Now the Iraqi officer and Zadko both stood up in full view of each other and began a bitter shouting match in Arabic, which MacGregor only partly understood.

'What are you doing up here?' Zadko demanded at the top of his voice.

'We're going to the top,' the Iraqi officer shouted back.

'Not up here,' Zadko shouted. 'Why don't you leave us alone? You want to make trouble?'

'What are you firing mortars at me for?'

'You go back and mind your own business for a couple of days,' Zadko shouted. 'You're not supposed to be up here.'

'I'm not going to turn around with your mortars on me.'

Zadko laughed. 'Are you scared, habibi? They won't hurt you.'

'Don't be a bent organ,' the Iraqi shouted back.

Zadko clapped his hand appreciatively. 'Come back in two days' time and we'll be gone. I swear it.'

The Iraqi hesitated a moment, then he leaned down and said something to the crew of his armoured car. MacGregor waited tensely for the heavy-calibre machine-gun to open up again. But Zadko shouted, 'Don't be a fool. I've got fifty men across the road behind you.'

The Iraqi straightened up. 'You've got nothing,' he shouted back, 'and I was asking my driver where he could turn around. So what are you afraid of?'

'Sweetheart...'

'I'll be back on Friday with a lot more stuff than I've got now,' the Iraqi said, 'so get out of the way, Zadko.'

'Don't worry. I don't want to take anything away from you. What use would all that stuff be to me?'

As the column began to back and turn they went on shouting insults at each other which got better and better until Zadko was laughing and slapping his sides in appreciation, not only for his own inventions but for the Iraqi's as well.

MacGregor sat down and let out his breath. 'You were very lucky that time,' he told Zadko.

'Why?'

'Because he could have finished you off if he'd backed away a little.'

'Why should he? We're not quarrelling with the Iraqis at the moment.'

Schramm was standing up now and watching the column roaring off down the asphalt road. 'What made them turn around and go back like that? What did he say to them?'

'He pointed out that we have the advantage,' MacGregor said.

The Frenchman laughed. 'Opera singers,' he said.

The rest of the Kurds were now climbing up the hillside like children, dragging mortars and steel ammunition boxes and tripods; but they were all laughing as if they were taking a circus to pieces.

'You really expect me to make a Kurdish liberation army out of that lot?' Schramm said.

MacGregor knew that if he tried to argue he would make it worse. The truth seemed only too stark and obvious. So how would anyone ever be able to explain to this particular Frenchman the way the Kurds lived and breathed?

When they reached the road Schramm slapped Zadko on the back the way you slap a drunken friend on the back to humour him. 'I'd love to spend six months up here with you, my friend,' he said.

'What did he say?' Zadko asked MacGregor.

263

'He says he would love to stay up here with you for six months.'

'Welcome,' Zadko said, and they got back in the jeep and returned to the village where they waited for darkness when the Qazi and the Iraqi would come down from the slopes where they had been hiding.

MacGregor had to admit to the Qazi that the Frenchman was not impressed.

'He's obviously a soldier,' the Qazi said. 'He probably takes a military view of everything he sees.'

The Iraqi and the Qazi were sitting together in the Qazi's little room. A white petrol lamp hissed from the ceiling between the two bunks. Both men, sitting on the separate bunks opposite each other, seemed to be pushed into the wall with the shadow and the light.

'It's a pity,' the Qazi said sadly.

'Does it really matter?' the Iraqi asked MacGregor.

'Yes, I'm afraid it does,' MacGregor said.

The depression of the room, the place, the village, the howling of some sick saluki in the mountains, the mud outside after a mountain shower, and the deep blackness that grew up like some jungle plant in the vast high plateau around them were all too much for him now.

'Don't be upset,' the Qazi told him. 'You did your best. In any case I've prepared you some letters for the other Frenchman in Paris—Cumont. Perhaps he'll understand what this soldier fails to understand.'

'That's about all we can count on now as far as the French are concerned,' MacGregor said.

The Qazi held the letters in his thin fingers for a moment and said, 'Do you think we should still go on dealing with the French?'

'I keep asking myself that question,' MacGregor told him. 'But I can't see any alternative. There's also a time factor. The French want to get those arms out of France by the end of the month, whatever else happens. And at that point they won't care who gets them.'

'Which obviously means the Ilkhani will get them if we don't persuade the French ourselves.'

'Of course.'

'All right,' the Qazi said. 'We'll stick to the French as long as we can.' And he gave MacGregor the two letters. One confirmed MacGregor's authority to speak for the Committee. The other welcomed the prospect of a commercial agreement with the French, and a long-term future of good relations. 'Do your best with them,' the Qazi said.

'The trouble is that I'm still a bad diplomat,' MacGregor said as he took the letters. 'I don't put the Kurdish case very well to them because I'm simply no good at political argument.'

The Qazi leaned forward to touch his sleeve. 'Whatever you say, they'll believe you. I'm sure of it.'

They were silent for a moment, and MacGregor knew it was time to go. He got up, but the Qazi held him by the arm for a moment.

'The important thing is that the Ilkhani must not get those guns and ammunition. It would set us back years if the old man managed to get his hands on any of it.'

'I understand,' MacGregor said.

'But don't do anything desperate. Don't risk your own safety, or your own family,' the Qazi said. 'I beg you.'

Zadko pushed aside the cotton door and said, 'The Frenchman's trying to leave secretly. He's been trying to bribe Gala.'

'Do you want us to stop him?' the Qazi asked MacGregor.

'No, no,' MacGregor said. 'I don't think I can influence him anyway, so you might as well let him go.'

'If we let him go with Gala,' Zadko pointed out, as if he

265

was reluctant to let the Frenchman go at all, 'how will you get back to Teheran?'

'I don't know. But it's better that I don't go back with him. Actually I was hoping that you could get me across to that old border town of Qarabas,' MacGregor said. 'I can get a bus from there.'

'All right,' Zadko said. 'But we'd better start the moment the Frenchman's gone.'

He began then to say his farewells to the Iraqi, and the Qazi embraced him gently. 'If you hear that we are being attacked,' he said, 'or that we've been killed, or that the Ilkhani has made an agreement with the foreigners, just go on doing whatever you think or feel is necessary. You must go on speaking for us and acting for us until this whole affair is over.'

'Of course,' MacGregor said, and as he left them he saw the Qazi preparing to wash his wounded neck in a plastic basin which he kept under the bed with his books and his fibre suitcase, and a neatly folded green banner of the 1946 revolution.

PART IV

Chapter Twenty-nine

MacGregor sat in Cecie's Citroën and watched the wet English countryside suck itself away into softer English horizons. Cecie's knees and elbows were at work, and even though the French steering wheel was on the wrong side, he felt safe enough to look for the English spring which crowded up everywhere to the edge of the road. Clematis, forsythia and camellias filled suburban gardens. After Rochester, apple blossoms. And after that wet lambs and low-flying crows.

'I forgot to get an extra can for petrol,' Cecie said. 'Every petrol pump in France is closed, so I'll have to get one at Dover.'

France was locked up tight in a general strike. He had come home to a national upheaval. The British press said that nothing was functioning in France, anywhere. Paris had been taken over by the students. Nothing moved, nothing was bought or sold, nothing was received and nothing manufactured. Even MacGregor's jet to Paris had been diverted to London, where he had found Cecie, not Kathy, in the Battersea house watching Paris burn on TV. Kathy had told him on the phone from Paris that she had gone back to look after the two children, but because there was so much fighting in the streets between police and students and crs, Kathy had sent Cecie back to London, while she had stayed on in Paris with Andrew and Aunt Joss. He had expected Kathy to protest when he told her he was bringing Cecie back with him, but she said: 'Oh, bring her back then. She was obviously going to defy me and come back anyway.'

Cecie had heard it on the extension. 'She's quite right,' she said. 'I wasn't going to stay in London another day. I swear it.'

'Well don't say that to your mother,' he told her. 'I'm taking you back, so leave it at that. Don't provoke her.'

'Everything provokes her these days,' Cecie said.

On the ferry, which was empty because no one would risk going through France, Cecie pointed to a man reading the *Evening Standard* whose headline said 'De Gaulle may resign before the plebiscite'.

'What plebiscite?' MacGregor asked her.

'Oh, something for or against the constitution. There's a pitched battle in the streets every day.'

The French roads were so deserted that Cecie drove the old Citroën down the middle of the highways at seventy miles an hour, even through the empty villages. Paris was littered with the wreckage of barricades, burned-out kiosks, uncollected refuse, sawn-off trees, and large drifts of dirty newspapers and cartons.

It was Kathy who opened the big gate for them. 'Where have you been?' she said anxiously. 'I expected you hours ago.'

'The ferry was late and we got lost in the Bois,' Mac-Gregor told her as he opened the other side of the gate so that Cecie could get the Citroën in.

'What were you doing right over on the Bois?'

'We didn't want to risk driving across Paris,' he said.

He was kissed on the cheek, and when he had closed the gates and they were walking up the outside steps he asked her how she was. She said she was perfectly all right.

'I mean your health,' he said.

'There's nothing wrong with my health,' she told him, and he felt a fool for asking.

When he had washed and they were sitting down to the

dinner which she had been keeping hot for them, he asked where Andrew was.

'I sent him home with Jizzy Margaux because she's alone except for the servants. Someone smashed in all the front windows of her house last night. Her husband's in Rome now. He just stays there.'

They ate dinner in silence, and when Cecie had left them to go to bed they sat opposite each other over the walnut table saying nothing, as if this was neither the time nor the place to come to terms with each other after ten days' separation.

'Why didn't you cable me from Teheran?' she asked him.

'I didn't want too many people in Iran to know I was there. I had to get in and out without anybody taking too much notice of me.'

She asked him if he had seen Jamal Janab at the NIOC.

'No, I didn't go near him.'

'Did you go home?'

He shook his head.

'Did the Persians know you went into the Kurdish areas?'

'I don't think so. I did most of my travelling by bus.'

He felt that she wanted to ask him what had happened with the Kurds and he waited tensely. She kept her discipline very well for a little while but then it had to come out.

'They're obviously counting on you again, aren't they?' she said. 'Even more than before. They trapped you again, didn't they?'

'Only for the moment,' he said.

Kathy had a way of holding herself poised with her head a little forward and her natural force and authority somehow packed into the air around her. 'So you're going to go on being single-minded about it,' she said. 'Regardless.'

'Obviously.'

He wanted to ask her what she had been doing for ten days. But he didn't ask, because he decided that anything was all right, almost anything at all, even Guy Moselle, so long as it kept her calm and sensible until he had finished with this business.

'I'm going to bed,' she said.

'I'll wait up for Andrew,' he told her, and she left him sitting in one of the old leathery chairs, so exhausted with tension that he fell asleep. Half an hour later Andrew woke him with a gentle nudge.

'You should be in bed,' he said to his father.

'I waited up to hear what's been happening,' MacGregor said, getting up.

'At the moment two separate things seem to be going on at the same time,' Andrew said. 'It's a fantastic revolution as far as the students are concerned, but to the unions and everybody else it's just a general strike.'

'Aren't they part and parcel of the same thing?'

'They may look as if they are,' Andrew said, 'but in fact they're really quite separate, even though everybody is treating them as one and the same thing.'

'So what happens next?' MacGregor asked as he turned the lights out.

'Good God, I don't know. Nobody does. Did Mama tell you that we read in *Le Monde* that someone had taken another shot at the Qazi when you were there?'

'No, she didn't mention it.'

'She was sick with worry.'

As they stood for a moment on the landing talking in whispers he remembered that Andrew had been to Jizzy Margaux's, and he asked his son if she was all right.

'She wouldn't leave the kitchen,' Andrew said. 'She sent all the servants away and we sat there talking about Iran and Kurds and you. We must have been the only people in the whole of France not arguing about the situation in France. I thought she was trying to keep awake because of the broken windows. I told her not to worry and to go to bed. But she said she couldn't care less if they smashed up the whole house. Then Mama rang and asked her if she wanted me to stay the night. She said No and she just got up and took me downstairs and sent me off.'

'Was she wearing all that maquillage on her face?'

'No. I don't think so. Why?'

'Oh, I just wondered,' MacGregor said and they parted for the night.

Chapter Thirty

His morning view of Paris astonished him. It looked like a wartime city living under siege. Shops were shut, the buses had stopped running, the Métro was closed, pickets were on the Métro entrances, the post offices, on gates and doors and even on the unwashed steps of '*100,000 Chemise*'. Red flags were hanging on balconies, on houses, stuck into the trees and on parking *panneaux* which were bent over like broken lilies.

MacGregor had walked up the boulevards and along the silent quais to Cumont's office in the Department of Procuration. He had telephoned ahead, and though he had not spoken to Cumont, he was told to come anyway. Soldiers with sub-machine-guns were posted outside and inside the courtyard and they wouldn't let him in until he had shown them his passport. Once inside he was not shown up to Cumont's office but into a small musty room, a ministry room, the kind where petitioners at all French ministries were left to *faire l'antichambre*.

'Sit down,' the Frenchman behind the ministry desk said, glancing at MacGregor and fumbling with papers as if no one had ever thought of doing such a thing before. 'Monsieur Cumont is not here, not here at all,' he said. 'Perhaps I can help you. My name is Forrest.'

'My business is with Monsieur Cumont,' MacGregor said. 'When will he be here?'

'I can't really say. But I have all the information here. I know your business with Monsieur Cumont.'

MacGregor glanced at the file under Monsieur Forrest's fingers. 'I don't think I can discuss my business with anyone but Monsieur Cumont,' he said.

'I assure you,' the Frenchman told him, 'that I'm perfectly well-equipped to deal with your business about Kurdistan. It's all here.' Forrest tapped the folder, and MacGregor felt that tapping things with his fingers was Forrest's work.

'It's a very complicated matter, and I can only discuss it with Monsieur Cumont himself.'

MacGregor understood immediately what they were doing to him, but he could remember Lord Essex telling him in Moscow twenty-three years ago that if you knew some Ministry fool was trying to diminish you by putting you on to an underling, 'Never discuss the issue. Just walk out.'

'It's not possible,' Forrest was saying.

MacGregor stood up. 'In that case, there's nothing else I can say.'

Forrest opened the folder to forestall his departure. 'I have been instructed...' he began.

But MacGregor said: 'No. I'll say *Au revoir* to you, Monsieur Forrest.'

'Just a moment,' Forrest got up from his desk and hurried around to MacGregor. 'I'm sorry, but Monsieur Cumont is not here. In fact I was going to tell you that he might not be able to see you at all.'

MacGregor knew he must be careful. 'If you tell me that,' he said, 'I'll be very sorry to hear it, and there's nothing more to say.'

'But wait a little,' Forrest insisted. 'You must know, Monsieur MacGregor, that nobody in France is quite himself at the moment.'

'I understand.'

'There are other difficult problems for all of us. In a few days, when this trouble has been decided...'

'That may be too late,' MacGregor pointed out. 'Monsieur

275

Cumont himself set a deadline. The end of the month.'

'Yes, I know.' Forrest hesitated. 'I'll see what I can do for tomorrow,' he said. 'But I can't promise anything.'

MacGregor thanked him, shook hands, and went out quickly because he knew that if he went on being polite his real disappointment would show, and that would have been a mistake.

But once outside in the street his disappointment had no difficulty getting the better of him because it was obvious that France was too preoccupied with itself to bother with his problem. It was written all around him in the syntax of liberty: *transparence, opacité, étoffement.* As he passed Solférino a student with a khaki sack full of aerosol paint tins was writing on the side of a Métro shelter, *'Un seul privilège, celui du travail. Une seule aristocratie, celle de l'intelligence et du courage.'* The boy kept running out of air-filled paint, and when he tried to continue it with a new tin he was attacked by a small worked-out Frenchman in espadrilles and baggy trousers and carrying a plastic shopping bag. The old man tried to snatch the aerosol tin away.

'Jesuit!' the old man shouted angrily.

The boy went on writing. The old man tried to smear the slogan with his sleeve but it was already dry so he began pushing the boy away.

'It's a scandal,' he shouted. 'A menagerie!'

The boy was obviously afraid of hurting the old man so he snatched up his khaki satchel and walked away, shouting cheerfully behind him, 'Don't be angry, old man. It's all done for you. You don't understand.'

The old man tried again to smear the slogan with his shopping bag, and in his failure he became furious. 'You're all mad with words, aren't you. But you've got nothing to say...' he screamed after the boy. 'Nothing...'

MacGregor did not know whose side to take—the man's or the boy's. The French were quarrelling about France on

every street corner. He passed the Ecole Spéciale de l'Archi-
tecture, and its new stone façade had been painted over
with mock red brick as an insult to its bourgeois formalism,
and a student picket at the gate wearing a battered top hat
with a cockade in it said mockingly to MacGregor as he
passed: 'Peter O'Toole!' It obviously meant something,
but MacGregor didn't know what it was. He didn't understand any of the fragments which seemed to be occupying
everyone at the moment. He only knew that nobody in
France could speak for France, not even the few words he
needed for the Kurds. At the moment there was no France at
all.

But there was always Guy Moselle, who was sitting in the
leather chair in the dining-room of Aunt Joss's, reading
Le Monde. He shook hands and sat down again as Kathy
said quickly that Guy had come for lunch.

'Schramm beat you back,' Moselle said. 'Pity.'

'Is that why Cumont wouldn't see me?' MacGregor asked,
taking the apéritif Kathy gave him.

'I saw Cumont yesterday,' Moselle said, 'and he told me
that Schramm says your Committee is shattered, and is unlikely to get itself off the ground. So Cumont thinks there's
no longer any point in committing himself in that direction.'

As they sat down to a luncheon of cold meat and salad
and a glass of wine, which Moselle wet his lips with and
put down and did not touch again, MacGregor told him
that Schramm couldn't possibly understand the situation in
Kurdistan. 'He simply took everything at face value.'

'Then you'd better convince Cumont of that.'

'I can't convince him through his clerks,' MacGregor said.

'I know,' Moselle said, and questioned him about the
Committee and whether it was really as run-down and exhausted as Schramm seemed to think it was.

'If you feel it might do some good,' Moselle told him,
'I'll fix it for you to see Cumont again.'

277

MacGregor glanced at Kathy, but she wouldn't look at him. She was being busy between them in silent attendance. She filled coffee cups, put sugar in front of them, shifted plates, made sure there was a neutral area on the table between them. But she said nothing, as if they would now have to solve the problems of their peculiar relationships themselves.

'Obviously I need help,' MacGregor said.

'Then I'll arrange it and telephone Kathy,' Moselle said as Kathy left them. 'But what happens this time if you don't get those trucks?'

'Someone will blow them up,' MacGregor said.

'That sounds foolish.'

'Of course. It's a foolish situation.'

Moselle obviously didn't like it at all. 'If you have any influence on such fools, tell them to wait. There's still a strong faction in the Ministry that would gladly give that stuff to your Committee. If you can give Cumont one more push and convince him that Schramm is wrong, you might just succeed.'

Kathy returned wearing a raincoat, ready to go out. 'I'm going down to the Odéon,' she said to Moselle, 'since you and Andrew and everybody else have painted such an insinuating picture of the place.'

'I'll drop you off,' Moselle said, getting up.

'I'll go with you,' MacGregor told them, and he followed them out, taking his raincoat from the hall. 'In fact Kathy and I can walk,' he told Moselle on the steps. 'It's not far.'

They went out through the gate, and when Moselle had disappeared in his inconspicuous little Renault, they walked silently up rue Barbet de Jouy in a light drizzle of rain.

'Which way is it?' MacGregor said to Kathy.

'I thought you knew where it was.'

'It's on the other side of Saint-Germain-des-Prés,' he said, and pushed his hands into his raincoat pockets.

278

'In that case I don't feel like getting wet,' Kathy said, and stopped.

'We'll never find a taxi,' he pointed out.

'Then we should have ridden with Guy. Why did we have to walk?'

He knew then that their safe neutrality was finally coming to an end.

'Oh, come on,' she said impatiently and walked ahead of him, forcing him to follow. 'You obviously want to lecture me, so go ahead.'

He caught up with her.

'If you want to quarrel about Guy Moselle, then go ahead. He sits on your head like a crown of thorns. But you won't really quarrel, will you? You just want to provoke me. You'd like me to bring everything out into the open.'

'Why not?' he said. 'It's better than the way we've been behaving lately.'

'Blame yourself for that,' she told him. 'If I don't care much about your problems it's you that made me feel that way. So don't start accusing me.'

They walked on, side by side, sucked into their raincoats and trying not to bump into each other nor to touch each other. 'I told you,' she said, 'that if you went back to Iran I couldn't answer for the consequences.'

'What's that supposed to mean?'

'Do you want me to be explicit?' she said. 'Do you want me to tell you?'

'Yes,' he said. 'Go ahead.'

'You must be stupid,' she told him. 'It's better left as it is.'

'Then why are you being so provocative about it?'

'Because I'm trying to shake you and shock you out of your stubbornness.'

They avoided a group of students who were marching

half on the footpath and half on the boulevard behind a black anarchist flag.

'You've shocked me,' he told her. 'But I still don't know what you're doing it for.'

'Because you remind me of Mrs Fawzi's stupid dog.'

Mrs Fawzi had been their neighbour in Teheran, and the Fawzis' dog would refuse to let go anything he got his teeth into, even though beaten, kicked or soused with water. 'There's obviously nothing I can do to make you let go this Kurdish mess. It's even worse than you think it is.'

He guessed then that Moselle had told her something more than he had been told himself. 'I can't let go, Kathy. Not yet.'

'Then all I'm trying to do is make you aware of what it's costing you,' she said. 'So think about that.'

'But I told you I'll come back to Europe for good when this is finished. Why don't you let it go at that? Why do you insist on all this upset now, when it's almost over? Just another few weeks...'

'You know very well it isn't only this Kurdish affair that's between us now.'

'I know that,' he said. 'But if I've agreed to stay in Europe,' he repeated stubbornly, 'what more can I do?'

'You can try to understand how I feel.'

'But I do understand.'

'No you don't,' she said as they passed the crowded tables of the Deux Magots where a lot of money and effort was being spent by people proving they were somebody.

'If sleeping with Guy Moselle will rouse you out of that ridiculous submission to the Kurds, then I'll sleep with Guy Moselle.'

'Now you're just being destructive,' he said angrily.

'Of course I'm being destructive. How else can I influence you?'

'But what the devil set you off on this, Kathy? What do you want me to do? What is it?'

'I don't want you to do anything,' she said. 'I simply want you to come back to being what you once were—a simple man of some sort, an individual. Then I'll go back to being what I was.'

'Oh, I'm sick of the individual,' he said. 'I'll never understand it this way.' He waved his hand at the city.

'Too bad,' she said drily as they went up the colonnaded steps of the old Odéon theatre.

They were stopped at the entrance to the theatre by a girl with pony-tail hair and a red armband which said 'Service'. 'If you're a couple of foreign badauds,' she said to them, 'you'd better keep quiet in there. Even Sagan was booed the other day, so just mind your own business.'

MacGregor followed Kathy into the pretty little red plush theatre which had been handed over to the students by Jean Louis Barrault. Its red carpets were clotted with dirt, and they had to walk around the circular passage behind the boxes looking for one they could get into. They stood at the back and looked down on the packed audience of the dimly lit amphitheatre.

There was no organised platform and the stage was sealed off by the safety curtain, across which there was a banner saying 'L'ex-Odéon est une Tribune Libre'. The free tribune was arguing about revolution from the parterre and the boxes and the baignoires. A woman was shouting, 'Don't be provoked,' and another was replying amid catcalls: 'They'll use machine-guns if they have to. I know. I come from a mattress factory.' MacGregor saw Cecie in the front row, sitting with Taha, and shouting from time to time, 'You're right.' 'You're wrong.' He pointed her out to Kathy.

'I know,' she said. 'I saw them when we came in.'

Where was Andrew?

He looked for his son. He found him leaning against the end of the stage with his arm draped casually around the shoulder of a girl who leaned against him affectionately, occasionally pulling the back of his hair.

'You shouldn't be smoking,' a girl said to a bearded student of thirty who was smoking a pipe in the box. 'It's dangerous. . . .'

'*Interdit d'interdire,*' the smoker said. Forbidden to forbid.

They stood uncomfortably for half an hour, and Mac-Gregor lost track of what was being said, because the kind of revolution they were talking about changed with every speaker. But Kathy listened carefully until she said she couldn't stay on her feet any more, and they found their way down a fire escape and out to the street.

'This time you'll have to do something about Cecie,' she said. 'He's going to involve her. . . .'

'Oh, it's not that, Kathy.'

'How do you know it isn't? Taha's a plotter. He'll use Cecie, he'll use anybody. And Cecie's still susceptible.'

'She's over all that,' he said as they went blindly up Saint Germain to Mabillon. He felt now as if the whole city was so loaded with quarrels that he didn't want to look at it any more.

'How do you know she's over it?' Kathy said. 'Do you know what an eighteen-year-old girl is like? Do you know what tortured nonsense goes on in their minds all the time? Particularly Cecie.'

'I told her to find Taha because I want to see him. That's all it is.'

'My God,' she said. 'I wish I had your blind and boundless faith. . . .'

They had reached the dog-leg of the Rue de Rennes, and though she didn't say anything more he knew that she had not yet finished with him. The rain had stopped, and now it was six o'clock and the disorganised streets began to look better because it was time for all the onlookers to go home; to leave the tribunes and to see the rest on TV.

'Why don't you ask me if I've been unfaithful to you or not?' she said to him suddenly.

'You're not going to make me angry saying things like that,' he said. 'So don't try.'

'Why don't you ask me?' she persisted. 'Ask me.'

'You'd never tell me if you were. So why should I ask?'

'And that's all the fuss you're going to make about it?'

'If you go to the couch every night with a loved one,' MacGregor said in Persian to her, 'who nonetheless locks her rose garden against you, there comes a moment when the rose is dead, and the passion is in ruins like a broken water jug.'

'That's a terrible thing to say to me.'

'Nonetheless it's true,' he said. 'You don't want me to touch you these days, do you?'

'How do you know what I want you to do?' she said. 'You don't even ask any more.'

'If I ever ask,' he said, 'you manage to crush me even before I've begun. And if there is a rare moment when you do want to make love, it doesn't help much any more, does it?'

'Well I'll be damned...' she said. 'I can't believe it. My God! After twenty-three years of married life my stumbling husband has finally become sexually explicit. I *must* be succeeding.'

'That's true.'

But Kathy was in tears. 'Why don't you ever understand that I can't help feeling the way I do?' she said. 'I can't help my skin hating you sometimes. It's you ... you ...'

'I understand all that,' he said. 'And I'm sorry. But why do you taunt me with people like Guy Moselle?'

'Because there's a time limit to everything, even marriage. That's what you are risking now. And I want you to know it. All the time.'

They were almost home, and with the habit of a lifetime when children must not know about a quarrel, or a Persian servant must not hear, they would not take the argument inside with them from the street.

'Anyway, you're the one who needs help, not me,' she told him. 'I'll just go on hurting you and provoking you until you start to think of yourself again. With or without me, that's what you need. You need help....'

'Not that kind,' he said.

'Even sexually? Not even that?'

'I'm perfectly normal,' he said.

'So it is all my fault.'

'Yes, it is. You want something I can't give you, Kathy. I'll never be able to give it to you when you're like this.'

She was in tears again, and as they opened the gate she said to him: 'I hate that cold and secretive and singular and stubborn mind of yours. I hate it now ... I hate it...'

Chapter Thirty-one

While France argued, Cumont met MacGregor in one of the rich but aseptic little rooms of Moselle's banking offices in Pillet-Will. Cumont apologised for not seeing him on his visit to the office in the Department of Procuration. 'But the situation had already changed a great deal since I saw you last.'

'That's why I wanted to talk to you,' MacGregor told him.

'I've already spoken to Schramm,' Cumont said. 'So I have a lot more information now than I had before, and he's convinced that your Kurdish Committee is not a real force.'

'Schramm's information can be wrong.'

'Of course.'

'Schramm had no possible way of judging whether the Committee is a force in Kurdistan or not,' MacGregor said. 'He only saw it as a soldier, and under very difficult circumstances.'

Cumont was sipping orange juice, and MacGregor was hot as he watched Cumont's eyes wandering on a patient route from orange juice to table and wall, and to his fine yellow fingers. It was an old man's tour of the room.

'I know that Schramm's judgement is a military one,' Cumont said. 'But that's the only one that can count at the moment, because it is the only effective measurement we have for the future prospects of your Committee.'

MacGregor knew he would never be able to argue the sense and justice of the Kurdish cause, because he did not know what the real arguments were to a European mind. 'All I can say,' he said to Cumont, 'is that whatever you decide now is going to be remembered for a very long time in Kurdistan.'

'Of course,' Cumont said. 'But France simply cannot commit herself now to something that might emerge in decades to come.'

'Why not?'

'It isn't practical. Moreover...'

Cumont got up and poured some orange juice from a jug on the table under the window and came back. 'There are other rivalries in this that France can't ignore. I have to tell you that.'

'What other rivalries?'

'We now have a better picture of the sort of grip the Americans and the British still have on the area, even among the Kurds themselves.'

'You mean the Ilkhani?'

'I mean that France couldn't get very far alone in the circumstances. It wouldn't be worth the risk.'

MacGregor made a Persian gesture of impatience. 'I don't suppose I could interest you in the justice of the Kurdish cause,' he said.

'You could interest me,' Cumont told him gently, 'but justice is never a good argument in international politics. I thought you knew that.'

'All right,' MacGregor said. 'Look at it in another way. You have those arms in Marseilles. They are in your hands. If you let them go to the Ilkhani the Committee will always blame France for arming a hostile faction.'

'The arms have simply passed through France,' Cumont said. 'Nothing more.'

'In that case, impound them or destroy them,' MacGregor suggested, suddenly feeling that the pale blue light of

Moselle's little banking chamber made this sort of bargaining natural and normal.

'I haven't any legal right to do anything like that,' Cumont said.

'So far everybody seems to have a legal right here except the Kurds,' MacGregor said. 'It's a European madness.'

'The only right I can consider here is the right of France.'

MacGregor got up. 'In that case the Kurds will just have to deal with those trucks in their own way.'

'I'll ignore that suggestion.'

'As you please.'

Cumont held him back. 'I'm very sorry that we can't do this, Monsieur MacGregor. I genuinely am. But we can't risk it in the face of other interests which are much stronger than ours, and also better able to do what they like.'

'Goodbye,' MacGregor said.

'Wait a minute,' Cumont said. 'There's one other way of doing this.'

He steered MacGregor firmly by the elbow towards a double white door which opened into two more small rooms in Moselle's domestic counting house. One was a thickly-carpeted board-room and the other was a little drawing-room where a board could relax, with couches and deep armchairs and glass coffee tables with drinks and coffee and fruit. He saw Guy Moselle first because Moselle was on his feet walking towards them. But then he saw Lord Essex sitting in a patch of sun near the window with his head back as if he were sunbathing on a beach. The American, Caspian, was sitting, almost squatting, in a deep armchair next to Essex, and he had a map across his knees. Caspian looked up and winked at MacGregor. Two other men, whom MacGregor had never seen before, were a little apart and leaning over a low coffee table, their black portfolios zipped open in front of them like experts in waiting.

'No luck?' Moselle half-whispered to MacGregor with a little shrug. 'Maybe it's just as well. This may be better.'

Essex raised a hand languidly, and Caspian almost made fun of Essex by doing the same thing with his plump cynical fingers.

'This is Mr van Klop and Herr Deutler,' Moselle said of the two strangers. 'They are from the funding secretariat of the Inter-international Bank.'

MacGregor was offered a red leather chair near the long coffee table, and the others watched him silently. They had already had their martinis, and Moselle gave MacGregor a cold glass with beads of sweat rimming the top. In the silence Caspian whistled for MacGregor's benefit a Persian song which said: 'The mountains are cold, so the wolves are staring hungrily at me with frozen eyes...'

Essex said, 'I suppose the best way to approach you on this, MacGregor, is to come right out with it. So what we want to know is do you still have the credentials of the Kurdish Committee? Do you still claim the right to speak for them?'

'Of course.'

'How can you qualify that?'

'I have a letter of authority from the Qazi, if that's what you're looking for,' MacGregor said.

'In Persian?'

'No. In French.'

'Oh, let's skip all that guff, Harold,' Caspian said to Essex. 'I can vouch myself for MacGregor's Kurdish bona-fides. So let's get on with it.'

'All right, I'll try again,' Essex said. 'We all know what the situation is like in those mountains now, MacGregor, so we've worked out a rough plan for giving the Kurds some sort of elementary federation.'

'You've worked out a plan....'

'Yes. And if you're willing to take the idea back to your friends, and if they accept it in principle, then we are ready to organise considerable financial aid and investment for them as part of the deal.'

'Who exactly is planning all this?' MacGregor asked, looking around him.

Six men in the little drawing-room seemed to wait for one of them to give an answer.

'You're a Scot,' Caspian said. 'You know all about porridge.'

'Caspian's exaggerating,' Essex said. 'We're all interested parties.'

'Where are the Iranians and the Turks? I don't see them.'

'They'll agree to anything we propose here,' Essex said.

'In that case what are you proposing?'

'It's quite a simple plan,' Essex said. 'We want your Kurdish Committee to set up a sort of loose federation which will include all, or most of, the Kurds in Iraq, Iran and maybe Turkey. Of course it's always a complicated business deciding where such a disparate sort of federation is to be administered from, but we think this one could be organised and administered from some central place—probably a Kurdish town in Iran. Now wait...' Essex said to MacGregor before he could ask a question. 'What we are thinking of is an arrangement that will allow the Kurds some kind of dual status....'

'You're wasting your time,' MacGregor said.

'... On the one hand,' Essex went on, 'all Kurds will remain as minorities in their present parent states, as they are now, and they will go on accepting the existing laws and codes of each country. But they will also have an independent central body of their own, which can deal with economic and political problems, and which will be able to speak for all Kurds. And that is where we could offer a great deal of help, technical as well as financial.'

'Is that what you want me to take back to the Committee?' MacGregor asked.

'In essence, yes.'

'I came to Europe in the first place,' he told Essex, 'to

recover money which was stolen from the Kurds. Why don't
we discuss that first.'

Essex looked at Moselle and then at Caspian. 'That's
a dead subject, MacGregor. Nothing to talk about.'

MacGregor plunged on. 'Then forget the money,' he said,
'and let's talk about the two trucks of arms which the money
bought and paid for.'

'That too is a dead subject,' Essex said.

'In that case so is your so-called federation. The Kurds
have heard all that a hundred times before anyway.'

'Just a minute,' Caspian said as Essex was about to go
on. 'Who are we kidding, Harold? The truth is, MacGregor,
that brutal situations like this one can only have brutal
solutions. The old Ilkhani is going to get those bloody
guns, because everybody here wants the Ilkhani to get
them. And rather than try to blackmail you with lying
promises to the contrary, you might as well face the truth.'

MacGregor was grateful for that, even though it made
him feel as if a long, long period of his life had finally
come to an end. 'That's all I wanted to know,' he said to
Caspian. 'So I don't suppose there is anything more to say.'

'Now don't go off feeling hurt,' Caspian told him in a
friendly way. 'Think about it for a bit. What we're offering
you, crude as it is, will more than make up for the Ilkhani
getting that handful of hardware.'

'Maybe. But it's not what the Kurds have in mind.'

'All right. It's a horse trade,' Caspian said. 'But at least
we're offering to do a deal with your Committee if they'll
do a deal with us. That's not bad, MacGregor. Not bad at
all.'

'But it wouldn't impress the Qazi,' he told Caspian.

'Why not?'

'Because all you're suggesting is a sort of Saigon solution.'

'But listen,' Caspian appealed. 'Can you honestly see any
alternative for the Kurds? Just ask yourself that.'

'I don't know. But no Kurd is going to consider himself

independent if you're telling him that he has to accept your sort of guidance, or go on obeying Turkish or Iranian laws which have always oppressed them. They wouldn't listen, and you know it.'

'Okay. It's not so good. But we're not offering you the moon. Just a beginning.'

MacGregor leaned forward to an empty glass, but when Moselle filled it for him he decided not to touch it. He glanced at Moselle, another honest man like Caspian. Perhaps they were all honest men. In any case the only important man here was Caspian, and it was satisfying after all these years to see Essex finally diminished by his historical replacement. 'Do you know what's really wrong with your proposition?' he said to Caspian.

'Christ yes, but . . .'

'You expect the Kurds to sit down with the wolves that eat the chickens that pick out the eyes of the children?' he said in Persian to Caspian.

Caspian laughed. 'I'd forgotten that one.'

'Well, isn't it true?'

'Of course it's true,' Caspian said. 'But the trouble is you're still dreaming, MacGregor. Absolute Kurdish independence is not practical. It's a hopeless proposition at the moment, and that's something *you* know as well as I do.'

'Yes, but we'll never admit it,' MacGregor said, and he realised that he liked this American because he could talk to him honestly. 'It's more than just a practical problem.'

'Well, whatever it is, why don't you at least take the suggestion back to the old man?'

MacGregor shook his head. 'I don't think so.'

'Why not?'

'Because I know what it really means.'

'You're making a mistake,' Caspian insisted. 'Maybe they'd listen.'

'Maybe. But not coming from me.'

'Look. We're bound to win the point one way or the

other,' Caspian persisted. 'We can easily keep the Qazi locked up in those empty mountains.'

'Don't be too sure,' MacGregor said. 'It's bad at the moment, but you can't occupy every hill and valley of that place, not even with the Ilkhani.'

'There are other ways.' Caspian turned to Moselle then and said, 'Where's the Greek or whatever he is?'

'Just a moment,' Moselle said.

The Frenchman opened a side door and called someone. 'The Greek' came in, a little fat man like Punch; his head was all out of proportion and he obviously wasn't Greek.

'Monsieur, monsieur, monsieur,' he said, bowing to each one of them.

'This is Suleiman,' Caspian said without looking at him. 'He's one of the signatories of that concession agreement which your Committee gave to the Leanco Company. He's the one who originally paid the Committee the money you were trying to locate. You know about him?'

'Of course.'

'In effect,' Caspian said, 'we have bought from him a big enough piece of the Leanco agreement to get the whole concession. Perfectly legal....'

'Even that?' MacGregor said.

'Yeah. Even that.'

MacGregor got up. 'Where did I leave my raincoat?' he asked Moselle.

'Now listen, MacGregor,' Essex said. 'You can't just walk out like that.'

MacGregor pulled on his coat. 'Sorry,' he said to Caspian. 'But you and I ... Oh well...'

And as Moselle showed him to the door he said quietly to MacGregor 'I'm sorry it finally had to end this way. But it was a very good try, MacGregor. A very good try.'

Chapter Thirty-two

When MacGregor told Kathy that it was finally over and that he had failed, she let out a long breath. 'Well, thank God for that.' But then she added, 'Anyway, the Chinese are right. The only way the Kurds will ever change their condition is if they do it themselves without outside help. And nothing you could have done, one way or the other, would have made that much difference.'

'The Chinese only got back China,' he said, 'after the Japanese had been defeated by considerable outside help.'

'All right,' she said. 'I'm not going to argue politics. I'll never argue with you about it again, just so long as you've finished with it.'

It was after seven, and they were dressing to go to Jizzy Margaux's for dinner. Kathy held up a stocking that needed to be inspected closely, but she was inspecting him instead. 'I suppose you *have* finished with it?' she said.

He waited a long time before deciding to be honest about it. 'No. Not quite,' he replied.

She came across the room and stood near him. 'What more can you do now? What else is there?'

'I don't know yet,' he said. 'But it's a little like the situation in France. Everybody is on the streets and the students are talking revolution, but the situation remains exactly what it was before.'

'I don't see what that's got to do with it?'

'We all seem to be dealing with an invisible opponent, some untouchable enemy.'

'If you've failed, you've failed,' she insisted, going back to her dressing. 'So let's pack up now and go back to London. Tomorrow.'

'No. I can't go yet,' he told her.

'Why not? What are you holding on to now?'

'I'm not holding on to anything. But those arms are still in Marseilles, and the Ilkhani is going to get them. I can't just walk away and leave it like that.'

'Oh yes you can,' she said before he had finished the sentence. She began to pull on one of the stockings as if it were made of iron. 'I know exactly what's in your mind,' she burst out, 'so don't even think of it.'

He said he was not thinking of anything at all.

'They know very well what Taha plans to do,' she warned him. 'And you're not going to have anything to do with it. That's when I say No.'

'All right,' he said. 'But I don't see what else can be done.'

She did not argue. 'Leave it just as it is,' she warned him. 'I don't even want to talk about it, because I'm calm now and I'm going to stay that way.'

He said 'All right,' and went downstairs to wait for her. Cecie had saved fifty litres of rationed petrol in a drum in the old stables in the courtyard, and when MacGregor went outside she was spitting out petrol which she had sucked into her mouth when she had siphoned it out.

'Disgusting stuff,' she said.

She was still spitting and coughing when Kathy came down, and Kathy said, 'She should have been a boy.'

'She's all right as a girl,' he said, knowing he had to fit in with Kathy's mood. There was no other way to behave now.

Cecie drove them through the empty Left Bank streets which were still under siege and waiting for catastrophe. The whole quartier now looked like an empty fairground. Rubbish and papers blew up and down the Sunday boulevards, and people wandered about collecting in argumentative groups as if they were unable to decide what to do or what to expect.

'I'll be at the atelier,' Cecie told him as she roared off. She was sulking because she had had to wait for them and because she had been anxious to get back to her *collectif* and because she knew they were being silent and careful with each other which she thought wasteful and silly.

At the house in Rue Jean Goujon Jizzy met them at the little lift that came up in a cage to the Japanese room, and when she saw MacGregor she put her hand up to her naked face and said: 'You see?'

Jizzy was wearing a very simple black dress, so simple that a fortune was cut and sewn into its bias and hem and waistline. She rubbed cheeks with Kathy and then she pushed her arm through MacGregor's and whispered in English: 'This dinner party is not my idea. I hate all this French community of eating. It was Guy's idea because he wants to make sure that you will all be friends, no matter what they did to you today. Guy doesn't want a mess. But I don't believe any of it. Look. There's my husband.'

Aristide Margaux was a thin, swaying, slightly alcoholic Frenchman who looked closely at everything with strained eyes. He shook hands carelessly, and MacGregor was passed on to the rest of the guests: Moselle, Lord Essex, Cumont and Madame Cumont. It was the cocktail hour and Jizzy had already arranged a chair for Kathy between the Cumonts, and one for himself next to Moselle. When the bonne brought a tray with a dry martini on it Jizzy said to the girl: 'No martini for Monsieur. Get him some vermouth.'

Moselle raised his eyebrows.

Then Essex took a new unlit pipe out of his mouth. 'Is Jizzy saving you from the gin mill, MacGregor?' he said.

'It looks like it,' MacGregor replied.

The girl put the vermouth on a table near MacGregor

and he sat still and listened to the French discussing their torn and tattered France. He listened to Cumont and Moselle and Aristide Margaux's thickened voice, and Mac-Gregor knew that France had become a strange copy of everybody. Everybody talked of France, and France talked of itself. The army, they said, was ringed around Paris. Mitterand was a fool. Mendès-France was waiting for a white horse.

'It depends on the communists,' Cumont said.

'But why the students, always the students?' Essex wanted to know.

'Because they've been trying for years to get some sort of reform in our archaic system of higher education,' Moselle said.

Jizzy told him it was time for dinner, and MacGregor knew Jizzy was going to rescue him. He was seated on her right. Opposite him was Essex and then Kathy and Cumont, and Aristide Margaux at the other end with Guy Moselle and Madame Cumont on his own side. Margaux stayed silent and bored.

'I separated Kathy and Guy,' Jizzy said to him as he glanced down the table, 'so that they'll have to talk to each other right across the table if they want to talk at all.'

'Don't start worrying about Kathy,' he said, 'she'll be all right.'

When the first course came, an avocado, Jizzy dug her spoonlike fork into it as if it were a piece of wood. 'Kathy also needs some protection,' she insisted, 'because it's always the man's presence that corrupts. Can't you go back to London and take her with you?'

'Not yet. I can't leave Paris now.'

'Then please don't wait too long,' she said. 'Guy is poised for something. I can feel it.'

She was leaning forward and talking to him with her protected eyes, her face and her body, ignoring the rest of her guests who ate and talked and watched and did what they liked. MacGregor managed to look away from her for a moment and he saw Essex talking to Cumont's very bronzed wife but at the same time watching Jizzy with interest. MacGregor knew what Essex was looking for. Was there something between MacGregor and this untouchable French beauty? Like every man who was ever face to face with Jizzy, Essex was obviously absorbed by her extraordinary beauty and he was asking himself why, for God's sake, was MacGregor being so favoured?

'They're going to be cruel to you,' Jizzy was telling MacGregor. 'They're all getting ready for it, so be careful.'

'There's nothing much left to be cruel about,' he told her.

'They'll find something,' she said. 'They're just waiting. So talk to me so that they can leave you alone. Talk.'

He laughed. 'What about?'

'Anything.'

'They say in Persian that if you talk for talk's sake you become defenceless even against a moth.'

Jizzy laughed. 'Then look at my silent husband. He'll never be knocked over by a moth. Won't you be glad to get out of this stupid sort of life?' She swept her hand towards the table.

'Leave them alone, Jizzy,' he told her. 'You're being too hard on them.'

'You don't understand,' Jizzy said to him. 'Tomorrow, I'm going to give it all up. You've convinced me. I knew from the first you would.'

MacGregor could see that Essex was unashamedly trying to hear what they were talking about. 'How did I convince you?' he asked her. 'What on earth did I say?'

'You didn't say anything,' she told him. 'I trust you, that's all. Tomorrow all this goes too.' Her long, freckled fingers went up to her coiffeured hair.

'You're not going to cut it off?' he said. 'No, Jizzy.'

'Just no more coiffeur. Never again. I don't need it, do I?'

'You don't need anything. In fact if you did cut it off it wouldn't make any difference.'

Jizzy put her hand across the corner of the table and tugged happily at his sleeve. 'It's extraordinary to hear things like that from you,' she said. 'I'd hate it from someone else.'

'But it's true,' he said.

'What are you two talking about up there?' Kathy demanded then, and MacGregor realised how utterly absorbed they had been in each other.

Everybody else at the table now stopped their own affairs to hear what he would say. He stared fixedly at the fish which was on a plate in front of him, and he wondered how it got there. Where was the uneaten avocado?

'We were talking politics, like everyone else,' Jizzy said.

'What politics?' Kathy asked.

'My politics,' Jizzy said.

'I didn't know you had any,' her husband said to her in French.

'Don't be stupid, Aro.'

'Well, what are your politics, Jizzy?' Kathy asked.

'Jizzy's a royalist, like Guy,' Cumont said good-naturedly.

'I'm nothing like Guy,' Jizzy said. 'Not a thing.'

'Jizzy is quite beyond politics,' Guy told them. 'She always was.'

'No I'm not,' Jizzy said. 'But at least I'm not a Royalist, nor even a Gaullist like the rest of you.'

'*Tiens!* Then what were you at the last election?'

'I wasn't a Gaullist.'

'A month ago, Jizzy, *ma chère*, you were denouncing Cohn-Bendit,' Madame Cumont reminded her. 'Wasn't that Gaullist talk?'

'What a silly thing to say, Marie-José. I don't like Cohn-Bendit,' Jizzy mocked. 'Who does? The trouble is you all wear political overcoats, but I keep myself quite naked.'

'That's a lovely condition to be in,' Essex said, 'and I'm sure MacGregor approves of it.'

They laughed and MacGregor realised that Jizzy had been switching their attention away from him, whereas Essex was determinedly switching it back again.

'Well, MacGregor's not naked,' Guy Moselle said. 'The English non-conformist, the famous Scotch Cameronian heresy—always morally *engagé*.'

'No, no,' Essex argued. 'MacGregor really despises politics,' he told them. 'Isn't that so, MacGregor? Now come on. Answer.'

'Why should I despise politics?' MacGregor said.

They waited for more.

'Is that all you're going to say?' Cumont asked him. '*Et alors* . . .'

'I don't despise politics,' MacGregor repeated firmly, trying not to be baited. 'Moreover, you all know it very well.'

'Explanations, MacGregor!' Essex said. 'They are due.'

'What are you saying?' Jizzy almost shouted at Essex. 'Why should he explain anything?'

'Because words mean something, Jizzy,' Essex said, suddenly troubled to be on the wrong side of a beautiful woman.

'Pascal said that an honest man's politics are always best unspoken.'

Moselle dropped his knife and fork on his plate. 'He said no such thing, Jizzy,' he told her indignantly.

'Then it was Lamartine.'

'Nonsense.'

'Then who cares who said it?'

'Nobody cares, my dear,' Essex said gently. 'All I'm trying to do is find out what MacGregor's attitudes are,' Essex said. 'After all, this is a rather political city at the moment.'

'He does what he has to do,' Jizzy told Essex. 'That's his attitude.'

Essex laughed. 'He does what?'

'He does what you can't do,' Jizzy told him. 'That's obvious.'

'You mean shooting Turks?' Essex said cheerfully.

'Why not?' Jizzy said contemptuously. 'If he shoots Turks at least they are dead. But at least he's done it and doesn't talk himself silly about it.'

'Nonetheless,' Essex insisted, obviously stung, 'things like that need explanations. Don't you agree, MacGregor?'

MacGregor had no chance to reply.

'An explanation of anything at a dinner table like this would only be a lie,' Jizzy told Essex.

'Then let him lie for himself,' Kathy told Jizzy, and Jizzy's speared fingers and naked eyelids and the rapid knots she tied in the French language were collected and ready to defend him even against Kathy. But MacGregor stopped her.

'I don't even know what you're all talking about,' he said to Essex.

'We're talking about you, sweetheart,' Kathy said sweetly. 'Or didn't you hear it?'

Again they laughed, except for Margaux who ignored everything.

'Don't explain yourself,' Jizzy ordered MacGregor. 'Never explain to them.'

'But why, in God's name, are you protecting him, Jizzy?' Kathy demanded. 'He can talk. He can look after himself.'

They were being served with delicate little pot roasts in individual copper ramequins, and as the little pots were put in front of them they were still crackling with heat and pressure.

'They're just teasing me, Jizzy,' MacGregor said. 'So let them be.'

'But I'm not teasing,' Essex insisted. 'I'm quite serious.'

'About what?' MacGregor asked him.

'I'd honestly like to know how you divide yourself in two. Half east and half west. Or half scientist and half Turk-killer. Half and half of everything, MacGregor. So which

300

one are you? For instance, which half of you is going to do something about those trucks or lorries, or whatever they are, filled with guns for your Kurds? After all, that's why you're here.'

'What am I supposed to do with them?' MacGregor asked.

'That's a question for you, not for me. And if you'd only answer it we would all have a clue to the way you really think.'

MacGregor looked at Cumont and then at Essex. 'Those trucks are out of our hands,' he said. 'You saw to that,' he said to Essex. 'There's nothing more to say. You got them.'

'I did?'

'You or Flanders. It's the same thing,' MacGregor said, suppressing his anger.

'Well, since some of your Kurdish friends have a plan to blow those trucks sky high, why don't you tell us about that?'

'I know nothing about it,' MacGregor said, 'and even if I did I don't think I'd be here talking about it. So there's nothing to tell you.'

'I would hope not,' Cumont said with a little laugh.

But Jizzy was furious again. 'You're right,' she said. 'They're wrong. Don't tell them anything,' she told Mac-Gregor. 'Don't ever tell them anything.'

This time it was Kathy who interrupted sharply. 'Jizzy. He can't tell them what he doesn't know. And he knows nothing about those trucks.'

'Personally,' Cumont said, 'I don't care what you do about that wretched arms shipment, providing you don't do anything about it on French soil.'

That should have been the end of it, because they all looked at Jizzy and knew that they would be in danger from the cat in her cage if they pursued it.

But Essex refused to let it go. 'As I see it,' he said to MacGregor, 'you either have to arrange for those trucks to be destroyed or you'll be going back to Iran with your tail between your legs.'

MacGregor had already burned his tongue twice on the little pot roast, and he was being cautious and preoccupied with his fork as they waited for him to defend himself. 'You're quite right,' he said to Essex.

'Oh, but this is ridiculous,' Kathy put in angrily. 'Ivre is not even going back to Iran. He's finished with Iran for good.'

'Oh? Oh?'

'We're going to stay in Europe, and there's nothing more to be said, so let's drop it.'

Jizzy pretended to be shocked by the news. 'You can't be serious, Kathy.'

'Of course I'm serious.'

Cumont raised his glass of burgundy. 'To the end, then, of a fascinating and romantic little episode.'

Again that should have been the end of it but Essex seemed determined to defend something vital and personal against MacGregor. 'I've known MacGregor for more than twenty years,' he said, 'and I don't think he gives up quite so easily.'

'This time he will,' Kathy replied.

'Now, now, Kathy. Are you also afraid to let him speak for himself?'

'Kathy's right,' MacGregor told them. 'We are staying in Europe.'

'So let's drop the subject,' Kathy said again, 'because it's nobody's business but our own.'

'It's my fault and I apologise,' Essex said.

'Yes, it was your fault,' Kathy told him. 'You seem to be afraid that he was finally going to beat you at something.'

'I think you are all stupid...' Jizzy began.

But MacGregor touched her lightly on the elbow to silence her, and she shrugged and said, 'Well, I don't think it's all over. Nor does Guy. He told me....'

302

'I didn't tell you anything,' Moselle said sharply. 'And it *is* all over as far as this conversation is concerned. So drop it, Jizzy.'

'Orders from Kathy,' Jizzy said contemptuously to Mac-Gregor who had decided, after one long look at the men around him, that tomorrow he would find Taha and plan with him the best way of destroying those trucks.

Chapter Thirty-three

But Taha had disappeared. Neither Andrew nor Cecie knew where he was. He was not in the room he shared with the Kurdish medical student, and the Kurd MacGregor found there next day didn't know where he was except that he was out of Paris. The Kurds selling pamphlets in the crowded Sorbonne courtyard didn't know.

'I think he went to Geneva,' one of them said.

'No. He's in Paris,' the other one argued. 'I swear it.'

MacGregor guessed that he was in Marseilles, and he went home to listen to the two o'clock news, wondering if Taha had already blown up the trucks and if there would be some report of it. But there was only the news of the national crisis: no bread in Toulouse; the strike was complete in Le Havre and twenty thousand workers had marched to the centre of the city; footballers of France had refused to recognise the government sports centres; and nine million people in France were now on strike. Today, at the Charléty stadium where the students were meeting. Mendès-France was expected, finally, to declare himself.

MacGregor was pacing around the gravel when Marin shuffled out of the coach-house and gave him an envelope. 'I found it under the gate,' Marin said. It was a note in Persian from Taha, telling MacGregor to meet him at the Sorbonne, under the elbow of Victor Hugo, before five o'clock. It was very important.

He didn't bother to tell Kathy where he was going but

pushed the gate open and hurried away, and only when he was on Rue Vaneau did he realise that nobody had been waiting to accost him outside the gate. Were they so sure of their victory now that they could abandon their harassments and leave him alone?

He walked down the deserted Rue de Rennes and cut across the Jardin to the Sorbonne. But when he got into the crowded courtyard he had to push his way through the students who were talking and arguing in groups, or crowded around the hundred factional bookstalls set up around the walls. He stood on the steps under Victor Hugo and noticed that the old stone man had red flags stuck in his elbows. He waited patiently, watching a group of student revolutionaries burning something to ashes in the courtyard.

'Uncle...'

Taha looked tired, but his eyes were still able to mock everything less than himself, and even his threadbare clothes looked more and more like the careless skin of a dedicated man.

'I was told you were out of Paris,' MacGregor said.

'I was. Listen, Uncle. We'll go through the Amphitheatre so that nobody can watch where you're going to.'

He turned quickly and MacGregor followed him through the courtyard into the Sorbonne, and into the busy old Grand Amphitheatre which was packed to the walls with student revolutionaries, onlookers, foreigners, *badauds* and secret policemen. On the platform, seated at an old desk, was a bearded student in a maroon jersey holding a microphone and squeezing condensed milk from a tube into his mouth. He was shouting into the microphone: 'I will now read this.' He waved a duplicated sheet at them. 'It's a declaration just issued by the Committee of the Enraged, and it says,' (he held it at arm's length), 'Revolution ceases the moment it becomes necessary to sacrifice oneself for it. Those people who speak of revolution and class struggle...'

(he looked up significantly at the auditorium and shouted angrily for silence) '... without referring explicitly to daily life, without understanding that there is subversion in love, and affirmation in a refusal of constraint—those people have the mouth of a cadavre. This is signed by the Committee of the Enraged, and by the Internationale of Situationists.'

There was a lot of noise from the floor as they reached the door on the other side and went out, left the Amphitheatre and walked down under the dark arches, past a student guard with a baton who knew Taha and who let them go down another floor of grimy steps. They avoided a Roneo machine in the dingy corridors which was slapping and click-clacking as it turned out material which covered the walls of the corridors, and they had to turn around lavatories and statues until finally they went into what had obviously been the Sorbonne's morgue for old furniture, desks, chairs, bookcases and unwanted busts of forgotten scholars. Taha closed the door behind them and turned on a light, and he immediately began to unfold a document he had been carrying.

'All right, Uncle,' Taha said with his dry little tiger's smile. 'How did your persuasions go?'

'They didn't,' MacGregor said. 'The trucks and the money have gone to the Ilkhani. I failed to get anything at all.'

'I knew it,' Taha said with a little shrug.

'Are you being cynical or did you actually know?'

'Of course I knew. Everybody knows.'

'Then I suppose you've got some sort of plan of your own,' MacGregor said.

'A plan for what? You mean a plan for myself?'

'I don't know. I'm asking you,' MacGregor said.

'Of course we're planning something. Are you saying that you are now willing to help us?'

'Why not?' MacGregor said. 'There's nothing else I can do now.'

Taha inspected him. 'Would you do exactly what we asked you to do?'

'No.'

Taha smiled a little.

'But I'll do anything within reason,' MacGregor added, 'so don't try to be too clever, Taha.'

'I think you are finally listening to us, Uncle,' Taha suggested.

'Perhaps.'

'You are agreeing with us....'

'Not at all,' MacGregor interrupted. 'If anything it's a gesture of despair because I wasn't able to do anything. And something ought to be done.'

They could hear feet shuffling on the gritty stairs outside in the cellars. Someone tried the door.

'Go away,' Taha shouted in French.

They sat down at an old metal table and Taha spread out the documents he had kept in his hand. 'Unfortunately you're too late to help us with those trucks now,' he told MacGregor. 'They've been taken away again.'

'I expected that. But where to?'

'The dockyard at Toulon.'

'That's a naval dockyard,' MacGregor said. 'You'll never get in there.'

'Maybe ... Maybe...'

Taha pushed the papers towards MacGregor who read the faint and flimsy duplicate loading instructions and manifests issued by the Port Captain of the Naval Dockyard at Toulon to the Master of the Greek ship *Alexandre Metaxas*.

'They're going to unload it all at Eshek, the Turkish port in the Black Sea. Then they'll be shipped overland to the Ilkhani.'

'Through Turkey?'

'Of course. Doesn't that tell you something about that old bastard? Is there a true Kurd who would even touch the hand of a government Turk? And now they're actually going to deliver the arms to him.'

'It's hard to believe, even for the Ilkhani,' MacGregor said. 'Are you sure, Taha?'

Taha pulled his moustache until its bristly roots became tiny spikes. Taha had never been bitter. He would never be so wasteful or self-indulgent. But he almost gave way to it for a moment, before he recovered and smiled again. 'Do you think Kurds can ever keep anything to themselves? Do you know how stupid those Kurds from Geneva are? That collection of arses who follow Dubas like dogs?'

MacGregor waited, knowing that Taha had something more to offer, or something to ask, or something to plot.

'What we want is your help at the other end of all this,' he said.

'In Turkey?'

'No. No. With the Qazi and the Committee.'

'You don't expect me to go back and ...'

'Wait,' Taha interrupted. 'We know that Dubas himself is going to take those arms across Turkey. He's going to use the new Turkish road from Eshek to Shahpur, crossing into Iran along the Qotur valley.'

'So?'

'That's where we intend to ambush him.'

'With what? Half a dozen students?' MacGregor said. 'The Ilkhani will be waiting there with every man he's got under arms.'

'That's why we want you to help.'

'How?'

'Will you go back to the Qazi and to my father and persuade them to attack the Ilkhani before he gets there— to draw him off?'

'They wouldn't even listen to me,' MacGregor pointed out.

'Why not?'

'Because attacking the Ilkhani is exactly what the Europeans want. Kurds fighting Kurds again. I'd never be able to persuade the Qazi to do it. Why do you think he's hiding away in those Iraqi mountains?'

'You could persuade him,' Taha insisted.

'No I could not. In any case,' he went on, 'they're too weak now to do anything as ambitious as that. They're both worn out, Taha.'

'Listen, Uncle. They know very well that if the Ilkhani gets those arms he'll be killing us all inside a month, like a butcher slaughtering goats. So what's the alternative? Tell me.'

MacGregor felt his spirit soaking up the wrong atmosphere in this dirty and depressing little room. He could hear the faint cries and shouts of the revolutionaries above them in the Amphitheatre. 'I suppose you're right,' he said. 'Of course you're right. But what makes you think they'll listen to me if I tell them to attack the Ilkhani? I'm not a soldier and I'm not a Kurd.'

'The Qazi trusts you as much as he trusts my father,' Taha said. 'If you explain the situation to him he'll understand it. In fact you're the only one who could make him understand.'

'I don't agree. Anyway, what do you expect them to do?' MacGregor asked. 'Attack the convoy?'

'All they have to do is draw off the Ilkhani with everything they have, so that he's completely occupied between 30 June and 1 July when the Mercedes trucks will be coming into Iran. We'll do the rest. We can arrange the details once we are there. It's as simple as that.'

'It may be simple for you, Taha...' MacGregor began, but he didn't finish it.

'I know all your problems, Uncle. I know your difficulties.'

'I doubt it.'

'Aunt Kathy will object,' Taha said. 'I know all about that. She's forbidden Cecie to talk to me, and now Andrew as well. But even she'll understand.'

'She'll understand all right, but it won't make any dif-

309

ference. She's fed up with all the violence, Taha, and I can't blame her.'

Taha shrugged. 'Of course. That's a European privilege,' he said, and raised his eyes towards the Amphitheatre upstairs. 'Like the French. Violence. Non-violence. It's an intellectual game to them,' he said. 'But it isn't a game to us, Uncle.'

'That's why your Aunt Kathy won't listen this time,' he said. 'She knows what it means.' He shrugged off any further explanation.

'But it'll be the last time for you, Uncle. Afterwards you can go home and forget about us for the rest of your life.'

'What do you think will be left of my life, Taha, without my family?'

MacGregor listened to the footsteps above them, and looked around at the dismal hole they were in. He didn't want to make any fateful decisions in a place like this, but what other place was there? It was the only place he knew —the back door, not the front door.

'All right,' he said. 'I'll go—God help me.' He looked at the remnants of food left by some of the Katanga mercenaries who had been living with the students. 'There's no other way out of it, I suppose. None visible, anyway.'

'Then welcome,' Taha said in Kurdish.

'Don't welcome me to anything,' MacGregor said. 'It was my stupid failure that allowed it to happen, so I'd better do something about it. That's all I'm interested in.'

'You could never have stopped it, Uncle.'

'Perhaps if I'd been cleverer...'

'You?'

'All right. But all I care about now is seeing that the Ilkhani doesn't get those arms. Everybody here is so sure he's going to get them that it's almost a point of honour to see that he doesn't.'

Taha took the chair away from the door and they went up through the gritty stone corridors and under the arches.

When they went outside into the sudden daylight of the street they saw six students (four girls and two boys) collecting themselves behind a sign which said that they were going off to take back the post office on Rue du Cardinal Lemoine from the CRS. He stood with Taha for a moment and watched them marching off behind a red flag.

'They'll be *matraqué*,' Taha said.

'Nonetheless, they'll make the point.'

'What point?' Taha said. 'Do they imagine they're at Smolny, and do they think Cohn-Bendit is Lenin?'

'Nonetheless,' MacGregor persisted, 'they've got a lot of courage.'

'Ahmed the Carefree's got a lot of courage,' Taha said as they walked a hundred metres behind the little group up Boulevard Saint-Michel. 'But Ahmed is a well-known Kurdish clown who is about as truly revolutionary as they are.'

Chapter Thirty-four

He was surprised to find Jizzy Margaux waiting for him in Aunt Joss's study, watching the TV which Kathy had hired. She was watching a film report by a *'jaune'* on the big meeting at Charléty, and she looked up at MacGregor and then down at the pictures, as if she wanted both. Then she switched it off.

'Why do anarchists wear black?' she asked him. 'I don't understand.'

'It's their conventional dress,' he said. 'Why shouldn't they?'

'If it's conventional they ought to be against it,' she said, and he waited for her to tell him why she was here. 'I came to take you to my place,' she said.

'I have to wait for Kathy,' he told her.

'No you don't,' she said, walking out into the hall so that he had to follow.

'Wait a moment,' MacGregor said. 'Honestly. I have to see Kathy.'

'You can't,' she insisted. 'Kathy's gone to Cannes with Guy in his plane.' She stood in the hall and shouted: 'We're going now, Aunt Joss.'

'All right, Jizzy darling.'

She took his arm and forced him to go with her. 'Don't worry. They'll probably be back tonight, some time,' she said. 'Kathy rang me and said she'd been trying to telephone you all afternoon. She didn't know where you were. She said to tell you where they were, and to give you dinner, which she knew I would do *avec empressement*.'

He resisted her warm hand at the door. 'Did they say what they were doing in Cannes?'

'She and Guy are obviously involved in something complicated. They must be if they went off like that. But I warned you...'

He put some of the surface parts of himself together and Jizzy got his raincoat for him. 'All I know is that it was Guy who arranged it,' she told him. 'And it's some scheme they've been talking about for weeks.'

'Wait a minute,' he said again. 'What about Cecie?'

'She's gone to the atelier to collect her goods and chattels. She was caught in another demonstration this afternoon, and the police have told her to leave France by tomorrow night. Kathy wouldn't let Guy interfere.'

'My God. What's happening? Where's Andrew then? He ought to be here.'

'Aunt Joss will tell him where you are, and they can follow you if they want to. So please stop disputing me.'

He did not resist but pulled on his coat, and when they were in the courtyard she stood near him in the light under the steps. 'You haven't looked at me yet,' she said and put her finger up to her face.

He saw then that she had washed out her coiffured hair, which looked now like a little pile of autumn leaves covering her head, a natural tangle on the freckled, autumnal beauty that, even in this light, was so startling. She held up her finger to show her nails, clipped to nothing.

'Well?' she demanded.

'Yes, I noticed,' he told her, trapped, because in stripping off her beauty Jizzy was only adding to it.

'No you didn't,' she said. 'But I'd hate it if you did. Anyway, now that I'm depending entirely on myself I'll have to learn how to forget myself. Like you.' They went outside the gate and got into Jizzy's Renault and she went on in a subdued voice as if she was imposing calm on herself and good sense: 'I suppose all this is a very silly beginning, even stupid, but the trouble is, I don't know how else to do it.'

'You don't have to explain it,' he told her. 'You're doing all right.'

'That's because you taught me about abnegation,' she said. 'And now I understand everything.'

MacGregor had been trying not to notice Jizzy's way of getting through traffic by ignoring it. 'I can't have taught you abnegation, Jizzy,' he told her, 'because I don't even believe in it myself.'

'You don't have to believe in it,' she said, 'because you were born with it and you must have been soaked up in it all your life.'

He kept quiet, and once more they went up to Jizzy's glittering kitchen and occupied it like a middle-class couple on the servants' night out.

'How did they manage to fly to Cannes?' he asked her. 'I thought all the airports were closed.'

'Not that little one near Mandelieu nor the private part of Orly.'

'Can he just get up and leave Paris like that, when everything here seems to be in danger?'

'Nothing of Guy's is in danger,' she said as she walked around getting plates and food together. 'And it never will be. Don't question me about them. They'll be back. That's all you can hope for. Don't let it pain you.'

'I don't understand it,' he said as Jizzy put a plate of smoked salmon in front of him.

She leaned over and touched his china-clear cheeks. 'It's that lovely innocent skin,' she said. 'Isn't it a pity to lose it so easily, or just give it up so gladly? What for? What is so marvellous about not being innocent any more?'

He tried to eat but he knew it was impossible. 'Life these days seems to be one long process of giving up something and never getting it back again,' he said.

'Yes, but you shouldn't say things like that. You ought not to.'

'Why not?'

'Because you're the one that guards the door. You're the one who must always be there to protect *la forteresse de la vie*. I don't care what else you do, but don't start despairing of yourself now. I won't listen. I will never hear it.'

'You make too much of everything.'

'And you underestimate yourself,' she said.

'Why? What strength am I supposed to have? What fortress of life am I supposed to be guarding, for God's sake?'

She got up and came around to him and put her hands lightly on his shoulders from behind, but he sat still.

'Why don't we at least try?' she said to him. 'It would be so peaceful. I would never let it hurt you or upset you.'

He kept his hands on the table. 'There's no point to it, Jizzy.'

'Does everything have to have a point? Anyway, you wouldn't be betraying anything if that's what you're worried about.'

'How do you know I wouldn't?'

'Is there anything left to betray with Kathy? Here?' She gripped his heart.

'I don't know,' he said. 'But as far as I am concerned it's still there and I can't go against it. It would make everything hopeless if I did.'

'You mean you won't believe the worst. You stick ...'

'I half believe everything.'

'Do you know what's really wrong between you and Kathy?' she said.

He said he wouldn't discuss it.

Jizzy took her hands away. 'No. And I don't really want to either. So if you're not going to eat,' she said, 'I want to take you somewhere.'

'Now?'

'It's not far,' she said. 'The roads will be empty and I've

315

telephoned Monsieur Moreau, the guardian, to leave the gate open for us.'

She got a jacket and they walked downstairs through the hole in the house. He asked her in the car where they were going.

'To Port-Royal des Champs,' she said as she started the Renault.

He didn't ask what for, and Jizzy drove through the washed-out streets of the city without policemen or protection or guards or administration. Paris was nothing more now than a blur, it was open to the winds, and after Pont de Saint Cloud he saw Mantes flash by on the signposts and then they were on the Autoroute de l'Ouest. Jizzy kept her course and speed like a pilot flying a serious mission. When they left the autoroute they turned back a little way towards Versailles, and in a deeply-wooded valley Jizzy stopped and parked the car. They walked through dark woods, in the crystal blue of the French country night, until they came to some shadowy buildings on either side of a path. Jizzy stopped when they reached a gate, and he realised it was a sort of enclosure formed by lime trees.

'What is it?' he asked.

'It used to be the old nunnery of Port-Royal,' she said. 'In the seventeenth century it was a Cistercian convent where Jansenist heretics were sheltered and looked after by a devoted abbess called Marie Angélica de Sainte Magdelena.'

All he could see in the darkness was the square of *tilleuls*, and all around them a wet, clear, country night was dripping dew from the sky. 'Why did you bring me out here?' he asked her.

'Because I wanted to show you something that I understand with my soul. I've never brought anyone here. Why should I? They wouldn't understand it. But I've always admired this place, ever since I was a girl.'

'Are you a Jansenist?' MacGregor asked her.

'How could I be a Jansenist?' she said. 'In any case I haven't got a conscience like that. I suppose I'm an Augustinian, which is what Jansen really was. Anyway it doesn't matter. The point is that Marie Angélica never deserted them. She looked after all *ces messieurs de Port-Royal*. They were called *hommes de valeur*. Pascal was one of them. The Jesuits told Louis to burn the place down, and that's what he did. He razed it to the last stone. But the abbess never deserted them.'

The invisible cloister was still, and above them they could hear pop music from some roadside café or auberge. But down here there was no connection with it at all because Jizzy was trying desperately to explain herself without any outside interference.

'If I had lived in the seventeenth century,' she said, 'I would have been a nun here. I am sure of it. It's the only place in all France that I feel so strongly about. You see— I am certainly a nun at heart, and always have been. And perhaps a puritan and a heretic too. Do you follow me? Do you understand these infractions ...'

'Of course,' he said, and he realised that he did understand her. He took her arm and they walked away from the *tilleuls* and along a wild rose pathway which they could smell in the night air but couldn't see.

'You're the first person I've understood in my life,' she told him. 'I know what you think, and I know what you feel. Even without talk. But I am a terrible secret, even to myself. Guy says I'm an animal, and that's the trouble. Everything about me is a secret that nobody has ever bothered to look for, although I know that if you wanted to, you would find it for me. I know it.'

MacGregor also knew that if he wanted to he would have no difficulty finding it for her: that there would be no difficulty matching Jizzy's secret with the same sort of secret that he had lived with all his life. The similarities were revealing, even upsetting. But he wondered why everybody had missed this woman not by a mile but by a chasm.

'You may be right, Jizzy,' he said to her sadly. 'But even so, I'm of no use to you.'

'It doesn't really matter. You live with your own terrible secrets and I live with mine. The difference is that you do things with them, whereas my life has been stupid and wasteful,' she said with a shrug. 'Perhaps all I can do now is to ruin all the beautiful surface of it. Like that...' She pulled her hair out from her face with a fierce, hateful tug. 'But I don't know that I can do any more. Not alone. I'm too old, I think, to do much more than demolish a little of myself. After that...' Jizzy shrugged like a piece of the sea filling up a hole in itself. 'I can watch you,' she said, 'and I can wait...'

She did not cling to him or offer any more explanation, and it was only somewhere on their return along the Autoroute de l'Ouest that he realised he had forgotten about Kathy. Jizzy filled the rents and the wounds, and he had even stopped asking himself why she had gone off like that with Guy Moselle. Did it even matter?

'Stop the car a moment,' he said.

She pulled off the Autoroute on to the green verge and waited while he made up his mind what he was going to say.

'I have to go away,' he told her in French. 'I have to go back...'

'Don't. Please don't tell me anything more. If you're not going to be here I don't want to know where you are or what you're doing, because it will be something unsafe and I don't want to be sick.'

'What I'm really saying,' he said to her, 'is that I'm too old to start undoing my life and trying to do it up again.'

'Perhaps Kathy'll save you the trouble.'

'Even if she does, I can't change anything, Jizzy. It's too late. If I tried to undo one part of me now, all the rest would simply fall to pieces, because all I can do is hold myself together with the simplest rules I know. Perhaps I'm hopelessly single-minded. I don't know. But it seems to me that some sort of fidelity has to survive somehow, because if it doesn't why should we go on caring about anything at all? What would be left?'

'If you have to explain,' she said in her indignant, affectionate French, 'it means you're in doubt. And it's Kathy you doubt, not yourself.'

'I'm simply trying to put an end to something before it's even begun,' he said. 'And I don't want to leave you without explaining.'

'You're too late. It's already begun. And anyway, I'm like you,' she went on in English. 'I can wait and wait and *wait*!'

'But there's nothing to wait for. That's the point, Jizzy. Believe me.'

'You don't know when a woman is strong or weak, do you? Now I'm much stronger than Kathy because I don't want anything. Nothing at all. So I'll just watch her and wait...'

'That won't do any good,' he insisted.

'*Nous verrons,*' she said and started the Renault.

At her house they found Andrew waiting sleepily for them in the kitchen, and when Jizzy asked him if he wanted something to eat he said he had eaten a piece of chicken and a tomato from the icebox. Jizzy kissed him on the cheek for having cleared up the dishes after him.

'Polite English boy,' she said.

At the door of the street she kept MacGregor back while Andrew continued a few steps away. 'Don't let any of them, not even Kathy, do anything to you,' she told him fiercely. 'Remember all the time that the fortress of your life is only ruined when someone else dismantles it; and I know it was Edmond Rostand who said that.'

He walked with Andrew along the edge of the Champs-Elysées for five minutes without saying anything, and when they were level with the Place de la Concorde he asked

Andrew if his mother was back.

'She rang when I was in Madame Margaux's kitchen,' he said. 'She's waiting up for you.'

It was about 2 a.m., and MacGregor watched the dark wavy edges of the blue river, sick these days with too much mercury light and too many cement shadows. Nonetheless its surface was shivering and flickering, like a row of Caspian birches. And as if the same thought had occurred to Andrew, the boy told his father that he had come to a decision.

'I've decided to go back home,' he said.

'To London?'

'No,' Andrew said. 'To Iran.'

'Now what makes you say a thing like that?' MacGregor said to his son.

'I'm not sure yet,' Andrew replied. 'I only know that I don't want to stay in Europe any more.'

MacGregor let their footsteps pass over the seconds and minutes and hours of his life. 'And what do you think you're going to do in Iran?' he asked.

'I suppose I can get into Teheran University,' Andrew said.

'You might. But that's not intelligent, Andy. In fact it's stupid.'

They had been walking along the murky edges of the pont, and they fell into step only when they came on the asphalt of the boulevard.

'Nonetheless, I've made up my mind. I'm convinced that I'll never be a European,' Andrew said. 'I didn't think so in England, and I don't think so in France. In fact if I stayed in this city I wouldn't even want to be a student.'

'Now just a minute.' MacGregor sat down on a bench which was slightly damp, but he didn't want to arrive without some attempt to stop this. 'It doesn't even sound like you,' he said. 'So who's been influencing you?'

'You,' Andrew said.

'I don't appreciate that at all, so you'd better explain it.'

'I don't want to make a personal career of political conviction, any more than you did. That's all it is.'

'But why should you give up Europe, or even Oxford, on that account?'

'Because I don't care about either of them any more. Just let me study something else in Iran where the problem is the problem. Then, if I have to, I can get into trouble the way you did—not for myself but for whatever it is you have to get into trouble for. Who, for God's sake, needs all this *individualité, opacité, volonté*?'

'All right, all right,' MacGregor said defensively, knowing already that he probably would not argue Andrew out of it. 'But you'll have to be far more precise about what you want to study in Iran before I'll even think of letting you go back.'

'I can specialise in Persian language and Iranian history,' Andrew said. 'That's precise enough, isn't it?'

'Your mother will never hear of it.'

'Why not?'

'Because she's trying to break the family connection with Iran—once and for all.'

'Do you want to break it?'

MacGregor felt as if all the corners of silence he had depended on for so long were slowly being taken away from him. 'It's time we all came back to Europe,' he said, 'where, in fact, we all belong.'

'Cecie might belong here. So does Mama,' Andrew said as they walked on again. 'But I don't, and you don't.'

'Everything you're saying is too full of contradictions to be even half-way credible,' MacGregor said. 'So you're not convincing me.'

'Can you tell me anything,' the boy replied in his calm, sensible, unarguable way, 'that I can do, or that you can do, or that anybody else can do that isn't full of contradictions?'

'That may be true,' MacGregor said. 'But it still doesn't convince me about you.'

They were already home, and they stood for a moment looking at the acid-stained gate. 'Let me think about it,' MacGregor said unhappily. 'In any case you're not to do anything until I come back from Iran. I expect that much of you.'

Andrew hesitated for a moment. 'All right,' he said.

'And don't say anything to your mother about it, or about me going back. I'll tell her everything in my own way.'

'Don't worry. I understand,' his son said with his natural tendency to help anybody in trouble, even strangers he met on railway stations or wounded pigeons that he sometimes found fluttering around the gutters of Battersea.

When he went upstairs, MacGregor found Kathy sitting up in bed writing a letter, although it was after 2.30 a.m. The swollen French furniture and the bed lamp made heavy round lines on walls and faces and curtains. She looked tired and tense, as if at the end of a long day she was refusing to give in to exhaustion.

'What took you so long?' she asked him.

'I went out to Port-Royal with Jizzy, and then Andrew and I walked home.'

'I sent Andrew in Guy's car for you.'

'I preferred to walk,' he said. He guessed that Andrew had sent Moselle's car away on his own initiative.

As he began undressing she watched deliberately, waiting for him to say something. 'Why don't you ask me why I went to Cannes with Guy Moselle?' she said.

'Because you'll tell me when you feel like telling me,' he said. 'And anyway,' he added, 'the right time for asking questions seems to have run out.'

'In that case you're obviously afraid to ask.'

'I suppose I am,' he said and realised that Kathy had chosen her own moment to talk to him. He was ridiculous, standing in his underpants and shirt and shoes and socks, struggling to undo his cuff-links to get the sleeves of his French shirt over his hands.

'Let me do that,' she said to him.

'I can manage,' he told her, although it was hopeless, as every tangle with his clothes was always hopeless.

'Well,' she said calmly, 'you'd better ask me why I went to Cannes because I'm not going to tell you unless you do ask. And since it concerns you it would be better if you weren't so reluctant about it.'

He thought he would be better off if he got his shoes and socks and his underpants off. Then he could cope with his shirtsleeves. She watched him relentlessly.

'What am I supposed to say?' he said to her. 'I know you went to Cannes, and I know you went with Guy Moselle. What else am I supposed to know?'

'Ask.'

He was silent.

'As usual you're afraid,' she said contemptuously. She folded the letter she had been writing and put it carefully in an envelope and licked the flap as if that was really what she was doing, while their conversation was no more than a supplementary affair. 'Oh, for heaven's sake give me that,' she said, and he held out his arms and she took off the cuff-links.

'I haven't the faintest idea why you went to Cannes. That's all I'm going to say,' he told her.

She scooped up some of the papers on her bed, selected one, and tossed it on the bed in front of him. Attached to it was a coloured photograph of a small, red, Provençal villa with olive trees on either side, an arched door, and a large tiled patio.

'I've decided to buy that house,' she said.

He glanced at the agent's particulars. 'Where is it?' he asked.

'Beyond Mandelieu, where Guy's house is. Near Pégomas. That's where I was today.'

The description of the house, in French, called it an old *Mas* which had been modernised and given central heating. It had four hectares, a stream, olive trees, *pinèdes*. . . .

'Why? Do you intend to live in France?' he asked her.

'I hate the English climate, and when it gets too much I can come down here. That way I'll survive the worst aspects of Europe.'

He handed her back the paper and the photo.

'Well?' she demanded.

'It's very nice, it's a good idea.'

'Knowing that you hate it, and hate the whole idea of it, particularly since it's so near Guy's place, I release you from all obligation to be polite about it. So if you don't like it you need never come near it. I'm buying it for myself.'

'I like it. It looks very attractive.'

'That's not what I mean. Why do you always avoid the real issue with me?'

He went into the bathroom to clean his teeth, and when he came back to the bedroom she had swept all the papers and letters to the floor.

'In fact,' she went on, 'I thought it would be a good idea if sometimes we got away from each other. You hate it down there. But I love that coast, so it'll probably improve my temper if I can be alone somewhere that I like.'

'I'm not arguing with that,' he said. 'If that's what you want why worry about it? Buy it.'

'We have not been away from each other enough. A couple of weeks apart every now and then won't hurt us.'

'I suppose not.'

'You won't commit yourself, will you? You're still determined to avoid everything.'

'One way or the other,' he said, 'you'll do it anyway, so it's no use quarrelling about it. Do it, Kathy. Just do it.'

'That almost pathological fear you have of quarrelling

with me is becoming an obsession. We quarrel anyway, so for God's sake why don't you say what you feel and think, so that I know what you feel and think?'

'Quarrel with your enemies,' he said to her in Persian. 'Why with your beloved?'

'Don't ever talk to me in Persian again. Ever!' she told him.

They were both sitting up in bed, side by side, and she put her hand flat on the blue eiderdown and he noticed that the tips of her fingers were trembling.

'If you'd only give me something else, anything to be hopeful about, I wouldn't buy that house,' she told him. 'Anything...'

He knew then that this was not the time to tell her that he was going back to the Kurds. 'I told you, Kathy,' he said. 'I'm still trying to finish what I promised to do, and that's what's really between us, isn't it? So why argue about it? Just let me finish it.'

'How are you ever going to finish with it? Tell me that.'

He kept silent.

Kathy slumped back on the bed and switched off her bedside table lamp. 'If I buy that house,' she said in the darkness, 'it will be the end of something between us. I can't tell you more plainly than that.'

'I suppose not,' he said.

Chapter Thirty-five

They saw Cecie off in the morning: Cecie in angry tears. Even Aunt Joss appeared. She stood at the door briefly in sabots to wave, as if Cecie was setting out on some gay expedition with friends. When Cecie had driven off, Mac-Gregor waited until the others had gone inside. Then he let himself out and walked across the river to the BOAC office in the Champs Elysées to ask them whether it was still possible to get a plane to Teheran. At least that would be one method of deciding it.

The BOAC clerk told him that there were buses running to Brussels, from where the BOAC planes were flying to Teheran. 'We can still book you,' the clerk said, 'but we can't guarantee a flight. You can probably get a total refund if you don't use your ticket.'

'I see.'

On the wall above the clerk's head was a BOAC poster showing an Indonesian puppet, and across it BOAC announced that it would not only get you there, but bring you back. The logic of it seemed irrefutable.

'Do you want a booking?' the clerk asked.

'Yes.'

'What day?'

'Friday if possible.'

'That's three clear days from today.'

Three clear days from today might give Kathy time to understand what he was doing. It would also give him time to tell her.

'That should be okay,' the clerk said and asked MacGregor

his nationality and his name and address. Did he have an Iranian visa?

MacGregor said yes and gave his name. But he said he didn't have an address at the moment. He would let them know where he was when he came in tomorrow for the ticket.

'If you come tomorrow make it in the morning,' the clerk said. 'There's going to be a big *manifestation* here at noon which will block all the streets. Today it's the communists at the Place de la Bastille, but tomorrow the Gaullists will be over here in the Champs-Elysées. And this time they will find out who is the strong man in the circus.'

MacGregor thanked him, and when he arrived home he heard Kathy calling out from the kitchen to Aunt Joss that she was going to prepare lunch. Andrew met him in the hall and MacGregor said quickly to him: 'I still haven't told your mother that I'm going back, so don't mention it yet.'

'Tell her now,' Andrew said.

'No,' he said. 'She's still upset about other things.'

Andrew told him then that Taha wanted to see him. 'He'll be in the *manifestation* this afternoon with the CGT and the unions. He wants to talk to you. I know where he'll be, so I'll take you.'

'All right,' he said hurriedly as Kathy came out of the kitchen.

Kathy seemed to guess what they were talking about. 'You're not going on the demonstration today,' she told Andrew.

'Why not? Today and tomorrow will be the final confrontations. None of the others mattered.'

'Guy warned me about you yesterday,' she said to Andrew. 'You've been spending your time with Taha and the Kurds and the Iranians. So if they catch you, the way they caught Cecie, you'll be thrown out like her. And this time I won't lift a finger to help you. You'll just have to suffer the punishment.'

Andrew leaned over and kissed his mother affectionately. 'Don't worry, Mama,' he said. 'I'm not as pretty as Cecie, so I don't attract so much attention.'

'I'll be going with him,' MacGregor said.

Kathy looked at him suspiciously and kept determinedly silent during lunch.

As they walked across Paris, Andrew read aloud from a newspaper which said that today would be one of the decisive days for France. Even Cohn-Bendit had been smuggled back into France for it. 'But all the students, including Cohn-Bendit's March 22 movement, are boycotting today's CGT *manifestation*,' he read, 'because the unions won't accept the students' slogans.'

'The students won't boycott it,' MacGregor told him. 'They need the unions more than the unions need them.'

'They say,' Andrew went on reading, 'that de Gaulle left Paris at 11.30 yesterday morning and didn't turn up at Colombey until 17.30 last night. Everybody wants to know where he was all day. The army is already ringing Paris and waiting.'

When they reached the Boulevard Beaumarchais they couldn't go any further because the thick columns of marchers were already on their way from the Place de la Bastille to the Place de la République singing *'Adieu, de Gaulle, adieu.'*

'We can wait here,' Andrew said, 'until we see the Kurdish students. They're near the end somewhere, and Taha will be with them.'

Banners were a form of coda, and the banners in a march like this one made everything very clear. At the end of a long list of nurses, doctors, teachers and quartiers they saw Taha, who left the march, came over and took them both by the arm, and told them to get into it with him.

'No,' MacGregor said.

'I need to talk to you, Uncle,' Taha said. 'And what safer place?'

A hole was made for them among the Kurds and Persians and Arabs and Turks (Turks!) who were hiding their foreign identity in every way except their appearance. They passed a sign for the Cirque d'Hiver and someone shouted *'De Gaulle au Cirque.'* They all laughed except Taha who ignored it because he wasn't here for that. He asked Mac-Gregor when he would leave for Iran.

'On Friday.'

'Three days?'

'I can't leave before,' MacGregor said, without explaining why.

'That means you'll see my father or the Qazi by next Monday or Tuesday.'

'If I'm not stopped.'

'Who's going to stop you?' Taha said.

'The Iranians, if they know what I'm doing. Anybody who catches me. Even here, perhaps. Everybody's got their eyes open now, Taha.'

'Nobody knows what you're doing, Uncle. Not yet.'

'Someone always finds out. You know that.'

'That's true.' Taha waited impatiently until the students in front had finished shouting their slogans.

'We found out,' he said, 'that those boxes of arms will be landed at the Turkish port on 7 June, and that the Ilkhani expects the trucks on the 10th, but not where I thought. So Zadko will have to get to the Qotur valley on that summer portion of the Ilkhani's lands by the 9th.'

'How reliable is that sort of information?' MacGregor asked. 'I don't want to tell the Qazi anything you're not absolutely sure of. So check everything carefully.'

'We have Turkish friends who confirm it.'

'Couldn't they be planting false information?'

'No. We trust them.'

'All right, I believe it. But how do you expect Zadko

to get to Qotur?' MacGregor said. 'It's almost on the Turkish border, and he'd have to go right up the long line of frontier posts if he has to attack the Ilkhani there.'

'He'll just have to go through Turkey, along the Kemi ridge.'

MacGregor put up his arm to ward off a banner which was flapping in his face. 'He's too weak to do anything as daring as that. Can't you think of something else?'

'He'll do it if he has to,' Taha insisted. 'But there's something more, which is really what I wanted to see you about. There are now three more truckloads of arms and ammunition at Toulon. They've given the Ilkhani a lot more stuff which they've sent from Belgium. It will go on the same ship.'

'I suppose that bit of trickery was inevitable,' MacGregor said bitterly. He waited while more slogans were shouted and sung, and then he asked Taha when he would be leaving.

'Tomorrow or Sunday,' Taha said.

'How?'

'Don't worry, Uncle. I'll get in touch with my father when I arrive. You just persuade them to be at Qotur on the 10th. My father will know what to do.'

They had now reached Chez Jenny and they stood jammed up together in the march. They noticed a man standing on the first floor balcony of a small building with a 16-millimetre cine camera. It was aimed at the nameless foreigners. When MacGregor looked up the camera seemed to be on him, or Taha, as if they were the specific objective.

'*Salaud!*' someone shouted.

Taha detached himself like a kingfisher, and in a moment he was in the main door of the building so quickly that the man had obviously failed to see him. Then they saw Taha come out on the balcony, and after a brief struggle the film was torn out of the camera and exposed over the balcony like a paper streamer. By the time they moved on again Taha was back with him, and the others cheered.

'You know,' he said, calm but out of breath. 'You're always in danger, Uncle, so you ought to take more care.'

'That's perfect advice, coming from you,' MacGregor said.

Taha shrugged. 'Maybe. But I told Andrew he must look after you.'

'And I told you, Taha, that I don't want him involved in this,' MacGregor said angrily.

'He's not involved. But if something happens to you wouldn't he feel unhappy all his life if he hadn't looked after you?'

'Nothing's going to happen to me. Not here, anyway.'

They had reached the Place de la République, and now there was nowhere else to go. The Service d'Ordre, with green armbands, were trying to organise two hundred thousand marchers into a useful mass that could fit into the square. Now they were shouting popular front slogans, and then songs that were drowned by chanted slogans and insults on the President.

'Well...'

Andrew had his father's arm. 'Let's get out of this before the whole place is clogged up for hours.'

Taha said in Kurdish he would stay awhile to listen for noise. He said *das-a-bas* which meant noise-and-talk which meant news. He told MacGregor he would come to see him and Aunt Kathy before he left. They pushed their way out of the singing crowd to the edge of the *manifestation* where someone was listening to the radio which reported that Mendès-France had finally mounted his white horse. Mendès-France said he would not refuse to be called upon if de Gaulle announced his resignation tomorrow.

Andrew laughed, but they did not stop to listen. As they pushed their way along the crowded footpath they heard the disappearing radio say that de Gaulle had been seen today walking in the park at Colombey.

'The helicopter was standing by. The pilot was in khaki with a map in his hand ... But for what reason ...'

'Tomorrow,' Andrew said in French as they got free of the dusty avenues, 'the French will pull out the plug.'

Tomorrow, MacGregor was thinking, he would have to tell Kathy that he was going back to Kurdistan.

He waited next day until Cecie had made her morning phone call from London to prove she was there and to report how stupid it all was. Then he waited over breakfast. Then he read what was happening on this decisive day for France: de Gaulle was back in the Elysée; the federation of the left was asking for a meeting excluding the communists; and the communists were saying that there could be no return to the politics of the third force or to the rule of a miracle man. Andrew read aloud from *Combat* (with the *Canard Enchaîné* printed inside it) that a choice of de Gaulle or the communists was the last and final step. Anybody else involved was really an ally of one or the other.

'I'm going back to London on Monday,' Kathy announced, and got up and left the breakfast table.

MacGregor exchanged a glance with his son and followed her upstairs. He closed the bedroom door behind him, as if closing a door defined the area of their battlefield.

'Do you have any money?' she said to him.

'You mean French francs?'

'Yes.'

'About two hundred.'

'Well give them to me. I need to pay Aunt Joss for all those drinks and wine she's been buying. Is that all you've got?'

'Yes, but I can get some more today.'

'I need another hundred at least.'

'All right.'

'It's the least we can do,' Kathy said.

MacGregor felt as if so far he had been refusing to pay, but he knew it was Kathy's way of putting him on the defensive, preparing herself for anything he had to say. He watched her hunting for a pair of shoes in the fat wardrobe.

'I've booked a ticket to go back to Teheran tomorrow,' he told her. 'I've got to go back and try to rescue whatever is left. I've got to explain to the Qazi what has happened here.'

She waited only an instant. Then she walked out, slamming the door on him. He followed her down the stairs. 'Listen, Kathy,' he said. 'It's only a little thing, so let me do it in peace, and then I'll gladly keep off it for the rest of my life. They have to stop that stuff getting to the Ilkhani. That's all I need to tell them. Otherwise everything else, everything I've ever done there will have been wasted....'

She did not say anything and she did not stop but walked on outside. He followed her silently but helplessly. She pushed him back roughly when he tried to walk through the big gate with her. Her face and manner were neither harsh nor brutal, but final; and her eyes were soaked with tears.

'I don't even want to be in the same house with you any more. I won't even talk to you.'

'But for God's sake...'

'Somebody,' she said, biting out the words fiercely through her tears and struggling to close the gate against him. 'Somebody in those mountains will kill you this time...' She could not control herself for a moment, but then she pulled the gate firmly closed. 'And that's what you'll deserve,' she cried through the old wooden wall. 'It's what you want, isn't it?' she shouted at him.

He stood still for a moment as he heard her hurry away.

Then he went back to the house and Andrew was running down the steps.

'I was just coming out to get you,' he said. 'There's a phone call from London.'

MacGregor expected Cecie. It was the London operator asking him if he was Mr MacGregor senior.

'Yes.'

She said she had a call from Teheran, which had been routed through London because they could still use the automatic London-Paris exchange while the PTT international operators were on strike.

'Hello, it's me.'

It was Jamal Janab at the NIOC office in Teheran, and MacGregor could hear him shouting in his glass office as a gesture to the distance and the situation.

'What is it, Jamal?' MacGregor asked. 'What's up?'

'You'll be very pleased,' Jamal shouted in his plump voice. 'Do you hear me?'

'Yes, yes.'

'The NIOC are going to ask you to be our permanent representative on the Committee for World Resources and Reserves in Geneva.'

'I see. When did this happen?'

'Just now. Today. Are you pleased?'

'Of course.'

'But more important,' Jamal went on excitedly. 'We are going to nominate you as its director. And because everybody knows you and your theoretical work you will easily get the appointment, I swear it. And that, habibi, is a final justification for you after all these years.'

MacGregor looked at his handsome son standing by the window of the lifeless study, at a bowl of dried leaves that had been sitting on the window sill for twenty years.

'Are you there?' Jamal asked.

'Yes. It's very good news, Jamal,' MacGregor shouted in Persian. 'Wonderful! And I know who did it for me, Jamal.

334

So I embrace you a hundred times, Jamal, a thousand times.'

Jamal used the Persian justification again and again. 'My friend, my friend,' he said emotionally, and MacGregor knew that Jamal's consuming belief in family and friends and loyalty were overflowing.

'But...' Jamal said dramatically.

He waited, and MacGregor was forced to ask what the 'but' was.

'Please, habibi. Don't do anything that will spoil it. Don't upset anyone. Don't get involved in anything ... in our mountains. You know what I mean.'

In our mountains. MacGregor laughed sadly despite himself. A thousand ears listening would know exactly what Jamal meant.

'I'm worried about you,' Jamal said.

'I'll come and see you,' MacGregor told him. 'Don't worry too much, Jamal. I'll be all right.'

'Please!' he appealed again. 'Please be careful.'

'Of course. I'll walk on roses,' he said.

They exchanged information about family, and Jamal said that his daughter was now making wonderful little animals in English plasticine. 'I've got a whole zoo on my window ledge, but the elephants drop off their trunks and the monkeys lose their tails.' Jamal laughed and repeated his congratulations to MacGregor. Then he said it all again, and after the half-dozen mutual Persian protestations of affection, regard and belief in each other, MacGregor hung up.

'Is everything all right?' Andrew asked.

'Yes. Everything's all right,' MacGregor replied, but he didn't tell him what Jamal had said.

Chapter Thirty-six

It was his last day in Paris and Andrew went with him to pick up the tickets at the BOAC office. Twice in the night there had been explosions at the end of the street, and the Left Bank was still full of night noises. When they collected the ticket the BOAC clerk told MacGregor to be at the Hôtel Continental at nine o'clock in the morning, where there would be a bus to take him to Brussels. 'But I would advise you—not much luggage,' the clerk said. 'There won't be much room on the bus.'

They went back to Aunt Joss's and MacGregor wrote Cecie a short letter telling her to obey her mother. At lunchtime Kathy was still not back, and he asked Andrew, who had been silently watching both of them, where he wanted to lunch.

'The best place to wait for de Gaulle is the Rotonde, where Lenin once used to wait for Longuet.'

But when they reached the Rotonde they found it was now half-cinema, half-restaurant. So they went to the Coupole and sat on leather benches. It was two o'clock and de Gaulle would speak at four o'clock, but the Coupole was already jaded with anticipation. MacGregor asked his son if he had ever read Zola's novel, *Paris*.

'Only Hugo's preface to it, which we were given at the Lycée,' Andrew said.

'It must have been written here,' MacGregor told him.

The food came. MacGregor had forgotten what he had ordered, and he was surprised to see a trout on his plate.

Andrew kept looking at his watch and then a waiter turned on the radio. They heard a Frenchman singing 'Marie', then a warning overture of classical music, and finally de Gaulle's old-fashioned, indignant, metallic voice addressing Frenchwomen and Frenchmen.

The President said he was not going to resign. Nor would the government resign. The chance for France was his way or the communist way. The communist way was not for France. Instead there would be an election and a referendum, and if this idea was rejected he would use his physical powers to restore order to France. 'My physical powers,' he said sternly. In the meantime, he said, the entire National Assembly was dissolved, and there was absolutely nothing more to say to France.

There were shouts all around them. 'The 18th Brumaire, the 2nd of December, the 13th of May...' It was like the floor of the Stock Exchange on a bad day.

'They don't like it. They hate it,' Andrew said.

'It doesn't matter whether they hate it or not,' MacGregor said. 'It's over.'

They paid the bill, and when they were outside in the pale green sun they crossed the river to watch two hundred thousand Gaullists marching along the dusty avenues of the Champs-Elysées singing the Marseillaise. MacGregor loved the song, but watching these *commerçants, propriétaires,* businessmen and Gaullist women in camel-hair coats, it seemed incredible to him that the peasant soldiers of France should be sitting in tanks and armoured cars in the outer arrondissements of Paris, waiting to protect the little paper tricolours the Gaullists were wearing in their hats.

'And that's the true dead end of the great Paris revolution,' Andrew said as they left.

Behind them as they returned to the Left Bank they could hear the Gaullists shouting *Liberté, Liberté, Liberté.* It seemed to be the last word he would hear of France, and MacGregor was sorry when they reached the tall, acid-stained, wooden gate which would close Paris off behind them.

Incredibly, Aunt Joss was sitting in the study with Kathy and Moselle, talking in her high-pitched voice as if this was the occasion for her voice and herself to come together at last. She ignored MacGregor, but gave Andrew a warm kiss on the cheek and another on the lips, and Guy Moselle laughed. 'Why don't you embrace the father as well?' he said.

Aunt Joss straightened her neck and said: 'I don't understand him. He frightens me...'

'MacGregor! My God!' Moselle laughed.

'Andrew,' Aunt Joss said. 'Go and get my sabots. I'm going outside.' When Aunt Joss went outside she wore a pair of Breton sabots which were badly stained with the lotion she slapped on her face and legs to protect her skin from gnats and air. She got up and left them, and MacGregor, who had not been looked at or spoken to, stood up as did Moselle, and they heard her asking Andrew to stay with her in case she fell.

'I suppose that's the nearest she'll ever get to being tactful,' Kathy said to nobody in particular, but MacGregor had the feeling that he had interrupted some sort of family cabal among them.

'We've spent most of the day arranging for Kathy to pay for her house,' Guy said pleasantly to MacGregor, and despite himself MacGregor knew that he would respond pleasantly because you could not do anything else with this man. 'In fact we tried to get you,' Moselle went on. 'French law needs the husband.'

'We went over to see the Gaullist demonstration,' MacGregor explained.

'Gaullist demonstrations are bad punctuation,' Guy said. 'Actually we dropped into the Coupole for lunch and we saw you and Andrew. By then we didn't need you, and you two looked so complete that we decided not to interrupt.'

MacGregor knew he was in no position at the moment to come to grips with this extraordinary but intangible take-over of his family, and even of his responsibilities.

'Oh, tell him, Guy!' Kathy said impatiently.

MacGregor felt himself sicken with anticipation. If Moselle was going to tell him that Kathy was about to leave him, he knew Moselle would do it with the same matter-of-fact charm and good sense which would make it no more than a fair exchange between one decent man and another.

'I hear you're going back to Teheran tomorrow,' Moselle said with a little smile, as if he had to straighten this out first.

'Yes...'

'Do you really have to go? Is it so important?'

'I need to clear up a few things, that's all,' MacGregor said.

'It's a mistake,' Moselle told him. 'Believe me...'

'Why?'

'Because you're not going to prevent the Ilkhani getting those guns, and you'll only put yourself in a worse position with everybody.'

'Not quite everybody,' MacGregor said.

'Even the Kurds won't thank you. Not now. You know very well that the Iranians won't tolerate your interference. Neither will the Americans nor the British nor the French, nor, God help us, the Turks. So what do you gain by going back?'

'I don't know,' MacGregor said. 'All I know is that they can't be allowed to decide it their way—just like that.'

'But you're in danger,' Moselle said, ignoring the argument. 'You must know what to expect if you go back now.'

'I'm in no more danger now than I was before,' Mac-Gregor said. 'So I don't have to think much about it.'

'That's a silly lie,' Kathy said angrily, speaking directly to him now.

MacGregor was beginning to watch Kathy, because it seemed incredible that she should have asked Moselle to come here and influence him. But that was what it looked like. It was suddenly very satisfying, even though he didn't really trust it. 'It's nice of you to worry,' he told Moselle, 'but obviously you don't understand what they're going to do to the Kurds.'

'Maybe I don't. But Kathy is worried and I do understand that. So can't you reconsider?' Again Moselle made him feel that he, MacGregor, was no more than a family friend to his own wife. 'Your crazy scheme for those trucks is obviously a hopeless one,' Moselle was saying.

'What crazy scheme?'

'Kathy says you're obviously going to ambush those trucks somewhere on the Iranian border.'

'Why did you say that?' MacGregor said incredulously to Kathy. 'Who told you?'

'You did,' Kathy said. 'You told me enough. And I could guess the rest.'

'Did you have to gossip about it?' The extraordinary pleasure he had felt a moment before, when he had realised she was using Moselle to put pressure on him, evaporated. Her blind belief and trust in the Frenchman had gone too far.

'Wait a minute,' Moselle said in a conciliatory way. 'I'm not going to start blabbing anything Kathy tells me. But is it true, MacGregor?'

MacGregor sat grimly silent.

'I ought to warn you,' Moselle went on gently. 'The Americans have about twenty helicopters in the Bustan base in Turkey watching all those mountain routes. The Americans haven't told the Iranians what is happening to those arms, but obviously the Turks know. And the Turks will be on to it too.'

'You seem to know everything,' MacGregor said. 'So there's nothing I need say to explain the situation.'

'You haven't a chance. Don't you see that it's now a hopeless cause, MacGregor?'

'It's always been a hopeless cause,' Kathy said. 'That was the trouble from the very beginning, but you refused to see it.'

'I don't care one way or the other what it is,' Moselle said. 'But I can certainly recognise inevitable tragedy when I see it.'

'Furthermore,' Kathy put in angrily as if she could not resist it any longer, 'they don't need you. It's too late now to go there and advise them or whatever you planned to do.'

'I'm not going there to advise them. I'm going to tell them what has happened here, and to warn them.'

Moselle got up to go. 'Don't do it, MacGregor,' he said. 'Don't go anywhere near Kurdistan for the time being. Keep out of it.'

'They've got everything organised against you,' Kathy told him. 'Can't you understand in simple language what Guy is trying to tell you?' she said.

'I can guess, so you don't have to make a point of it.'

'Then keep away,' Moselle said sharply this time. But then he smiled in a friendly way. 'Just for a little while, MacGregor.'

MacGregor said nothing so Moselle shrugged and gave up. They shook hands and Moselle walked to the door with Kathy beside him.

'I can't abandon them now,' MacGregor said after them. 'It's not possible.'

Moselle was about to say something in reply, but Kathy put her hand on his arm. 'For God's sake don't bother,' she said to Moselle. 'He'll never listen.'

'I'm sorry, MacGregor,' Moselle said. 'I tried, for Kathy's sake. And I thought you'd understand.'

'That's all right,' MacGregor said.

He waited for Kathy, and though she was not weeping

when she came back, her eyes suggested it. She was cold and menacingly reasonable.

'In that case there's nothing more I can do now,' she told him. 'So you can do what you like, and you can take everything of yourself with you, because there'll be nothing left of me when you come back, not as far as you're concerned.'

He would not answer her.

'You don't believe me, do you?'

He shook his head.

'You don't believe I've been unfaithful, do you?'

He shook his head again.

'Then go away,' she said to him. 'Just go away and don't come back.'

'Don't you see,' he said, 'that I don't want to go anywhere near Kurdistan. I really have finished with it. But I told you, this is the one thing I have to do. I *have* to do it.'

'Then do it,' she said. 'But just go away, because it's no use talking to you any more. You'll only understand when you come back. Then you'll know...'

'Don't say that,' he said angrily.

She looked at him as if he were already miles away and disappearing from her sight. 'Just go away,' she said flatly. '*Go away!*'

He pushed a finger gently into the air towards her.

'Don't touch me,' she said sharply. 'You think I'll behave like a stupid and obedient wife. Never!' she said, and he could hear her repeating loudly as she went up the stairs. 'Never! Never! Never...'

PART V

Chapter Thirty-seven

The mountains were no longer wet with snow, and the gunmetal rivers that usually cut nervous veins into the eastern slopes of the Dalanpar were dry this year. It didn't look like the end of May, it already seemed to be midsummer. MacGregor knew what was happening on the other side, and he pointed out two long ridges called by the Kurds Kar and Kari (which together meant 'adorned') and said to Taha, 'It's dry on this side, but it will be full of flowers on the other side.'

'Why?'

'Because when the snow melts so early on these slate slopes, it always runs down the west side and leaves this side dry and rather barren.'

Taha was not interested in the giant horned poppies, the astragaluses and earth nuts and primulas and the parasitic philipias (which looked like wild orchids) that MacGregor had expected to find on these slopes. They were not here.

'It'll take us another two days to cut across these hills,' Taha complained, 'and I don't see why you are doing it this way.'

'They'll all be looking for us,' MacGregor said, 'so we might as well be careful.'

'Listen, Uncle,' Taha protested. 'I have to go further than you, and I'm in a hurry. So why don't we take the road and just walk through all the Kerki and Zarga villages?'

'We've been cautious this far,' MacGregor insisted, 'so we'd be fools to take risks now.'

Taha himself had been cautious enough to deceive every-

345

one when he had left Paris, even MacGregor. He had gone to Frankfurt by bus and taken a plane there for Athens, via Rome. But he had disembarked at Rome and transferred to the BOAC plane going to Teheran, the same plane that MacGregor had been on. MacGregor had only recognised Taha when he had been nudged on the gangway as they got out of the plane at Teheran.

'What the devil,' he had said. 'And what in God's name have you done to your face?'

'It's all right,' Taha had said simply. 'I cut my moustache and shaved off some of my eyebrows to fit the picture on my passport.'

'If it's forged,' MacGregor pointed out as they walked into the hot airport building, 'you'll never get through.'

Taha said it wasn't forged, it was genuine. One of the Persian students in Paris had given him his own.

'What's he going to do without his passport?' MacGregor had asked as they filtered through the passengers to the Iranian police barrier.

'He'll report it stolen in a week or two, and by then I'll have burned it and nobody will remember me.'

There had been no embarrassing questions and after changing some money they had both walked out of the airport without any difficulty. Since then they had been travelling in country buses, first to Tabriz and then the long way around Lake Rezaiah through Baham and Mahdad and Millus. Then they had picked up village buses and trucks and horse carts, and now they were on foot, walking across the slender Kurdish valleys, skirting around Mount Delaga and heading towards the corner of the world where Iran and Iraq and Turkey all came together.

It was there that they would part. Taha would go on and collect his revolutionaries and head for the Qotur valley. But he said he would only leave MacGregor when they had picked up some definite news of the Qazi or Zadko, and so far the Kurdish villagers knew nothing. There was no sign of either man or any of their supporters.

'They're all frightened and it's getting worse,' Taha said gloomily as they walked towards a crumpled sheep- and goat-herders' village, almost invisible on the slaty sides of the dry mountain.

'Flanders must have done it,' MacGregor said. 'He's the one that's been preparing the way up here for Dubas and the Ilkhani.'

There had been reports in the low mountain villages that the Englishman who looked after children was going about warning the villages to be careful for their children's sake. There was going to be trouble...

'Too many stupid rumours,' Taha said.

In the last village the headman had told them the Qazi was dead in Iraq, and that Zadko had been captured in Turkey and hanged.

'Who says so?' Taha had demanded.

'A sick smuggler who passed through here a week ago. No ... ten days ago.'

Taha had used words like *quirk* (traitor) and *rus* (coward), and the village headman had recognised an educated political Kurd who was dealing with bigger affairs than village politics. 'It's not my fault,' he complained. 'Don't get angry with me.'

'Then don't repeat stupid rumours,' Taha said.

When they came to the slaty village of Asnaf, which was little more than a collection of semi-caves dug into the depressing hillside, they found only old women and children and one or two tattered old men chewing seeds. In the absence of everybody else the old men suddenly became dignified spokesmen for the absent herders. They said the Qazi had been camped on the high Kurdish plateau only a few days ago.

'How do you know?' Taha demanded.

'We know everything that goes on up here,' the old men replied aggressively.

Taha told them they were too old to know anything. Instead, he asked the village boys who were holding back the village mongrels, and the boys laughed and crowed like cocks at the old men.

'They don't know the *who-ness* of anybody up here,' the boys said. 'It was the Ilkhani's men who were up on the plateau looking for thieves.'

'The Ilkhani's men are over this far?' MacGregor said incredulously. 'Are you sure?'

'Why should we lie?' the boys said indignantly.

By now the old women and the boys and the old men were all arguing with each other in high-pitched voices, and the dogs were barking.

'Enough!' Taha shouted.

MacGregor suddenly laughed at the every-day Kurdish situation they were in and he suggested that they spend the night here. 'We're almost at the Iraqi frontier,' he told Taha, 'and if we don't hear something from the village men when they come in tonight, I'll head for that Iraqi village on the other side of the mountains.'

'Right through the Iraqi army outposts,' Taha said cynically.

'Nonetheless, if the Qazi and Zadko are still avoiding the Ilkhani, that's most likely where they'll be.'

The women gave them a corner of a village shed, and they had already eaten their stale bread and tinned beef by the time the men and young women came in from the pastures. They were ragged and poor men, and the herds were thin. They said the lambs and kids were starving on the dry pasture. It was going to be a bad year. They sat around a moss and dung fire talking about their miseries, and MacGregor went to sleep sitting on his haunches listening to Taha telling them it was time they got rid of their primitive ways and began to think of a true Kurdish revolution against all feodals and foreigners.

'Every Kurd must be willing to die for his duty,' Taha

348

was saying. The rest of it disappeared in the night air and MacGregor heard no more until Taha woke him up. The fire was out, the men had gone, and now it was dark and damp and cold.

'It looks as if you were right,' Taha said. 'They say that the Qazi and Zadko have been living on the other side. But the Ilkhani's men have been sitting up on all the passes picking off any Kurd that crosses into Iraq along the old smuggling routes.'

'How did the Ilkhani's men get across this far?' MacGregor said. 'Who's helping them here?'

'One of the villagers said that helicopters are flying around, and he swears that they take away some Kurds and shoot at others.'

'Whose helicopters?'

'They don't know,' Taha shrugged. 'In any case everybody here believes that Zadko was kidnapped weeks ago and taken to Turkey and shot. But I think that's a Megrik rumour put out by the Ilkhani.'

'It could be true,' MacGregor said gloomily. 'Particularly if they're using helicopters.'

Taha was lying on his back in the shed with his hands stretched out behind him, and he was cracking his fingers in the Moslem ablution, something he would normally consider stupid and primitive.

'What is the best way to deal with a helicopter, Uncle?'

MacGregor said he didn't know. 'One or two good shots from a couple of rocket launchers would probably do, if you had the rocket launchers.'

'We'll have to get them,' Taha said, but MacGregor fell asleep before Taha could tell him where he planned to get them from.

In the morning they were half-way up the rocky valley with the herders when they saw two horsemen, in tribal gear and carrying rifles, riding up and down one of the mountain paths that led to the village below.

'They'll be the Ilkhani's men hunting for you,' one of the young men told them. He wore Iraqi army boots which some smuggler had given him.

'In God's name,' Taha said bitterly, 'what sort of network have they got up here? How do they know we're here?'

'They use radios.'

'On their horses?' Taha laughed savagely.

'They're only little thingumajigs.'

'I know, I know,' Taha said.

They left the herders when they found a reasonable gap in the rocky sides of the slope, and they began to climb a high dry watershed to a neglected but high-hung footbridge that had been put up years before between two sides of a deep slash in the high ridges.

'They can't follow us across that old bridge on a horse,' MacGregor said, 'and it will take them days to go around it the long way.'

'And where will we be if we get across that bridge?' Taha said, staring up at the high ridge they had to climb, impatient again with MacGregor's caution. 'We'll be stuck on the top of that mountainside, and God knows how long it will take us to get down the other side.'

'If I know your father,' MacGregor pointed out, 'and if he's still alive, he'll have a telescope man on the other side of that old bridge, and he'll probably be able to tell us what's happening.'

'It's all wrong,' Taha said.

'What is?'

Taha swept his hand angrily at the vast countryside. 'The barren stupidity of all this,' he said. 'What use has any of this ever been to us?'

'Your Kurdish mountains,' MacGregor reminded him breathlessly as they climbed up and up. 'Don't insult them.'

'Emptiness,' Taha went on.

350

MacGregor had never before known Taha to say anything so hostile about his birthright. 'You're a city boy at heart,' he said teasingly to Taha. 'So cheer up.'

'We should have abandoned these mountains years ago,' Taha insisted. 'We should have been revolting in the streets and ateliers of the cities.'

'With a handful of students?' MacGregor said lightly, but he had to lean against the warm rocks to catch his breath and allow the sweat to free itself from his shirt and trousers.

'I thank thee for that lesson, Uncle,' Taha said.

'You're in a bad mood,' MacGregor told him and they climbed, not like rock climbers but simply taking a steep zig-zag course up steeper and steeper surfaces, trying not to slip when the shale was loose.

'There they are again.'

Taha, well ahead now, was sitting on a lump of loose shale and pointing to the other side of the valley. MacGregor scrambled up and looked across the mountain gap at two horsemen. Even as he saw them one of them had raised his rifle and fired at them.

Taha laughed. 'He must think he's got a cannon.'

They saw the puff of black powder, heard the shot, but not the whine of the bullet.

'He's signalling someone,' MacGregor pointed out.

'But who? And where?'

MacGregor was breathing heavily now and Taha was watching him carefully. 'Are you all right, Uncle?' he said.

'Of course.'

'You look done in.'

'I'm perfectly all right.'

'You're too old to be doing this sort of thing,' Taha told him seriously.

They went on climbing, but MacGregor noticed that Taha deliberately slowed his pace, and he was watching for the difficult lifts and slippery funnels. When they had almost reached the bridge, which looked like a little grey pencil mark across the top of a ragged and deep gorge, MacGregor sat on a soft lump of damp moss and Taha pointed below to the horsemen again.

'It's a mistake to cross these hills unarmed,' Taha said.

'I've been walking all over them for thirty years,' Mac-Gregor told him, 'and I've never been armed.'

'You've never been in a situation like this before,' Taha said. 'They're hunting us like dogs.'

They continued the climb, and MacGregor had taken off his shirt and tied it by the sleeves around his waist. He began to feel better, as if his body and his flesh could finally breathe, even if his lungs couldn't.

Taha said then that he would go up ahead, and Mac-Gregor watched him climb the rest of the slope like a garden spider. Taha still wore the thin, useless clothes he had bought for Paris, and as MacGregor watched him scramble up like a schoolboy on holiday he closed his eyes for a moment and wondered where his own unthinking youth had gone. On what hillside had it worn itself out? In what city streets, in what glass-walled offices or mud-walled houses? In what vast, empty fields where the sun seemed always to be setting on a lemon-coloured day?

'There's nobody on this side,' Taha called down when he reached the bridge.

MacGregor followed him, and when he finally reached the huge rock, which the rusty cables of the bridge were bound to, Taha pointed to some excrement and a little pile of cashew nut shells.

'The Kurd in his mountains.'

'Probably yesterday or the day before. So we'd better get across now,' MacGregor said.

He knew it had to be done, but he looked doubtfully at the two sagging lines of rusted cable which were held together by a footwalk of wire and rotting wood. Beneath it there was a chasm a thousand feet deep that seemed to disappear infinitely under itself, and to stretch either

way like a hungry, empty, jagged mouth. It was not difficult to cross the span on hands and knees, but MacGregor
clung with his fingers to the pendulous, broken footwalk,
and by the time he was across it Taha had already unwrapped the flat bread which had dried hard in the
mountain air although it had been fresh and damp that
morning. When they were eating it, with pieces of white
cheese and balls of cold rice, they heard someone laughing
in the ruins of an old Turkish watch-tower just above them.

'Where's your gold?' they heard a Kurdish voice boom-
ing crazily above them.

They stood up.

'I scared you.' There was a delightful cackle.

MacGregor wondered when he had heard all this before.

'Come out, Ahmed,' Taha shouted.

A Kurd in coxa jacket and stiff baggy trousers stepped
out of the Turkish pile and pointed his rifle down at
them, and MacGregor recognised Ahmed the Carefree, the
mounted Kurd who had once scared Kathy with his coarse
Kurdish exuberance.

'Come on down,' Taha ordered. 'Come on.'

'I scared you, didn't I?' Ahmed said happily. He slid
down the rock face with his rifle held high above his head.
He almost landed on top of them as he tumbled the last
twenty feet.

'Where's the khanoum?' he asked MacGregor, and he
looked around for Kathy with his wicked, childish eyes.
'And that sackful of gold?' He laughed and held out his
hand for some of the bread.

'They're both far away,' MacGregor said, pleased to see
the crazy horseman again. 'How are you, Ahmed?' he asked,
and then said it again. 'How are you, old friend?'

'I was up there looking for last year's honey,' Ahmed
said as he bit ravenously into the bread. Last year's honey
was the honey left by wild alpine bees that sometimes holed
up in a rock and then abandoned it. The honeycomb itself

was usually preserved by the high, cold winter. 'I was digging it out.'

'Never mind the honey,' Taha said. 'Just tell us where Zadko is. Where is the Qazi and the rest of them?'

'Your father is on the other side of the Meladi,' Ahmed said. 'He's been living with the Herati family. We've all been living with them.'

'Is he all right?' MacGregor asked.

'He gets red in the face, furious, because his feet are so swollen. Like that.' Ahmed shaped his hand around his ragged boots.

'When did you see him?'

'Four midnights ago.'

'That's three days ago,' MacGregor calculated to himself in English. 'Is the Qazi with him?'

'The Qazi Mohamed is very sick. That's why we are all living with the Herati family, because the Ilkhani has men all over these hills with new American rifles. What a weapon...'

'What about Zadko?' Taha persisted.

'I'm coming to that. It's all these sticky helicopters, sticking themselves in the air all over the place, like blowflies. I've been hiding from them all day, waiting for Zadko to come, but something must have happened to him.'

'When did you expect him?' Taha asked.

'Yesterday. Today. Maybe they're all down there playing cards.' Ahmed laughed like a child, then he became worried again. 'There was a lot of shooting and helicopters there yesterday, so I didn't move. Am I a fool?'

MacGregor didn't wait. 'You'd better come with me,' he said to Taha as he got up.

Taha was already packing up his small bundles. He gave Ahmed some of the bread and cheese. 'Wait up here until we come back,' he said to Ahmed. 'And if they start shooting at you, get out of the way. Where's your horse?'

'He's hungry, so he's up there sniffing at old dung,'

354

Ahmed said. 'I can only let him loose at night, but he makes too much noise because his teeth are worn....'

They left Ahmed telling them a long story about his horse's teeth, and they hurried down the other side of the slope without paying any attention now to whether they were being followed or not. In an hour they could see the nearest Herati village in the distance, pinned between two barren little valleys, and MacGregor began to head for it.

'Not that one,' Taha said. 'Keep up high and we'll come to the old summer village, which is where they're sure to be. It's safer.'

They walked along the mountain paths for four hours without talking or stopping, and just before the sun disappeared over the mountain tops they came to the Herati summer village which looked so poor that it resembled an archaeological site rather than a living place.

'They've obviously gone,' Taha said.

'Everybody's gone,' MacGregor said.

There was nobody in the village. It had been shot up. Spent cartridges lay in the ditches, and the mud-stone walls were powdered with bullet scars. There was a dead horse in the middle of the dirt road, and an abandoned jeep which was midnight blue.

'It's Zadko's,' Taha said. 'Look at the blood on it.'

They ran along the old street looking into all the huts until they came on two men crumpled up in a doorway.

'Hamza and Rashid,' Taha said. 'They would never leave my father.'

Both had been shot dead, the primitive furniture in the stone hut had been smashed, and pots and pans and quilts scattered about.

'How did anyone get up this close?' Taha said. 'How could it happen?'

'The helicopters,' MacGregor said. 'I noticed a place back there where they had churned up the dirt. Zadko must have gone into the mountains.'

They began to climb up the narrow path over the slopes behind the village, and when they were almost on top they heard someone calling them by name from a shepherd's winter hut.

'It's the Iraqi,' MacGregor said, and they ran up the slope as he called out to them to be careful.

'Where is everybody?' Taha said as they arrived, breathless.

The Iraqi waved tiredly at the mountains. 'All the villagers are hiding from the helicopters,' he said. 'They'll come back at night.'

'And Zadko and the Qazi?' MacGregor said.

The Iraqi, who was obviously sicker than usual, pointed into the hut, and though he said 'wait ... wait...' Taha had already gone in, and MacGregor followed.

Lying yellow on the floor, wrapped in a polka-dot bedcover, was the Qazi with his eyes closed, and lying feet to head near him was Zadko in his Kurdish jacket and trousers with carpet slippers still on his feet.

'They were killed when two helicopters came over the village,' the Iraqi said, standing at the open door. 'They landed some of the Ilkhani's men up the road, and when the Qazi and Zadko tried to escape in the jeep one of the helicopters came back and chased them and killed them....'

Taha slapped his hands over his ears so that he didn't hear anything more, and MacGregor leaned against the wall. Then Taha leaned over and closed his father's eyes and covered the dead face with an old French newspaper he had been carrying in his pocket to light fires with.

'Whose helicopters were they?' MacGregor said. 'Who brought them here, Ali?'

'Who knows?' the Iraqi said, his face covered in tears. 'They could have been Turkish or Iranian or American. Anybody. Does it matter? It was the Ilkhani's men, that's all we know.'

They went outside, and MacGregor could see no tears in

356

Taha's eyes, nor were there any in his own because it was already such a matter-of-fact sort of death that it seemed as if it had happened a very long time ago.

'They didn't find me,' the Iraqi said, 'because I was sick, and I was lying in one of the goat pens trying to get my breath. I heard it, it was all over in a few minutes, but I didn't know what had happened until they stopped shooting and the helicopters had gone.'

'Where are Zadko's men now?' Taha said.

'Up there. But leave them, Taha. I told them to keep away until nightfall. The Ilkhani wants to kill as many of Zadko's men as he can find. But I don't think he wanted to kill the Qazi. They went through the village looking for the Qazi, and they were frightened and started hitting their heads when they discovered that they had killed him in the jeep with Zadko.'

Taha did not say anything but stared for a long time at the acres of opal shadows which the peaks made in the silent valleys as the sun got behind them.

'You know what I discovered in Europe, Uncle?' he said after a while. 'I discovered that the only oppressions Europeans know anything about are the oppressions of personality, or the oppressions of clean cities with painted walls and educated children, every one of whom can write his name and get sick and die in a hospital bed. What a mockery this is.' He pointed to the hills and valleys. 'This place must be a comedy to them.' He made a gesture of distaste. 'I suppose all this ignorance has to come to an end somehow. But is it gases and chemicals and metals and helicopters, Uncle? Is that what we need on our backs?'

'God knows,' MacGregor said.

'They win so easily, don't they,' Taha said. 'And they leave us nothing. Not even sick old men. Not a thing. They just finish us off.'

MacGregor looked at the Iraqi, expecting him to argue, but the Iraqi was leaning against the wall of the stone hut struggling slowly and carefully for breath, and MacGregor wondered for a moment how many revolutions had been led by sick old men, worn out by pursuit and misery. The Qazi's dead face had looked a hundred years old.

'We'd better try to pick up the others in the hills,' MacGregor said.

'You'd never find them now,' Taha said. 'They've gone.'

'Some of Zadko's men must be waiting up there somewhere.'

'Waiting for what?' Taha said. 'Nothing will persuade our frightened Kurds to come out of the mountains now. They've gone for good this time, Uncle, and they've taken the Kurdish cause with them.'

'Then we'd better go and find them before it's too late. It's only a matter of convincing them ...'

Taha laughed. 'There's nothing left to convince them with. Don't you understand? It's all over up here. Half the Kurdish cause is lying dead in there, and the other half is running away as fast as it can, and there's nothing you or I can do to stop it now.'

'Are you giving it all up to the Ilkhani?'

'Sooner or later I'll kill the old man,' Taha said. 'That's about all that he's left for me to do up here.'

'Oh no!' MacGregor said, taking out his maps. 'You're not going to dissipate everything in a piece of personal, stupid, wasteful Kurdish revenge like that.'

'What else is there?' Taha shouted in reply. 'Do you think we can ambush those trucks with six men and Ahmed the clown?'

'Listen, Taha,' MacGregor said. 'All you have to do is get to those frightened Kurds and tell them exactly what happened, how the Ilkhani murdered the Qazi and Zadko, and they'll still do what you want done.'

'You don't understand our Kurdish weakness, Uncle,' Taha argued. 'Kurds are cowards when they're sad. They're like whining babies when they despair.'

358

'Then you'd better not indulge in it yourself. We'll go up after them.'

'I'm indulging in reality. Let the old bastard have these mountains. Let him get his arms. It's the cities and the ateliers that count. That's the truth of it.'

'There are about forty villages and twenty big families between here and Qotur,' MacGregor said over his map. 'If we fail to pick up enough men en route, then you can call it off. But it'll be dark in an hour, and if we can persuade some of these Herati villagers we can start by morning.'

'Qotur is too far for me...' the Iraqi said. They had forgotten him, and he sat cross-legged now in the doorway of the hut as if he had fixed himself there in some sort of ritual. '...but I'll talk to the Herati. Although Taha is right, Agha,' he said to MacGregor. 'They're frightened now. But you're also wrong, Taha,' he said. 'If you tell a man to cough when he's afraid, sometimes it's enough to make him courageous.'

'A cough also hurts your balls,' Taha said. 'That's what's happened up here.'

'In any case,' the Iraqi said, getting up slowly, 'we have to bury the dead before dark. It's the second day, and since you're the owner of your father's body, Taha, you'll have to recite the service over them.'

'Not me!' Taha said. 'I'll never bury my father up here. I'll only bury him when I've buried the Ilkhani.'

'Then you'll have to dig a grave,' the Iraqi told them. 'We can't leave them like this.'

They dug two graves with some of the tools they found in the village, and when they put the Qazi in the grave, head to the north and feet to the south, MacGregor got down and turned his head to Mecca. Then the Iraqi placed his hands on the lobes of his ears and said, 'God is great,' and they covered the Qazi with dirt and stones. They put Zadko in the other grave in the same way, leaving no mark to show where they were, and when the Iraqi touched his earlobes over Zadko, MacGregor waited for Taha to say one word from the traditional *takbirs*.

But Taha refused to do it, and as they walked back to the village almost carrying the Iraqi, MacGregor said: 'I don't care what you do afterwards, Taha, but we'll head towards Qotur tomorrow, and we can pick up whoever we can on the way. Then we'll organise it exactly as it was planned.'

'You're a fool, Uncle,' Taha said.

'I know that. But I'd sooner be this kind of fool, than the kind they make of you.'

'It's a fool's end,' Taha said. 'It's a waste.'

'Nonetheless...'

Chapter Thirty-eight

They went on quarrelling in and out of a dozen mountain villages while MacGregor looked for someone to help them. Taha wouldn't argue with the villagers, but he listened to MacGregor trying to persuade the ragged herders and the wool-gatherers and the grass-cutters that it was in their interest to resist the Ilkhani now.

'In God's name,' they said, 'you're right.'

But didn't he see that with the Qazi's death it was hopeless? Didn't he see that it was a repetition of the 1947 tragedy? Didn't he see that the Kurdish cause had been crushed again? And didn't he see that the only thing to do now was to reorganise their principles, and start all over again?

'You won't be able to start all over again if the Ilkhani gets those arms up here,' MacGregor told one of the old men whose family and tribe were half in Turkey and half in Iran. 'The foreigners are going to drive him into you like a nail.'

'All right. All right,' the old man said. 'But there have always been foreigners in our affairs.'

'This time they want a hundred years of your life,' MacGregor shouted.

But like most of the others before him the old man wept and threw up his hands in dismay and said God is good.

'You're wasting your time,' Taha insisted when they lay shivering on the cold hillside high above a herders' village, eating from a five-pound tin of meat they had bought from a village herder who had obviously stolen it from an army truck. 'They're not going to listen to any of your parliamentary English arguments. Why should they?'

MacGregor got up to stamp the numbness out of his feet. 'What will they ever listen to then?'

'Nothing.'

'So?'

'I'll go and kill the old man, Uncle. Then we can leave these mountains to the goat herders and start again the city streets.'

'Killing the Ilkhani won't stop the arms getting here.'

'Can you stop them getting here?'

'It doesn't look like it, does it? Even Zadko's men have gone.'

'Then stop stamping around and I'll show you, Uncle, that there's nothing else I can do but kill the old man.'

'If you can ever convince me of that,' MacGregor said, squatting on his haunches and huddling himself into his jacket, 'I'll pack up everything and go with you.'

Taha threw him a fragment of sheepskin. 'The trouble is, you still don't understand us, Uncle. You can't help thinking like an English parliamentary gentleman. But up here you have to look at the situation with our thinking, not theirs.'

'That's what I've been trying to do for thirty years, Taha.'

'Then look what's happening to us now. We have no arms, no real organisation left, no money and no sympathy from foreigners. Who cares about us, Uncle? Aren't we a backward, quarrelsome, divided, and swarthy people?'

'Don't, for heaven's sake, start that.'

'Nonetheless it's true. So don't start worrying because we have to kill one man. What are we supposed to do, Uncle? How are we to face the foreigners and their arms? Am I supposed to worry up here what your nice Englishwomen with hats and Sunday culture will think when they open their morning papers at breakfast and read that we have

362

killed a man? How many men are they killing while they sit and eat their breakfast of eggs and bacon?'

MacGregor stood up again and stamped around as he talked. 'You're deliberately misunderstanding me, Taha. What's the use of killing one man if, by doing so, you unwittingly persuade your own people that someone is doing their fighting for them? Why should they bother?'

'That won't be the case.'

'You're doing what those students in Paris were doing. You're acting as if you're the élite, and as if that gives you the right to call yourself the Kurdish revolution. Well, you're not.'

Taha sighed and groaned as if it was stupid trying to argue. 'You're always forgetting one thing, Uncle.'

'What?'

'When the Ilkhani chopped off our two clean thumbs, he didn't kill two fat Prime Ministers whom everybody will forget in a week. He was trying to kill the only upright things we had.'

'I'm glad you finally understand it.'

'I've always understood it. But how can English businessmen and housewives taking their children to school and English lawyers and white doctors understand it? They're the culture of the guns. But I can't go to England and shoot them, can I? I can't take a Kalashnikov and kill the clean children and wives and priests and businessmen in their English villages, can I? How awful that would be. But how awful was it to them when their RAF once bombed a hundred defenceless Kurdish villages one English Sunday in 1933? You've even done it yourself.'

'Me?'

'Listen, Uncle. You once had the same single-minded morality you deny me.'

'Not me.'

'If I can show you that you once behaved in the same way, will you tell me to go ahead and kill the old man?'

'I told you,' MacGregor said, finally giving up the effort to keep warm on his feet. 'If you can convince me that you're right then I swear I'll go to Qotur with you.'

'I'm not asking you to come to Qotur with me.'

'Nonetheless that's what I'm saying.'

Taha shrugged. 'As you wish,' he said. 'But do you remember in the war setting out with eight soldiers to kill the German General Rommel in the Egyptian desert?'

'Oh, that!'

'Weren't you the navigation officer? Didn't you and your friends kill four German officers without them firing a shot, and only miss General Rommel because he wasn't there?'

'Who told you about that?'

'Aunt Kathy read it to me from a book when I was eleven. She was very proud of you. Didn't you get an English medal for your part in trying to kill the German General?'

'I'm too tired to argue with you,' MacGregor said, and got into his sleeping bag which was already damp with mountain dew. 'Anyway, even if you kill the old man, there's always Dubas who will go on doing what his father was doing.'

'If I kill the father,' Taha said, 'I'll certainly kill the son as well.'

'Go to sleep,' MacGregor told him. Then he sat up. 'And no disappearing into the darkness when I'm asleep.'

'I won't disappear,' Taha said. 'But tomorrow we will have to do this one way or the other.'

'All right ... Tomorrow...' MacGregor told him, and knew as he went to sleep that his arguments would be no better tomorrow than they were today. The only difference was that tomorrow he must make up his mind, once more, about what was right in life and what was wrong with it.

Chapter Thirty-nine

In the morning Taha was not there. MacGregor watched two mountain crows flying high above him, looking for the morning sun that was already up behind the mountains.

'If he's gone he's gone,' MacGregor said and was glad for a moment that he had been spared an argument and a decision. 'Taha,' he called.

'I'm down here, looking for water.'

'Did you find any?'

'Enough for a little coffee.'

Taha came up the wet mountain slope, soft with mist, holding a blackened powdered-milk tin which they used for boiling water in. 'It's rock water and it looks like Coca Cola,' he said, 'but it's drinkable.'

He had already gathered enough berberifolia to make a small fire, and while they waited for the water to boil they cut up the meat and watched the crows. But they didn't talk until they were both standing up getting ready to go.

'You'd better go on down to Keraj, Uncle,' Taha said. 'You can catch the Mercedes bus to Rezaiya, then you can go on home.'

'I can't talk you out of this, I suppose?'

Taha shook his head. 'I'll go on to Qotur and work my way up the valley until I find him. So give me your maps in case I need them, and you go on home.'

'No. I'm coming with you.'

365

Taha pulled on the rucksack. 'What for? You're dead against it.'

'I'm only half against it.' MacGregor was pulling on the Kurdish coxa jacket he had bought in one of the villages. 'I suppose it's the English and European and parliamentary half that's against you. Whereas a whole lifetime here is for you. The trouble is, I can't honestly say which one I am in this.'

'Don't try to be a Kurd, Uncle. Just give me the maps.'

'I'm trying to be myself,' MacGregor said. 'If I had to kill one man and be praised for it, why not another? So maybe I'll help you kill the old man. Maybe it's the only way. I don't know. But I'll go with you in any case.'

'Then we'd better hurry.' Taha pointed over the bubbly peaks to a dark little incision buzzing in the morning sky. 'The old bull is on his way.'

They began to hurry across the open slope, and it took them the rest of the day to reach the Herati summer village where Zadko and the Qazi had been shot. The Iraqi had gone. But the jeep was still there, the Kalashnikov automatic and the .303 were still lying in the back of it, and the village was deserted.

'I suppose in another year or two,' MacGregor said as he looked at the desolation, 'every mountain Kurd for miles around will be making pilgrimages up here the way they still visit the graves of the 1947 martyrs.'

'Thus,' Taha said, 'burying their cause in death and hindsight.'

They were working on the jeep, which had been jammed tight in second gear. They had to rock it and push it, and when they finally got it rolling down hill Taha shouted 'Jump on' and MacGregor leapt into the back and clung to the sides as Taha let out the clutch. After half a dozen coughs and shudders the engine burst into life.

'Where are we heading for?' MacGregor shouted.

'We'll find a place to paint the jeep. Then we can go on

to Qotur and drive up the valley to the border.'

'You're crazy,' MacGregor said. 'It'll be packed with the Ilkhani's men.'

'It's still a public road. And the old man's not going to shoot at every jeep that might be using it.'

'We'll never reach the border.'

'We don't have to. There's a village called Habashi Ashagi on the north side. The old man will certainly be there.'

'How do you know?'

'Because—that's the only village that can house him fittingly with all his tribal trappings.'

MacGregor had not asked Taha what his plan was, because he didn't want to know it. But he guessed now that Taha was going to do this the Kurdish way—everything out in the open—where honour must be seen to be done and where the advantage had to be with your cowardly opponent.

'You're going to drive right into the village?' he said as he clung to the bouncing jeep which Taha drove like his father.

'Of course.'

'Don't be a fool, Taha. It's not practical.'

'If I did it in your practical way, Uncle, by some clever English trick, it would signify nothing to a Kurd.'

'But at least you'd have a better chance.'

Taha didn't bother to reply and they went on down the hillside. Ten miles from the black road they ran out of petrol and they had to wait an hour until they could buy two gallons from a passing truck. It was enough to get them to the south-north road going to Khoi, and at Rezaiya they filled the tank and two spare cans and bought half a gallon of brown paint and filled their bottles with water. Twenty miles out of Rezaiya they turned off the road and hurriedly painted Zadko's midnight blue into a dirty, dusty brown.

'Isn't this being dishonourable?' MacGregor said as if Kurdish honour had to be teased a little.

'They'd recognise Zadko's blue,' Taha said, 'and we'd never get up the valley.'

They had eaten a three-course lunch in one of Rezaiya's Europeanised restaurants, but they had also bought enough food and tea to last them a week, which they now packed in their rucksacks. Then Taha unwrapped Zadko's Kalashnikov and checked its action before attaching a magazine to it. He did the same with the .303 and laid both weapons under the greasy sheepskin between the seats.

MacGregor tried again. 'You still insist?—No plan?'

'It can't be planned,' Taha said.

They returned to the black road, and in two hours they turned off west along the new road that ran up the Qotur valley to the Turkish border. Eight Kurds packed into an old Peugeot passed them, and they knew they were the Ilkhani's men.

'Look for an open place where we can get off the road,' Taha shouted.

MacGregor pointed to a dry gulch ahead and Taha swerved into it and kept going up the gulch until the road was out of sight. He stopped the jeep and turned off the engine. For a moment they said nothing. Then Taha took his hands off the steering wheel, as if there was still a last choice left for them.

'I still think it would be better if you wait here for me,' he said.

'Why? What are you arguing about now?'

'It's not the right way for you, Uncle. We can only drive in, and, if we're lucky, drive out. That's about all we can hope for.'

'Then you'd better let me do the driving.'

'They may even recognise us before we get there.'

'Then in God's name let's hope they don't have time to think about it,' MacGregor said, and walked around and

368

got into the driving seat of the jeep. 'All set?'

'All right. All right,' Taha said. 'But be careful of yourself, Uncle, I beg you.'

MacGregor took the jeep back to the road, and as they turned into the valley and went along the river towards the frontier he began to feel the way he always felt in these mountains: that what you did in them was only measurable here, that there was nothing extraordinary in what they were doing, that these hillsides had been soaked in violence for so long that they had become the natural battlefield for ragged armies who always fought each other face to face, hand to hand, man to man. That was the kind of thing they were going into themselves, and the only problem that still bothered him was the lack of adequate preparation for it.

The road to Qotur followed the river, and the river lined the stony valley, but the river was almost dry and they passed shepherds with flocks of astrakhan sheep looking for water. Then they began to see men on the roadside, and once a motorbike passed them. It was ridden by a Kurd who looked curiously at them as they went by. They passed a sagging, laden truck; then more Kurds shouted at them from the roadside.

'I can't understand what they're saying,' MacGregor shouted above the groan and whine of the jeep.

'Something about soldiers.'

Kurds, khan's men, were scattered along the roadside, and MacGregor knew that sooner or later they would be stopped by one of them.

'Get all your Kurdish explanations ready,' he said to Taha.

'If we have to explain ourselves we'll be dead in two seconds,' Taha replied. 'Don't stop for anything.'

They were negotiating one of the wide, rising bends of the road when they saw a line of Iranian Army trucks ahead of them.

'We'll never get past that lot,' MacGregor said.

'Don't try. Stick close to the last truck and nobody on the roadside will see us until it's too late.'

Everything they did now was an improvisation. The jeep still had Zadko's responses built into it: it performed recklessly in top gear but objected to this third gear crawling, and MacGregor felt that it was going to stall any moment.

'Keep it going, for God's sake,' Taha shouted.

They both had the scarves of their Kurdish headgear around their mouths to keep out the dust, and they ignored all the shouting they heard from the Kurds who ran down the hillsides after them, or stepped out on to the road as they passed.

'They might be using walkie-talkies,' MacGregor said.

'It won't make any difference now. Turn off here where that old signpost is.'

The old painted signpost was chipped, faded and shot at; but MacGregor knew it was an Iranian Army sign warning travellers they were entering a military area and were not allowed to leave the road or take photographs and must stop when ordered to do so.

'Now watch out for everything,' Taha said as they left the convoy and began to bump and twist and lurch along a climbing, rutted, unmade road.

'How far is the village?'

Taha didn't answer but pointed quickly to the hills on either side. There were two or three look-out men scattered along the peaks. Taha waved to them, and one of them waved back.

'Is this the way you drove up to your German General?' Taha said.

'No. We did it sensibly and intelligently at night.'

'Assassins. Terrorists, by God.'

MacGregor couldn't remember the last time Taha had joked like that.

'There's the bodyguard.'

Taha was pointing ahead to a Volkswagen bus which was parked on a bend. Four Kurds were sitting on the roadside cooking something on a fire.

'If they're up here, then the old man is too,' Taha said. 'Don't stop. For God's sake don't stop or we'll be recognised.'

They watched the Kurds taking an interest in them. Two stood up. One of them hurried down to the Volkswagen, and MacGregor realised that none of them, here or in the valley, seemed armed. They were obviously too close to the Iranian Army to carry arms openly.

'Get around him before he comes out of the Volkswagen with a rifle,' Taha said.

MacGregor accelerated, and as they came up to the bend Taha began to shout to them in Kurdish that Mahmoud was having trouble with the army, and that they were going to get someone to help.

'What?' they called back.

Taha stood up and repeated what he had said at the top of his voice, and then added something unintelligible —gesticulating with both arms.

'Go on, go on,' he said to MacGregor.

MacGregor swung the jeep around the bend, and Taha, still shouting and gesticulating, stayed on his feet until they were out of sight.

'Who is Mahmoud?' MacGregor asked as he twisted and turned the worn wheel of the bouncing jeep.

'There's always a Mahmoud. . . .'

They saw the village now, and Taha told him to blow the horn.

'What for?'

'Blow it.'

MacGregor pushed the button, and the klaxon echoed off the hills.

'Again . . .'

Taha leaned over and kept his finger on the button and

they saw women running out of the village houses.

'Over there.' MacGregor pointed to the other end of the village. 'Can you see it?'

Outside a house at the far end was a big Chevrolet and another van. Two armed men came out of the freshly-painted door of the house, and MacGregor drove towards it.

'Keep the engine going,' Taha said.

'I know.'

'And don't say anything at all. Nothing.'

'All right. All right.'

When they were fifty yards from the house, approaching it slowly, Taha shouted to the armed men: 'Where is the khan?'

'He's inside,' one of them replied.

'Then tell him I'm here, and I'm in a hurry.'

One of them went inside, and by the time the jeep stopped outside the house there were four armed men at the door.

'Tell him I can't wait long,' Taha said angrily, coarsening his accent.

'What's happened?'

MacGregor looked quickly at the four men, each with an automatic rifle, and he wondered where the road ahead went to, because that would be their only way out of this.

'In God's name . . .'

It was the khan in his black riding boots. He was wearing a napkin tucked into his neck on one side, like an Italian, and his big pointed ears were red. He was still chewing food.

'Khan. Ilkhan,' Taha said to him.

'What is it? What are you making all this fuss about?'

'No fuss. Where is your son, Dubas?'

'He's in Rezaiya. What do you want?'

Taha had kept his hand visibly on the windscreen. 'You are an old man, Ilkhani, older than my father, so there's not much justice in death, is there?'

'What's that? What are you talking about?'

372

MacGregor waited rigidly for the old man's moment of recognition and what it would bring. He couldn't take his eyes from Taha's hands which were filthy but white with their grip on the windscreen.

'It has to come to an end....' Taha said.

'I don't even understand you, you fool.'

'You don't have to understand me.'

It was then that the Ilkhani seemed to recognise Taha. He jerked the napkin from his neck and pulled out his spectacles which he put on roughly as if he was naturally rough with everyone, even himself.

'There's nothing for you here,' he bellowed at Taha. 'Go away.'

But the old man seemed puzzled. He looked up at the hills as if he expected Zadko to be hidden in them somewhere. Then he peered closely at MacGregor through his spectacles, and this time the recognition was startling, as if all Taha's provocations had failed but this one had succeeded.

'Isn't it enough that he insults me,' the khan bellowed at the hills and the sky, 'without bringing this foreigner to shit on our mountains ... Hassan ... Hassan ...'

MacGregor did not wait. Even as he saw the Kurd called Hassan lifting his automatic rifle, he revved the engine and let out the clutch and drove at the man. At the same time he heard Taha shouting something at the Ilkhani, and as he ran down Hassan with a glancing blow he heard another automatic behind them. He heard each one of the shots hitting the jeep as he drove on with spinning wheels burning in the dirt.

'Wait...' Taha shouted as he struggled with the Kalashnikov.

But MacGregor drove on as Taha twisted around and fired the Kalashnikov without getting to his feet. Then the windscreen was shattered, and there was another burst of fire from behind them.

'Wait,' Taha shouted again. 'For God's sake, wait.'

He had been firing continuously, but MacGregor could see the dirt road ahead bending around a last clump of crumbling houses, and, as he got himself ready to twist the careering jeep around it at full speed, he turned quickly to see what had happened behind him.

He could see the old man curled up on the ground; he could see another Kurd holding himself up against a wall, and the third one, Hassan, lying on his face where the jeep had knocked him down. One man was left, and he was running to the Chevrolet, but long before he reached it he fell over as if he had been tripped, and MacGregor knew that Taha had shot him, although he wasn't aware of Taha firing.

'But where are you going?' Taha shouted as they reached the corner.

'Wherever this road goes.'

'It goes up, and they've got men all over the mountains.'

'We can't go back.'

'Why didn't you wait?'

'What for?'

The village road degenerated into a mere track on the side of the slope, and the higher up they went the more of a steep mountain footpath it became.

'You should have gone down,' Taha shouted.

'We'd be trapped.'

'We're trapped up here. They can see us better.'

'Not for long.'

They could see one of the Ilkhani's men running down the slope ahead of them. Taha stood up ready to deal with him, but then it became clear that he was running away from them, and MacGregor turned off the track and began to climb up the bare slope over rocks and brush.

'Are you all right?' Taha said.

'Yes, but for God's sake knock a hole in the windscreen. I can't see.'

He had been twisted to one side to see around the shattered windscreen, and as Taha knocked a hole in the sticky glass with the Kalashnikov he felt the jeep trying to stall.

'Keep it going.'

'I can't. It stalls in low gear.'

'Put it in top.'

MacGregor changed up but the jeep simply died as if struggling like a dog to do what it couldn't do any longer.

'Let me do it,' Taha said as MacGregor failed to restart it.

They heard someone shouting, then more shooting, and a car starting. MacGregor got the jeep going again but when he put it in gear it jammed and skidded to a stop and they knew this time that they would not be able to free it.

'Come on.'

MacGregor picked up the rucksack, and as Taha picked up the Kalashnikov and the .303 they heard someone firing at them from the hillside ahead and they heard every shot pass over them.

'Never mind him,' Taha said. 'We'll have to go higher up now.'

It was steep, bare ground, and as they ran upward they could hear more firing. They heard the shots hitting rocks and dirt fifty yards behind them, then in front of them.

'Come on ... Come on,' Taha shouted and began to pull MacGregor by the arm up the steep slope.

'You go on. I'll catch you,' MacGregor said. 'Go on ...'

Taha let go and climbed straight up to the only shelter there was over the slope—a dip and then a little fold leading to two large outcrops. Two men were firing at them, but as soon as Taha reached the outcrop he fired three single shots and there was no more firing.

'They're on the far side,' Taha said as MacGregor collapsed into the little dip.

'Just give me a minute,' MacGregor said.

'We can't wait, Uncle. They're all over these hills. Our only hope now is to get above them.'

'All right ... All right ...'

They scrambled out of the dip and climbed the slope, using their hands and knees. Again MacGregor heard firing from somewhere above them.

'Don't stop, whatever you do,' Taha said, and he was also breathless now. 'I'll go on ahead of you and settle that one. Just keep climbing Uncle, don't stop.'

'Go on then,' MacGregor said.

Taha threw the Kalashnikov ahead of him up the steep rocky ground and then scrambled up after it. He did it again in the little scarp that rose above them, and MacGregor realised how much of a mountain Kurd Taha was, because only a mountain Kurd would throw his rifle up ahead like that without damaging it. It allowed Taha to move so fast, however, that MacGregor soon lost sight of him, and by now he was so exhausted that he fell into a stupefying rhythmic clawing with hands and feet as he climbed blindly up the slope.

'The other way ...'

He heard Taha but couldn't see him, and as he looked up the narrow gap that led to the high ground five hundred feet above him he shouted: 'Where the devil are you?'

'Go to the right. The other way.'

MacGregor staggered to the right and Taha kept giving him instructions as single rifle shots began to seek him out.

'You're all right,' Taha shouted.

But MacGregor knew he was not all right. He knew that he was resigning himself at every clawing step to the certainty that he was never going to leave these mountains.

'Where are you?' he shouted at Taha.

'Here. You're almost here.'

He made one final effort to get through a high narrow gap which was too tight to climb over. Then he heard the shots and didn't know where they were coming from. There was no cover, only this open alpine hillside. When he heard the next shots he felt them at the same time hitting his back and his legs.

'Oh no...' he said.

Rock chips flew in his face. His grip on the rock gave way when there was another burst of the American rifles that Ahmed had admired so much, and MacGregor felt himself disappearing into instant darkness. Then he found himself back in the dim sunshine, lying on his back against the hot muscular rocks, staring at the blurred sky, aware instantly that he was smashed like an egg. He could feel no pain and could hardly feel life. It was far away.

'Taha...'

Taha did not answer. MacGregor could turn his head, and he could see faintly from some enormous distance Taha's jacket hanging over some rocks. There was nothing to depend on there, so it was only the sky that he depended on for a little while, afraid that he was finally going to disappear into it.

'Taha...'

He called twice but Taha had gone.

It didn't matter. He managed to turn his head and then he saw Taha leaping across the alpine hillside he had just climbed. He knew that Taha was looking for cover as more shots chased him. When he reached some rocks Taha began firing and then he shouted at the top of his voice: 'Can you hear me?'

MacGregor knew he couldn't answer, so he waved his right hand.

'I'll have to keep them busy so that you can move. Crawl into that little gap on your right,' Taha shouted.

The little gap was the one he had been trying to negotiate. But he decided to lie still for a while until he could feel his arms and legs. He would have to be very practical about this.

'I can't move,' he said.

'*Essaie,*' Taha shouted in French.

MacGregor tilted his body so that he fell over. Then he pulled at loose stones and rock until he got a grip on something solid which allowed him to pull himself along on his stomach to the little sheltering gap. But the effort drained away his reserves, and he watched the darkness come in on him like one curtain after another until it blotted him out.

'Uncle...'

He knew it was Taha, but he seemed to be screwed up in his clothes like toffee.

'I got you up here,' Taha was saying, 'but you'll have to help me.'

They were in a little flower of bare rock on the top of the hillside and he was on his back again, but the sky seemed to have gone pale and dim.

'What time is it?' he said.

'God knows. Almost five o'clock. Can you sit up?'

'Are they still firing at us?'

'No. We're safe here for a while.'

'I must have passed out.'

'Listen, Uncle, I've got to bandage your legs with your shirts from the rucksack. You're bleeding.'

'Where are my shoes?' he said as Taha began to take his trousers off.

'They're here. Don't worry. For God's sake give me some help.'

'Sit me up then.'

Taha pulled him back against the rock and MacGregor felt his back raw and agonising against its surface. He looked at his legs. They were so bloody that at first he couldn't see what condition they were in. But as Taha swabbed at them with a wet handkerchief he could see the wound on the right leg above the knee—a deep, clean hole that exposed severed grey muscle, nerves, and an untouched vein, but all amazingly dry. Below the knee was another jagged, very bloody wound that was smaller and disappeared into the shin. On the other leg he couldn't see the wound because it was on the calf muscle.

'I'll have to tie them up to stop the blood and keep the dirt and flies out,' Taha said.

MacGregor told him to go ahead, but when Taha tried to close the open hole above the knee and hold it tight the blood drained from his head and he fainted again. By the time he could see light penetrating his eyelids he was bound up and lying on his back.

'Listen, Uncle. Can you hear me?'

'Yes, I can hear you.'

'When it's dark,' Taha said, 'I'll have to leave you and try to get into that village and find a horse or a mule. It looks as if nothing else will get you down these slopes. I'd kill you if I tried to get you down on my back.'

MacGregor closed his eyes for a moment. 'There'll be a hundred men in that village now, Taha.'

'Well? What do you suggest?'

'Even if you get a mule or a horse, how far do you think we'd get?—I'm losing blood, and even if you got me down to Rezaiya or Khoi I'd be arrested and locked up forever. So there's no point trying to move me.'

'Only the Ilkhani recognised you, Uncle, I'm sure of that.'

MacGregor felt himself breathing very slowly. 'And my legs full of bullet holes?'

'There are friends in Khoi.'

MacGregor tried to sit up. 'There's no point to it, Taha. You go on.'

Taha stood up because there was more firing, and this time it seemed nearer. 'Are you thinking of staying up here, Uncle, and dying like a hero?'

MacGregor watched a patch of blood soaking slowly through the bandages below his knees. 'Nowhere else I can go, Taha. Not this time ...'

Taha squatted down near him and watched him. 'You're

too weak to think properly.'

'That's true,' MacGregor said, eyes closed, almost drunk now with the need to abandon himself to pain and exhaustion and weakness. 'It wasn't the right way, was it,' he was saying.

'Just keep your eyes open.'

'I know we had to kill the old man, but ...'

'We had to kill the old man and we have to get out of here and get back to the city streets where we can start it all over again, where the future is waiting for us, Uncle. So keep your eyes open and think of that.'

MacGregor knew he was being humoured, and when he wanted to point out angrily that though he was blurred with pain he was perfectly coherent and clear-minded and sane, he felt himself losing his grip again.

'Uncle ... Uncle ...'

It was dark this time.

'I have to go now,' Taha was saying.

'All right.'

'I've left everything here for you. The water and the food are in the rucksack. The .303 is on your left side and the Kalashnikov is on the right. Just there.'

'That's silly. Take the Kalashnikov.'

'I don't need it. Listen, Uncle. It might take me a few days, and you might be able to get yourself up on the rock and keep watch. But I'll try to make it look as if we've both left here. Understand?'

'I understand.'

'I don't know how long it'll take me.'

'I'll be all right. But take some food ...'

'I'll be back, Uncle. I'll get you home, I swear it on my father's grave. Only you'll have to hang on here like a tortured Simurg in the pit.'

'Don't worry. I'll just sit up here and decide what to do with myself.'

'Think of Aunt Kathy.'

'Of course.'

'Everything will be all right when you get home.'

'Yes, I'll think of that.'

'You're ready, then?'

MacGregor nodded and realised that he was covered with one of the sleeping bags. Taha had packed the other one under his back.

'Sit me up,' he told Taha.

Taha pulled him up against the rock and padded his back and said: 'Remember. I'll give you plenty of warning when I'm on the way up again, so shoot at anyone else you hear.'

'I shan't see them.'

'Then just keep thinking of yourself, Uncle. That's all that counts now.'

'All right.'

Taha had stepped over the little lip of rock petals and in a moment he was gone. MacGregor heard him slide noisily down the first slope, then he heard him shouting, then several shots and more shouting which he supposed was Taha confusing the hundred men who could always be hiding in the hills around them.

'This way, Uncle,' he heard Taha shouting somewhere far below.

He was aware now of the saturated black sky, the ice-cold stars which had always sucked Kathy into the night-time loneliness of these high ranges.

'This way, Uncle,' he heard again, very faint.

A few shots followed, then the alpine silence, and he knew he must keep awake now, because being awake was being alive. And when he groaned aloud with the pain of it he remembered his father telling him as a boy that the great poet Haidary of Tabriz had said 'Life is pain; but pain is not life.'

Nonetheless, he knew it was pain that was going to keep him alive. It was pain, trouble and inconclusion that you had to live with, not petals and nightingales and rose-blended water. The great poet Haidary had said that too. Haidary had drawn up 986 conclusions on pain, life and love. 'Separate them if you can,' Haidary said, 'and you'll die of emptiness.' He was therefore not going to die of emptiness up here. There was the wound and the agony of Kathy to keep him alive. The enticing pain of Jizzy Margaux with petals instead of hair. Even the enormous inconclusions ...

In the meantime he must be practical. He must keep his mind on what Taha was doing. He must think clearly of the odds the boy was facing. He must put his faith in the resilience and invincibility of his youth. He must depend on the boy's passionate conviction, his true sense of honour, his faithful comradeship, his certainty in a cause, his affection, intelligence, cunning, health, courage, strength, skill. The true Kurd in the faith of his fathers ...

'This way, Uncle,' he heard, surprisingly, from very far off in the night, so that he knew Taha was safe.

He didn't know if it was the distance, or if it was his own mind that was turning to icy darkness again. But he pushed on his back once more, and when he felt the exquisite, agonising pain he knew he was alive and that it was only a matter of time before the boy came up the hill again, calling his name, telling him to get ready, and perhaps looking for the giant horned poppies, the astagaluses, the earth nuts, the primulas and the parasitic philipias which made these mountains a place to be lived in and enjoyed, not fought over bloodily and destroyed.